THE UNFINISHED

The Unfinished

Jay B. Laws

Boston ♦ Alyson Publications, Inc.

Typeset and printed in the United States of America.

This is a paperback original from Alyson Publications, Inc.,
40 Plympton St., Boston, Mass. 02118.
Distributed in England by GMP Publishers,
P.O. Box 247, London N17 9QR, England.

This book is printed on acid-free, recycled paper.

First edition: June 1993

5 4 3 2 1

ISBN 1-55583-217-2

Contents

Come closer.
The Dead have stories to tell
—and we don't like to shout.

But the rain is full of ghosts tonight,
that tap and sigh upon glass,
and listen for reply.
—EDNA ST. VINCENT MILLAY

The Unfinished

Spooks

1

"Now. Don't. Move." Dr. Grant brought the laser scalpel into view. "This won't hurt one bit."

Yeah, sure, thought Jiggs. *Like I'm really going to move my head and have you cut my eyeball out.* This was the one aspect of the entire operation that he had dreaded the most: the fact that he had to remain awake. Plus the ominous fact that his right eye was clamped open by some metal terror straight out of *A Clockwork Orange,* so there was no way to close that eye's lids. Thank god for the tranquilizers they'd fed him, not counting the Valium he'd swallowed on his own to keep up the nerve to get to the clinic. Sure, they'd dripped enough numbing painkillers onto his eyeball to ensure he wouldn't feel a thing, but *you* try to stay calm with a scalpel coming straight for your face.

Here it was. The Moment. He was awake. Alert. His eyelids wouldn't budge. Dr. Grant was poised on his right side, a vision of tight surgical gloves, green hospital cap, and a weathered face. He smiled reassuringly. Jiggs wasn't reassured. All he saw was the tip of the scalpel now inches from his right eyeball. Despite all the drugs floating through his system, he tensed.

Dr. Grant was saying something. He'd missed it. He frowned with confusion, and this time the doctor added a gesture of pointing a finger up toward the ceiling. "Look up."

Jiggs drew a breath and did as he was told. He always did as he was told, if he could read their lips. The ceiling was smooth and white. A shadow leapt in, quick, and his world swam red with blood. His eye was dabbed with something, the smooth ceiling returned for an instant, and then the red wave broke once again across his vision.

He didn't feel a thing. He relaxed, but just a little.

The procedure dragged on, though Jiggs knew from all the brochures and through his previous consultations that the radial keratotomy operation to fix nearsightedness was supposed to be fast and painless. A dozen or so laser-thin cuts on the eyeball, to make it expand slightly, and good-bye nearsightedness. Good-bye glasses. Good-bye to his aborted attempt with contacts. Finally, he was having an adventure. It made him giddy.

Soon enough, he felt the clamps holding open his eyelids release their iron grip. What a relief to blink again. His right eye was bandaged with gauze and tape. Dr. Grant patted his shoulder and said, "That wasn't so bad, now was it?" Before he could respond, several sympathetic nurses helped him off the table and into the waiting room at the front of the clinic. They made faces of concern at him, probably trying to soothe him with words he could not hear. He accepted a cup of water and waited for Dr. Grant to come in with his final instructions for care. A few waves of dizziness lapped at him, especially whenever he tried to move his head. The good doctor finally came in and perched on the chair opposite him. His instructions were brief. Jiggs watched his lips and caught most of it.

Keep the bandages on overnight. Wear sunglasses inside and outside of the house for the first few days. Try to avoid bright sunshine for the first week. Besides, with your red hair and fair skin, you should limit yourself in the sun as a matter of rule. Keep your head as level as possible. No bending down or leaning forward. Give the incisions plenty of time to heal.

"When will I see results?" Jiggs asked as he and the doctor strolled toward the office door. He put on the pair of shades he'd brought. They were tight against his bandages, and felt awkward on his face.

"About four days, if you're average. Is a friend. Up?"

He'd turned his head. Jiggs supplied the missing words — "picking you" — and nodded. A flare of pain and dizziness. Ouch.

"Now. That's. Avoided," Dr. Grant cautioned. He wagged a finger for emphasis. "Let's call you a cab and get." He turned to his receptionist and cut off his last words. Jiggs knew what was meant. He'd had years of practice interpreting broken phrases and swallowed words. If only people didn't move their heads so much when they talked.

"I have a friend coming to get me," Jiggs said. "As a matter of fact, I think that's Luke coming up the walkway." And what a relief. Now that the worst was over, a brighter anticipation was beginning to shine through him. Soon enough, perfect vision. Perfect.

Dr. Grant had already lost interest. Or maybe he'd said his good-byes and good luck to his back, forgetting Jiggs could not hear him. It happened all the time. A nurse brought him a mimeographed sheet of care instructions right as his friend Luke pushed through the glass doors.

"Well, well. Jimmy Jiggers, look at you!" Luke snickered. He wasn't being mean. He just wanted to lighten the mood, right off the bat. It was his way.

"Get me home," said Jiggs. "And you've got to help me in that sun. It already hurts my eyes."

They went through the doors. Luke had him by his elbow, guiding his hesitant steps. "Did it hurt?"

"Huh? I can't see—"

Luke spelled h-u-r-t with his free hand and shrugged, making the word a question.

Hurt? Jiggs smiled. He was too busy having an adventure to worry about hurt. "Naw. Piece of cake."

It was an attitude about to change, forever and always.

2

"I've made a decision," Jiggs told Luke three days later. "I want to move."

Luke, working at the tiny stove in Jiggs's studio, was adding the finishing touches to his beef stroganoff. He turned his head so Jiggs could see his lips. "Don't you think you should handle one change at a time?"

"I'm bored."

"You're always bored. You just have cabin fever."

Jiggs had to admit that part was true. Keeping a level head — both physically and mentally — was requiring an effort he hadn't anticipated. His eye hurt like hell. He could not look down upon himself while lathering up in the shower without courting wave upon wave of dizziness. Dressing himself had become a game of contortions. Tying his shoelaces was especially fraught with danger, usually in sync with a pounding headache just beneath his eyes. For the past several days he had stayed home in his little studio off Haight Street and let Luke and the rest of the world come to him. He could not read. Television aggravated his eye. He could not listen to it, and the words at the bottom of the picture for the hearing impaired went by too fast and too blurry for him to read.

"Don't rush it," Dr. Grant had cautioned. "Your eye will correct itself in its own time."

Okay. Jiggs could accept that. He'd pulled the bandages off the second morning, losing a few rust-colored eyebrow hairs in the process. The drops he placed into his right eye were very soothing, but still his world was blurry and inscrutable, unless he tried to use only his left eye, which Dr. Grant wanted him to avoid. The whole point was to strengthen his right eye.

"Can you notice any changes yet?" Luke asked.

Jiggs removed his pair of sunglasses. He squinted against the glare of overhead kitchen light. He shook his head no and immediately regretted the motion. A shooting jab, right behind his right ear. He cupped a hand over his good left eye and tried to focus his right. Luke remained a stubborn blur in a checkered shirt. He narrowed his eye and looked at the far wall. He focused on the bright Ken Done picture calendar he'd hung up last January. The painting was an abstract explosion of oranges and blues. He could make out the smear of numbers beneath the picture, but distinguish anything specific? Forget it.

"Nope. I'm still legally blind without the wire rims."

Luke shook his head with amazement. "You have more guts than I have, I'll say that again. Letting some doctor come at your eyeball with a knife — yuck."

"What?"

"Y-u-c-k," Luke spelled with his hand. He was getting pretty good at signing, but language was still constantly filled with mine fields that required spelling out unfamiliar words. "All I know is, I wouldn't let them near me unless I knew for sure it'd give me twenty-twenty vision."

"The worst that can happen is the cuts will open too much, and I'll become farsighted."

"So *they* say. Come on, let's eat. This is ready." He made a big show of draining the noodles and ladling out huge portions of the stroganoff.

They ate in companionable silence, with the TV flickering images in the corner. It was too hard to read lips while eating, and too complicated for Luke to lay aside his fork and use his minimal signing skills. But Jiggs didn't mind. They'd worked as cooks in the same restaurant for several years, and had slowly nourished a true friendship. It was funny, in a way, because Luke was such his opposite: tall, with wiry black hair and a gray-speckled beard that frequently rotated as goatee, mustache, and back to a beard for the cold and rainy San Francisco winters. Right now, in June, he wore only a mustache. None of his clothes were new. He roamed the secondhand clothing stores in the Haight for used jeans and comfortable, well-worn shirts. He'd come to the city from Fresno, and would always consider himself a country boy. He'd probably never even have left Fresno at thirty-four had Luke not decided that a husband, not a wife, was what he saw in his future. He had a yen to try all the pleasures and sins a big city could offer.

Whereas Jiggs, after ten years in San Francisco, felt jaded, bored, and no longer in tune with the political trumpeting of the younger gay community. Or queer community, as they labeled themselves now. There wasn't much the city could offer him that he hadn't already tried or rejected. He'd always been more comfortable as a loner. His flaming red hair set him apart in a world where it seemed everyone had brown or black hair, and his being deaf was usually misinterpreted by strangers as a snobbish aloofness.

That's what was unique about his friendship with Luke. Luke didn't ask many questions. He didn't mind silence. He was fascinated with the logic behind sign language, and was mastering it in his own clumsy way. Otherwise they talked in simple sentences that Jiggs could usually follow. Like right now.

"So why do you want to move?" Luke asked. He was stabbing his stroganoff with quite a vengeance.

Jiggs watched him, puzzled. "I just want more elbow room, now that I can afford it. Something with a view, or a backyard. In town. Though the Russian River area up north has always interested me."

His friend's face darkened. Luke stared at his plate. "Don't worry," Jiggs quickly said. "I won't leave you to the city wolves all by yourself."

Luke was frowning. "Why this need for change? Most people I know want everything to stay the same. But you: you inherit a g-o-b of money, and the next thing I know you're having risky eye operations, talking about quitting your job, and now this. Moving. You're so lucky to have this money. I'd hate to see you blow it all at once."

Jiggs stiffened. "Lucky? You think I'm *lucky?*"

"You know what I mean."

Yes, he knew. But Jiggs would never, even in jest, refer to his parent's accident as lucky. Having a back tire blow loose at sixty-five miles an hour on a freeway was not his idea of luck.

Luke reached across the table. "I'm sorry. I didn't mean to stir up painful memories. Forget I said anything, okay?"

Jiggs made the sign gesture for "I'm fine": thumb against his chest, fingers extended. After a moment he cleared his throat and pushed away his plate. "They wanted so much for me, but I think I disappointed them. They never accepted my being gay. They just tolerated it because I was their son. They never understood me. How could they? *I* never understood me. I'm thirty-two years old and still haven't a clue what to do with my life. Their insurance money, and the freedom it brings me, only reminds me of that truth. That's why I want to take time off, and figure out what's important."

Luke was nodding. He elbowed his own plate away and shook out a cigarette from the pack in his shirt pocket. "Then that's what you have to do."

Yes. It was a feeling that had been building in Jiggs, something as subtle as a shifting breeze. He was quietly and systematically being urged into a new direction, an uncharted terrain. The eye operation was a part of it. Oh, maybe that was too melodramatic an explanation for what really amounted to guilt over his stagnant life. He had been given the means to change his life. Now if he could only figure out what to do with it.

It never occurred to him that the cause was already stalking *him.*

3

He had the dream again that night.

The worst part was knowing how it would end. How it always ended. What changed — with no rhyme or reason — was the beginning. This particular dream started with him about eight years old, sitting in the backseat with a picnic basket wedged between his legs. Good smells drifted over him. Potato salad. Fried chicken. Baked beans with lots of brown sugar. He could still hear then, and they were singing songs as Dad drove to the park for a picnic. He tried to warn them that something was wrong with the car, but his mom and dad were too busy singing. They didn't hear him shout that the bolts on the left back tire were coming loose. They ignored his pleas to turn around and go back to the Mighty Lube and complain that the two new tires had been improperly mounted. No matter how much he waved his arms or shouted, he remained invisible, a guest to witness the inevitable.

Somehow, he always knew when to throw open the back door and jump out. He was never hurt. Only his mom and dad got hurt. Hurt bad. From the shoulder of the highway he'd watch as the back tire exploded out of its sockets. The skidding car, flipping over three times. He could hear in these dreams. Hear the squeal of metal grinding against concrete, and a high-pitched falsetto cry that could only belong to his mother. He could smell burning rubber from the other cars as drivers frantically braked to avoid a crash.

No, he never knew how these torturous dreams would start, whether he'd be a little boy who could still hear or a grownup visiting Austin from San Francisco. But it always ended with the fire. The exploding fireball put an end to any hopes of rescue. Though of course he always tried. He'd run close enough to the car to see his parents writhing in the flames, their hands pounding against the glass windows. The inhuman screams.

On this night, dreaming about that terrible day, Jiggs saw himself lunging for the door handle. The heat was terrifying, the flames full of menace. If only he could get the door open. His mother would spill out then. She'd be burned, but alive. He knew he could save her, and *if* he saved her, then surely he could save his dad.

With a mad snarl he threw himself against the door, his hand gripping the handle. Pain exploded up his arm and out the back of his head. Smoke sizzled up from his palm. A seared, sweet-sour smell of cooking flesh filled his nostrils. Somehow he depressed the button, and the door swung open. A great furnace of heat and flames roared out. He ducked against the flames, and looked. His mother was sitting calmly in the inferno. Her hands were clasped in her lap, a white purse tucked neatly against the fold of her arm. Her hair was on fire, swirling and shrinking in the heat. She turned her head and looked at him.

"Help them, Jigger."

He frowned. "I want to help *you*."

His mother shook her head. Her pink face was strangely expressionless. "Your father and I don't matter. Help them, when they ask."

"Help who? *Who?*"

She smiled then. It was a creepy smile, full of mystery and secrets. "But be careful, my son. They are full of tricks and deceptions."

Jiggs startled awake. He was slick with sweat, his heart pounding with a disco beat. The dream and its imagery lingered like a smoky haze in his dark studio. He was aware of an ache: hearing his mother's voice again, and the ache that was a hole, all the space that his parents had formerly occupied in his life, which was now empty. His imagination was vicious when it came to constructing this horrible event he had never witnessed. It provided nightly tortures. This was the first time he'd managed to open the car door in the dream. Usually he would just wake up as he reached into the heat.

And hearing his mother. What a strange thing for her to say: *"Help them."* Help who?

He settled back against his damp pillow. His parents were two years in the grave, buried in twin plots outside of Austin, Texas. It had taken one and a half years to bring their case before a court. The jury found in his family's behalf, and ordered the auto repair shop to pay compensation of half a million dollars, to be split equally between his older brother Doug and himself. It couldn't bring his mom and dad back, but it did bring a certain satisfaction, and justice. Even so, when the first of many checks arrived in the mail he held it at arm's length, repelled and nauseated by what it represented. Weeks passed before he'd eventually taken the check to his bank, and watched how in a single day his meager account quadrupled in size.

Jiggs rolled onto his side and searched out the luminous hands of his alarm clock. 3:20 a.m. A dangerous time of night, unless he could slip back into sleep before unwanted thoughts crowded his brain. But wait. Wait a minute. He was missing something. Something so clear it dangled in front of his nose.

And it hit him.

He glanced back at the clock. For a second or two the clock's face was a glow of green light. Suddenly, startlingly, wham! The numbers snapped into clean focus. 3:22. He could even make out the sweep of the second hand. Just as suddenly he lost it, the numbers disintegrating into chaos. He narrowed his eyes and the clock face once again leapt out at him.

He could see it. Actually see it! Look, Ma, no glasses!

He found the lamp switch beside the bed and clicked it on. He stared at the periphery of light, willing objects into focus. His bookcase was stacked high with books and magazines. He could make out a few of the titles. Oh, this was great, great! What a thrill, to see without glasses. He held up a hand and cupped it over his left eye, to make sure the right eye was truly working.

But before he had a chance to test it out, he noticed an ache in the palm of his hand. He'd been so excited he hadn't paid any attention. Now it hurt, and throbbed when he touched his face. He lowered his hand and put it under the light. His breath just died when he saw it.

The hand was raw with a burn. Two blisters rose out of his palm. And some of the red hairs on the back of his hand and fingers had been singed away.

4

The next afternoon he and Luke drove out to Land's End, a dramatic jut of windblown trees and craggy cliffs with spectacular views of the Golden Gate to the right, and the vast expanse of the powerful Pacific to the left. It was also home to rocky nude beaches populated by hardy gays inured to the constant cold wind, and dense thickets of underbrush that had once been an infamous natural playground.

They walked out to the very edge of one cliff. With a fanfare that amused Luke, Jiggs ceremoniously tossed his glasses over the edge and watched as the hungry Pacific chewed them up.

"Are you sure you want to do this?" Luke signed with his hands instead of shouting over the wind. He watched Jiggs remove his contacts holder from an inside shirt pocket.

Jiggs nodded. "Even if I eventually have to wear glasses again, this prescription will never be right. Why keep them? This just proves the operation was a success." And with that, he threw the contacts case high into the air, and watched with delight as it crashed among the rocks.

They popped a bottle of cheap champagne Jiggs had brought along and took turns guzzling straight from the bottle. Jiggs was ecstatic. His right eye was improving, his focus stretching longer and longer between short bouts of blurring out. It had been a thrill to so clearly watch himself in the mirror that morning when he stepped out of the shower. But it had also proved puzzling, when he held his right hand up to his face. Except for a strange tingling in his palm, there was no sign of blisters, or of having been burned in some way. Dreams. Crazy, their power over his imagination.

Instead of dealing with the overcrowded Geary Street traffic, they took the long way back, going up Sloat and Portola to the crest of Twin Peaks. It was a Sunday in June without the usual fog, so the tour buses were out in full force, lined up like dominoes at Scenic Point.

Luke turned to him, a mischievous twinkle in his eye. He made their sign for a drink, a smart cocktail detour into the Castro.

"Sure," Jiggs answered with a nodding fist, the sign for yes. He was already giddy from the champagne. Besides, it was fun to go into a bar and gossip about the other patrons in sign language. Today was a day for celebrating.

Luke cut down Clipper Street and drove into Noe Valley. Jiggs looked with new interest at the row upon row of Victorian homes. He'd forgotten what a pleasant part of town this was: cozy, residential, good mix of gays and families with young kids, and most of all, sunny. His studio in the Haight was often fogged in during the summer months. He probably wouldn't see the sun until September. Luke hooked a left onto Bourbon Street and aimed for the Castro District up and over the hill.

Jiggs held up a hand. "Stop the car."

"What's wrong?" Luke asked, but Jiggs didn't see him. He was staring at an attractive gray cottage sandwiched between two taller Victorian homes. A red "For Rent" sign was taped against the glass of the front door. Luke nudged him. "You want to take a look?"

A few minutes later they stood in front of the house. It truly was no bigger than a cottage. A white picket fence separated the postage stamp–sized front yard from the sidewalk. It was over-run with ivy, while the yard exploded with flowering plants and ferns. Its wildness held a certain appeal, but it could all be quite attractive, if tended to by someone with a green thumb.

The front door opened as they stood admiring the house. A prim man in a business suit stepped out. He was talking to a silver-haired woman who followed him out. Jiggs could only pick up a word or two, but it was obvious from the business-man's sour expression that the house had not met his qualifica-tions. The woman acknowledged their presence with a smile and wrapped up her pitch. As the man walked away she turned to Jiggs and Luke and made a retching gesture with her hand and mouth. That cinched it; Jiggs liked her instantly.

Her name was Kate. She lived with her partner Susan, several houses up the street. She was an attractive woman in her midforties with spiked hair who seemed delighted to be showing the house to another gay "couple." Jiggs introduced himself and explained that *he* was the interested party, not Luke, and would she mind talking so he could watch her lips?

They stepped into the main hallway. The master bedroom was on the immediate left, with a smaller room that had served as an office on the right. Jiggs was surprised to see each room furnished with a successful blend of modern and antique furniture.

"Susan and I were hoping to rent the place furnished," explained Kate. "Our last tenant — our last *two* tenants, as a matter of fact — just up and left, with no notice. The last one left behind all his furniture but no last month's deposit. Stupid, huh? If we have to put it all in storage, or sell it off to meet our bills, we will."

"I like it," Jiggs said, and meant it. "They had good taste. Besides, all my piddly stuff could fit into that front office. Studio living, don't you know."

"Oh, that's wonderful," she beamed. "Naturally, we're looking for someone with stability who'll honor his lease. Now here's the main living area."

The house revealed a lot of charm, but Jiggs decided it sure was set up funny. Whoever heard of a house with bedrooms in the front, right next to the street and traffic, with the main rooms on the inside? He followed Kate as the hallway flowed into a living room. Chilly in there, but a window on the eastern side was beginning to warm the air from the sunlight streaming through. The room was handsomely furnished, with a forest green couch, a wooden rocker, and an overstuffed chair. A whole mess of stereo and electronic equipment was stacked against one wall, with a big television in its center.

"Your last tenant must have been in *some* hurry," Jiggs said with a whistle. He glanced to his right, where he saw another small den with a narrow window. The only bathroom in the house was set off from it, gorgeous with paneled walls and a skylight for plentiful natural light.

The living room opened into a huge kitchen, divided by a wooden counter. Here, the hardwood floors gave way to a red brick tile. The kitchen was more than adequate, with an abundance of storage space and cabinets. Off in a corner sat a small black potbellied stove, which would come in handy during the fall and winter. The overall effect was one of coziness and unpretentiousness. Jiggs liked it.

But he was especially drawn to the back porch just beyond the kitchen door. This seemed to be Kate's ace in the hole, the way she swung open the door and encouraged them to step outside. Tall weathered fences surrounded a modest backyard. At the end of the property stood two pine trees, both about twenty feet tall. The yard needed some tending, with quite a few weeds to be yanked, but the potential was obvious. There were fragrant bushes of jasmine. Several rosebushes were in bloom. A section of the fence was woven with bougainvillea.

Luke signed his approval to Jiggs. "Here's your bit of country without having to leave the city."

That's what Jiggs had been thinking too. This house, at least from one perfunctory glance, seemed perfect. Not too big for one person to manage, yet big enough for two people. He'd been toying with the idea of asking Luke to be his roommate, at some future date.

"I can't imagine anyone walking away from a place like this," Jiggs said. They were all sitting in lawn chairs on the deck, enjoying the summer sun.

Kate shrugged. "Neither could we. This was our first house we bought together, Susie and I. We've made a point of looking for people who will help us take care of it. Maybe we've just had a streak of rotten luck, but you'd be amazed at the number of flakes running around this city."

"Number of what?"

"F-l-a-k-e-s," Luke spelled, and Jiggs nodded, smiling.

"So how much would this slice of paradise cost me each month?" he asked.

"Look," Kate said. "I'll level with you. Sue and I aren't trying to make a bundle here. We want someone who'll take care of the place. Someone who will stick around. The rent is $900, furnished, or $800 unfurnished."

"That's very reasonable, especially for this neighborhood."

"We've had a good number of people check out the house, but it's sat empty for two months. I don't know. For some reason, the house rubs them the wrong way. They don't like the master bedroom in the front. The traffic is too loud. The rooms are too small. Or they simply have a ... a ... feeling. We've invested a lot of love and time into renovating this place. Susie put in all those cabinets in the kitchen. She's the carpenter in the family. Me, I'm happy to take in the checks and keep the books balanced. Which brings me to one more point. Where do you work — Jiggs, is it?"

He nodded, feeling himself put on the spot. "I work in a restaurant in the Haight, but I might be quitting this week."

Kate raised a quizzical eyebrow.

"I've come into some money recently. I wouldn't have any problem meeting the rent. And I assume you'll want a first and last month's deposit, in case I join your list of disappearing renters?"

She nodded, clearly embarrassed. "That furniture in there paid for the last mistake. I don't think we'll do that again. Anyway, I think I'll let you two talk in private." She stood up and went into the house.

"This *is* the first place you've looked at," Luke pointed out. "Are you sure you want to be surrounded by someone else's furniture? Not to mention plunking down almost a thousand a month in rent."

Jiggs glanced across the yard to an area back by the pine trees. Puffs of dry dirt flew up from the ground. Probably a squirrel, or a groundhog. The idea struck him as absurdly quaint. He returned his attention to Luke. "This house is a steal. A *house*, Luke; not some boxy modern horror with bad plumbing and rude neighbors. If it becomes too much of a bite each month, maybe you could join me once your lease is up on your place in the Sunset."

Luke did a double take, and then grinned ear to ear. "You sure about that?"

"Sure." The gopher or whatever it was seemed to approve the idea; the mound of earth shook from below, causing pebbles and dirt to roll down its sides. Jiggs felt an immense satisfaction settle upon his shoulders, as warm as the midafternoon sun. Why, it had taken no effort. None at all.

After signing a contract with Kate, events snowballed for the next week and a half. Jiggs sold most of his belongings in a sidewalk sale (where he'd picked up most of it the first time around). What he had left fit easily into the back of a pickup truck. Between Luke and the hired hand with the truck, moving day felt like an extended, all-day party.

There was pizza and beer, and lots of kidding around. Kate bustled over to help and introduced Susie, who was a younger, squatter version of Kate with a quick wit and friendly manner. Susie's sweatshirt was barnacled with a dozen political pins, and she took great pains to explain each one whenever Luke shook his head and pleaded country-boy ignorance. Despite their differences of political opinions, she and Luke got along famously. They were an invaluable team running wires discreetly around furniture and setting up all the electronic equipment. They also attached the special doorbell contraption Jiggs had bought and wanted installed. It flashed a bright light in the living room whenever someone rang the doorbell, which would alert Jiggs that a guest stood at his front door. Kate and Susie thought it the greatest gadget they'd ever seen. They also praised his ability to read lips. It was a hard-won reward, Jiggs explained, after years of speech therapy and schooling at Austin's renowned School for the Deaf, where their family had moved from Dallas after his illness destroyed his hearing. Jiggs didn't have a chance to tell them that he usually only caught about seventy-five percent of a conversation — they were too astonished to learn of his recent eye operation.

Susie shrieked in mock horror. "I'd pass out if I saw a knife coming toward my eye! Gross mama!"

Day and twilight had long since segued into night. Weariness was beginning to etch into everyone's face. Jiggs saw the time, thanked them all, and herded them toward the front door. Yes, he would be fine on his first night alone in the house. Piece of cake. He watched Susie and Kate walk arm in arm up the street toward their house, and he waved good night as Luke revved up his car and drove away. A stillness settled in him as he stood at the front door, breathing in the June night. Maybe it was contentment. Taking charge. And a feeling that after so many empty months, he was finally trying to make good out of misfortune.

He grew so lost in his thoughts that it was startling to glance across the street and realize he was staring at a gorgeous white Cadillac limousine. It was parked in his neighbor's driveway. Moonlight reflected off its shimmering milkiness and the late-fifties-style fins at the back. Perhaps he'd meet the owner and ask about the car. After all, how many neighbors owned a vintage limousine?

As he stepped back inside and began to shut the front door, he thought he saw movement in the limo's backseat. Out of curiosity he stood still. But the motion must have resulted from the moonlit shadows of the trees bordering the driveway. Jiggs walked into his living room and settled onto the couch. How odd, as he turned his head to survey the room, to see his belongings blended with the belongings of a total stranger. What had that person's life been like? Why had he abandoned the house? Now, it was almost as if he and these former tenants had been roommates, their mutual possessions tangled together. As if they shared something.

A creepy-crawly anxiety spread up the back of his neck. First-night jitters. He glanced uneasily into the hole of darkness that was his new den and wished he'd turned on a light in there.

All of this tension would pass as soon as he got comfortable with the house. It was just a matter of time.

He found a Rex Stout mystery he'd been reading, and settled in. To read without glasses was a new and cherished joy. But try as he might, the words didn't make their familiar connection into a story. While he read, his peripheral vision kept insisting there was movement in the other dark room. Whenever he popped his head up from the book, he saw nothing. Not that he *wanted* to see anything — that would have been worse.

Finally Jiggs turned the book upside down to keep his place and flipped on a lamp in the small adjacent den. The soft light warmed the room, even though darkness clung like stubborn cobwebs in the high corners and on the floor. *Come on,* he scolded himself. *This is silly. There's no reason to be afraid.* He went into the kitchen and checked out what was in the fridge to drink. Two bottles of beer left, and a small carton of milk. Maybe it was a sissy thing to do, but he chose the milk, hoping it would calm his nerves and help him sleep. His own dishes and glasses lay wrapped in old newspapers in a box, so he pulled down one of the stout glasses in the cabinet. He poured the milk and went back to his mystery novel, determined to get into it.

Jiggs had been reading awhile, the sentences and paragraphs making sense now, when he reached for the milk. He made to take his first sip, and stared. One side of the glass was already white, the milk half gone. He saw faint tattletale signs of lips against the glass. He pulled the drink away from his face. Yuck. Before he started reaching for dishes, he'd better make sure they were clean. He set the glass away from him on the coffee table.

He read some more. Dosed. When he woke up he felt blurry with sleep, his eyelids glued together. Jiggs stumbled into the bathroom to brush his teeth and take a leak. No problem about falling asleep now; he couldn't wait to lay his head on his pillow. He came back out and glanced at the coffee table. Even in his fuzzy state he gradually became aware that something was different. It hit him when he saw the watermark ring on the glass coffee table: his glass of milk was gone.

His mind clicked with possibilities, the most logical answer being that he didn't remember taking the glass back to the kitchen sink. On impulse he checked the sink, just to be sure. No milk. No glass anywhere.

5

Jiggs thought he had called it a night and could use sleep to wipe all the strangeness away. Instead, deep into the wee hours, he rolled and tossed fitfully in his sheets as an old familiar anxiety dream played itself out.

He returned to that first morning when his fever broke in the hospital. All was quiet. He was an exhausted ten-year-old, wrung through the ringer of illness and persistent fevers, the days having turned into weeks on this strange white bed. His mother looked up from a book she was holding, noticed his stirring, and rushed to his side. Her red lips moved with what looked like talking. Her eyes sparkled. She stroked his wet brow. She was going on and on, fluttery and happy and seemingly chatting away. Only no words were coming out. It looked like they did, the way her mouth opened and closed, and the way her Adam's apple bobbed.

If there was such a thing as recognizing darkness in the heart, Jiggs felt it then, felt a premonition so black he opened his own mouth to order it away. He heard his words in his head. He recognized the usual networking companionship of tongue and throat muscles which indicated speech. But nothing came out. Nothing. It was a little like drowning, as the truth sank in. Drowning, because he did not want to swallow its bitter fountain even as it gushed into his mouth. Yet even as he accepted it, it could not stop his wild shrieks — nor could his mother's frantic grasp at his shoulders — from echoing against the hospital walls as he tried in vain to pierce the silence which had now made a home within him.

The memory dream ended there, with his screams bursting his head wide open, and abruptly switched into a completely different gear.

Now he was walking across the street in front of his new house. He stared with longing at his neighbor's white limousine, which was frosted with moonlight. As he approached, the back door popped open. Jiggs hurried up to it and peered in.

His mother and father sat primly in the backseat. They were dressed to the nines, his father handsome in a formal tux, his mother radiant in a slinky black gown and simple strand of pearls around her neck. Too bad their skin bubbled and sizzled like pieces of frying bacon. Clouds of smelly smoke clung within the confined interior of the limo. All his mother's beautiful red hair had burned down to blackened stubble. Something gluey and sluggish twisted down the side of his father's face. Jiggs recoiled, trying to blink away their impossible presence. His parents patted the empty space between them and motioned with their skeletal hands. He shook his head.

His mother made a face — what was left of it — and shrugged her shoulders in exasperation. "You know what they want, don't you?" Her mouth sounded full of gravel.

"No," he answered. He had no idea who "they" were.

"Well," sighed his mother. "Then I'll just have to show you." She drew her right hand toward her face, polished nails flashing like colored scissors. She tugged down the skin directly below one blue eye and—

Jiggs couldn't look. His shock at what she was about to do blew a fuse in his brain. There was an explosion of white light. He sprang back in panic, his feet crossed paths, and with a wordless whoop he tumbled backward, landing with a hard thump upon the dewy grass.

Something seemed to snap inside his head. He was shaking head to toe like a wet dog fresh from its bath. He looked at his surroundings with an amazement that instantly doubled into full-fledged terror.

The dream had ended, but this new nightmare had only just begun. He was sitting on his neighbor's front lawn, his boxer shorts — the only clothing he wore — drinking in the dew from the wet grass. He had fallen at the edge of their driveway. The limousine of his dream had been replaced by a perfectly ordinary Volvo complete with a baby seat in the back.

A profound shudder whipped up his spine. Jiggs hugged himself. He glanced across the street and saw his new home. The front door stood wide open. The house's interior was as black and uninviting as a hole in the ground. His mind became a tape recorder with only one repeating message: *I sleepwalked. I honest to god walked in my sleep. Walked in my sleep!*

He pushed himself to his feet. A lone car drove past. Jiggs ducked into the shadows of the leafy trees bordering the driveway. His exposed flesh erupted into goosebumps. Christ. Nearly naked, and standing in some neighbor's front yard. He couldn't get over it, he just couldn't. He started to leave. His foot skidded in something slick and viscous on the driveway. Repulsed, he yanked it away and squinted to see what exactly he had stepped into. Motor oil. A small dark puddle. For an instant his mind lined up the puddle with the position of his dream limo, and with a lurch in his guts he knew that the positioning fit.

The cold pulled him out of his daze. Plenty of time to mull this over later, but right now he stood in his underwear, in public. Streaking had gone out of style along with disco, and his presence would certainly be frowned upon. He peeked beyond the trees, saw that the coast was clear, and dashed across the street with a barefooted hop and dance as he avoided anything shiny on the pavement that might be glass.

And his only thought was, *Dear god, this is just the first night.*

6

"You were actually stark naked in your neighbor's yard?"

"Sleepwalking. Can you believe it? I've never been more scared and disoriented in my entire life." Jiggs had to spell out "disoriented" with his fingers. "But I had on a pair of boxers, so I wasn't exactly imitating Adam with no Eve."

Luke shoveled out two scrambled egg platters with a side of bacon and scooted them underneath the heat lamps aimed at the counter. He twisted his waist to talk with Jiggs. Jiggs had decided living inside the house day after day wasn't such a hot idea. Said the house spooked him. Jiggs enjoyed the clack of plates against the counter, the hop-to rhythm of the busy kitchen. Something like that, or close to it. So he said.

"Jiggs." Luke talked with a one-handed shorthand; the kitchen was far too noisy for normal conversation. "Everybody freaks a little when they move into a new place. Aren't used to the house settling."

"That's what is so crazy. The house doesn't *feel* 'settled.' Pass me the tuna melt, would you?" Luke complied. "Frankly, it's just the opposite. I swear I feel eyes staring at me. I thought it would stop after the first night and all, but I was wrong. It's every day now. Every day. Especially the nights."

"Well," shrugged Luke, "I'm not surprised. You're sitting in rooms filled with other people's furniture. It'd take *me* a while to shake the feeling of being a guest in my own home."

"I don't want to be anybody's guest," Jiggs groused. "I want a house and a life. Is that so difficult? To not have a home that plays hide-and-seek with milk glasses? Yesterday I couldn't find my old pair of Nike's. Guess where I found them. Guess."

"Jiggs, you're beginning to wear thin around the edges. We need those pancakes flipped." Luke shook his head and pried out a slightly burned waffle from its metallic womb. "Okay. Uncle. Where did you find them?"

"In the backyard. They were partially buried in that gopher mound over near the pine trees."

Luke faked an exaggerated shudder and grinned. It made Jiggs fume.

"This wouldn't be so funny if it were happening to you," he snapped.

"Oh, lighten up. I believe you," Luke assured him. "But don't you get it?"

"Get what?"

"You must still be sleepwalking." He cracked three eggs for the omelette needed for table four. "The only reason items in your house are getting moved around is because you're doing it in your sleep. Like finding that glass of milk up high in your medicine cabinet. You put it there and don't remember. Same with your shoes."

Jiggs thought for a moment, the wind temporarily knocked out of his sails. The logic made sense. It was the implications that scared the hell out of him. "Luke," he said, "as far as I know I've never sleepwalked in my life. Not until I moved into that house. Why? Why should it start up now?"

Luke chanced burning the omelette and gave his friend a squeeze on the shoulder. He was smiling again, though serious. "Golly, I can't imagine why, unless it's because you're in a brand-new house. Fresh from a serious eye operation. Or that perhaps you're still trying to get over your parents' deaths. Not to mention trying to put your life together so you can use that settlement money for an honorable purpose. Gosh, I don't see any reason why you'd be so anxious that you might start pacing the floors at night."

Jiggs held up his hand. "Okay, okay. I get the point. You're right. And you're much too old to be using words like 'golly' and 'gosh.'" They smiled at each other and worked in amiable silence as they finished off the rush produced by brunchtime customers. Only after it had calmed down did Jiggs admit his true fear. "What should I do about it? See a doctor?"

Luke raised his eyebrows. "If it gets worse, yes. Otherwise, my friend, don't be afraid to admit this whole thing makes you anxious. Give yourself time to ride it out. I'll bet it will stop as quickly as it started."

Jiggs nodded with relief. Luke's words made complete sense. The scary dreams were just his mind's interpretations of that anxiety. He felt so much better, he hated to remember what he'd forgotten to add to his story. How the mound of dirt where he'd found his tennis shoes no longer looked like a mound. It was bigger, the ground freshly turned. Almost as if something underneath was churning it up in an attempt to free itself.

7

It got worse.

8

A few nights later Jiggs came awake right before dawn. He flipped his pillow to the fresh side and settled back into the sheets. He had a feeling he'd been dreaming, but the dream's details were already growing soft, its power over him ebbing away. Half-awake and half-asleep, he was comforted by the warm pressure against his side. He curled into it. How nice. How nice to draw in strength and pleasure. How ... how...

His eyes snapped open. His hand lay draped across the covers, and was resting upon a rounded shape. The shape moved rhythmically, as though breathing. Jiggs forced himself to move his hand. He traced his fingers downward along the covers and came to rest upon what felt like the outline of a hipbone, and then a leg. *What in hell...?* He jerked his hand away, frightened, and rolled away from the shape. His hand groped for the small lamp beside the bed. He found the dangling cord, but at first was too paralyzed by what he might see to use it.

Darkness exploded into light.

For a split second Jiggs saw a human outline framed by sheets and blankets, the body curled into a sort of S shape. Just as suddenly the bed covers shuddered, drooped, and with a strange dignity settled against the mattress where they belonged. Jiggs patted the empty area and threw back the sheets. Nothing. Nothing at all.

But there was a dent in the other pillow, the subtle outline of a face.

9

And worse.

10

Every night, several times a night, at all hours, his doorbell light flashed that someone stood at the front door. He'd grudgingly get up and swing open the door, only to find the stoop empty.

Luke didn't call Jiggs's problem "anxiety" anymore. He wasn't sure what to call it. But he no longer spoke of doctors, though that's what he thought.

11

"You haven't been sleeping well?" Dr. Grant repeated. He shined a light into Jiggs's right eye.

"No, sir."

"Does. Eye. Pain. Night?"

Jiggs sighed. How in the world did Dr. Grant expect him to read lips with this spotlight trained directly into his right eye? All he saw was a poor silhouette that moved its lips.

"Oh. Sorry. Finish." Dr. Grant tapped Jiggs on his knees and shoulders, indicating which direction he was supposed to look, up, down, right, left. After a few minutes of this the doctor rolled his chair away from him. He removed the funny contraption strapped over his head which had allowed him to peer as though through a microscope. Dr. Grant rolled his chair even further back so he could flip on the overhead lights.

Jiggs squinted in the sudden volcano glare. His right eye had been dilated about forty minutes earlier. Now it ached and burned, its surface gluey-feeling from the drops they'd used.

"Can you understand me now?" asked his doctor. Jiggs nodded. "Your eye is right on schedule. No undue swelling, or signs of infection. The incisions haven't overexpanded. You're turning into a model patient." He smiled, waiting for Jiggs to grin at his good fortune. Jiggs only nodded. "So what are these problems?" he prodded. "Aside from looking tired in the face, and not getting enough sleep." The expression on his face was tempered with a subtle plea, Don't take up too much of my time, boy.

Jiggs stalled. A blush of heat stained his freckled face. Maybe he should keep this to himself. Try it out on Luke, and gauge his reactions. But he was in the doctor's office. Here was the authority. If anyone might be able to answer his questions, it'd be Dr. Grant, right?

In a soft voice he blurted out, "Sometimes I see things."

"What kind of things? Floaters? Flashes of light?"

"Flashes of light. Yeah." He chewed on his lower lip, remembering this new strangeness that had been added to an already strange brew. "It's like I see a ... a ... double image."

"Of what?"

"That's what I'm trying to figure out," he said in exasperation. "It's like an image from a movie comes between me and whatever I'm staring at at the time. I see a shadow. Well. Not exactly a shadow. More like the waves of heat that rise off hot concrete."

"Nothing specific?"

Jiggs frowned. "No. I'll blink a few times, and it clears up. Or it kind of dissolves, if you know what I mean." But the good doctor obviously didn't know.

Dr. Grant leaned in. "When did this start? Right after the operation? You didn't mention anything at our first post-op appointment," he scolded.

"No. I didn't notice any problems for the first few days. It started when I moved into my new house."

The doctor threw up his hands. "Well, that may be your problem right there. You've put yourself under a lot of pressure and stress. I warned you that your eye would heal at its own rate."

"You just told me my eye looks normal."

An irritated frown, immediately replaced with a replica of a smile. "It does. Look, what you describe is probably simple eye strain. Don't be afraid to use those eye drops I gave you. They should help. If your little mirages persist, get back in here and we'll run a few more tests."

But Dr. Grant would never run more tests. Jiggs had come to the conclusion that tests wouldn't help. The puzzling forces at work in his house had little connection to his eye operation.

An eye operation doesn't make a glass of milk disappear, only to be found two days later on the top shelf of his medicine cabinet, next to an unmarked bottle of pills. Or hide tennis shoes in a pile of dirt with dirty smudges of what may have been handprints on each shoe. Or put frozen steaks into his pantry. Or ring doorbells.

Returning home from the eye clinic that afternoon, Jiggs paused at the front gate. A picture postcard, his house. He'd cut back much of the wild, unchecked ivy threading through the picket fence, and trimmed off the dead leaves and wilting Calla Lilies. Now it looked like someone who actually cared lived there. Kate had told him the house was once featured in a book of San Francisco cottages, and he understood why. It was beautiful. Attractive, without calling attention to itself.

So why in the world did he always feel reluctant to open the front door and step inside? Why this sinking heaviness, almost like sadness, stealing into his heart. It wasn't fear, exactly. More a growing wonder over what might happen next.

He had barely completed that last thought when a shadowy, amoebalike shape rippled across and up his front door. Jiggs rubbed at his dilated eye and blinked. It didn't go away. Whatever it was moved like a heavy liquid, fingers of it spilling upward toward the eaves of the roof. Without being aware he was doing it, he squinted shut his left eye. There — again, the elusive shimmer of heat-fanned waves as it curled and seemingly reabsorbed into the boards of the house.

He took a moment, not knowing what he should do. He could run up the street to Kate and Susan's, but what then? Tell them about these hunches, these intuitions, these visions which might possibly be just a trick of his eyes?

His hand trembled as he turned the key in the lock and pushed open the door. Almost instantly the hairs on his arms stood on end. His skin went clammy. The interior hallway was dim, despite the midday brightness of the sunny afternoon. As he stepped inside he was suddenly, absolutely sure he was not alone in the house.

Jiggs curbed his impulse to shout, "Hello?" His breathing grew shallow as he shut the door. The sensation of someone watching from a hidden corner latched onto him and would not loosen its grip. There was a pregnancy to the stilled air, a heaviness that stole light. Something was thickening the air into syrup.

God, this was crazy. Crazy. Where was he going to live, if he was afraid of walking into his own house? He forced himself to walk down the hallway and stare into his living room.

The rocking chair was moving. Back and forth, back and forth. The leather seat sagged under an invisible weight, and something unseen pressed against the pillow strapped to the back of the chair.

Jiggs stumbled backward, and may have even cried out in surprise. He felt shot through with an electric jolt, sure that every hair on his body now stood on end. His vocal cords were paralyzed; it was all he could do just to swallow. While he watched, the rocker began to slow its rhythmic back-and-forth movement. It came to a gentle halt. The cushions sprang back to their normal shape, as though a weight pressing against it had lifted.

He cleared his throat. "Don't mind me, guys," he whispered, hoping his voice was soufflé-light, masking his tension. As soon as the words fled his lips he was struck by what they implied: a kernel of belief that suggested not some*thing* in the house, but some*one*.

A breeze rustled his hair, accompanied by an abrupt drop in temperature. A biting cold moved through and around him — a meat locker cold, like something frozen solid pushing past. If Jiggs had been shaken by the sight of the rocking chair moving by itself, his fear then was nothing compared to finding himself enveloped by this Arctic blast. The silent wind tugged at his hair and clothes and seemed to want to burrow into his gaping mouth; he snapped his jaw shut in reflex. He was afraid to breathe, afraid he'd see his breath plume out in frosty, ghostly defiance of reality. He sucked in a breath and tasted a horrible gravelly sludge in his mouth. The pebble-and-mud taste made him gag and his stomach revolt. His eyes clamped shut. He raised fists next to his ears. Very clearly he heard the scrape of a shovel as it skimmed across metal.

His eyes blinked open. Something was above him. He tilted his head further back and saw a shovel hanging in the air. Poised above his head, it tipped. All at once a sludgy muck splattered onto his face.

"Hey!" Jiggs cried out. His hands flew to cover his face. The cold released him. The stunning image of the shovel released him. His mouth still reacted to the taste of whatever it was, bitter and rocky. He peeked through webbed fingers and lights danced across his vision, lights that warned he'd better plant his behind onto a chair before he passed out. His legs were loose and wobbly. In one fluid motion he collapsed onto the couch.

It was only much later, as he tried to put the experience into perspective, that Jiggs realized he had *heard* the shovel dig its cargo from the wheelbarrow.

It was the first sound he had consciously heard in over twenty-two years.

13

Sometime in the dead hours of that morning, when night wielded its tightest grip, a car horn shattered the silence. Jiggs came awake with the blare of the second horn, and sat upright in bed, heart in his throat, with the shrill of the third blast. His hands gripped each other, as though the pressure would assure him he was awake.

Awake, and that he had heard a horn. Actually *heard* it.

He threw his legs over the side of the bed. He was definitely awake, no ifs, ands, or buts about it, and if he heard the car horn one more time he was going to spring from the bed and investigate. He didn't dare to think what it could mean.

He waited. The silence with which he had made an uneasy truce over the years spun on and on, uninterrupted.

But the mystery nagged at him. Jiggs got out of bed and padded over to the front door. He tugged back the flimsy curtain covering the peephole window. Beyond the gate, sleek in the moonlight, waited the limousine. With his face nearly pressed against the cool glass, he thought he could actually hear the chug chug chug of the limo's exhaust pipe. He felt his testicles crawl into hiding at the sight — and sound — of it. His skin erupted into gooseflesh. *This isn't happening.* But the illusion moved. A back window glided open on electric skates. The interior was a black maw against the gleaming white, with no hint of what lay inside. Until the arm appeared.

It was shaped like an arm. Jiggs saw the crook of elbow, and stubby fingers spread wide as though in signal. It just didn't look like an arm. It was covered with something viscous and gray. Blobs of it dripped onto the side of the car as the hand motioned for Jiggs to step out of the house. It reminded him of bird droppings.

"No," he whispered. "No." He could hear the engine of the great machine idling, but he could not hear his own voice. The insanity of this pulled him away from the curtain. He could look no more, and double-checked the locks with trembling hands.

But he heard the limousine shift out of park into drive, as it rolled away into the night.

14

Why? Jiggs asked himself the next morning over a bracing cup of coffee. He pushed aside the daily paper he'd been trying to read. *Why should anyone — or anything — be interested in me? I have no experience with any of this. I have nothing to offer.*

That afternoon he was grateful when Kate came by and suggested he join her on a grocery run to Safeway. Perhaps, if he broached the subject properly, she'd have some answers for him. But it was impossible to talk while Kate drove the car; she turned her head too much, or she stared at him so intently he was afraid she'd forgotten she was behind the wheel. At any moment he expected to crash. And Safeway was a harried mess of shoppers swerving carts around little old ladies and impatient kids.

He waited until they were back at his house, the grocery bags piled onto the kitchen table. Kate wore a frown on her face. Her nose crinkled up, as though she smelled something bad.

"What is it?" Jiggs asked her.

Kate shrugged. "Is your house always this gloomy?"

"It's the day." Summer fog had swept away the blue sky, painting the afternoon in chrome.

His landlord shook her head. "No. It's more than that. Doesn't it seem stale in here to you?"

This was his first hint that someone else felt the peculiarities of the house. Jiggs waited, silent.

"Oh, don't take offense. We should open the doors and windows and give this place a good airing out."

He nodded. It was easier than expressing his true fears, that no amount of fresh air would rid him of whatever had decided to take up residence there. He started to pull groceries from the plastic bags. "Kate, have you or Susan ever noticed a white limousine around here?"

She stared at him as though he had spoken Greek. "A what?"

"A Cadillac limousine. It's white with big fins on either side, from the late fifties. I saw it in my neighbor's driveway the first night I moved in, when everyone went home."

Kate moved her mouth around, as if she had to taste the words she was about to say. But after all that preproduction buildup, her answer was simple. "No. Not that I know of."

"You didn't notice it parked in the driveway across the street?"

"No. Sorry. But then, who pays attention to things like that?"

Jiggs shrugged. Who indeed? He dug out more of the groceries.

"Well," said Kate. "I've got ice cream melting in the backseat of the car..."

"Kate, did any of the earlier tenants who lived here complain to you about anything ... anything weird with the house?"

"Weird?"

He took a breath. "Funny noises. Objects being misplaced. Seeing things they didn't understand?"

"You mean like poltergeists? Ghosts?"

"Ghosts. Yes."

"No. Never. Why? Do you think this house is haunted?" An incredulous smile was spreading across her face until she saw he was serious.

"Well — maybe. Is that so unbelievable? It does suggest a reason as to why your tenants skipped off without even bothering to take their furniture."

"Oh, I don't believe it. Honestly. This is a perfectly normal house." But she lowered her eyes, and grabbed each elbow to support them across her stomach.

"Which, of course, explains why you couldn't rent such a normal little house for two months — and in this neighborhood. You told me yourself: the place rubs some people the wrong way."

A wall crashed down in front of Kate's eyes. Her gaze grew frosty. "What exactly are you implying? That I rented to you under false pretenses? Didn't warn you to watch out for spooks?"

Jiggs raised his hands in front of his body. "Please understand. This has nothing to do with rent. Did anyone renting here ever say to you the house is odd, or that items disappeared without explanation, or that they may have seen things they didn't understand? Because if they did," he breathed, "I will, too."

Kate mulled it over. She scratched at her starchy spiked hair. The frost in her gaze had thawed. "No. Never a word. Sorry. I know that's not what you wanted to hear, but it's the truth. Look, I've got things defrosting. Maybe I'd better hustle on. Have you seen my purse?"

"It's on the counter." Jiggs turned away from her in dejection. This had gone badly. He should have waited for the next night, when Luke was coming over for dinner. He'd see what his best friend had to say.

Kate plowed across the kitchen floor. She was making bird motions with her head and shoulders, quizzical, pecking. "You're not trying to make a point now, are you? I know I brought in my purse. I put it right there." Her fingernail clicked against the empty counter in punctuation.

They searched the kitchen and living room. Nothing. Kate had a hand over her mouth, trying to suppress her giggles of frustration. "Don't say I told you so, or I'll brain you! This is *un*believable! I'd better go call Safeway even though I *know* I didn't leave it there. This must be punishment for using politically incorrect plastic grocery bags. I knew I should have said paper. Call me — I mean, come over if you find the purse. Or if one of your little ghosts decides he doesn't like my shade of lipstick." She waved halfheartedly and strode down the hallway. At the door, she remembered something and turned.

"Just for the record, two men used to live across the street. Married. One of them ran a small repair shop out of his garage for high-priced specialty cars. Mercedes and the like. Maybe your limo came to him for service. Except that doesn't make sense either. They moved."

"Moved?"

"One of them did, anyway. I think the mechanic's business up and closed. Maybe his work got too popular for a residential area, and he had to move to a bigger place. Only thing is, his boyfriend hung around for a while longer before he also moved. Maybe they broke up. They were an odd choice for a couple, one in fancy business suits, and the other always covered in grease and overalls. But hey: oil and vinegar. It works for Susie and me."

"Thanks, Kate. Really. I'm just trying to make sense out of nonsense. If I find your purse, I'll bring it over."

Kate opened the door, but hesitated yet again. "Susie and I loved this house the moment we set eyes on it. We never noticed anything to complain about the whole time we renovated. If something *is* going on here, it started after we began renting it out." She waved a final time and left.

Jiggs put away the remaining groceries. He thought about what Kate had told him. Maybe she did occasionally sense stirrings in the house, but it frightened her to label it as ghosts. Frankly, he wasn't sure he could either. Perhaps strong emotions had somehow imprinted themselves in the walls, with the mood of the house shaped by the people who occupied it. He shrugged. It was as reasonable an explanation as any.

He reached into the last plastic bag, felt something oddly shaped, and pulled it out. It was a thick blue spiral notebook. He dug back into the bag and brought up two new Bic ballpoints. A premonition rippled through him.

I didn't buy these, Jiggs told himself. *I know I didn't.*

He flung the items onto the kitchen table.

15

That night the feeling was back, stronger than ever, of being watched.

He avoided looking into the corners of the room, where shadows pooled. He wiped clammy palms against his sweatpants. A steak dinner had settled like lead in his stomach, making him nauseated.

It was a long, empty time before sleep pulled covers over his eyes, and he eventually dozed. Images swirled behind his eyes. Whispers seemed to tickle his ears.

He awoke suddenly in a full sweat, startled as if by a loud crash. Jiggs sprang up in bed and gulped for air. His temples pounded. He was afraid he was going to be sick. With great care he swung both legs over the side of the bed. *If I hear a car horn, I'm going to scream and never stop. I swear it.* There was no car horn, just this nausea that urged him to the bathroom. With arms outstretched to claw his way through the darkness, he aimed for the bathroom and groped for the light switch just inside the door.

He didn't scream. He was too shocked.

But he banged up against the wall, thrown back by the explosive sight in front of him. Jiggs's throat made funny gagging noises as though he were a man having his life choked out of him.

Kate's purse lay in the sink. It had been emptied, its contents strewn across the counter. Checkbook. Makeup. Credit cards. Photos of the happy couple, Kate and Susie. Kleenex. A tampon. Several books of matches. Next to the hot water spigot was the opened tube of lipstick. Its end had been cruelly blunted, held by clumsy, unsophisticated hands.

Scrawled across the mirror in huge childish letters, blood red:
COME TO US

16

"Why?" Jiggs asked the mirror. "Why are you doing this to me?"

No reply. Not that he expected any. Not that he would have been ready or prepared to see that tube of lipstick lift into the air by invisible hands and start to scrawl an answer.

Wearily, a headache pounding right behind his eyes, he piled the contents of the purse next to the sink. He took a sponge and a spray bottle of Glass Plus from beneath the sink and worked on the mirror. The lipstick made stubborn, bloody smears before surrendering its message. He worked on automatic, consumed by the task at hand, not thinking. It would be too dangerous to think.

The mirror cleared and gleamed beneath his hand. He dumped the contents of Kate's purse back into the handbag. The only item he had not touched was the tube of lipstick with its blunted end. Jiggs felt a superstitious dread just looking at it: as if he knew, somewhere in his heart, that picking it up would escalate this madness. But he could not leave the lipstick there beside the sink, a red exclamation point to what had occurred there.

He scooped it into his right hand, snatching it the way one would sneak up on a nasty crawling bug. Its bulletlike shell was cool to his palm. He half turned to toss it into the open mouth of Kate's purse when his hand flooded with raw cold, as though he'd stuck it into a bucket of ice water.

Air hissed between his teeth. His hand jerked and twitched, even as the numbing cold stole up his arm. All at once his hand attacked the mirror, the lipstick drawing one tortured letter at a time, as words assembled themselves onto the glass. Jiggs snatched at his right wrist and yanked his hand away from the mirror. He had not been fast enough. Now the mirror said:

TALK TO US

His lips trembled with wordless horror. "How?" he whispered.

Again his right hand reacted violently, and shot to the mirror. Beneath the other words, the tube of lipstick wrote:

LISTEN

Jiggs dropped the lipstick. It clattered into the sink. He clenched his eyes shut and accordioned down into a tight ball, the bathroom tile cold against his naked ass. "I don't know how, I don't," he chanted, a kid's lost plea against the bogeyman. "Please go away. Leave me alone."

He awoke with dawn's first gray strokes of light filtering through the bathroom's skylight. Jiggs was numb and shivering. Beside him lay the spiral notebook, turned to the first blank page. Sticking out of his right hand like a blue bone was one of the ballpoint pens.

17

"Why didn't you say something sooner?" Luke scolded.

Jiggs swallowed. "You believe me?"

He shrugged at that, unable to immediately answer. He pushed away his empty dinner plate and turned his chair to the side for more leg room. "What I believe," he said, "is that you have no reason to make up such a farfetched story."

Jiggs relaxed a little. Anticipation of this talk with Luke had wound him tight all day. "I'm telling you, Luke, I haven't had a moment's rest since the very first night I moved in." He scooped up the dirty dishes and took them to the sink.

His pal shook his head. "Limousines that only you can see — and *hear*, for god's sake! Feeling yourself being watched. Those wild dreams. And writing on the mirror." Suddenly he grew somber. "What do they want from you?"

Jiggs rinsed his hands and came back to the kitchen table with a dish towel to dry his hands. "That's what I have to figure out. I think they want to talk with me."

"Like a seance?"

"No." A shadow crossed his face. "I think they want me to go with them."

Luke caught his eye, deadly serious. "You're alive. They're dead. The two don't mix."

Jiggs turned his face to the ceiling in exasperation. "Why didn't they pick Kate or Susan? It's their house!"

"You think the other tenants went through this?" Luke asked once Jiggs lowered his head to continue the talk.

"Yes. Scared them so badly they split." He looked at Luke with a new curiosity. "Do *you* feel anything odd about the house?"

His frown said it all. "I'm freaked by what you told me. But the truth is, no. The house doesn't give me the creeps the way it does you. Although I *was* uncomfortable the first time we viewed the house."

"You should spend the night, and see for yourself." Jiggs's eyes popped wide. "Could you? Stay? I'd really appreciate the company." His face glowed with his idea. He should have thought of this before.

Luke looked bewildered, then pleased. "If you want me to, sure. Long as I get to work tomorrow on time. I can't afford your part-time hours."

"No problem. I'll even sleep on the couch."

Luke scooted away from the table. "Then let me grab a few things from my car."

"What could you need that I haven't got?" Jiggs asked as he followed his friend down the hall to the front door.

"Oh, I keep a toilet kit in the glove compartment for special occasions — or emergencies. Toothbrush. Cigarettes. Perhaps a toy or two. A few rubbers."

"Boy, you *do* come prepared," laughed Jiggs. They went outside. The nighttime air had a bite to it. Fog slouched over the hills of Twin Peaks. "I'll bet you were a Cub Scout, huh? 'Fess up."

Luke stepped to the edge of the sidewalk. His car sat directly across the street. "Always willing to help a friend with ghost troubles." He looked both ways and started across the street.

Luke looked both ways. Jiggs was sure of it. He remembered it. He saw him do it.

But neither one saw the limousine until it was too late.

There was a white flash, like gunsmoke, only bigger. Like a space shuttle blasting against the reins of gravity. All at once it was just there, roaring up the street. Jiggs heard the engine growl and watched it shoot forward with its predatory pounce.

The limousine struck Luke at midwaist. He had begun to turn in the limo's direction, reacting to the violence of noise and the sudden appearance of the broad white hood. There was a moment of upraised hands. He had time for that, barely. A thud, like the booming of thunder. And then the sickening snap of breaking bones. Luke soared over the wide hood and smashed into the windshield. His lanky arms and legs flopped at angles Jiggs would have thought impossible, even for a life-sized rag doll. He rolled toward the passenger side, twisted and flung, and fell legs first to the uncaring pavement.

Jiggs flew to his friend's side. He knelt beside him, desperate to help. Luke lay on his back. His face was chalk dust, clammy. A monumental bruise was rising from his left cheek. His ashen lips moved with what Jiggs could only guess were moans. His eyes had rolled to the back of his head, eyelids fluttering madly. Luke's jeans were soaked with blood around his thighs. His legs didn't lay straight. And his left side, where the hood of the car had struck him, seemed somehow dented and mushy in a way that brought bile into Jiggs's throat.

He looked up the street and raised a fist. "You bastards!" he shouted. "Why'd you have to hurt him?"

But the street was empty with an eerie twilight, so still and unmoving the night might have become a photograph.

18

Tubes. More tubes. Monitoring devices that scrawled Luke's lifeline up above his crumpled body. Men and women in white jackets who poked and prodded and put their hands to their chins. Luke's left leg already in a plaster cast. His ribs taped. And the dreaded diagnosis, delivered as Kate and Susan held Jiggs's hands in support: "Coma."

Kate drove them home from Kaiser Hospital. Their silence was full of despair. Jiggs had wanted to stay. Wasn't it true that people in a coma could hear a friend's voice, and might actually respond? But the doctors urged him firmly to go home and get some rest. There was nothing more to be done that night. Plenty of time to sit at his bedside and help Luke recover. The police were searching for the elusive white limousine, confident that such a unique car would easily be found. Jiggs had scowled and said nothing.

"Why don't you stay with us tonight?" Susie asked as Kate pulled up to Jiggs's house. "We've got a really comfortable couch..."

"Thanks, but no." Jiggs shut the rear door and glanced toward his feet. He was almost standing right were the hit-and-run had happened. He stepped back, afraid he might get sick.

Susie rolled down her window, but it was Kate who leaned across, her face tight with concern. "Aren't you afraid to go inside?" Her eyes flicked toward the house.

It had remained unspoken between them, what he'd told her about the house and mysterious limousine. Her eyes reflected a fear that had never been there before.

"Yes," he answered truthfully, and stepped onto the sidewalk. With words of encouragement and promises of getting together in the morning, Kate slowly drove further up the street to their own house.

The night had turned wild. Gusts of wind tugged at his clothes and jacket like the grasping hands of madmen. Tree branches thrashed above his head. And in that moment, a wildness stole into his heart.

He wasn't afraid. He was angry.

Standing in the center of his living room, arms crossed in defiance, Jiggs said, "You had no right to hurt my friend. If you wanted my attention, you have it. Show yourself and tell me what you want."

A steady silence was his only answer. His heart thumped against his chest.

"Come on," he challenged. "You've already shown yourself once tonight. This is your big chance. Let me see you."

Sweat popped out along his brow. The air grew dense in a way that was difficult to define. An electric charge spiked the hairs on his arms. A cold swirl of that freezer-burned air brushed past his shoulder. The branches of his houseplants began to sway and undulate. His nostrils flared with the scratchy smell of dirt and bits of pebbles, steamy with decay.

Jiggs licked his lips. "That's it," he prodded. "Show yourself."

Quite clearly, a wailing moan. He jerked in the direction of the sound. It was followed by a confusion of whispers that came from all sides, wild and as unpredictable as the stormy wind pounding the outside of the house. The whispers raced up and down the walls. Skirted across the ceiling. Spoke directly into his ears, causing him to flinch at the exhale of stale cold air.

The rocking chair began to sway back and forth. An empty soda can jerked off the coffee table and clanged to the floor. It rolled to the far wall, where Jiggs saw other loose, light items like coasters and his paperback mysteries were now flinging themselves to the floor. One of the gay weeklies flapped loose sheets of paper and stuck to the blank wall.

It felt like a vacuum, as if a rip in the fabric of whatever he recognized as reality was about to tear apart the wall. He imagined himself being sucked into some monstrous pit to the other side, where he'd be lost forever.

And here it came: the same inkblot shape that he'd seen slithering up the front of the house. It rose out of the floorboards like oil, defying gravity, and spread out tentacles as it went. At about midheight on the wall, the stain expanded and became a more solid shape. It looked like a drooping doorway, or an old movie screen improperly set up.

And still the air was frantic with movement. One of the pages from the weekly flew up, stuck to the stain, and before his eyes was absorbed into the wall. The same fate was repeated by the soda can, and one of his paperbacks.

By this time Jiggs had had enough. He backed away and grasped the door frame leading into the den. No way was he going to be drawn into that maw of black emptiness. But as he watched, he saw movement from within its darkest core. Something gray and white was surfacing with a fountain of oily bubbles, floating up from some unfathomable depth. All at once the figure of a naked man broke through to the surface. Jiggs gasped.

The man in all that black was Luke.

Sort of.

He possessed none of the round sturdiness of three dimensionality. Luke's features seemed as though painted onto a surface of wet clay. His eyes blinked wildly. He was trying to focus them, but couldn't quite succeed. His body jerked with a marionette's clumsiness, and each movement caused Luke's puppet face to twitch. There were strange nubs, almost like large teeth, punched through him at various places along the edges of his body. They seemed to support him up out of that liquid pool. His cheeks were pulled tight with these strange needles—

Oh god. Oh no. Jiggs wanted to cover his eyes.

Fingers. That's what they were. Fingers that held Luke from underneath and hooked through the flesh of both cheeks. There were hands in his shoulders, his thighs, his feet. Hands that were partially rotted with decay, the bones stark against Luke's skin.

The frantic currents of wind died down as this macabre image completely asserted itself.

Jiggs found his voice. "My god, Luke, what have they done to you?"

The fingers sticking out of his friend's cheeks tugged and pulled. Luke turned his head, facing him, but whether he could actually see Jiggs was anyone's guess. A sleepwalker's trancelike voice rasped out, "I'm with the dead. The dead took me."

He was so startled by this he didn't stop to consider that this was the first time he'd heard Luke's voice. "How could they do that? You're in a coma in the hospital. I just left you there."

"My body is there, yes. But they took me as I lay on the street. It was part of their plan."

"Plan?" Jiggs stepped closer to his friend, no longer worried about being yanked into that inky dark. "Tell me what they want."

Luke worked his throat with difficulty.

"Your eyes. They want your eyes."

19

"My ... my eyes? Jiggs's fingers rose in a protective gesture to the hollows above his cheeks.

"Your operation. It did something utterly unique. It allows you to sense them. To see them. And because you are deaf in the living world, they have opened up a channel so you could hear them as well." His voice was so flat and unemotional Jiggs wondered if it truly was Luke speaking, or if he was simply an instrument for their voices.

"Luke, who are they? Do you know?"

"Here, they are called the Unfinished. Earthbound. Their lives were interrupted, their desires, incomplete. It chains them to this place."

The bony fingers curled and raked at Luke's face, contorting it with pain. They obviously did not approve of their secrets being revealed.

"Why couldn't they have told me themselves?"

"They tried. You were too afraid. So they took me as ransom."

Jiggs felt his heart derail. "Ransom?"

"For three nights they will come to you. Each will tell their story. It is the only way to break their chains, to complete the circle." Suddenly Jiggs saw a flash in Luke's eyes, a glimmer of his true friend. For the first time Luke seemed to actually stare at him. "But know this: being earthbound changes them. It doesn't matter what kind of life they led when alive. The Unfinished are poisoned by their own unfulfilled desires, and angry in their predicament. They brought you to this house. They will remain trapped here forever unless you help them. It's very dangerous—"

One of the hands hooking through Luke's cheek suddenly shot even further out and clamped over his mouth. His eyes bulged under the assault. His muffled whimpers were like a dog that had been kicked in the face.

"Stop it!" Jiggs shouted. He was furious. "Leave him alone! I'll do it. I'll do as you say. But you must release him when we're finished. You harm him and the deal is off."

A great cyclone of wind abruptly filled the room. He watched helplessly as Luke was yanked back under that shimmering oily surface, still in the terrible hooklike grasp of the dead's hands. As though there was a leak on the other side of the wall, the black stain began to drain into the wall. Within seconds, it shrank to a few inches in size before the wall completely reabsorbed it. Only the wind-scattered papers and fallen pillows from the couch testified that anything had been there at all.

Jiggs collapsed onto the couch. He was so overwhelmed that for several minutes he could not move. He dragged his hands across his face and suddenly remembered the dream with his mother. "You know what they want, don't you?" she had started to say as her painted fingernails rose toward the flesh of her eyes. She, too, had warned him of danger.

His eyes. They want his eyes. His ears. And his hands, no doubt, to write their story into the notebook they had lifted from the store.

Jiggs shook his head in misery. What else could he do? Now he was as trapped as these earthbound.

A car horn honked in front of the house. He jumped at the sound, a wave of revulsion shuddering through him. His doorbell light flashed on and off. Couldn't they give him a few moments to collect his wits? To sleep off some of his exhaustion?

He thought of Luke with those fingerbones sticking through his face, and he stood up. Wearily, he went to the front door and stepped outside.

The white limousine waited for him, its engine idling. Moonlight winked off the red taillights and sharp fins of its backside. Without bothering to lock his front door Jiggs passed through the ivy-covered gate and approached the limo. There was a splatter of red stain on the hood and windshield; he averted his eyes.

"Okay," he whispered, and held out his palms in supplication. "Here I am."

The rear passenger door popped open. No light came on, but there was a phosphorescence of some kind, greenish blue, which suggested the interior and the figure within.

"Get in," rasped the passenger. His voice was curt, and somehow gravelly.

Jiggs understood as soon as he stepped in and shut the door. He remembered the gray, goopy arm motioning for him a few nights earlier.

The figure on his left was naked, and encased in concrete. It was still wet — perhaps, as part of his earthbound condition, it would always be wet — and dribbled an endless mushy stream of pebbles and gray goop. The man snapped his head toward Jiggs. Bits of gravel flew off his chin and stuck to the leather seat. All at once the man reached out and grabbed a fistful of Jiggs's shirt.

"Hey!" Jiggs flinched under the assault. His fright was so great he was having trouble catching a breath. "I'm here to help you, remember?"

"Driver, get going," the man growled. The chauffeur dropped the gears into drive. The man leaned in close. His eyes glowered from deep gray sockets. "This better work," he hissed. "Or you're staying with me. Just like him." He flicked a glance toward the chauffeur and released his wet grip on Jiggs's shirt.

Yes, Jiggs thought. *This sure better work, or I'm as dead as they are.*

SAM SPEAKS:

Backstabbers

Lust

1

won't go until I settle the score. Until I get even. I won't.

2

My own damn fault, this mess. I'm man enough to admit that now. I had brushed aside a growing army of suspicions, ignoring them even as they continued to pile up. When you don't want to see something you simply don't see it, no matter if it's staring you eyeball to eyeball.

And what started it all for me was that limo. That beautiful white Cadillac of precision machinery and magic, gliding past my garage where I work. From that day forward, my fate, as they say, was sealed.

I saw it maybe half a dozen times over the course of a few weeks. I always keep the garage door open when I work on a client's car to catch a bit of the spring sunshine. The garage stays cold, chilly in the mornings almost year-round, but about one-thirty, two in the afternoon the sun would begin to creep along the cement floor, pushing cold and shadow into final retreat. In the summertime I had to run a fan to keep the garage bearable, but for months on end, like that month of April with spring in full bloom, the sun was a welcome companion, as comforting as my lover Rich's arms about my shoulders.

The first time I saw the limo whiz by, my hands were buried deep in the guts of a BMW brought in by some fastidious guy from Pacific Heights. I happened to look up, wiping my brow with the sleeve of my jumpsuit when I saw it go by. I know beauty when I see it and this car was the real thing, a classic over thirty years old. Sleek and gorgeous. Perfect set of whitewalls. Classic set of fins and red taillights. A '57 or '58, was what I figured with that first look.

When Rich came home from work that night I told him about spotting the limo. He looked at me oddly, frozenly, before breaking into a tolerant smile. He knows zilch about cars, and like so many of my clients, could care less, just so long as their own car runs when they need it. Still, to Rich's credit, he's always indulged this little passion that I'd turned into a profitable business, and he tries to take an interest since he knows how much it means to me. Hey, I've gritted my teeth a few times as I sat through those obscure art films he used to drag me to early in our relationship. Even when they were in English I couldn't follow half of them. Rich had to fill in all the gaps afterward. Operas were hopeless.

The second time the white limo went by I was standing in the driveway having a quick smoke. It passed slowly, as though trawling for something. I caught a glimpse of the driver. He wore a classy little cap on his head, and a flashy dark suit to contrast nicely with all that white. Maybe I'm reading more into that moment, now that I know Joe and got to see that suit up close. But I *do* know I caught enough of that man's glance to assume he had something on his mind, and my working on cars was the least of it.

So I pulled the cigarette out of my mouth and offered up a return smile, what the hell, when horns started blowing. My part of Bourbon Hill can be a busy street, and those drivers didn't take too kindly to a limo cruising along at fifteen miles an hour. The driver — who by now was almost out of sight — tossed me a little acknowledging wave and sped up. On impulse I flipped him a thumbs-up gesture, a bit of appreciation for *his* appreciation.

And that was it. I didn't see him go by the next day, or the next. I forgot all about him. After all, I was a busy man. Lots of work. With spring in full bloom, guys were getting their fancy cars all tuned up for Easter trips out of the city, little getaway adventures. Since I'm just a one-man operation except for my part-timer Bill, I was really hoppin'. Rich was busy himself with his job at Bank of America. I look back on it now and I see we were coasting, both of us up to our elbows in work, too tired at night to do anything much more than flop onto the sofa and watch TV. Our relationship had a few years under its belt so I don't think either one of us was worried. Once tax time was over, we'd both catch a breather.

Then I saw the limo again. Just cruising by. A wave from the driver, and a flash of white teeth. I figured he must live nearby, and used our street a lot. I began to make up fantasies about the guy. This is embarrassing to pass on, but hell, that's the whole point, isn't it, to tell all? My guts are already spilled, so to speak.

You know what I'm talking about. Guys like us, we love the fact we know no boundaries. That our attractions to each other are based on a whole host of circumstances. Look at Rich and me: him a banker, in his three-piece suit; me a mechanic. But together, we're terrific. And lots of guys who bring me their cars — I see that glimmer in their eyes. I know they're looking at me in my dirty jumpsuit and a little grease under my nails. Once in a while I glance back. I suppose I'm a sucker for three-piece suits, for men who think they're above it all one minute and then begging for it the next. Since I'm telling all here, I may as well admit to a few blow jobs in the shadows of the garage, or in the front seat of their cars. I fulfilled some kind of fantasy for those guys — the straight-looking car mechanic who'd dig into his pants and pull it out for them. I used to tell Rich about these digressions but he told me flat out he didn't want to know about them. He wanted me to be careful, yes, but he wanted no knowledge of them. Fine. I could respect that. Truth is, these were very rare occurrences. I had a business to run, after all.

I guess what I'm driving at is that events were quietly slipping into place. Rich and I were hardly talking to each other. A touch of spring fever. I hadn't had any sort of outside adventure in months, not since the previous September. And like something waiting in the background, here were this man and his gorgeous limo, slowly building my interest, stoking the fire of my fever, giving me that itch that demanded to be scratched. One day, I used to joke with myself. Maybe. One day ... Never dreaming it would actually happen...

Right up until that sunny morning when the limo pulled into my driveway. The day it all started. The day it all ended.

3

The man shut off the engine and stepped out of the limo.

"Hi," he said.

"Well hello there," I answered back. "What's the occasion?" My tone of voice let him know I recognized him from his driving by. I'm too old for coy, and so was this guy in his chauffeur's outfit. The man hooked his thumb toward the hood.

"Do you have a minute to look under the hood? Something's whining under there, making a lot of racket. I didn't think I'd be able to make it back from the airport."

He was gushing, words tumbling out with a nervousness that hinted — now that I look back on it — at other reasons for this meeting. There was a brush of red rouging his cheeks.

"Sure," I said, all good-naturedly. "Pop the hood and start her up for me."

He nodded obediently — strange that I thought that at that time: obedient — and started the car. Sure enough, a whine cut through the air, rising from a tangle of wires and hoses. Took me two seconds to locate the source of trouble. I motioned for him to kill the engine.

"Can you fix it?" he asked after he climbed out of the driver's seat.

"Here's your problem right here," I said, and pointed at a badly frayed piece of cloth — all that remained of a fan belt. He studied it with the respect due a serious injury or accident: a furrowed brow and big, interested eyes. He really was on the slender side, up close. I had the impression that if I pulled that suit off him he'd drop another few pounds of padding. No love handles on this guy, and we were probably about the same age, midthirties. Me, it's a losing battle. But his eyes were a pastel blue, sort of the china blue color of the spring sky. His blond hair was actually a woven combination of white and gold and brown strands; an uneven, bleached-on-top look that might have been natural but was more likely the result of past tinkering with Clairol. His mustache looked like a thatch of straw under his nose.

It was a swift appraisal, this glance, while he studiously peered into the foreign territory of the limo's engine. I began to realize the black suit and jaunty little cap of his chauffeur's outfit created much of the illusion of his attractiveness. Mind you, he was no dog. He had that boy-stuffed-into-a-man's-outfit look. You know: someone wanting to appear very professional, dressed in the right clothing, who comes close to achieving the desired effect, but who falls short just the same. It's that mismatched look — like his hair — not for everyone, but cute and appealing in its own way.

"Don't worry," I consoled him. "Its bark's worse than its bite."

His eyes lit up. "You'll fix it, then?"

I nodded. "But first I have to finish playing with the BMW in there," I said, and indicated the dark gray car sitting in the April shadows of my garage.

An odd smile pulled his lips. He blurted out — but oh so smoothly, amusement and proposition neatly intertwined: "And once you're finished, you'll be ready to play with ... mine?"

We stared at each other. His eyes drank me in, watching for my reaction.

"Perhaps," I said.

"It'll be worth your time," he volleyed back, his tone satin smooth, like a shot of Jack Daniel's.

I was a lot of things at that moment. Amused. Interested. Cautious. Flattered. It had been too long since I'd had any proper attention. I felt rusty with these coy remarks, these hints and innuendoes. It should have tipped me off about his character. He was not, I was about to learn, a man of forthrightness. He hid behind detours and ellipses, preferring to leave intentions and words dangling so that I had to scoop them up, and come to my own conclusions. He was someone who thought bad deeds could not touch him or impinge on his character if the words never crossed his lips.

Awkwardly, he thrust out a hand.

"I'm Joe," he said.

I shook his hand and countered with my own firm grip. "Sam."

"Sam," he repeated, and his eyes darted over me once again. "It fits you."

"Yeah," I agreed self-mockingly, "an average name for an average guy."

"Oh, I wouldn't say that. Not too many guys of our ... persuasion ... choose your kind of job. I mean, auto mechanics rates right up there on the avoidance scale with high school gym class."

"What about you?" I challenged.

He waved a hand dismissively. "My lack of expertise is rather obvious, wouldn't you say? I just drive this thing. My partner's the one who knows all about cars."

"Why didn't you let him take a look at it?"

Joe looked at me funny, as though he'd made a gaffe, then dropped his eyes to the ground. "He's running some important errands today." His glance lifted, his eyes full of unspoken promises. "Frank won't be back all afternoon."

"Is that a fact?"

He nodded, and then burst into a little chuckle. "Look at me," he said, shaking his head.

"What?" I didn't get the joke.

Joe hit me with the punchline. What his mouth would not divulge his hand decided to reveal. His right hand dropped down and brushed against the striking upward bow of his erection. It seemed monstrous, huge, pressed against the confines of his dark gray slacks.

"Where did *that* come from?"

Joe's cheeks were pink. He gestured toward the street. "Guess it's from watching you all this time," he admitted — one of his few straight answers.

My own cheeks felt hot, but not from embarrassment. The sight of his hardness so close to me had ignited a flame that was rapidly becoming a small fire. Time to leave coy behind. "I've been watching you, too. Wondering if you were ever going to stop by and say hello."

"No time like the present."

Cliches and euphemisms: I blamed it on nervousness, on the awkwardness of the situation.

"I really do need the limo worked on," he hastily added. "I have an airport run in the morning."

"This won't take me long," I said.

"So you'll be ... free, later this afternoon?"

"Maybe. If I get hustling, that is."

Joe pushed a card into my hand. "Why don't you call me when it's ready. When you're ... ready."

"I'm ready right now," I whispered huskily.

That pleased him. He ran his tongue over his lower lip and then jerked his head toward the garage. "You want to...?"

Reluctantly, I shook my head. By this time I had my own bulge in my pants saying yes, but my head had to say no. "I've got too much to finish at the moment. And my part-timer's gonna be here in another half hour."

Joe leaned in close. I wanted to taste his lips, his mustache. "Then call me when you finish. You can see on the card I don't live too far away, about ten blocks. I could be here in no time. Or you could swing by my place..."

"I may do just that," I surprised myself by saying, my voice low.

A car horn honked in the street. I jerked at the noise, the connection drawing the two of us together broken by the harsh sound. The day and its duties were waiting for me.

"Go home," I told Joe. "The sooner I take care of my babies over there, the faster I'll see if I have any spare time in my day left over for a rendezvous." My mouth was saying those words but in my heart I'd already made my decision. With a bit of retuning I could manage a couple of hours on my own this afternoon. Plenty of time to get wild and woolly with this man in his jaunty cap. A quick harmless fling on a warm spring afternoon.

"Okay," Joe agreed. "I'll get out of your way. For now. Just be prepared to deal with *this.*" And with his back still to the street he groped himself quickly, grinning at me with a bad-boy leer. He turned and sauntered off, his legs slightly spread.

4

Excitement stoked cool fires as the hours ticked by. I thought my concentration would be shot through with forbidden images and lusts, but like a surgeon performing a delicate operation, I remained levelheaded and steady. I would not allow myself any dalliance if it meant I performed a slipshod, hurried job. My customers want the best, and me, it's what I demand of myself.

Still, anticipation jangled my nerves, dramatically heightening my senses like a drug. Only for a job well done would I reward myself with this rendezvous with Joe.

I finished with the Stauters' BMW and broke for lunch. My part-timer Bill would be in at one. He could handle the tune-up on the Hutchinsons' car while I changed Joe's fan belt. I could disappear for a couple of hours while Bill minded the shop, then return by four-thirty or five. I had it all worked out.

Right up until Rich called from the bank.

"How's it going today?" he asked after our hellos. "Busy?"

"As a matter of fact, yes. Just got a rush job on that beautiful fifties limo I've told you about. Can you believe, a chauffeur who doesn't even know how to change a frayed fan belt?"

I expected a laugh, but all I received was silence. Lots of it.

"Hello? Rich? You still there?"

"Yeah. Sorry." He coughed into the phone. "I guess I just needed to hear your voice." Again the silence, hued with streaks of purple, if something like silence could be assigned a color. Rich could be a master at hiding his true feelings or intentions whenever he needed to, so it made this fumbled silence of unspoken words all the more odd.

"Listen," Rich said in a rush. "I'm really sorry we haven't spent some quality time together lately. All my late nights at the bank, trying to get their tax accounts in order ... They're busting my balls, I swear."

"That could prove interesting, given the right circumstances," I countered in my best porno truck driver voice.

Finally, a chuckle out of him. "It *has* been a while since we got down hot and heavy, hasn't it? I could go for a little raunch, and maybe a toot up the nose."

"You told me you'd given that up."

"Hey, I'm not dead. But wouldn't you know it, I *do* have to work late tonight. It's why I called, to warn you. Think you could handle a late dinner?"

My mouth was sandpaper. "Yes."

"Good. See you about seven-thirty, my hunky proletarian. Love you."

"I love *you*, Rich."

A knife right to the heart, right to that part of me anticipating that afternoon's playtime. Accusations and reprimands flew through my head. Coward. Cad. Backstabber. We had been coasting, Rich and I, but while he was making provisions to close that rift, my plans could only tear us further apart.

I pushed away the other half of my tuna sandwich, recriminations stealing away my appetite. A tuna sandwich on light rye: I didn't know at the time it was a condemned man's last meal. Would I have finished it, had I known? For as I sat there new directions took hold of my thoughts, and resolutions. New directions I was convinced would lead me away from secrets and infidelities. What I didn't realize of course was that the path, once chosen, would allow no detours.

I called Joe later in the afternoon. I'd finished replacing the fan belt. Bill had arrived a little after one and had set to work replacing spark plugs and fine-tuning the Hutchinsons' car. My decision had been made.

"The car's ready? That's great news," Joe gushed over the phone. His voice roughened, dropped in pitch. "And it's still early."

"Joe, listen—"

"Uh-oh. I recognize that tone of voice."

"How could you? We barely know each other."

"Doesn't matter," Joe said. "This is the part where you say the day's gotten away from you. That you have a dozen unfinished errands left to take care of. Or where you say you weren't really interested, after all."

"No. That's not true. I *am* interested. I've just had a change of heart."

"What does that mean?"

"It means I need to spend some time with my lover," I said. "It's nothing personal. The timing for this is just all wrong."

"What did he do, call?" He sounded irritated. "You talked to him and now you're feeling guilty."

"As a matter of fact, yes."

"We have the whole afternoon to ourselves. How could the timing be wrong? Look, Sam, I'm not expecting to go steady here. You don't have to give me your class ring. We *both* have someone in our lives. I like that. It keeps this ... uncomplicated. Up-front. We have no illusions. Do you understand what I'm saying?"

"Yes," I reluctantly agreed. True enough, this would be no illicit romance. This would be a straight-to-the-point, one-time-only shot. Clean and simple. Or so I thought.

"So how about it, handsome? The afternoon is young."

We continued to go back and forth, Joe whittling away my resolve with his sexy banter until I agreed to drive the limousine over to his house. How long I might linger at his place once I got there, I couldn't have said. My body was still voting yes, stay, while my heart picked up a dissenting cry. I told him I'd be over in half an hour and hung up. The debate still raged inside my head, but now it would not be influenced any further by Joe's talk.

Even as I convinced myself of a decision to say no, I found myself brushing my teeth, combing my dark hair, freshening up. An odd, knowing expression skipped across Bill's face when I told him I'd probably be gone most of the afternoon while I ran some errands. He pointed to the limo.

"Since when do we provide door-to-door service?" he asked.

I felt my cheeks go hot, and turned from his inquiring eyes with a deliberately flippant motion. "Are you kidding? This is a treat to drive a beauty like that. Maybe I'll tool around town first before I return it."

Had he noticed I'd freshened up? He watched me with a bemused expression as I climbed into the limo. Maybe it was my own guilt I saw on his face, reflecting back at me. But once I was seated inside the luxurious interior of soft black leather, I thought, *Do it. Drive to Joe's house and get this over with.* The road to hell, as they say.

5

The address took me to a nondescript house in a long row of houses all built back in the fifties. It was in one of the city's many neighborhoods of houses smacked up against each other, with a tiny square patch of lawn out front, a garage, and manicured shrubs lining the sidewalk up to the front door.

Joe's house was a little on the undernourished side. Its white facade had faced too many brutal seasons and ocean winds, so that what might have been referred to kindly as "weathered" was actually blistered and cracked, white dulled to a dirty gray. No one had put a pair of shears to the riot of shrubbery climbing the walls in haphazard fashion for quite some time, and the brown lawn had given up the ghost ages ago, victim of drought and neglect. But hey; I wasn't here to give a critique of Joe's house in his neighborhood. People get busy, choose other priorities. My house was my workplace, and was therefore a reflection of my pride. For Joe, this immaculate limo. No guest rider would ever need to see this beauty's home.

I pulled into the driveway, maneuvering the grand car carefully up to the garage. No sooner had I shut off the engine than the front door to the house slid open and Joe popped out. His grin was huge as he walked toward me. The nervousness was back, as though he wasn't sure what to do with me right off the bat, now that I was present in the flesh. He was dressed casually, in a pair of blue jeans and green t-shirt that hugged his lithe body. Personally, I still craved a view of his uniform, and imagined peeling it off layer by layer as I pinned him against a bed.

Joe read my mind.

"Once we get inside," he said with a knowing leer. He glanced around nervously at his neighbors' houses as though he didn't want us to be seen. "Speaking of which..."

I nodded my agreement. We walked toward the house and slipped into its dim interior.

"As they say: excuse the mess," Joe apologized with a wave of his hand. "Frank and I are in the throes of remodeling. At least I won't give you a tour of the basement, where it's *really* a mess."

No problem. And while they were at it, they could remodel their furniture as well. My eye for fashion is about as cultured as a mud wasp's — Rich is the one with that talent in our family — but even *I* shuddered at the appalling lack of finesse with which these men had decorated their home. It was an embarrassing mishmash of motel blandness: utilitarian, dull, and cheap. Oil paintings of California seascapes competed with oh-so-cute mountain vistas of a cabin by a stream. The only saving grace of these starving artists' show rejects was that they hung so high on the white walls my nose came almost even with the bottoms of the frames. All that was missing was a velvet painting of a crying clown. Then again, I hadn't yet seen the bedroom.

There was a gate about three feet high strung across what looked like the entrance to the kitchen. I started toward it, curious, when a German shepherd lunged for the gate, sleek and silent as a bullet. His snout drew back to reveal amazing rows of sharp teeth. The sight of him knocked me back a step.

"Boris, sit!" Joe commanded.

The dog lowered its behind to the floor, but pranced with its front legs, seemingly eager to make a meal out of me, if necessary.

"Sorry about that," Joe apologized, though he didn't appear to be all that sorry. Maybe he didn't realize how hard the conga drums were beating against my chest. Now a bit of pink flushed his cheeks. "Frank and I sometimes get unwanted guests in the house. Boris is our insurance for when we want them to leave."

"Oh? What happens when you decide it's time for *me* to leave?"

My companion only grinned, and hopped over the makeshift gate. "How about a drink? Scotch okay?"

"Fine." I glared at Boris with my best evil eye, but the damn dog wouldn't even flinch. So I glanced into the kitchen, which reflected the same slightly seedy taste — or lack thereof. Open cabinets revealed mismatched plates and glasses. Tacked to the wall was a Colt calendar of naked men draped in various articles of leather. On a small table, a portable thirteen-inch TV. Beside the TV, a gaily printed cookie jar that looked straight out of Donna Reed's kitchen. My eyes rolled skyward and I saw the scales partially hidden on the top shelf. I recognized instantly that these intricate twin scales of weights and measurements were never used for food. I looked at Boris, guard dog, and thought about what Joe had said: *I sometimes get unwanted guests.* Yeah. I'll bet.

Joe added a splash of water to our drinks and then handed me a hefty one. He climbed back over the gate and raised his glass in salutation. "To the afternoon," he said, and we clinked glasses.

The scotch was strong, a heated ribbon that warmed my throat and gut.

"Do you know why people do that? Clink glasses?"

I shook my head. Joe gestured toward an awful plaid couch and we sat down.

"It's an old custom. The devil is supposed to hate the sound of breaking glass. So you clink glasses before you drink to keep the devil away while you get drunk."

He beamed at me expectantly, a student waiting for his pat on the head from his teacher.

I smiled indulgently and turned the glass in my hand to avoid a chip on the rim.

"What's the matter?" he suddenly asked.

I let out a long sigh. I felt too tired to lie. "I'm sorry. I feel distracted."

"Maybe this will help." Joe reached across the glass coffee table to an antique wooden cigarette box. He pulled out a joint, smiling wickedly.

"Oh, I don't know about that...," I muttered.

"Come on. Relax. We've got the whole afternoon."

"With this drink and a few puffs of that, I'll be floating in the ozone." But I dutifully dug out of my pocket my engraved silver lighter.

"That's the whole idea, butch." He lit the joint. His hand appeared on my knee and slid along my inner thigh. His sly smile made a return visit, lighting up his narrow face in a manner that immediately melted some of my resistance. What did it matter, the mess of his house, the lack of style and grace? I was there for an hour, two at tops. I ran fingers along Joe's arm and gulped down more of the scotch. When he handed me the joint I eased in a few puffs, mindful of not coughing up the smoke.

"You don't have a driving job today," I said suddenly. A pulse thumped at the side of my head.

Joe gave me a quizzical look. "Yeah. So?"

"I saw the scales in the kitchen."

I don't know why I said it; the combination of smoke and drink was making me cocky. I wanted to see how Joe's face would arrange itself into a save.

He only grinned, nonplussed. "Yeah, Frank and I take care of a few friends with a yen for nose candy. Candy, and smoke. That's it."

"I believe you."

"It helps pay the rent." His face lost that defensive look and suddenly brightened. "Why? You need some? I'll give you a fair price."

"No, thanks. The most I do is a little smoke now and then, and Rich gave up coke a few years ago, though he still does it occasionally."

It crossed my mind suddenly that Rich might appreciate a little present. A present to appease my own guilt for this afternoon dalliance, though he wouldn't know that. Rich had liked nothing better than to snort a toot and get down and dirty. For someone as conservative and highbrow as Rich, he had a streak of wild man running through him. He loved me with grease under my nails, dirty from the guts of some engine, to paw at him in his three-piece suit. Rich would probably get off on the shabbiness of Joe's house, on the whole idea of having sex in such a cheap room, watched by a German shepherd.

I shook my head and giggled.

"What's the matter?"

"Nothing," I answered, and leaned back on the couch, spreading my legs in invitation. I was woozy with alcohol and smoke, pleasantly buzzed. I had to go with this feeling, keep it uppermost in my mind. Otherwise the reality of this unimaginative place and meeting would intervene. Already I envisioned yanking my pants on minutes after shooting my load. I would waste no time beating a hasty retreat.

I looked at Joe. "So where's that uniform you promised me?"

"More fun to be *out* of clothes than in them. But come on: I've got a surprise." He stood and pulled me up from the couch. I wobbled unsteadily, quite frankly startled to find myself so intoxicated.

"Where are we going?"

"To the playroom."

"*Play*room?"

He took my hand and guided me through the living room. I stuck my tongue out at Boris as we passed the kitchen entryway. I felt a pleasant stirring in my crotch. Maybe this was going to work out, after all. The booze and grass had certainly aroused my randy side.

In a narrow hallway beside a bathroom we came to a halt. On our right was the open door to the master bedroom. Joe reached high above him and grabbed hold of a dangling cord. A mouth yawned in the ceiling, a rectangular patch that creaked open onto darkness. My stomach did a lazy somersault at the sight of that darkness: it was like staring into a hole in the ground when it should have been the heavens I was seeing.

And then Joe was yanking on the folded-up ladder, unfolding it until it touched the floor. "Voila!" he beamed. "Your gateway to pleasure."

He started up the stairs still facing me and then stopped when his crotch was level with my face. "Come and get it," he whispered huskily, and pawed at himself through his jeans.

Before he could go any higher I suddenly buried my face in his crotch, grinding Joe against the ladder as I felt that enormous bone against my cheeks and lips. He grabbed the hair at the back of my neck and squashed my face against him.

We grinned at each other, our eyes dark with pleasure. This was going to work out just fine. He quickly turned around and clambered up the creaky narrow stairs.

I followed. No spring sunshine intruded upon the attic shadows; we were immediately cloaked in dusty mauve. Dust motes swirled about me. Most of the attic was bare except for a collection of cardboard boxes shoved against the far walls. This "playroom" essentially consisted of a double mattress raised off the floor by a single piece of plywood. Joe had already thrown himself upon the mattress. I found myself wondering, fleetingly, if the sheets had ever been changed.

As I stood above him, Joe peeled off his t-shirt with one fluid motion and tossed it onto the floor. His chest gleamed whitely in the shadows. A nest of blondish brown hair sprouted between dime-sized nipples. He kicked off his shoes and raised himself expertly to slither out of his blue jeans. He kicked them into a crumpled pile by my feet. Fully displayed before me, his body seemed boyish and thin, his enormous erection a ludicrous attachment to such a slender body. I was afraid of moving my mouth, afraid my smile would give away my thoughts.

Then Joe saved me from any such embarrassments. He stood up, his head bowed in obsequiousness, and helped me out of my clothes. He knelt at my feet and untied my tennis shoes, pulling them off one by one, followed by my socks. I have to admit it was wildly arousing, this sudden subservient attitude on his part. He finished undressing me, pulled me around and pushed me onto the bed, my feet still touching the cold attic floor. In a silence charged with sexual tension he leaned forward and took me into his mouth.

So much for foreplay. So much for a delicate touch. Joe fell upon me as though determined to prove something to himself, as though he'd been challenged and by god he was going to kick some butt. In my intoxicated state I was a little overwhelmed at the fierce attention, but gladly submitted to Joe's pawing. My head whipped side to side in pleasure. Even while at the height of it, my nose crinkled slightly at the sour smell of the sheets. The things one notices...

But I did not want to travel this one-way street alone; a bit of reciprocation was necessary. I wanted to grab and taste that monster dick that had brought me here in the first place. I wanted to share, if that makes any sense. What seemed to be happening between us was nothing more than a lopsided masturbatory fantasy. I touch you, you touch me, then I touch you ... We were two men cocooned in our private thoughts and pleasures.

I made Joe stop, though his tongue had discovered a delight-ful stretch of my inner thigh. I swung him around so that he now sat at the edge of the bed, and I knelt on the floor. The plywood board bit into my kneecaps.

He leaned back, and the monster was before me, curving up and across a skinny thigh. It was pink as a baby, richly veined, waiting for attention. A stoned smile stretched my lips: this would be a memory worth hoarding, this moment of first touch.

I bent to take him.

And we both heard it, the car pulling into the driveway and shutting off its engine.

Joe scooted onto both elbows. We stared at each other, his erection waving like a windshield wiper between us.

"Frank," he said.

6

A hot electric current whipped through me. I've no doubt that if a mirror had been placed before me, it would have showed my hair standing spikily on end. I was caught in the cheapest and tawdriest of situations, and it hadn't even been worth it. That thought kept buzzing lightning fast around and around in my brain: *It hadn't even been worth it.*

We heard a car door open and slam shut with a screechy bang.

I leveled Joe with an accusatory stare. "You told me he'd be gone all afternoon." Despite my anger, I'd dropped my voice to a whisper.

Joe shrugged with aggravating calmness and smiled apolo-getically. I had a sudden urge to throttle him. Instead I snatched at my pile of clothes, pushing aside socks and pants for my underwear.

"Don't bother," Joe said. "He'll be here before you can get dressed."

"Just watch me!" I snarled. If there was to be a confrontation — and there seemed no way out of it — I'd be damned if I'd be caught with my pants down. I would not be caught naked in someone else's apartment. But I was shaking so badly I couldn't even slip on my underwear.

"It'll be okay," Joe tried to assure me in his best placating tone. He threw me a conspiratorial look. "This has happened before — to *both* of us. He won't be too mad, I think."

Again I had to squelch an urge to grab him by his neck. Great. Just great. The reason for the state of this attic playroom became abundantly clear. In these danger-filled times of unpronounceable and deadly diseases, I'd picked myself a man who regularly tricked out on his lover. Correction: probably *both* of them tricked out, this playroom their snug hideaway, as though doing it in the house — but not in their own *bed,* heaven forbid — was somehow safe.

A wave of revulsion rolled through me, neatly overlapping my fear. I cursed my predicament and fervently wished there were such a thing as a teleporter, like out of "Star Trek." I wanted to vanish in a cloud of humming dots and reassemble in my own house, Rich at my side.

Rich. Never had I wanted my lover so badly as I did at that moment. Never had I felt so much a cad and coward.

Joe abruptly rose from the bed and searched for his pants. "Let me go talk to him," he announced. "You wait here."

Where the hell do you think I'll go — out the window? I stared at him coldly as he grabbed for his pants and slid into them. His erection, like mine, had shrunk into hiding. He stuffed himself into his jeans and buttoned his fly. Without bothering to pull on socks or a shirt, he descended the ladder.

Up until that moment I would not have believed a grown man could be so consumed by terror — and that that man could be *me.* I had no frame of reference for the horror pounding my heart. No nightmare was so acute as I stood there yanking on my jockeys while I heard Frank unlock the front door to their house and step inside. Boris was barking a greeting, anxious to be let out of his kitchen prison. I heard Joe tell Boris to shush, and then an exchange of hellos.

A voice I didn't recognize asked, "What's going on? Were you sleeping?" It was a pleasant voice, calm. It was a voice that had no reason to accuse of mischief.

Joe murmured an answer I couldn't hear. I took the opportunity to play Olympics and threw on the remainder of my clothes in record-breaking time. I thought I just might possibly throw up, my heart was beating so fast. Maybe it *would* be okay. Maybe they'd laugh it off, the two of them downstairs. The very fact they had a playroom spoke to a certain amount of understanding between them.

I tried on these different thoughts like various hats, desperate to find one that would fit and comfort me.

Their voices grew louder. Hurriedly, I laced up my sneakers.

"You're sure?" I heard Joe ask.

"Sure I'm sure."

They were directly below. My chest thudded with drums.

"Frank, I want you to meet Sam."

"Hello," came that voice. Still calm.

I sucked in a breath to steady myself. Showtime, folks. "Hello," I croaked in an artificially cheery voice.

Weight on the ladder. A head popped up. Salt-and-pepper hair, like mine, but tight to the scalp. Amused brown eyes. Frank studied me for a moment, and I, him. A salty mustache twitched above his upper lip. "Come on downstairs," he said at last. "I won't bite."

Air forced itself out of my lungs and out my mouth in silent exhalation. I relaxed — but only a little. At least we weren't screaming at each other. At least accusations weren't being flung. I climbed down the ladder.

"I have to go," I immediately announced when the three of us stood face-to-face in the now crowded hallway.

"Nonsense," Frank said, and took hold of my shoulder. His hand was hot, burning through my shirt. He propelled me into the living room, and gestured for the couch. "Joe, how about a round of drinks, huh? Oh. Looks like you two already had a head start. Freshen yours and pour me a stiff one while I entertain our company."

"Look," I stammered. "I'm sorry for this. Really. But it's late, and I have to get back."

Frank's lips slit open. "What's your hurry?"

"I have some errands to run."

"Oh. I see. This—" He gestured around the room. "—was just part of your day of running errands?"

I shook my head, flustered.

"Sit down." For the first time I detected a cool thread in his voice, cool as the long afternoon shadows that now invaded the living room. No one reached for a lamp; Frank seemed to prefer this semidarkness. What he did reach for was the unfinished joint sticking out of the ashtray.

"This is the best way to end a day, don't you agree? A joint, a drink, a little conversation." Frank tipped his head and lit the reefer with my lighter, admiring its unique design. His face bloomed orange, lit from beneath like a kid shining a flashlight upon his face. He had a wiry, tough look about him, like he'd once been a boxer in his youth. His dark eyes gave back no reflection of himself. Whatever thoughts swirled behind those flat eyes were his private property. When he talked, he had the ancient remains of a New York accent.

I decided to try again, though already my heart knew my pleas would be useless. "I really do have to get home. I'm expected."

"Oh?" He passed me the joint, which I waved away. His hand hovered in the air, refusing to budge, until I took the cigarette from his fingers. "What's his name?"

"I don't think that's relevant."

"Relevant?" That amused him to no end. "You can tell a lot about a person through their name."

I sighed. "Rich."

"Rich. Not Richard, but Rich. Now see: that sounds like the name of someone who would be very upset to learn you were here."

I felt myself bristle at that, but in a steady voice I said, "Look, Frank, I don't know how many times I can say this. I'm sorry. Okay? This is not one of my finer moments." I passed him the joint. "I fixed the limo and I tell you what. It's yours, gratis. Okay? But now—"

"You're responsible for fixing the limo? Well then we really *must* celebrate. Sometimes we have to work ... odd jobs ... to help take care of our expenses, but that car, as Joe probably told you, is our lifeblood. Where the fuck are those drinks?" This last bit abruptly whipped out of him like a lash.

Joe appeared at once at the kitchen door. "Let me put Boris out."

"No, open the gate. He and I haven't said our hellos to each other." Frank studied me with cool appraisal. "You aren't afraid of dogs, are you?"

I shook my head. Inside, I felt a coiled spring of tension twist up another notch.

"Good. I didn't picture you the type. Come'ere, Boris."

The German shepherd bounded into the room and knocked against Frank's knee. My whole body tensed up tighter than a Nebraska farmboy's asshole. Boris spun around, allowing Frank to scratch him behind the ears while keeping a determined eye on me.

Joe slipped into the room like a living shadow, a triangle of three drinks balanced within the web of his fingers. He set the scotch rocks onto the glass coffee table and scooted a drink toward each of us. His bare chest, I was dismayed to notice, was prickled with gooseflesh. He was either badly frightened, cold, or both. I opted for both.

Frank hooked a thumb toward their bedroom. "Go put on a shirt, for Christ's sake," he instructed Joe. Joe disappeared without a word. I watched him go with a growing sense of unease. He would be no help, should this situation turn nasty. The role he played in this household was becoming abundantly clear. I'm surprised he'd found the nerve and tenacity to get me over here in the first place.

I reached for my new drink, anxious to give my hands something to do. Without warning Boris snapped at my fingers. "Hey!"

"Bad dog," Frank admonished, and gave the dog a light smack across the snout. "Sit. Stay."

For a moment I wondered who he was commanding: the dog — or me.

"Boris is a little overprotective," Frank went on to explain. There was no hint of apology in his explanation, however. He seemed, in fact, secretly pleased at the start the dog had given me. "Sometimes we have guests who overstay their welcome. Boris is our insurance, should any of them become unpleasant."

"Why should anyone become unpleasant?" I heard myself snap. "That is, unless they feel they've been cheated out of their money's worth."

Now it was Frank's turn to rear back with amused surprise. His brown eyes twinkled, but the effect was more akin to light bouncing and reflecting off two dimes.

"I know how you take care of your friends," I heard myself say. Don't ask me why I was pressing my luck; I guess I'd wearied of him holding the upper hand.

"Joe should learn to keep his mouth shut," Frank said evenly, and stared at me with those flinty eyes.

Joe sauntered back into the living room at that moment, his head snapping to attention at the sound of his name. A t-shirt hugged his chest.

"He didn't say a word. He didn't have to. I could tell what the story was about this place from practically the moment I walked in."

Silence spun out, as though Frank was trying to decide if he was angered by my bit of knowledge. Eventually he said, "Well, as you can see, it gives us plenty of free time. Maybe too much time. What do you think, Joe?"

"There's never enough free time," he answered darkly, and downed half of his drink in one swallow.

"Speaking of time—," I ventured.

"Oh please, enough with that record," Frank said, dismissing me impatiently. "We're all friends here. We're all *pals* here, wouldn't you agree? We can say anything we want to each other." He gave me a once-over with those dark dime eyes. "A big handsome mechanic like you is proof my lover has good taste in men. So did you at least get your nuts off?"

My neck flushed warm. I kept my silence.

"No," Joe answered for us.

Frank twisted his face into a parody of dismay. "Say, that's too bad! If I'd come home another thirty minutes later I wouldn't have spoiled your good time — ain't that right? In fact, you might have been zippered up and outta here without me ever knowing about it. Like the other times."

"I don't know what you're talking about," Joe said in a low voice. His eyes were downcast, his voice sullen.

I glanced at Joe, then back at Frank. Joe was trying to act casual but his back was ramrod stiff with tension.

Frank relit the joint and sucked in two quick noisy hits. "Oh. Oh I see. This was the first time, is that it? *Have I got that right?"* A ribbon of sarcasm wound his voice tight.

I jumped my cue, anxious to diffuse the electricity of the room. "Yes. This was the first time. Not *even* a first time, really, because we had just gotten started. And quite frankly, now it's the last time, because I don't have time for this little game the two of you want to play."

"What game?" Frank asked, all innocence and sugar. He held his palms up in a gesture that said he had nothing to hide. "I'm trying to thank the man responsible for fixing our baby out in the driveway, by sharing a drink and a smoke. Not as fun as having sex like youse guys, but then I wasn't invited to join in, *now was I."*

"Stop it, Frank," Joe warned.

But Frank bulldozed ahead, the hole he seemed so determined to dig getting deeper and deeper. "Then again, that could be a lot of fun, huh? I mean, who has a three-way in this day and age? Been a long time since I've had two for the price of one. Me, I think *watching* can be just as fun." He gave us each a lingering glance, a glance as cold as the long shadows filling the room. He dug into his pants pocket and produced a small glass vial filled with white powder. "Anyone for a toot?"

"Put that away," Joe said in a steady voice. I shot a look at him, surprised by what I detected underneath that smooth warning: fear. He didn't want his lover packing candy up his nose.

Frank ignored his partner and swiveled in my direction. "Want some?" He unscrewed the cap.

I shook my head no. My lungs were tight in my chest, like they'd forgotten how to expand for a good deep breath.

"It's fresh. And pure. Just like me." He grinned two rows of yellowing teeth. With practiced finesse he used the built-in spoon of the cap to snort cocaine into each nostril.

"How much have you done?" Joe croaked.

Frank shrugged. "Hey, it's a long drive from Mendocino," he answered vaguely.

"And the smoke? Do you have that, too?"

"Does he have to hear *all* of our business?" Frank snapped, a chink in that calm exterior finally revealing itself. "It's all there, the whole order. In the trunk. When it's dark I'll bring it in. Do you mind?"

"Frank, honey, calm down—"

"Oh shut the fuck up!" he exploded. Boris jerked away from his master's feet at the force of so much anger. "Don't call me *honey,* not with one of your tricks in front of me. I told you last night I'd be home early today, but you just couldn't resist copping a little extra on the side, could you? Too bad I came home and spoiled your little afternoon fun."

On impulse I stood up. Electric wires of panic were shooting through my legs, making me twitch with frightened anticipation. Enough of this: I wanted out.

"Where the hell do you think *you're* going?" Frank spat. The heat of his anger blew over me like hellfire.

I held up my hands and forced my wooden tongue to speak. Joe watched me warily. "This is between the two of you," I said as firmly as I could muster. "I'm leaving. Good-bye."

I'd taken all of three steps toward the front door, not even bothering to give Joe any farewell look, when I heard Frank say in a strangely dead voice, *"Boris, hold."*

Suddenly a snarling dark shape hurled itself against the back of my legs. My knees buckled out from under me. With an undignified cry I collapsed to the living room floor, hands fanning out to break my fall. I immediately rolled onto my back with a reflexive motion and Boris was on top of me, his front paws planted onto my chest. I raised a hand to protect my face and he snapped at me, nipping the flesh of my right palm. I cringed: this animal was all menace and fanged teeth. Like his master, he knew his job all too well.

"Boris," I heard Joe command, "let go!"

"Shut up. *Stay,* Boris. Hold. *Hold."*

"Frank, stop this. Right now. I mean it."

"I told you to shut up."

"This is crazy!"

"Crazy? I'll tell you what's crazy. Putting up with all your screwing around. You want to fuck with an occasional piece of trash, I don't mind. I get my own itch every now and then. But don't give me this shit about how this is your first time together."

"It's true!"

"I know you've been seeing him, so don't deny it. A dozen times I've heard you whispering on the phone, setting up dates. Hanging up as soon as I walk into the room."

"That's paranoid bull—"

"Don't call *me* paranoid!" Frank shrieked. He capered about the room, his arms waving. "Don't you try and weasel your way out of this. I know what you and him are up to. You want to steal this business out from under me! Well, I won't let you!"

Maybe I should have stayed invisible, pinned to the carpet by that damn Nazi dog. But I'd had enough of this. Things were running too fast, too heated. I had to inject a bit of truth and sanity into the situation before Frank turned *really* nuts. The booze, the coke, and the grass in his system were wiring him into one mean time bomb; we had to defuse this, and fast.

"Let me up," I announced, and tried to scoot into a sitting position. Boris snarled low in his throat and nipped at my stomach. But I held my ground, determined not to be pushed back onto the rug. "Frank, listen to me. I *swear* this is the first time I've been here."

Frank jumped into my view, towering above me like a furious ancient god. "What do I look like, an idiot? You think 'cause I do a little toot I'm *brain dead?* That I'm not aware of what's been going on in my own house for weeks on end?"

"I wouldn't know anything about that," I answered. "If Joe's been out on the sly it's been with someone else, not me. I came here today to return the car, and things got out of hand. But that's it. Now get this dog off me. I'm getting up and I'm going home. Period." Suddenly I didn't care if I had to hobble home with Boris's teeth embedded in my calf; I'd had enough. I should have just forced my way out of the house the moment Frank came home.

Had I said I'd been frightened when Frank discovered me up in the attic? That I had no yardstick to measure the fright and adrenaline pumping through me?

Was this a nightmare? All preliminary, my dear.

This nightmare didn't really get rolling until I heard the click of the hammer pull back and found myself staring down the barrel of a .22 caliber pistol.

Frank said in that dead voice, *"You're not going anywhere."*

7

The cold attic floor. The bite of kneecaps against wood. I shivered, naked, but not from the cold: the goosebumps fanning across my skin were the result of this weird déjà vu.

Joe sat before me on the bed, his legs spread open in whorelike invitation, naked. His hands pumped frantically in an attempt to make himself hard. But the pained expression on his face, as though he'd suffered a good kick to the ribs, more truly revealed his emotions than this awkward sexual situation. He looked like a man witnessing disaster, as though all his plans had gone horribly wrong, and now hurled down the wrong tracks. He was too wrapped up in his own fear and misery to cast a sympathetic eye in my direction.

"Go ahead," Frank encouraged, that butter-and-cream voice back. He stood a few feet behind me so that I could not see him. "Camera's rolling, as they say. Let's get this show on the road."

"Honey—," Joe pleaded.

"No talking. Didn't I say no talking?"

He'd made us climb back into the attic, of course. Boris sat downstairs at the foot of the ladder, positioned in case I somehow managed to run for it. Frank had made a quick detour into the kitchen, where I'd heard him rummage through a drawer. I didn't like the sound: it was too sharp, too pointed. *Some*thing was concealed underneath his sweatshirt, I knew that much. But all that truly mattered was the .22 caliber pistol he waved so casually at my face. I should have known, in his dirty line of business, he'd have all the accoutrements of protection at his disposal.

So back into the shadowed attic we went, the day's light and heat stealing away with each passing moment. It was a shame we "hadn't got our nuts off," as Frank put it. He said it was "unhealthy" to get all worked up and then not come. He wanted to watch us.

"And then I can leave?" I'd asked him as I unbuttoned my shirt. "You'll let me go?"

"Of course," he replied with that crocodile smile. "I just want you guys to have the fun you were denied by my intrusion. Since this *is*, as you claim, *your first time.*" Sarcasm dripped from his last words. Frank's face was ugly with blue shadows.

In silence Joe and I stripped out of our clothes. Fright had burned off any sensation from the drinks and smoke: I was stone-cold sober. I held absolutely no hope of resurrecting my limp penis. The cold, the fear, the gun: these things overwhelmed my consciousness.

I knelt in front of Joe like Frank demanded, but this position seemed a parody of our sexual hunger from an hour earlier. I doubted that even my mouth upon Joe would entice an erection out of him. His eyes were as bright as his lover's, lit not with cocaine, but with terror.

"Do it," I heard Frank whisper behind my ear in that flat dead voice. "Do it or I'll shoot your balls off, I swear to god."

I stared at Joe in desperation. Incredibly, he'd managed to manipulate himself into a semi-erection. We exchanged a glance that was charged with urgency. *Hurry,* Joe's glance said to me. *Hurry, or he'll hurt us...*

The room clamped down in purple nightmare hues, unreal and somehow faraway. I felt myself leaning closer to Joe, bending in. In my ears, blood sang a requiem. I opened my mouth, which was sandpaper dry, to take him.

A creak of floorboards behind me. I looked up and was startled to see upon Joe's slim face an expression of supreme horror so acute I'm surprised he didn't call out or faint.

No, I didn't see it coming. I *heard* it coming, but could do no more than begin to turn my head toward the noise when Frank rammed the butcher knife between my shoulder blades.

8

OWWW that hurts it hurts
Can't reach Get it out of me
No! No! No! Not again! Owww
Oh Jesus, he's killing me
Stop
Make it stop
I want to

9

STOP.

Vengeance

1

It really was the funniest thing, this crossing over. Well, not funny in a ha-ha sense. Funny odd. Funny amazing. I mean, you read and hear about stuff like this but you just don't expect to go floating out of your body. But when Frank stuck it to me good I just sorta peeled out of myself, away from the pain that hurt like a son of a bitch, let me tell you. I went floating up and bounced against the ceiling, around the attic beams and stringy cobwebs.

I could see everything plain as day.

My body lay facedown by the foot of the bed. I looked pretty good for a 34-year-old, my physique in solid shape from jogging and the gym three times a week. Yeah, I looked pretty damn good except for that butcher knife sticking out between my shoulder blades. It looked like someone had poured a big pile of spaghetti and meatballs across my back. Frank hadn't been content to cut me just once. No: the creep had played Thanksgiving turkey across my back, slashing and digging, keeping me pinned to the floor while all I could do was explode with pain.

So: here's the new tableau, laid out before me. My naked body on the floor. A few feet away, red hands thrust out before him, Frank. The front of his sweatshirt and jeans were all splattered with blood from yours truly. He tilted back his head and his eyes were two eggs sunny-side up, wild and crazy. And this jiggly smile on his lips, like he couldn't decide if he wanted to burst out laughing or scream till doomsday.

Joe wore a similar expression, except that his scales tilted in favor of a loud scream. He had scooted away to the center of the bed, his knees drawn up as though to cover his nakedness. His enormous dick had shriveled to the size of a pinhead, as if it wanted to go into hiding. I could see why. Who knew what mischief Frank was gonna do next. Now that he'd gotten a taste of what it was like to chop me up, he might just yank that knife out of me and go after Joe.

But he didn't.

They just stared at each other in stunned silence, their breath harsh in their throats. The scream wanting to rip out of Joe's throat was starting to break loose; his jaw snapped open and shut, making funny gargling noises like he was tasting his own vomit. Sorry if that's a disgusting image, but it's the truth.

Frank stepped forward.

"Shut up!" he snapped. "Stop making that noise!"

Joe went right on gargling "Dixie."

"I said shut up! I need silence. I have to figure this out."

Now Joe looked at him, his eyes sick with confusion.

"Why, Frank? Why'd you go and kill him, for Christ's sake?"

Yeah, Frank. I was mighty curious myself.

"Just shut your trap, all right? It's your own goddamned fault. I always said your dick would get you into trouble, and look what's happened!"

"You're the one who killed him!" Joe shot back. I guess since he couldn't scream, getting angry was the next best thing.

Frank paced the attic.

"Don't you go blaming me. We're both in this together, whether you like it or not. You started this ball rolling, not me. Now it's up to us to finish it."

Joe looked sick again. "F-Finish it?"

His lover nodded as though addressing a simpleton. "We can't keep the body here, now can we?"

And for the first time in my new condition I grew suddenly cold with fright.

2

"Put your clothes on," Frank ordered. He absently scratched at his chin, unaware of the muddy red streaks that stained his face from my blood.

My blood. Jesus, this was just too unreal. I wouldn't have believed it if it wasn't me bouncing around the cobwebs. And looking down at my poor body, it hardly looked like me anymore. It was turning all kinds of awful shades, a sort of Play-Doh blue around the edges. I couldn't smell anymore but I'm sure the attic stank of that iron-and-copper blood smell. Blood, and their fear.

"I can't put on my clothes," Joe whined. He gestured to himself, speckled with bits of me all over him. "I'm dirty with—"

"—And you're gonna get a lot dirtier before we finish here," Frank barked. "Now hurry it up. The sooner we take care of this body, the better. We'll clean up then."

"What are we going to do with it?"

Yeah, Frank. That's what I was wondering. And since when had I become an *it?*

Frank pushed his lover aside, scooting him off the bed. He pulled loose the top and fitted sheets. "We'll wrap him up in this," he mumbled, more to himself than to Joe. "Keep him from making too big a mess."

He planted a foot on either side of me, bent down, and grabbed the black stump of knife lodged between my shoulder blades. With a grunt of annoyance — as if it were my fault it was there in the first place — he began to extricate it.

Twinges of phantom pain scissored across my back. In death, as in life, I flapped my hands across my upper back, as though I could somehow stop that knife from its deadly purpose. The movement threw me off balance; I flailed about like an astronaut unaccustomed to weightlessness. And still the twinges of sharp pain as I watched Frank free his knife from my gristle and bone.

"What are we going to do, Frank?" Joe blubbered from his corner. He seemed incapable of movement or decision, aware only of two things: the knife in Frank's hands and my body on the floor.

"I told you to wrap him up," Frank hissed. He dropped the knife to the floor and stepped away. He rubbed his palms against his blue jeans.

Like a frightened child chosen to step before the front of the class, Joe came forward. He turned suddenly efficient, bundling me up with those smelly sheets stained from past trysts. My arms were laid at my sides, one corner of the sheet tucked beneath shoulder and side, then the other. I was still wobbling up there in the cobwebs, each movement of my body causing me to twitch and jerk like a fly caught in a web. With sudden sadness I realized that was exactly how I felt: caught and trapped.

Just when I thought this situation couldn't get any worse, Joe covered my face with the sheets, and I went blind.

Don't ask me how it happened, or the logic of it all. That sheet draped over me and a filmy darkness descended with the rush of eternal night. *Hey!* I screamed. *Don't do this to me! I can't see!*

Then I was moving, dropping down away from the cobwebs, falling into a pit as black as any childhood nightmare. Weird twinges rippled through me — a sensation I finally recognized as hands grabbing hold of my ankles and shoulders. I could hear their curses and the creak of weight upon that flimsy attic staircase as they tried to maneuver my body through the opening in the floor. I felt myself tip down headfirst, dragged as my poor draped body was dragged. Unable to control my movements, arms held by my side, and now blind: So this was death? This is what it all boils down to, this sensation of being buried alive, frozen into your body's last pose?

I screamed bitter screams, my mouth stuffed with those foul sheets.

I screamed for so long that only little by little did the outside intrude beyond my overpowering fear. Words as sharp as the knife that had violated my body:

"We can't leave him here."

"Let's take him out to Land's End and dump him there."

"How about the Tenderloin? Police'll think he's involved with drugs or something. We could plant a little dope on him..."

"No. I don't want him identified. He's got to disappear, like he never existed."

"Nobody can just disappear. There's always loose ends."

"Not if we plan this right. And I've got an idea."

More shifting and banging. Grunts of exertion as they took hold of my body once again. Once more I felt myself being lowered, but this decline was not as steep as the trip down from the attic playroom. I jerked and twisted within their hands, deadweight, and that pleased me to no end: happy to make their job as difficult as possible.

Then a voice, Frank's: "Here. Put him here."

I thudded onto cold floor. The sheet, mercifully, yanked free of my face. Colors and sensations exploded across my eyes, shimmering with a fireworks afterglow.

I was in the basement. Next to my body, a long ditch dug between pipes and floorboards. A sack of cement off to the side. Joe had said they were working on the basement, that the house was a mess, ha ha. I wasn't in a laughing mood now. I was too busy thinking what eternity would taste like with my mouth stuffed full of cement and eyes sealed in darkness.

Frank turned to Joe with a sly grin. "Who says you can't make someone disappear? They never found Jimmy Hoffa, right? Now give me a hand."

For the first time since dying, something began to well up inside me that wasn't crazy with fear. I made this feeling multiply, made it feed upon itself like a kind of cancer. I added kindling to the fire.

I would not let them do this to me.

Trouble, my friends. Trouble of the worst kind. I ain't going nowhere, not until I settle the score.

I turned away from my body and that bloody sheet. I had to stop thinking of that corpse as me. The me I had become was floating off to the side, watching Joe and Frank mix cement into a wheelbarrow. Even though I bobbed on the air currents like a float on a fishing line, my arms were still confined by the tightly wrapped sheets. I had to figure out how to move.

I was so busy figuring out what to do I stopped paying attention to Joe and Frank — right up until they tossed my body between the narrow gap of floorboards.

Darkness poured across my eyes.

Stop! I screamed. *Stop—!*

Gravel and dust plugged my throat, a heavy glue of it.

I plummeted into this silent darkness, rushing toward oblivion. I embraced it as a drowning man finally welcomes his liquid home. All choices but this had been closed off.

No more—

3

But there was. More.

Light filtered across the backs of my eyelids. A dreamy awareness pulled me up from eternity, as though the person I had been in life was now the dream. I opened eyes raw and gummy, and beheld myself.

I was naked, my skin soapy and white, like dried soap on a glass shower stall. My body — or, rather, this semitransparent vessel that apparently housed my soul — tingled in a most curious way. I felt elastic and smoky at the same time, my dimensions no longer harnessed by the encumbering confines of a physical body. Just beyond the outer line of my body was a phosphorescent glow. I held up my right hand and grinned at the shifting aura of colors flaming around my fingertips. It reminded me of stepping out of a scalding shower, my body steaming in the cooler air of the bathroom.

Could anyone see me? I wondered. Probably not. Frank and Joe had not noticed me playing Peter Pan earlier, up in the attic.

But I was different now, different from when I had peeled up and out of my body. Then, I had still been connected to it, tied to its throbbing pain of screaming nerves and sabotaged ganglia. This — whatever was happening to me now — felt more like I had taken an important step; a toddler learning how to walk. Maybe I was different now because I'd been buried.

I looked through myself. I was hovering inches above where my corpse lay buried by a gray frosting of wet cement.

Can I stand? I want up—

I stretched forward, a ghostly rubber band responding to my instant wish. So: *thought* governed my movement, not some outmoded conjunction between physical body and desire. I willed myself into a standing position and stared down at the slab of wet cement.

I felt nothing. No rage. No sorrow. The fear had vanished.

Only when I thought of Frank sticking the knife into my back did a knot tighten somewhere at my core. Bastard. Make me disappear, eh? Washed his hands of me? Surprise, surprise. I made a vow, right then: if it took the rest of eternity, I'd make him pay. Him and that cowering puppy dog of a boyfriend, Joe.

All at once a startling warm light fell across my shoulders. The light speared right through me, like I was something living in shadow that had inadvertently stepped out into the direct rays of sunlight.

A new kind of fear washed over me. I knew what the light wanted. If I turned around, faced it, it'd take me. I'd do all those metaphysical things I'd always laughed at whenever Rich brought it up: fly through a dark tunnel and emerge on the other side, baptized by a white, comforting light.

Another time, baby. Not now. Miles to go before I sleep, and all that rot. Bug off.

But the light baked into me, insistent. It tugged with restless fingers, wanting to pull me into its embrace.

I clenched my hands into fists. Shook my head. Stood firm. I had to make it understand I wasn't ready to leave.

The warm fingers let go. I was plunged back into shadow, and this time I shivered with the enormity of what I'd done. Had I just doomed myself to an existence of rattling chains from the great beyond, Jacob Marley style? Would the light come back for me at a future time?

I was suddenly hit with a loneliness so terrible I bent over double. My predicament exploded over me in waves. *Rich. Oh, Rich. I'll make them pay...*

4

Frank plopped down onto the couch. "I'm done in!" he muttered at no one, and wiped his brow with the back of a hand. He called into the kitchen. "Fix me a drink, how about it?" He was damp from a shower, his hair shiny and slick. He'd changed out of his blood-splattered clothes into a pair of gray sweatpants and white t-shirt with a flannel shirt over that, open.

I moved past him, silent and invisible, and floated into the kitchen. Joe was stuffing what looked like spotted rags into a tall plastic trash can. With an electric jolt I recognized my own clothes mixed up with Joe's pants and shirt. The last of me out with the garbage.

Joe straightened and turned in my general direction. He, too, was fresh from a shower, his straw hair spiky and combed back. A magnificent black eye swelled his cheek below his left eye. So much for his supposed limo job in the morning; he wasn't about to show his face in public with that shiner.

"Hey," Frank bellowed from the living room. "Where's my stiff one?"

Something dark flashed across Joe's battered face. His lips turned down and his good eye glared. Just as abruptly his whole face rearranged itself into a smooth mask, as though he was afraid Frank would pop into the kitchen and catch that other expression on his face. "It's coming!" he trilled.

He tossed a few ice cubes into each glass. He kept glancing in the direction of the doorway with odd quick movements. He glanced at the phone on the wall next to the freezer. Suddenly he lunged, catlike, and scooped the receiver into his hand. He turned on the faucet above the kitchen sink for a distracting noise.

Well, well. The boy has some backbone after all, I thought. Go ahead: call the police.

Joe looked stricken. He punched in the numbers, bit his upper lip, and watched the doorway with fearful anticipation.

That's the way. Bring the police. Show them your black eye, and take them down into the basement...

"Where the hell's my drink!"

Joe nearly jumped out of his socks. He stared at the phone as if it were burning his fingers and threw it back into its cradle on the wall.

What are you doing? Coward! Call them back! Call the police!

He shut off the running water and hurriedly fixed both drinks. Before walking into the living room he rearranged his face one last time. It was smooth and tight, an expressionless, blown-up balloon.

"About fucking time," Frank grumbled as Joe handed him his drink.

Joe fell into a chair. "I'm exhausted."

"Did we clean up everything?"

Joe nodded. "The attic still needs more work, but I got the floor around the ladder, and all the steps down into the basement."

Watching them, I wondered how much time had elapsed since my body had been dumped. They had been busy, these boys. Scrubbing out the last clues of my presence.

"Anyone see him this afternoon?" Frank asked. He brought out the dope pan from underneath the couch and nimbly rolled a joint.

"I don't think so."

"Hard to miss the limo," he pointed out.

"But the neighbors are used to seeing it around. Just because someone could have seen Sam arrive doesn't mean they waited around by their window to watch him leave."

Frank scowled and lit up his joint. "It's the weak link," he asserted through clouds of smoke. "Even if none of our neighbors saw him arrive. Someone back at his car shop is gonna know he's missing. Right? The last time he was seen, he was on his way to our house. The limo's here, so obviously he made it this far. Nothing we can do to cover that."

Joe watched ice cubes float in his drink. In a stony voice he said, "He returned the limo. I wrote him out a check. I offered him a ride back to his house, but he said he had some errands to run and would walk. End of story."

"Hey, that's damn good!" Frank breathed. "That's real damn good!"

If I had had blood, it would have been boiling. Doing a pretty thorough job of wiping me out, damn them. I floated around the couch to get a better look at Frank. I wanted to give him my best evil eye.

Suddenly Joe fumbled his glass. Amber-colored liquor splashed through his fingers. The glass banged against the coffee table top with a crack as startling as a gunshot.

"What the hell!" Frank muttered. "Want to watch what you're doing to our furniture?" He stared at Joe and realized Joe was staring into the space somewhere over his shoulder. "What is it?" He wheeled around, tense and ready to pounce.

I reared back in surprise, my cloak of invisibility yanked.

Frank's eyes narrowed to dark slits. "What? *What?* I don't see nothing."

Joe shook his head of cobwebs. "Oh god: what have we done," he suddenly blubbered.

"Now don't you go soft on me!"

"He was there, right behind you."

"Who was?" Frank spun around again, his worried face half a foot from my own. A thin line of sweat had popped out on his forehead, shiny as grease. He grimaced, angry with himself for having turned to look. "Aww, you're jerking at shadows."

Joe nodded, his pale skin bloodless. "Yes. That's exactly what I'm doing. I swear it looked like — him — behind you—"

"You want another black eye?"

Joe shook his head.

"Then shut up with that kind of talk. Don't spook us with crazy ideas."

Joe dove into his drink as though the liquid were oxygen and could save his life. A wave of unexpected pleasure rippled through me. How very interesting. I raised my hand near to the lamp that sat beside Frank, and glanced to the wall. A smudge of shadow whispered across the yellowing wall, delicate as a child's shadow puppet. I could be seen under strong light.

"I just wish we could have dumped him somewhere else," Joe said. He raised his good eye to Frank, wary of his reaction but determined to make his point.

"The basement is perfect," Frank said. He dismissed his lover's concern with a wave of his hand. "We'll finish the floor like we decided, throw a rug over it, and that will be that. No one will ever know."

"Except us." Joe finished his drink.

I hate to admit it, but I felt kinda sorry for the guy. His life here in this house with Frank had become appallingly clear. How often would Frank pop him one in the mouth, or the eye? What set him off — a burned dinner? A weak scotch and water? Joe's silly affairs? How exhausting it must be, constantly monitoring Frank's mood swings, or how much coke he'd packed up his nose, or how many drinks he'd consumed that night. Little wonder Joe protected himself by being so obsequious. Or that he struck back through clandestine affairs. His pride and respect had been whittled down so far that any hope he could pack a suitcase and leave was preposterous and totally alien.

Frank pushed his empty glass across the coffee table. "How about another round, huh?" He reached for a packet of shiny white paper folded into a triangle from the jar on the dope tray. With a razor blade he set to work chopping out two lines of cocaine.

Joe took both of their glasses and went into the kitchen.

I came around the couch, curious about what mischief I could get into. I reached out a hand to touch Frank's shoulder. Right as I was about to make contact, a jolt lightninged through me. I snatched back my hand. It had felt like pushing the repelling ends of two magnets together.

I wrenched away, disappointed, and in my wake white puffs of cocaine spun into the air.

"What the hell!" Frank bent over the white cloud in a parody of greed, as though he could suck the powder from the air. "Is there a goddamned window open?" he bellowed. "We've got a draft in here!"

Joe returned with the drinks. He glanced at each glass and nibbled his lower lip, as if trying to remember what went where. He chose a glass and set it in front of Frank. He plopped down into an armchair.

The doorbell rang.

Both men's heads jerked up in surprise.

"You expecting anybody?" Frank asked.

Joe swallowed and shook his head. "You?"

Frank thought about it. "Lots of our buddies knew I was picking up fresh this afternoon. Anyone call while I was out?"

Joe said nothing. He acquired a sleek feline posture.

Frank's lips split open into a smile. He looked like he was chomping down on sour grapes. "Maybe you was too busy this afternoon to pick up the phone."

"I always take care of business. Nobody called."

Instead of the doorbell, there now came a tentative knock, like a sinner inquiring entry to the gates of heaven.

Frank swiveled his head. "Where's Boris?"

"Out back."

"Bring him in. I'll answer the door." He picked up the tray of drug paraphernalia and scooted it back into its hiding place beneath the couch. "This better be good."

I watched the two of them spring away in opposite directions. Bring in that Nazi dog, I thought. Let's see if I can scare the hairs off him.

My anticipation was so great I almost forgot about Frank opening the front door until a voice chilled me with its familiarity.

"I'm sorry to disturb you so late at night," the visitor at the door said. "For all I know, I'm following a wild-goose chase. May I come in?"

"Why don't you tell me what's on your mind," Frank said. He was leaning against the edge of the front door, prepared to slam it shut, if necessary.

Cool nighttime air whistled down the foyer; I bobbed in its steady stream. The flaming sparks of color shooting out beyond my form went black with my dread.

Rich.

It was Rich at the door.

His face was agitated and distraught, though he was plainly trying to reel these feelings in, to not appear a lunatic at this stranger's door. He hooked a thumb back toward the limousine parked in the driveway.

"My name is Rich Bennington. My partner runs an auto repair shop out of our home. Did ... did you have your car worked on today?"

A pregnant pause. I could just imagine the thoughts speeding through Frank's feverish brain.

Frank shrugged. "I don't know what you're talking about."

Rich's mouth popped open. "You don't?"

"I just said so, didn't I?" Frank shifted his weight foot to foot; the boxer in him was coming out. "Now if you don't mind, you're letting out all the heat—"

"Maybe you'd better invite me in, then," Rich answered without missing a beat.

I wish I could have seen the expression on Frank's face.

"Now why should I do that?" he asked. His tone was all too familiar now: scraped ice.

Rich opened up his leather jacket and patted his shirt pocket. "Because of what I have in here." He teased Frank by revealing several inches of paper. "Proof that my partner worked on that car this very afternoon."

They sized each other up. Silence.

Joe abruptly strode past me and joined Frank at the door. I bounced away and slammed against the hallway, thrown by the repelling force of our nearness. Through my stunned surprise I heard him say, "Come inside for a minute."

Frank blistered Joe with a smoldering gaze, but Joe ignored it as he ushered Rich down the hallway.

I launched myself up and out of the way, up by the ceiling as all three men passed. From the kitchen whined Boris, who pawed at the gate that prevented him from entering. He was wagging his tail.

Joe motioned toward one end of the couch — the same place where I had sat hours earlier, in another lifetime. "I'm Joe and that's Frank. Now what's going on?"

Rich lowered himself to the couch. He sat on its edge, as though its fabric might be dirty and he didn't want to soil his pants. "Am I interrupting anything?"

"What do you think," Frank said.

Rich's eyes drifted to a forlorn glass sitting on the coffee table. Its ice had melted, and the glass sat in a puddle of its own condensation. Its contents was the color of weak iced tea. And next to it, my silver lighter.

Joe's eyes darted to the glass and went big as two eggs. He glanced away as Rich looked up. Their eyes locked. Joe twisted his gaze away and looked to Frank for support. The damage had been done.

They had scrubbed the walls with buckets of soapy water. Used an aerosol rug cleaner on the carpets. Wadded my clothes into the garbage. And yet they had overlooked the most obvious evidence of my having been in the house: my poor neglected drink and my one-of-a-kind lighter.

"Look's like I'm not the first one here," Rich managed with what tried to be a casual sigh. His observation hung in the suddenly stuffy air like a warm fog.

"We had some friends stop by earlier," Frank said in an oil-smooth voice.

"Can you verify that?"

"Verify?" Frank's salt-and-pepper mustache danced upon an otherwise stony facade. *"Verify?* What kind of shit is this?"

I circled close and overhead, fearing the worst. Rich was going about this all wrong. You couldn't barge into Frank's house and start slapping him around with accusations. *Frank* was the one used to doing the slapping.

Something broke in Rich's expression, a silent acknowledgment that he had overstepped his bounds. He raised both hands into the air, a mock surrender.

"Look. Guys. I'm a little upset right now. My lover has disappeared."

Frank picked up his cocktail. He did not offer one to Rich.

Rich coughed into one hand. "I know that one of you brought your car to the shop today. My lover told me so. And according to this copy of the receipt—" He patted the folded piece of paper in his chest pocket. "—the fan belt was fixed. He told our part-timer Bill he was delivering the car and would be back about four or five. He ... he ... never returned."

"So what do you want from us?" Frank took another gulp from his drink, and waited. I've seen mannequins take deeper breaths.

Rich smiled. "Your help. That's all."

"We'll help, if we can," Joe said.

Rich nodded in genuine gratitude. He raked a hand through his hair. "It just doesn't make sense. We had plans tonight. He wouldn't just ... keep me in the dark like this. I'm afraid something might have happened to him."

He looked very small, balanced there on the edge of that ugly plaid couch, his shoulders slumped with worry.

Oh, Rich. I'm right here. Here...

"Anything you can tell me would be helpful," he finished. His eyes implored first Joe, and then, with reluctance, Frank. "I'm sorry for sounding so melodramatic."

Joe fell into his spiel. "Your friend brought the car by about two o'clock," he said, and segued smoothly into his lie. "He took his check, thanked me, and split. Said he had a few errands to run."

"That's it?"

"He just said so, didn't he?" Frank shifted in his seat. "Your buddy left."

Rich sucked in a breath. "I don't believe you."

Frank blinked. You'd think he had just received a sharp blow to the jaw. "What?"

Rich pointed to the lighter. "Did you offer him a drink? A smoke?" No one said anything. "Why would you offer him a cocktail, if he just picked up a check and left? You haven't offered *me* a drink."

"A friend stopped by," Frank said. Now a twitch had developed in his right cheek. "That was *his* drink, not Sam's."

Joe looked at him, stricken.

Frank glared back at him. "What? What'd I say?"

Rich said, "How did you know his name is Sam?"

"Huh?"

"His name. Sam. You knew it. You met him today."

"So? What does that prove? Nothing." Frank shook his head. Bullets of sweat whipped into the air. He blinked his eyes as though an eyelash or dust had gotten into them. "You know what I think? This whole business of coming here tonight. It's a charade."

"What are you talking about?"

"Yeah, I met your friend. As he was leaving. He was in a hurry to leave, but maybe he wasn't in such a big hurry to *get home,* if you know what I mean. Maybe he had other plans."

Rich turned red in the face. "What is that supposed to mean?"

"Hey, it wouldn't be the first time someone went after a little afternoon delight. Maybe your boyfriend is snoozing on someone else's bed right about now." The words scored direct hits, and Frank grinned at the reactions they elicited from Rich. No jerk was gonna come into *his* home and act so high and mighty.

"Take that back," Rich said.

"Oh, come on. You're after the truth, aren't you? Isn't that why you're here? Maybe he came back home and youse guys had a fight. What'd you do to him? Huh? What'd you do that you had to make an ass out of yourself by coming here to cover up."

Rich stabbed a finger. "How did Joe get a black eye?" Silence. "The only fighting that's gone on today took place here, not my house. Now I don't know what the hell happened, but you're both acting guilty as sin."

"It ain't a crime," Frank said. "Whatever goes on inside this house is none of your goddamned business."

"Maybe not. But I'm beginning to think it *should* be my business."

"What's that supposed to mean?"

"Frank, cool it." Joe held out his hands, palms up, to both of them.

"Don't tell me to cool it. This is *my* house."

"I don't want trouble," Rich reiterated. "I'm just trying to figure out what happened to Sam. And why you have his lighter."

Frank wiggled fingers at Rich. "Let me see that receipt."

Rich hesitated.

Don't do it, I thought. *Don't—*

"Come on. This should clear things up," Frank coaxed.

Rich made a pouting face as he thought about it. He nodded to himself and reached into his shirt pocket. Before handing over the receipt, he felt compelled to say, "I have a copy of this at home."

"How very clever." Frank extended his hand. Waited. Rich put the folded piece of paper into his fingers. He stood up and began to move about the living room.

"You've already admitted Sam was here," Rich said. "What good is seeing the receipt now?"

A smile, thin as a razor blade. "Curiosity." Frank wandered over to the entrance to the kitchen. Boris stood up from behind his gate, tail wagging, eager for attention. Frank reached over the railing to pat the dog on the head. He straightened clumsily and planted himself with his back to the wall. He opened up the yellow receipt and blinked a few times in the poor light.

He's drunk, I thought with trepidation. He's drunk and he's mean. I looked at Frank and saw how close he stood next to Boris. Mischief, that's what he was up to. Trouble.

"You know what this is?" Frank said after a moment of silence. He dangled the receipt in his hand like a dainty paper handkerchief.

"Frank, what are you doing?" Joe asked. He was wary, his eyes dark with concern.

"It's bullshit."

Rich stood up. "Give it back."

"What do you need this shit for, huh?"

"I said give it back."

Frank refolded the slip of paper. "This means nothing. Absolutely nothing. It's shit. Garbage." He tore the receipt in half.

"Frank!" Joe blurted out. He stared at his lover and then quickly swiveled his head to see what Rich was going to do next.

Rich flushed with anger. His hands were two fists at his side. His mouth puckered wordlessly, opening and closing like a fish discovering itself out of water. It was almost comical, in a really horrible way, to watch. Rich was not going to back down. Neither would Frank.

In that icy voice Frank said, "Now get the hell out of my house."

Still speechless, Rich nevertheless took a bold step forward.

Frank blinked rapidly. "If you take one more step toward me I'm going to let Boris here chew your dick for dinner — you got that?"

Rich froze. He glanced at Joe, then scowled at Frank. "I'm going to stop you. Both of you."

"You and what army," Frank sneered.

Get out of the house, Rich, I silently commanded. *Don't say another word. Just get yourself out.*

But he didn't. He sealed his fate as neatly and completely as I had done hours earlier. Rich pointed an accusing finger. "I'm going to the police. And there's not a damn thing you can do to stop me." He turned to leave.

With surprising agility for one so drunk, Frank spun to the gate, fingers quickly finding the latch that popped the gate free of its suction across the doorway. In a liquid motion he lifted the gate off to the side, looked at Rich, and said, "Boris. Hold."

I swooped down, moving on an instinct primal and without thought. I rushed toward Boris as his snout snarled back to reveal teeth. He tensed his haunches, ready to spring. He had been cooped up in that kitchen for too long. He was ready for action.

Rich suddenly realized what was about to happen. He retreated jerkily, his hands already flung to protect his ashen face.

I pitched forward, determined to bounce against that damn dog if I had to, to give Rich enough time to flee.

Imagine my shock when Boris reared up and let out a sharp yelp of fright. Instead of springing toward my lover, he jerked away and to the side, retreating deep into the kitchen.

"Boris! Hold!"

Down went the dog's tail, tucked between the quivering brown fur of his hind legs. His snarls became whiny agitation, and his front paws danced as though the carpeted floor were scalding.

He could see me. The dog could actually see me — or at least feel my presence blocking his way. I forged closer, getting as near to the doorway as I dared without hitting that magnetic boundary that was Frank's aura, which would send me bouncing away.

Now Frank was crazy with disbelief.

"You little shit! Attack! Hold!"

I waved my arms and made a face of pure menace.

Boris leapt backward into the kitchen with another frightened yelp. He bumped into the tall plastic garbage can and then scurried away on clicking toenails as the can tipped and fell.

From behind me I heard Rich mutter, "Dear god."

Frank cursed.

I looked. Amid the clutter of opened soup cans and old newspapers was my wadded-up and obviously bloodstained clothes. They were maroon piles on the floor, like the ragged craters of Mars.

Boris retreated to the back door, plopped down on his ass, and whined. His whole body trembled.

"You did it," Rich said, his voice barely above a whisper. His eyes burned as innocence ripped away like a veil and revealed the true nature of what had transpired that afternoon. In a voice choked with incredulity he said, "You honest to god did it. You killed him."

There was a moment where no one moved. No one breathed. The truth, raw and unpalatable, settled with the odor of garbage, flooding the room.

Frank catapulted away from the doorjamb at Rich, who staggered backward, and for one awful moment they looked like a pair of country-and-western dancers doing a bizarre two-step. Then Rich lost his balance. His arms pinwheeled. A lamp crashed off a table and fell to the rug, followed by him hitting the floor. Frank jumped on top of him.

Everything began to happen very fast.

Boris sprang up, determined to defend his master one last time. But I blocked the doorway, and allowed him to come no closer.

Inarticulate screams issued out of Rich's throat as he tried to wrench Frank's hands off his throat.

Joe fell to his knees and grabbed Frank's arm. "Stop it!" he was shouting. "No more! I can't take any more!" In desperation he picked up the small lamp that had tumbled to the floor and jerked off its shade, exposing the still-lighted bulb. "I said stop it!" He raised the lamp above his head.

Frank recoiled, his fingers slipping away from Rich's throat. His face became a caricature of surprise.

But it was left to Rich to articulate their surprise as he gulped air into his bruised throat and lungs. "Sam," he gasped. "Sam."

I reeled back with my own surprise, and glanced with dawning understanding at the naked light bulb shining forth from the lamp in Joe's hand.

I shimmered in their presence like heat waves. I swelled with pride, wanting to glory in my role as avenging angel. By god this had better turn out all right.

Rich's face burned with fury. He tore the lamp from Joe's hand, and swung. The bulb shattered against Frank's left ear as

Rich swung with all his might. There was a muffled pop, like a bag full of air ripping open. Glass and blood abruptly rained into the air as the light bulb shattered against Frank's head.

I vanished from their sight, extinguished with the light. Not that any of them noticed anymore.

Frank rolled off Rich and fell to his side. Rich pushed him onto the floor, pinning Frank in his agony. "You son of a bitch!" Rich roared. "You filthy son of a bitch!" Red fingerprints stood in ghastly relief on either side of his neck, bright as a child's watercolor set. His right arm raised up and back and then his fist whistled through the air. It connected with the cartilage of Frank's nose, breaking it with a noisy, messy snap. Copious amounts of blood, a shocking quantity of it, gushed out of both nostrils.

Frank opened his mouth and now it was his turn to gargle "Dixie." Ugly red bubbles ballooned past his lips and dribbled down either cheek.

From behind and below me came a sudden snarl. With no other warning, Boris sailed through the air and pounced onto Rich's back. The dog tore into Rich's leather jacket. He gouged out a chunk of the heavy material and dove in for more, aiming for the back of my lover's neck.

"Get him!" Frank cried with supreme joy. He turned his head and spat out an incredible wad of blood and mucus. "Kill, Boris! Kill!"

The dog went into an orgy of attack, his teeth everywhere, saliva flinging from his mouth.

Rich collapsed into a tight ball and tried desperately to protect himself from attack. Somehow he rightly resisted the urge to stay the dog with his hands — which would have surely resulted in a few mangled or bitten-off fingers.

I swooped down in panic. With my bare hands would I rip that mutt off of him. But inches from the dog's fur an electrical charge slammed through me. I was knocked clean across the room. That dog might be afraid of me but he would defend his master to the very end. I wailed with frustration.

My only hope was Joe.

But he was scrambling away, the coward. Without a word he staggered to one knee and then the other, managing to stand on wobbly legs. He hurled himself toward the kitchen.

Come back! You chicken-shit coward! Don't let them kill my lover!

Rich was moaning into the rug now, rolling like a man on fire as he tried to shake the dog from his back.

Frank lay exhausted and bleeding, grinning through jack-o'-lantern teeth, watching with exultation.

I ordered myself into an upright position, floating above the floor. That repelling charge when I'd tried to attack Boris had blown a fuse of my energy; I was quite literally dizzy with exhaustion. But I couldn't bear to sit back and watch Rich go to his death. I couldn't. I moved toward them once again.

And all at once warm white light spilled across the back of my shoulders. It felt as if a door had opened a few feet behind me, and that if I turned to look I would immediately be sucked through, crossing over to whatever waited on the other side.

Not now! I shouted, resisting its pull once again. *Don't take me now!*

I slogged forward, like a mountain climber facing a blizzard and high winds. The white force did not want me to approach the cluster of men and dog on the floor. It tugged me backward.

Oh, god! Help me! Somebody help me!

Rich found the lamp with roving fingers. He grasped its base into his hand and batted it over his shoulders. The glass fragments jutting out of the light socket jabbed into Boris's flank. The dog yelped and jumped off his back, turning to attack from another angle.

But Rich was just as fast. He swung the lamp and batted the dog away. He jabbed, using the shards of light bulb as he would a bayonet. Boris backed away, prancing in frustration, a growl deep in his throat.

Behind Rich, Frank raised himself.

Look out! Rich—

Frank's hands closed over Rich's throat. He dug in with murderous intent, his grip from behind scissoring lungs from any benefit of air. Frank was a horror to behold: eyes glassy, his broken nose disgorging streams of blood. Yes, he'd truly gotten a taste for killing this afternoon. Whatever boundary had held him in check had snapped with the same finality as my death.

Something yanked my feet out from under me. I sprawled to the carpet, facedown, and dug in with my hands. *Don't take me...*

Rich could not break free of Frank's grip. He struggled in vain, eyes filled with disbelief, tongue sticking out of his round mouth, going purple.

No. No No No—

A dark blur swooped onto Frank. An arm raised, the steel edge of a knife giving a silver wink before being plunged just above Frank's shoulder blades.

"No more!" Joe was screaming. "No more!"

He rolled Frank onto his back, the steak knife from the kitchen pantry now a dull copper in Joe's hand.

"What are you do—?"

Joe brought the knife down. Up. Down. It made flat thick noises as it cut through skin and bone. Air hissed out of torn lungs with a farting sound. Frank flopped about, hands crab claws in the air, his protests wet, inarticulate moans.

"No more," Joe whispered, and brought down the knife one last time.

Boris had retreated, confused by the actions of his two masters, as though trying to decide what new game this was they had played on him.

Rich struggled to sit up, coughing and sucking for air, one hand comforting his bruised neck.

Joe scooted off Frank. The knife hasp stuck out of his lover's chest, but he acted like he no longer saw it.

The pressure tugging at my feet suddenly relented. Maybe it had changed its mind about me one last time, or taken pity on my cries. All I knew was that I wanted to stay just a little bit longer. I could handle anything, could move into any uncertain future, as long as I knew Rich was going to be safe.

I looked across the room and watched as Frank's spirit rolled out of himself. Like something wet and newborn he raised above his battered physical body, reclining on a cushion of air. He glanced around with obvious confusion and then saw me. His face pained with sickening understanding. He would remain connected to his body, I knew, until he was buried. Only then would the light come for him. Only then would the pain of his murder subside.

Joe reached out tentatively and touched Rich's thigh. "Are you all right?"

Rich nodded.

"It's over now. It's finally over. We did it." The relief in Joe's quiet voice was unmistakable, huge. The batterings. The verbal and physical abuse. Getting out from under that weight, at long last.

Rich pulled himself into a full sitting position. Their noisy exhales were the only sound in the room. "I thought I saw Sam."

"I know. Me too."

"But — how?"

"Hush. It doesn't matter. Not anymore."

Joe was right. It didn't matter. Things had turned out badly, at least for me. But I'd gotten my revenge on Frank. I could leave, knowing I'd bested him. My affairs were in order; Rich would be comfortable, if not exactly living the life of luxury. My only regret was that I couldn't tell him I was sorry for what I'd done. That instead of trying to fix our relationship I'd hopelessly torn it apart.

For the final time, the light fell upon my shoulders. It was comforting, immense, like sunshine on a tropical beach. Across the room Frank eyed me with envy. Perhaps this would not be too bad, after all.

Rich said, "I was so scared when you called tonight and signaled me with the two rings. That you'd managed to set everything into motion. There was no turning back from our plan."

"No," Joe agreed. "There was no turning back. And it worked."

"Look at us. You with your black eye. My poor throat. Wouldn't it all have been simpler if we'd used Frank's gun?"

Joe shook his head. "Simpler? Sure. There were too many moments tonight when I thought the whole thing was going to backfire. Frank knew more than I'd ever suspected. He knew I was having an affair. But look how we worked it out. We'll say Frank killed Sam in a jealous rage. I didn't have to kill him, after all. Fortunately for us, Frank took care of our little problem. He buried him in the basement. He went crazy, determined to kill us all. We had to stop him in self-defense."

Rich smiled. "And we've got the bruise marks to prove it for the police."

Boris, calm now, wandered over to Joe and Rich. Rich put out his hand and scratched the dog behind the ears. He patted him on his flank. "Good dog," he soothed, and Boris wagged his tail. "It's all going to be okay now. We're together at last."

5

The white light enfolded me with its warmth. A ringing sound invaded my ears. Frank and I stared at each other as the truth hit us at exactly the same moment.

I flew into the abyss, everything clear now, my own innocence burned away by the light. Betrayed. I had been betrayed. And the last thing I saw before the light pulled me into its whirlpool was Rich and Joe bending close and kissing each other passionately.

The Unfinished,
continued

The promise

1

Jiggs Martin came awake sweaty and disheveled. His ears hurt, as though they had been subjected to an unconscionably loud noise. A monster migraine held him firmly in its teeth. He was lying upon his bedspread fully clothed, his right hand dangling over the side of the bed. He tasted what he could only surmise was dirt and gravel in his mouth.

Last night's journey with Sam unfolded slowly through his thoughts. He had no memory of returning home. He raised himself to his elbows to flip over onto his back and was surprised to discover a ballpoint pen sticking out of his sweaty right fist. He removed the pen and pried open his cramped fingers. He felt his knuckles pop.

There were scratches of blue ink marring the sheets. They looked like the unfinished strokes to a connect-the-dots game. He scooted to the edge of the bed and there, on the floor, lay the spiral notebook, open. Words had been flung onto the lined paper, words that veritably steamed with last night's birthing: the heated guts of Sam's story.

Except that Sam was unaware of his own ending, wasn't he? He thought he'd gone into the light, lifted to a better place. Instead, incredibly, he had somehow clung on. He'd managed to infuse his spirit into the heart of the limousine, shackled to earth by his outrage over his betrayal by Rich. And his anger had been great enough to rope Frank's spirit to him, forcing him to be the chauffeur of their haunted limousine.

Jiggs propped pillows behind his back. He rubbed his eyes. Recording Sam's story in the spiral notebook was only the first step in freeing the man's tortured spirit. He'd have to think out the final solution, carefully.

He showered and drank cup after cup of coffee with breakfast. There wasn't much time; Kate and Susan would be coming by soon to drive him to the hospital. He wanted this business completed before he left. He dug out his old college typewriter from the closet and set it up on the kitchen table. For quite a while he just sat there, thinking. Finally he rolled a piece of paper into place.

He worded it as simply and as anonymously as possible. The police, he suggested, should recheck their files about a supposed self-defense case involving a Rich Bennington and a Joseph Houseman and the deaths of Sam Parker and Frank Tarlton. Their deaths last year, Jiggs wrote, were not the result of self-defense, but a well-thought-out scheme of murder and passion.

He debated adding a comment about the limousine being involved in Luke's accident, but decided against it. Better, for now, to keep that connection quiet.

Jiggs finished the letter and stuck it into an envelope. As he licked it shut he felt cold air swirl up from his feet and around his shoulders like a frozen blanket. "Are you satisfied, Sam?" he asked the empty kitchen.

The air currents rippled around him, and then settled into a peaceful calm.

2

The intensive care unit, though frantic with activity, was perversely silent in that hushed atmosphere of the injured and dying. Nurses blew past them like fluttering white sails. Kate held one of his hands, Susie the other. Jiggs welcomed their support.

After checking in at the nurses' station, they slipped into Luke's room. He lay in a pool of tubes and intravenous lines. Monitors above his head clicked with activity. The bruises on his face and arms had had time to swell into their full, ugly glory. Luke looked worse than when they had first brought him in.

They arranged themselves in chairs beside the bed. Jiggs took one of Luke's limp hands into his own, mindful of the intravenous cords they were using to feed him medicine and nourishment.

"Luke," they each whispered in turn, and mumbled words of encouragement.

Jiggs looked at the two women, and then let his gaze settle upon his friend. "Luke, I have something to tell you," he said in a soft voice. And with quiet and deliberate tones, all of the previous night's events flowed out of him. Kate and Susie glanced at each other often with growing alarm, but they managed to keep their lips buttoned, no matter how fantastic Jiggs's story became.

By the time he had finished, a nurse poked her head through the door and indicated they needed to leave, to give Luke some rest. Kate stood up from her chair, stretched, and pinned Jiggs with her stare.

"All true?" she asked.

Jiggs nodded. "All true."

Susie muttered, "I'll never be able to set foot inside that house ever again."

"Sure you will," said Jiggs. "It's me they want, not you." But his glance returned to Luke and the broken figure he had become, there on the bed. He cradled Luke's hand, rubbing his thumbs into his palm. *Hang in there, buddy,* Jiggs spelled into Luke's palm. *I'll get you free. Promise. Whatever it takes.*

3

The smell hit him as soon as he walked through the front door. Jiggs crinkled his nose. It was a strange, somehow chemical smell, weirdly organic.

He checked his garbage pail in the kitchen, but that was not the source of the odor. It didn't seem to have a source: the stench was everywhere, filling every corner of the house. He opened the front and back doors to create a little circulation of fresh air.

So, Jiggs thought. *What new surprises have they in store for me now?*

It's what Susie and Kate had been afraid of the most. He'd asked them to come inside, to have a cup of coffee and talk about the hospital visit. Susie had visibly blanched at the idea, and Kate had coughed into her hands.

"They have no reason to hurt you," Jiggs said. But even he knew he was trying to reassure himself.

Susie shook her head with dismay. "I can't. I like my enemies out in the open, where I can fight fair."

"Why do you call them an enemy?"

Kate piped up. "Look at what they did to Luke. How do you know the same thing won't happen to one of us if we interfere?"

"They need help."

"Then *you* help them. They need you. Susie and I are just ... in the way."

Kate was right, of course. Jiggs couldn't predict the Unfinished's next move. For all he knew, taking more hostages, as they had done with Luke, could be part of their game plan. Better he tackle this himself, and rely on this bridge that connected him to these disturbed spirits.

And now, the house filled with this foul smell, like something dead buried in a bunch of moldy leaves. Jiggs dug around in the kitchen drawers and stumbled upon a packet of incense sticks. He lit three of them and stuck them into various potted plants around the house. He wasn't crazy about the strong musky scent they produced, but it was better than nothing. Much better.

Even though anxiety had wound him up tight, he managed a few hours of sleep in the afternoon. The previous night's journey had extracted a harsh toll upon his body and soul. He'd be of no help that night without a little rest.

But the first shadows of twilight brought fresh waves of anxiety that could not be quelled. Jiggs felt a sinking premonition that this night would be his most difficult. The heaviness weighing down the air — not to mention the ingratiating, mysterious stink — suggested a rough time. He steeled his shaky nerves by reaffirming his promise to Luke.

He grabbed the spiral notebook from his bedroom and brought it into the kitchen, where he tossed it onto the table. Somehow it seemed the right thing to do, that he would need the notebook close at hand. In the meantime, he set about making himself a BLT for dinner.

As he walked past the stove, his feet encountered something sharp and crunchy. He hopped away, lifting one foot after another in alarm. It had felt as if he'd stepped onto broken glass. But the floor was clean, unlittered. He checked the bottoms of his socks. There were no shards of broken glass embedded in them. Yet he could not only hear it but feel it, as well, when he walked the floor: the grinding crunch of shattered glass beneath his feet. Disconcerting, to say the least.

It's part of whatever's going to happen tonight, Jiggs thought. *Like this awful smell.*

While frying the bacon for his sandwich, he found himself gazing out the kitchen window, his attention drawn to the backyard. Correction: drawn to the pine trees, and the mound of dirt below them. The mound of disturbed earth which even in the ripening dusk and from this distance looked larger, wider, and more churned up than ever. Jiggs felt the screws of anxiety twist even deeper. He had a bad feeling about this, and it was getting worse with every passing moment.

He turned on lights, but just as quickly shut them off after a few minutes. Instead of providing comfort, the light had speared his eyes and made him squint in such a way he actually considered putting on a pair of sunglasses. Since that struck him as a silly thing to do, he opted for a few low lights and several well-placed candles.

He ate his sandwich, but it may as well have been made of cardboard. His restlessness continued to build. Once again he was drawn to the kitchen window and surveyed the yard. *Oh, what the hell.* He grabbed a flashlight from his junk drawer and stepped outside onto the porch. The pine trees were whistling in the gentle nighttime breeze. He shouldn't have been able to hear it, of course, and when it dawned on him that he *could* hear it, it made his skin crawl with nervous anticipation. Whatever was going to happen that night was close at hand. He walked down the porch steps and went into the yard. Pine needles crunched beneath his stockinged feet. He clicked on the flashlight and trained its light onto the patch of ground below the trees.

Jiggs expected most anything, yet was unprepared for what the flashlight revealed: an opened grave.

Dirt had been flung into piles alongside a rectangular, body-sized hole. And even now chunks of earth were being tossed by unseen hands. No gopher, this. The piles on both sides of the hole grew ever steeper. Jiggs had to remind himself to breath. And when the flashlight suddenly trained upon a skeletal hand rising out of the grave he lurched backward in shock and clicked off the light. He couldn't watch, at least not under the unforgiving glare of bright light. But he couldn't move, either. His legs had turned into concrete posts.

A dirty, tattered shape pulled itself into a sitting position. It brushed clods of dirt from its shoulders. Its garments — or whatever it had been draped in — were in ruined strips that fluttered with the night breeze. Both hands raised to the unseen face. Jiggs heard a distinct ripping sound, like a sheet being torn apart. It was an ugly, hurtful sound, followed by the hollow gasp of the creature's first taste of air. The shredded cloth fell away, and the corpse's face appeared in the blue hues of the dark air.

Jiggs was beside himself. He felt an almost uncontrollable urge to urinate. The hairs on the back of his neck stood on end. The limousine, and even Sam's presence, encased in goopy concrete, had been easier to tolerate than this. This was boyhood nightmares revisited, the ultimate terror straight out of comic books and Hollywood's scream factory. Jiggs had to clamp a hand over his mouth.

The creature planted both hands on the edges of the grave, and with tremendous effort raised himself to his feet. He swayed like a macabre scarecrow, and found his balance. He stepped out of the shallow grave, each step a torture of effort.

Jiggs backed away, and climbed the steps of his porch. The corpse followed, heaving himself upon each step, arms swaying for balance. There were hints of bone and gray matter peeking through the rotted clothing, but Jiggs didn't want to look too closely. He also didn't want the thing to come into his kitchen, but that's precisely where it intended to go. Another flash of unreality, as Jiggs imagined Susie and Kate walking into the house and seeing him sitting casually at the kitchen table with a decaying corpse. *Don't mind us, we're just shooting the breeze over a cup of coffee. Care to join us?*

Jiggs waited uneasily, his hands gripping the back of the kitchen chair. The thing stepped inside, and immediately raised a bony hand to his eyes.

"Are — are you okay?" Jiggs asked. He glanced at some of the lit candles placed about the rooms. "Is it too bright? Should I—"

"Sunglasses."

Jiggs wore a blank face. He'd heard this creature speak, even though its stringy lips did not move. "What did you say?"

"Sunglasses. Do you have a pair?" The thing shrugged with an expression that almost approximated sheepishness. "My eyes ... aren't what they used to be..."

Jiggs turned away. *Yeah, I'll bet.* He walked into the living room and picked up his pair of sunglasses sitting on the coffee table. He remembered his earlier urge to put on the glasses because of the light, and now wondered how this all connected. He brought them into the kitchen and reluctantly set them upon the table. He cringed a little to watch the creature snatch them and put them onto his decomposing face. Some kind of fluid leaked out of his cheeks as the weight of the glasses sank into the spoiled flesh below his eyes.

"Ahh," he rasped. "Better."

Jiggs bit his lip to hide his revulsion. Never again would those glasses touch *his* face. No way.

The dead man gestured for Jiggs to join him at the table. Jiggs obeyed, sitting on the edge of his chair. His fingers rapped nervously on the tabletop.

The corpse pointed to the spiral notebook which sat between them.

"This isn't my story," he explained with apology. "Not really. But I made a promise with myself to stick around and tell what happened, if I was ever given the chance. I'm the only one left to tell it."

Jiggs flipped to the first clean page in the notebook. All at once the corpse shot out his hand and clamped it over the back of Jiggs's hand. Burning needles pricked through his skin. "Oww! That hurts!"

"Sorry," the dead man said. "It's the only way for me to take control. Your hand should go numb soon, and then we can start."

Jiggs silently cursed this thing in front of him, and waited. He surrendered control of his hand as a numbing cold took hold of it. His hand, which now seemed to belong to a foreign entity, picked up a pen and began to move across the page. Jiggs watched his hand move by itself with an uneasy fascination.

"This is about a man who had the Look..."

BRENT SPEAKS:

The Look

PART ONE

The Scarecrow Club

1

He could deny it no longer. There was no way around it. He had it. The Look.

He had become a member of a secret club. A secret society, coexisting within a brighter, everyday world that had somehow slipped from his fingers. Young men with canes smiled at him on the street. Men who were bundled into layer after layer of clothing — sweaters, jackets, scarves, gloves — these were the men who noticed him now, men who looked as if they had been dressed by overprotective mothers afraid to send their boys out into the cold, cruel world. He no longer caught the eye of men in muscled t-shirts and slim, tight blue jeans, men whose rosy health seemed a technicolor glow alongside his own gray pallor. These boys skipped in the sunshine holding hands with lovers and buddy friends, their laughter stinging his ears as they waltzed through the Castro.

He had been one of those men, once.

It murdered something deep inside him to be excluded, to be so cavalierly dismissed from the community that had once adored and admired him with naked longing. He didn't care what people said, your looks were *everything*.

Now he had it: the Look. The wrong look.

He'd been so careful. Twice-weekly trips to the tanning salon. The gym, three or four times a week no matter how lousy he felt, no matter how low his energy. He was going to beat this.

Except. The Look.

He could handle anything but that. Anything. The lingering colds, the constant fatigue, the joint and muscle aches that sometimes kept him awake at night. He could deal with these pains because he could do it in his own private way, out of sight of prying eyes.

But now he had joined this secret club. Its members acknowledged each other with knowing nods or telltale winks. They understood that they had been passed by, like jet-setters bumped out of first class into economy. They understood that they had become something outside the norm, something that lived in a twilight world of in-between, somewhat forgotten but difficult to ignore.

Not Brent. He had a beautiful name. He was one of the beautiful people. If he clamped down hard enough on this, pushed it away, he would undo his plight. He would make it go away. He was sure of it.

Until he stared at his reflection in the mirror one more time, and saw the message that had imprinted itself indelibly upon his skin. The Look.

2

"I won't stand for it," Brent told his psychologist the next afternoon, on his routine Tuesday visit. "I don't accept this. I don't."

"Now, Brent," said Dr. Anthony Able, his fingers steepled above his lap. "We've been through all of this. Part of your illness is accepting—"

"Look at me." Brent turned to stare at the gray-haired man in his turtleneck sweater. This was ridiculous. Beautiful men like himself did not need to air dirty laundry at seventy-five dollars a pop to men who wore turtlenecks in the nineties, for Christ's sake. He was standing, his agitation a need for motion that the leather couch could not contain.

"Yes. I'm looking."

"Look at these suitcases under my eyes. Even with enough sleep, I still look tired, every morning. My hair — I used to have such gorgeous blond hair. Men *loved* to run their fingers through my hair. Now it's all flyaway, just hanging on my head."

"AZT has a tendency to do that in some patients," said the doctor in a voice like that of a professor reading notes to an impatient classroom.

Brent brought his fingertips to his temples. "Look. Look at what's happening to my face. I don't like to go out in public anymore. People stare at me. The wrong people.

"You won't make friends with an attitude like that," admonished his doctor, gently.

Brent snorted. "Friends. Who has time for friends?" He didn't add that he had been too busy being admired all his life to have friends. Friends were just people who hung around because they wanted to get inside your pants. It was all very tedious, unless of course his pursuers were cute. And now they weren't even that, anymore. He had become a member of the Scarecrow Club, and he hadn't even applied for an application.

"Making time for friends is the one luxury you *do* have," Dr. Able said. "They may come in handy, one day. "

Brent turned his back on the psychologist. His right hand bunched into a fist. Sometimes he just wanted to hit things, he was so mad.

"I won't stand for this," he muttered.

"What? What did you say?"

"I am *not* going to lose my looks."

"Now, Brent, there isn't much we can do about that."

"I will not have my epitaph read, 'He died of bad dandruff.'"

"That's the spirit. Humor is good. Humor is healing. These feelings will pass. Remember how upset you were after your first stay in the hospital? How you swore you'd never let that happen to you again? This is no different."

Brent's fists tightened. No different? He was paying seventy-five dollars an hour to a man who couldn't recognize disaster when it stared at him eyeball to eyeball?

The doctor tried again. "If you made some friends—"

"I don't need friends," Brent snapped. "I need my looks back."

An indulgent sigh. Dr. Able glanced at his watch.

Brent mumbled something under his breath.

"Sorry?" A word had jumped out at him, like a punch. "What did you say?"

Brent decided to face this ridiculous man in his turtleneck. He turned with determination to watch the shock his words would cause. "I said I'd kill to have my looks back."

"Don't speak such nonsense."

"I would. I really would."

The doctor's face clouded with irritation, not the shock Brent had hoped to induce. "Don't speak of such things."

"Why not? It's how I feel."

"Careful. The walls have ears, you know."

"What's that supposed to mean?"

Now the older man was embarrassed as well as irritated, caught in a snare he did not want to articulate. He arranged his face into a humorous mask, as though this were all a big joke. "It's like saying I'd sell my soul to the devil. Don't tempt the fates. You may not believe in the devil, but maybe *he* believes in *you.*"

I believe in the devil, Brent thought half an hour later as he walked through the Castro on his way home. The February sky was rain-swollen, hugging the ground. The world appeared painted in shades of aluminum. *Because only the devil would allow this to happen to me.*

His gait was slow, deliberate, as though he were window-shopping the trendy clothing boutiques and not actually moving as fast as his aching legs would allow. He tugged on his coat as cold gusts of wind blew over him. Two men whistled past in tightly packed t-shirts, oblivious of the cold and damp. Brent buttoned up his coat another notch, wincing as arthritis — his latest torture — flared in his stiff fingers.

A figure moved toward him on the same side of the street. He leaned heavily upon an ornate wooden cane, his labored pace making Brent feel as though his own walk were a hundred-yard dash. Brown hair lay in dull wisps against his skull. The bottom of his face was all beard, as though the man's chin had disappeared, having been eaten away. Even at that distance, Brent saw the unmistakable: he was not long for this world. He wanted to turn his head. He wanted not to see, as others now chose not to see him.

Brent knew this man. They'd dated a few times, back in the early eighties. A lifetime ago, in another age. In another world. What was his name? John? Bob? No: John, that was it. Brent stopped in front of Crown Books and pretended interest in the latest best-sellers. He stood and stared without seeing until this frail, broken man hobbled past him.

Without meaning to, Brent followed John's reflection. His old dating buddy had half turned, recognizing. Their eyes met. And then, without a word — though their embarrassed silence spoke volumes — each glanced away, and continued walking.

Yes, Brent thought grimly. *I would kill to have it all back. I would.*

3

His life had become a melodrama of the lowest order: trite and cliched and utterly predictable. He knew exactly what was coming. He knew all the moves. He'd watched enough late-night Bette Davis movies ad nauseam, down to the last shredded Kleenex, to know. ("Play that song again, the one about time.") If he could not halt what was happening to him, then he wanted to just curl up on a king-sized bed amid the trumpeting of angels and be carried off to the great darkness, angel wings flapping. It was a fitting end, for a beauty.

Only he was no longer a beauty, was he. For months he'd adopted the habit of not looking at himself too closely in the mirrors. A quick glance to make sure his hair was combed usually sufficed. Now, he accepted the truth. The mirrors did not lie. His shoulders lately had slimmed down so much he was surprised they could support the weight of his shirts and sweaters. He hadn't told anyone, but he'd bought himself a pair of shoulder pads. At least it gave him the illusion of normalcy, out in public.

He'd been a gymnast once, in high school and college. Perfect strong legs and thighs that had always garnered him furtive looks from special teammates — and not a few coaches. Proud of his butt, which knew precisely how to fill out any pair of pants or swimsuit for full advantage. As a gymnast, he had understood the power of presentation — which was why he could only view his shriveled self in the mirror and sigh. Toothpicks. Toothpicks for legs. His butt had all but disappeared, the beach ball curves now pancake flat, skin sagging below his spine. How could he not have noticed this, before? Little wonder that members of the Scarecrow Club had initiated him into their ranks, even without his permission.

And of course — above all else — there was the sad matter of his face. He was losing his cheeks, so that he appeared to always be sucking on a lemon. Forehead seemed wider, but lacked character: it was gaunt, bony, as though his skull were determined to push through to the outside. His green eyes — once described by a short-time boyfriend as "pools of emeralds" — not bad — were turning muddy, brown. It was cause to shudder, to see this dying of inner fire, that spark that was his most passionate core.

Brent stood before the medicine cabinet. The hinged door squealed open. On the top shelf, an aspirin bottle. Only there was no aspirin inside, not anymore. Over the past year he had slowly collected what he could of all varieties: codeine and Valium, Vicodan, percodan, Xanex. A virtual jelly-bean soup of pills.

He would let what was happening to him progress only so far. So far, and no more. His pills would see to that.

He forced himself to shut the cabinet door and leave the bathroom. He had to be careful It was hypnotic, in its own awful way, to search out every change, every new purple lesion or sunken patch of skin. He wasn't ready for the pills, not quite yet, but if he didn't yank himself away from the mirrors he would be filling a tall glass with water all too soon.

He flopped onto the couch in the living room and watched TV. He must have dozed. A sharp noise roused him some indefinable time later, a noise his sluggish mind insisted had been the metal scrape of his mail slot in his front door.

A clock on his mantel chimed twelve times. Midnight.

Brent swayed off the couch, his thoughts oatmeal. He went to the hallway, and stared. In the dark at the front of the house he almost missed it there, lying flat on the floor. A rectangle of white against wooden floorboards. An envelope. Mail delivery at midnight?

He started down the hallway.

A feeling rose in him, a childhood premonition of monsters under the bed, of squishy dead things that should never, ever, be touched. He was not a superstitious man, never had been, and so it was all the more vexing to find his thoughts overrun with what could only be nonsense. Instead, he turned to the mystery of it: that someone had come to his door at this late hour, and pushed the envelope through the mail slot. Perhaps another noise had disrupted his sleep. For he could think of no good reason, none at all, as to why someone would come to his door. And there lay the source of his unexpected dread: there was no good reason.

Brent hovered before it. His fingers groped for the light switch by the front door. He blinked against the overhead hallway light and waited for his double vision to clear. His name was scrawled upon the envelope in spiderweb-thin ink, the lettering somehow Gothic with giant curlicues and a swirling underline supporting his name.

He stooped to pick it up. His knees popped like gunshot blasts. He clawed the envelope into his hand, pushed himself back onto sturdy feet, and nearly dropped it. For just a moment — the tiniest moment, really — the letter had seemed to ripple beneath his fingers. Like something reptilian rearranging its position: a snake curling into its burrow. Brent blinked against the illusion.

It was the thickness of the envelope, he saw, a rich vellum the color of old ivory, that accounted for that unaccustomed feel. His name stared up at him. There was not even an address below it. He flipped the letter over in search of a return address and saw only a red wax seal.

The child in him, innocence, rose up. *Don't open it.*

Brent's thumb hooked beneath the seal. The wax, though sealed to a hard crust, felt slightly warm, as though it had been applied only moments before. Inside was a card of the same texture and weight as the envelope. His breath held in his throat. He plucked the card from its sheath.

No salutation. No return address. One sentence, in that hair-thin writing, slicing the blank surface:

Would you really, truly, kill to have your looks back?

4

He thought he'd been prepared for those two words — "You're fired" — but he wasn't. Around him was the clickety-clack of fingers upon computer keyboards, the soft hum of co-workers assuring worried travelers that their plane seats were reserved.

"Brent? You still with me?"

Brent jerked out of his daze. Captain Kirk, his overweight, basset hound boss, had overflowed onto a seat in front of his terminal. This was not a good sign. And he'd been saying things to Brent, gobs of words strung together that he'd missed. This was also not good. "Sorry?"

"Are you feeling okay?"

He nodded, and then gave a weak shrug. He hadn't been able to sleep properly the past two nights, the dark shot through with silver and red. Something hovering...

"Have they put you on a new medication?"

"There *are* no new medications," he answered a bit too archly, a zinger arrow aimed at his boss's heart. But Kirk — Captain Kirk, as he was affectionately called by his mostly young, pretty-boy staff — seemed not to have heard it. He was a man with a mission, today.

"I'm afraid I have no choice but to be blunt," Captain Kirk told him. He squirmed uncomfortably in his chair.

There was a buzzing in Brent's ears. This was a part of his melodrama, too. He thought he'd been prepared.

"Take a look around you, Brent. We're a good group of guys. And you've been with me a long time, right? Three or four years, isn't it? You've been the perfect advertisement I've wanted to project for Captain Kirk's Travels to the Beyond."

A smile attached itself to Brent's face. It squatted there like a Halloween mask, wobbling as though held on with a flimsy rubber band. Yes, this clean and antiseptic office of brick walls and fashionable paintings and polished wooden floors presented just the right image to winter-weary gay men in search of sunny beaches and a cruise to the Caribbean. For several years he had been the perfect advertisement, tanned and gorgeous and blond below travel posters green and orange and tropical. Come embrace the exotic, he and the posters seemed to whisper, and perhaps you will find a beauty such as me.

Below his desk, out of sight, Brent bunched his hands into fists. Something raw and indigestible pushed on the back of his throat.

"You're just not working out anymore," Captain Kirk explained, his hound dog expression downcast with dismay. "You've been nodding off in the afternoons. Business is slow, what with the recession. I just ... think this is for the best. You understand, don't you?"

He understood, all right. Members of the Scarecrow Club were not the best poster boys for Puerto Vallarta. Not with skin the color of cigarette ash, and raccoon eyes.

Brent forced his lips to move. In a cracked voice he said, "Without this job, I'll lose my health coverage."

"Tell you what. I'll carry you for another few months. We'll work something out with Kaiser Hospital, get you off group and onto an individual plan. It won't cost you that much."

"Couldn't you just cut back my hours?"

"No. I'm sorry. Truly." He did not say the words that Brent knew were inside his head: You don't fit in anymore. You look like death warmed over. I can't have a poster boy who looks like a skeleton. *Don't you know you have the Look?*

No. Captain Kirk and his mighty crew of pretty boys were not about to set themselves up for a lawsuit. His work wasn't up to par. He fell asleep at the keyboard. Business was slow. Anything but the truth.

"I'll help you any way I can," said his boss, standing. He looked immensely relieved, the weight of his decision lifted, now that he'd gotten it out in the open. "One day you'll see this is for the best."

Maybe for you, Brent thought.

"Take the rest of the afternoon off. Come in tomorrow morning and we'll settle up, so to speak. Let's make this ... as equitable as possible. Okay?"

A cold wind funneled down Market Street. It hit Brent like a solid wall. He felt little corners of himself crumble against its onslaught. His looks, gone. His job, gone. If he couldn't pay the premiums on his health insurance, if he lost his coverage — what then?

He knew what then. A trip to the medicine cabinet.

Ahh, to what depths, desperation. What he would not do, to undo, this predicament.

As he inched himself up Market toward the Twin Peaks bar on the corner, his thoughts folded back to the mysterious letter he'd received a week earlier. Its message had scraped across his brain like a thumbnail down a chalkboard; it gave him the shivers.

But despite all the mystery of its arrival at his door, and cryptic invitation, the real puzzle had not started until the following morning. Right before going to bed he'd put the letter and its envelope onto the dresser next to his change jar. He'd forgotten all about it in the morning, though something had nagged at the back of his thoughts as he rushed around getting ready for work. Only when he stood before the dresser, sock drawer ajar, did his gaze float absently across its smooth surface—

—And memory slammed into him. The letter. He'd left it right there, next to the coin jar. Right where there was now the tiniest whisper of ash.

It wasn't on the floor. It hadn't fallen into a drawer. Seemingly, all that remained of the letter was this sprinkle of what looked like cigarette ash dusting the surface in a gray pile.

Brent ducked into a doorway, out of the unforgiving wind, and caught his breath. He hugged his coat tight. He hadn't imagined any of it, of that fact he was absolutely certain. The note's vanishing merely added one more facet to the cluster of oddities surrounding it. Just as, when he calmed down enough to really contemplate it, like now, he noticed his belly was filled with an absurd expectancy. Like the good food smells that envelop an apartment hours before sitting down to a banquet, his appetite had been whetted.

His heart brimming with these mixed emotions, Brent propelled himself out of the doorway — and smack into a man hurrying by.

"Sorry," Brent gasped, knocked to the side.

"No problem," said the man in a deep baritone. He sidestepped Brent in an effort to keep his momentum.

But Brent jerked out a hand and held the man firm. "John?" The name of his old friend was choked out in disbelief, as though addressing one dead, now alive.

The man turned crimson beneath freshly shaven cheeks, and tried to pry Brent's grip off his arm. "You've got me confused with someone else—"

"No, I don't. Don't you remember me? Brent?"

"No."

"We saw each other about a week ago. On Castro Street, in front of Crown Books. You and I had a few dates way back when."

The man nodded gamely. "Yeah. I remember. It's been a long time..."

"What did you do?"

"What do you mean?" The man glanced uneasily up and down the windswept street. He raked a hand across a handsome jaw which less than a week ago had been buried by a scraggly beard.

"Look at you!" Brent cried. He was awed by the transformation, and could assemble no words upon his tongue to adequately describe it.

John's cane was gone. So too the dark smudges beneath brown eyes that had glanced away with embarrassment at their last meeting. His skeleton no longer resided in his face, but had retreated beneath a San Francisco pale but nonetheless healthy skin. He had seemingly gained twenty pounds — and not fat gain, but the solid assured musculature that should only result from sweaty three-month marathons at the trendy gay gyms. In fact, instead of the ornate cane in his hand, he carried a black nylon gym bag. His hair piled lustful and rich, like sumptuous shaved flakes of chocolate above his eyes, that invited a lingering touch of hands.

Brent gawked. And then a desperation seized him as powerfully as his grip upon his old friend's arm. "Please. Tell me. How did you do it?"

John scowled. "You know."

"No, I don't."

"Of course you do."

Confusion. Panic, that this man would tear free before explaining himself. "I don't! I swear I don't!"

John leaned in. A smell blew over Brent, sour and unpleasant. In a conspiratorial whisper he said, "He's contacted you, hasn't he?"

"Who?"

"I know he has. I can see it on you—"

And he clamped his hand over his mouth in that ageless me-and-my-big-mouth gesture. His bright eyes blinked with fright. "Forget it," he hissed. "Forget I said anything. And do yourself a favor, Brent."

"What's that?" Again a ripe odor tickled Brent's nose.

"Say no."

"Say no?"

"It's not worth it. You may think so, now, looking at me. But if you only knew..." His eyes darkened with something Brent did not recognize, something that may have been despair. "If you only knew, you'd run the hell away. From him." John pried Brent's feeble hand from his arm. "And from me."

"I want my looks back," Brent whispered, irritated that he sounded more and more the petulant child. It was no use. John was in retreat. "I want to be like you."

Something wild leapt over his companion's face at that. He shook his head in disbelief and stepped away. A broken sound screeched out of his lips like a needle hopping over a scratched record. He fled down the street.

5

Brent was still trying to make sense out of John's amazing appearance as he slipped his key into the front door and stepped inside. A pile of mail scooted to one side of the hallway as the opening door brushed it across the floor.

Anticipation, at the sight of his mail. In the back of his mind he had wondered if today might be the day. Would be the day. He scooped the mail into his hands. Shuffled through bills and advertisements. His breath was hot and fast.

Here it was. The second letter.

His name was spelled out in a spindly script no wider than strands of hair. The envelope appeared old, as if it had spent years upon someone's bookshelf, forgotten. He gripped it uneasily; despite the burning curiosity, there was frankly something repellent about its surface, something between paper and snakeskin that encouraged his fingers to recoil.

But this was absurd. He had waited for this. Known it would happen. His previous letter had been too much the dangling question, the bait, not to be followed up. Unless it had been — and still was — some sort of prank.

Brent walked down the hallway to his kitchen. He absently tossed the other letters and bills onto the surface of his round antique wooden table. He meant to sit down, to open the envelope casually, as though perusing an electric bill. Anticipation tipped the scales. His fingers slid beneath the warm red wax seal. And he read:

Yes or no. Answer now. Aloud.

Brent's lower lip trembled. He saw the new and improved John standing before him: *"Say no."*

It hurt to draw in a breath. The air in his house seemed stale and weighted down, fraught with things that could not be seen in the light. But mostly he thought of this drowning pool that was his illness, that contained him on all sides and would not let him out. This illness would not be satisfied until he had slipped beneath the pool's surface, and floated with all the other dead.

Brent opened his mouth. "Yes."

The word reverberated as though inside an empty chamber, as though bouncing off the stone walls of a deeply buried well. Weak February daylight grew even more timorous, as fog and rain clouds crept over the face of the sun.

He pulled out a chair and sat down heavily with jelly legs. He dropped the letter and its casing to the table, and noticed distractedly that his fingertips were oily from its touch. He thought of his bright sunshine days of wild youth when bar friends had encouraged him to drop a tab of LSD; how, upon swallowing the tiny stamp of paper, his stomach would always clench with the knowledge that there was no turning back, that he had unalterably set his course for the next six hours. All he could do was wait through that first hour before the drug bloomed in him. Wait, and hope his trip would be a pleasant one.

He felt much like that now. If he had truly set forces into motion, there was nothing to be done but ride it out. Let him come, this letter writer with his sneaky proposals. Let him show himself, and lay his cards upon the table.

Outside the window of his kitchen, daylight faded to battle-ship gray. Brent sat in the cathedral silence and watched the afternoon leak away. His thoughts were too full for brightness, and required only this cottony silver for his inventory. The refrigerator hummed and gurgled in the semidarkness that was ripening to the color of plums.

When he could no longer adequately see, Brent walked out of the kitchen, one hand outstretched, and went into his bed-room. He clicked on a small table lamp. Hanging from the wall were half a dozen pictures of himself. The images of health: bronzed and baby-smooth complexion, blond hair almost white on top from trips to Laguna Beach. His green eyes, bright as M&M candies. Here was one, fetching and sexy in a bikini Speedo, the meat of his shoulders delectably accented by the tapering V of his waist.

Yes, Brent thought, studying his former self. *Whatever it takes, the answer is yes.*

From the living room, distinctly, came the snap click of a cigarette lighter, and the hot-air hiss of burning fuel.

Brent stepped away from the photographs and glanced beyond his bedroom door. He forced each foot to make a step, and then another, and another. Metal snapped against metal, an exhaled breath, and the faintest aroma of smoke stained the dusky air. He heard his arts-and-crafts rocking chair creak from weight and movement. He slipped down the hallway, his bowels rumbling with abrupt queasiness, and rounded the corner. Smoke was rising, a smudge of white drifting against the dark, from the red-dot coin of a cigarette's tip. A figure sat in the chair, ennobled by the dark the way a stone statue takes on an air of immortality and immenseness against the night.

The statue moved. "Hello, Brent."

6

Brent lubricated his tongue, which had turned into driftwood, with saliva.

"Hello."

"I don't blame you for admiring yourself," said the statue. "You were quite handsome, once."

"How did you get inside?" croaked Brent.

"I was under the distinct impression I had been invited."

"Yes. You were." He relaxed a little. There was no surprise. No fear. A calm inevitability.

"Forgive me for startling you. Your absorption with your pictures was so complete I'm afraid you didn't hear me come in. It was awfully kind of you to leave off the lights. My eyes, I'm embarrassed to admit, are not what they used to be. If you require light, perhaps a candle...?"

As if in a waking dream, Brent glided across the room. In various corners he had placed votive candles of vanilla and lemon. He fumbled a book of matches. The faint drift of lemon perfumed the room. He turned to light the second candle. As more of the mellow light invaded the room, Brent dared himself to look upon his visitor. Perhaps it was the fault of the flickering candlelight, but he found he could not properly focus his eyes. His guest was a quick series of impressions, like a strobe light, starting with the red punctuation mark of his cigarette tip. He wore a dark suit, navy blue and exquisitely tailored. An equally exquisite Panama hat was pulled down close to shade eyes shielded by a wide black pair of sunglasses. His guest's complexion seemed artificially white, almost powdered, but Brent decided it was the contrast between all that dark clothing and sunglasses. His lips looked painted on, as though he wore lipstick. A goatee lent a Freudian touch to his jaw.

"Why do you look at me that way?" asked the man, suddenly.

Brent shrugged sheepishly. "You're not what I expected."

A hairline smile. "And what did you expect?"

"I don't know." But he did, in some recessed part of himself that could never utter the words aloud: Pointed ears. Fangs. Demon eyes. Anyone but this urbane David Niven with a goatee. He laughed at himself and plopped down upon the couch.

"You expected some kind of devil, perhaps?"

Brent was grateful for the darkness, to hide the fire in his cheeks. He blurted out, "Aren't you — you know — here to make me a bargain? Isn't this what it's all about?"

The stranger took a drag off his cigarette. Yes, his face was theatrically white, somehow painted on. It pulled with amusement.

"Your imagination does you an injustice," he said after a moment. "I am a man, as you are a man. Believe that. As for your soul, if such a thing exists, I have absolutely no interest. It's your services that I require, your physical strength and stamina."

"Mister, I don't think you've taken a good look at me."

"Yes. I can see you were once quite special. I'm sure all the handsome boys flocked around you. Adored you. You would have been *my* type, in your day. It must have been wonderful to have anyone you wanted. But look at you now."

Brent hung his head, stung. This man owned a preacher's resonant voice, that of a minister who could gather his flock about him with just a choice word. Somehow Brent had to be chastised, first.

Another drag of cigarette. Red reflected off the sunglasses. "This disease is ruthless, is it not? First it strips away your health. Then your looks. And finally, your dignity. It toys with you, a cat with a mouse. Here a swipe, there a swipe." Red lips twitched. "It's enough to drive one mad."

Brent lifted his head. "Can you help me?"

"Oh, yes." Surprised by the absurdity of the question.

"And how do I help you?"

"Right to the point — I admire that in a business partner. I've no tolerance for pussyfooting around."

"You're the one who's been so secretive," Brent heard himself say.

"You would be too, given the circumstances."

"Which are?"

"Do you have an ashtray?"

Brent handed the man what was handy, a used water glass from the coffee table. The cigarette dropped in with a last gasp. "Like many other chemists in my profession, I searched for a cure to this epidemic. My own health had begun to decline, you see. For several years my efforts went unrewarded. This virus is too changeable, too complicated for one simple answer. I had almost given up. And then, through a happy combination of chance and good fortune, I hit upon the drug. A very unique drug, which the other gentlemen in my employ laughingly refer to as 'the cocktail.' It has, as you have seen with your acquaintance John, restorative properties that are quite remarkable."

Brent felt a glimmer of hope, a tingling of anticipation. "Why haven't you tried to market it? If it truly works, you could make a fortune. Have more fame than you can possibly imagine."

The man grunted and held up a pale hand; he had obviously considered such proposals before. "The cocktail's ingredients are a bit too specialized for mass-market consumption. I'm afraid the FDA would never approve it."

An alarm bell went off in Brent. "Okay. 'Fess up. What are the side effects?"

"Side effects?"

"There's always something with these kinds of drugs. Muscle aches and pains. Upset stomach. Fevers. Which is it?"

Brent's visitor shook his head. "As long as you take the cocktail every day, none. There are no side effects. Some gentlemen claim it gives them a bit of an odor, much like eating garlic and having it seep out of your pores. I think they exaggerate."

"How do I pay you for this — cocktail?"

"Through your services. And your silence."

Brent coughed into one hand; his guest's lingering cigarette smoke had produced a tickle. "I have no problem with keeping silent. But exactly what sort of work are we talking about here? It sounds ... well ... illegal."

The man laughed, a single guffaw that barked out with his amusement. "Oh, it *is*. Highly." He placed a hand upon his chest as though in effort to calm his mirth. "About once or twice a week, occasionally more, I will require your help in transporting various items. Sometimes I may ask for your assistance in procuring ingredients. The cocktail, as you may well imagine, is a complicated brew. The required combinations of chemicals and rare herbs are not always easily obtained. In your new, strengthened condition these tasks, I assure you, will not be difficult. I am a busy man. I can not always spare the time to track them all down. So: in return for these procurements, I provide you with a week's supply of the drug."

Brent nodded. He had a sudden vision of himself loping across dew-wet fields in search of exotic mushrooms and tree bark. Is this what he wanted for the rest of his life? "And if I don't care for your line of work?" he asked. "What then?"

"You may always purchase your supply." A hand floated up and played with the curls of his goatee. "But I believe you will take to your job quite readily. Otherwise I would never have contacted you in the first place."

"When could I get this drug?"

A wave of hand, white against dark. "Tonight, if you wish."

"Tonight?" Brent hardly dared believe it. In his mind's eye he saw his old trick buddy John, first as the man who walked arm in arm with Death, and then as he had been that very afternoon, sculpted and desirable, free of the virus's handiwork.

John: *"Say no."*

Why? He had played out all his cards against this disease, and owned no other aces. His doctor at Kaiser pretty much patted his hand these days. He was sick of the roller coaster ride of new treatments, new drugs, new therapies — and the whole ghastly gamut of odd and terrible side effects. Nothing that he had gulped down in the last two desperate years had ever produced even a tenth of the change he had witnessed in John that afternoon. Brent understood with an absolute certainty that he was staring down his final option. There would be no reprieves after this: only a short slide into the grave. Faced with such an appalling future, why was there now this hesitancy? If he didn't care for the work, he could always quit. He'd buy the cocktail, if necessary. If it worked. *Oh god, if it only works...*

Brent drew a breath. "I'll do it," he said. "Count me in."

If it was possible for a face hidden by sunglasses to beam with pleasure, his did. "Excellent," cooed the man.

Now that he had taken the final step, Brent felt abruptly flustered. He clapped his hands with nervous anticipation. "So what happens now? Do I sign a contract or something?"

"A gentlemen's handshake will be quite adequate."

Brent thrust out a hand. "I don't even know your name," he admitted with a little laugh.

"Skettle," the man answered "Call me Skettle." A powdered hand clamped upon Brent's frail fingers and palm. The grip was fierce, total, like a big fish swallowing whole a littler fish. Fingernails dug into the vulnerable pad of his palm. There was an exhaled wince of pain, and a quick apology: "Oh, I'm terribly sorry. I've forgotten my own strength. Allow me." And a handkerchief fluttered out of the gloom, Brent's hand turned palm up, as the man with the goatee dabbed up three drops of blood with mechanical, meticulous care. With these same precise motions Skettle folded up the dirtied handkerchief and secreted it into an inside vest pocket of his exquisite suit.

Without even knowing the words sat upon his tongue, Brent blurted out, "What if I had said no?"

"Dear boy," Skettle said with wry amusement. "We passed up that option long ago."

7

Now he stood before the stove in the kitchen and adjusted the gas flame. Brent grabbed an aluminum saucepan and measured out two cups of water, precisely. Skettle's instructions had been exact. The moment the water began to boil he was to add one of the packets left for him in the paper sack. Boil for three minutes. Strain. And drink, as quick and as hot as tolerable.

Brent replayed Skettle's departure in his mind while he waited for the water to boil. There had been a knock at the front door, and before he had even managed to raise himself from the couch, they tromped in, two men. Bodyguards, or simply chauffeur and assistant, he did not know. Big and powerfully built, they were silent as a mausoleum as one of the men lifted Skettle from the rocking chair in a gesture more suggestive of a servant-to-master relationship than of any fragility. The other man, his chiseled face implacable in the dying glow of candle-light, held within his hands a medium-sized paper sack. He thrust it, dainty as a woman's expensive purse, toward Brent. Brent took it, his heart quickening at the satisfying weight in his hands, this promise of restored health and vitality.

"Enjoy your reprieve," Skettle said to him after laying out precise instructions for taking the drug.

"I don't know what to say," Brent had stammered.

A hairline smile crossed Skettle's face. He was clearly enjoying this role of savior to handsome men. "Say nothing," Skettle cautioned. "Have your honeymoon. And do not hesitate when I call upon you."

"Oh, I won't. I won't," he had blubbered in a voice appallingly like that of a child enlisted by Santa for secret service.

Then they were gone, melting into the winter darkness beyond his front door. Brent heard no car engine rev up to drive them away. They were simply — gone.

And in his hands, the cocktail.

Boiling water hissed against the sides of the pan. Brent snapped out of his reverie, remembering with a panicky alarm that he was supposed to dump the contents of one of the packets immediately into the water. He yanked open the mouth of the sack and reached in. There was a note. He lifted it to his face.

Remember: silence. Even with the others.

Brent frowned. Yeah, yeah. All this hushed secrecy was too James Bond for his tastes. What was the big deal? Besides, he had no one to tell. His parents in Southern California had already given him up for dead, waiting for the final call from the hospital. His sister Mary Ann and her family, even though they lived in nearby Daly City, would have nothing to do with him. He had no friends. And he certainly wasn't about to tell that quack in the turtleneck, Dr. Anthony Able, who kept insisting Brent would like himself better if only he surrendered to the inevitability of his illness.

He reached into the sack and pulled out a small ziplock baggie. Grimaced at its contents. It was a liquidy pulp, like a bag of moist, undercooked oatmeal. Nothing distinguished its contents. Maybe that was for the best, especially now. He didn't want to know what made up its varied ingredients; he just wanted it to work.

Brent opened the baggie and a smell exhaled out, yucky as the witch's brew it resembled. He upended it over the boiling water and out it slopped, viscous and awful. His nose crinkled. His empty stomach clenched. This was better than AZT three times a day? Better than the acyclovir, the thousand milligrams of vitamin C, the B complex, the aerosol pentamidine inhaled once a month, warding off the voodoo spirits of Death?

He pulled a spoon from the silverware drawer and stirred the concoction, watching with a repulsed fascination as the water stirred up reddish and brown, like the tough clay of Texas farmland. His legs trembled with weakness, and with dismay Brent patted the damp moisture beading on his forehead. He really should have eaten something before doing this; his poor body was dizzy with exhaustion.

But in a way he was grateful that he had no time to think about what he was about to do. The cocktail boiled for three minutes, as per Skettle's instructions, and then he strained out a tall glass of the rust-colored liquid. It looked gritty, smelling of dirt. Bits of indefinable matter rested on top of the strainer. Brent knocked the debris into the trash can without staring at it too closely. He was secretly afraid that he would never manage his first sip if he studied the cocktail's liquid too closely.

Please help me, he prayed to the gods of medicine. The glass was too hot to pick up, so Brent dug out a potholder and used that to help him lift the glass. With his left hand he pinched shut his nostrils, to kill the smell and taste.

And there by the stove, at eleven-forty at night, Brent took his first sip.

8

An hour and a half later he was on the toilet, coming and going from both ends. He'd no sooner throw up than his bowels would break loose with a vile rush. He didn't even have time for the dignity of cleaning himself up with a tissue or washcloth. At one point, unable even to turn around and vomit into the toilet, he leaned over the bathtub and let go with shocking violence, only to plop back onto the toilet just in the nick of time to keep from dirtying himself.

It was humiliating and ghastly. His poor body, under siege one more time. In between bouts Brent shook a fist and cursed Skettle's name to the darkness. Liquid heat blazed off his forehead, the sweat like drops of boiling water. Through the haze of his fever he grasped the terrible truth: he had overdosed. Somehow in his excitement, he'd mixed up his instructions. Perhaps he was only supposed to drink half a glass of the vile stuff. But no; he clearly remembered Skettle telling him to gulp it all down, every last drop.

Brent shook his head in disbelief as another series of spasms rumbled through him. He gritted his teeth and rode it out. Years ago he'd gotten food poisoning from eating a dinner of spoiled ham and navy beans. The dim memory of that agony seemed a piece of cake in comparison with this present torture. His body moaned and revolted with a desperate urge to purge itself, as though every pore, every orifice had thrown open some secret chamber in an attempt to right this wrong. With hands clasped to either side of his head Brent sat cocooned in his misery, unable to think, unable to move. Every time he suspected he was finished and could attempt to clean up, a tidal wave of biblical proportions would swamp him afresh. Thank god he hadn't eaten any dinner or he'd be stuck here all night. Already he seriously doubted not just when, but *if,* he could return to bed, where he'd earlier awakened howling with pain.

The night yawned before him, hours upon hours before dawn would lighten the sky into a new day.

But like all things good and bad, the worst of it eventually passed. The knots in his intestines unraveled. Clammy with perspiration, Brent lifted himself onto rubbery legs and splashed cold water across his face. The smell and sight of his sickness in the bathtub almost drove him to a fresh bout of trouble, but he managed — barely — to control himself. He turned on the shower to wash the tub clean and then dared himself for the task of a shower. He felt soiled and inexplicably altered in some unforgivable way, as though he had reason to be shamed by this latest betrayal of his body.

Is this going to happen every time I drink the cocktail? wondered Brent as he stood beneath the hot spray of shower. He soaped and lathered every inch of himself. The very idea of drinking tomorrow's dose — and subjecting himself to this misery one more time — set his legs to trembling.

His fright sobered him. Exactly how much of the cocktail would he have to drink before he'd notice any benefits? *If* he had any benefits, he thought blackly. With his recent rotten luck he was probably allergic to the damn stuff.

Brent shut off the shower and toweled himself dry. He lay a palm against his stomach; it was asleep at last, but threatened to wake at any moment. Perhaps an Alka Seltzer? A little Pepto? He decided to leave his stomach empty.

He wiped a clear patch in the steamed-over mirror. Despite the restorative qualities of the hot shower, his face was drawn with illness, his eyes dark hollows punched below a pale forehead. Something moved beneath the pink of his skin. He leaned in close to the mirror. His veins were tight against his skin, busily pumping blood and the cocktail through every capillary. He blinked, and the illusion snapped away like a lost opportunity for a photograph. His bleak face stared back at him, unchanged.

Brent gave up with a desultory shrug. What he needed now was sleep, or he'd have to write off the next day. Not that he had to be anywhere, now. No; his schedule calendar had been swept clean. He had all the time in the world to think about death.

Stop it, he commanded himself, afraid of the grim back alley to which such thoughts would surely lead him. He crawled into bed, the sheets still damp from his bout of sweats. Fell asleep at once, though he never would have dreamed it possible.

And woke up an indefinable time later, his skin on fire, itchy and hot. Every muscle ached and moaned. It was like having hives and cramps, each separate agony now perfectly intertwined. Brent touched the flesh of his chest and felt it crawl beneath his fingers. He yanked his fingers away. So. It was not over, whatever this first dose of the cocktail was doing to him.

Years ago he had tried one of those passive exercise places in the Castro. The idea of not having to lift a finger while receiving the benefits of fifteen hundred situps had been immensely appealing. But the experience had been much too Frankensteinish for his tastes. First, they hooked electrodes all over his naked body. One by one certain sections of his anatomy were worked over with bursts of electricity. It had scared him, quite frankly, to watch his stomach muscles ripple and move under the direction of some outside force. All so he could have a tight stomach when he pulled off his shirt at the annual Memorial Day Madness dance party.

This sensation jerking through him now was similar, but less predictable. He was all motion and restlessness. Brent hauled himself out of bed and stumbled back into the bathroom. Wearily, he downed two of his painkillers. The itch of his skin was maddening.

Two steps out of the bathroom his legs collapsed beneath him. He had no warning. A pain careened through him as he hit the woven rug on his den floor. He tried to shout, but even the tendons in his neck stood out in shock. Brent folded into a fetal curl and surrendered to his sudden unforgiving pain.

Oh god, what have I done...

Morning light roused him some hours later. Brent woke up in a state of total disorientation. He was curled up on the rug. He raised onto his elbows and blinked away sleep. Around him were things he did not recognize, white-gray strips of matter that looked for all the world like dirty snowflakes. They lay in a snowy drift all about him. Brent glanced at his arms and legs and saw that many of these snowflakes clung to him. He rubbed a hand over his left forearm and its surface blistered away, erupting into a snowy dance.

Even in his confusion, it hit him.

Skin.

He had shed his outside self. He was peeling away the last of what his illness had wrought upon him. Most of his skin lay in discarded strips, like a weird pattern to an unfinished quilt. His new self lay just underneath, pink and gleaming. With another hot shower and his loofa brush and he'd look like a million bucks—

Brent's eyes widened. Disbelief.

His arms, which from his illness had withered away to the size of broomsticks, were now fleshed out, plump as Cornish game hens. He slapped hands against his chest, everywhere firm and pumped.

Delirious joy swept through him. Brent rushed to the bathroom mirror to gaze upon his reflection.

And screamed.

PART TWO

That honeymoon glow

1

Thus began Brent's honeymoon.

He stayed home the first day despite an overwhelming urge to run shouting into the streets. He wanted to announce to the world his restored vigor, his miraculous recovery. No wonder Skettle insisted on silence, for without that caution Brent would have been holding a press conference. This exhilaration was sharpened by the knowledge of just how close to the brink he had been standing. A man strapped into the electric chair would feel exactly like this, if the governor's reprieve came winging down the telephone wire moments before the thrown switch.

Of course — let's be honest here — it hadn't started out all rose petals and daisies. Brent had gone to the bathroom mirror expecting to admire his restored health — and instead he had shrieked at the shredded corpse leering out from the mirror. He looked like fruit ripened too long by the sun, strips of his dried skin dangling from his brow, his blond hair hanging like strings.

Oh, the shock of it, on top of all the agony he'd endured to reach this point! But then he'd reeled in his senses — not to mention his screams — and knew he had to help this process of change along. He took two baths, one after the other, and meticulously scrubbed away the dead skin. His muscles ached with a soreness akin to having run a marathon. His calves were unresponsive to his massaging touch. His shoulders, too, ached with a dull deep pain that seemed to shoot out from some central core. It reminded him of that passive exercise machine with the electrodes: while he'd slept, his muscles had worked and worked, restoring a former glory to his physique.

Well, glory wasn't the right word, until Brent broke down at noon and boiled up his second dose of the cocktail. Its smell seeped into every corner of the house; he threw open the windows and ignored the February chill. His stomach rumbled with reluctance as he drank down the gritty stuff. Not knowing what to expect, he hung around within bolting distance to the bathroom. About two hours in, weird flaming arrows of pain shot up and down his arms and legs. But it was not accompanied by any of last night's desperation to purge, he was thankful to note. He was tolerating this dose with nothing more than a queasy stomach and these painful joint and muscle aches.

It was a good thing Skettle had lied to him about these side effects. Would he have drunk the stuff if he'd known he'd be up half the night puking his guts out?

But the changes — the changes were worth all the pain, all the discomfort. And really, what had he expected, a fairy tale transformation? A wave of a wand, a magic potion, and poof: his former self, unsullied by years of illness? His purging binge from the night before encouraged him to believe he had thrown off everything toxic in his body. And these aches, what were they if not his muscles somehow springing back to life, rearranging themselves beneath his new skin? So Brent popped his pain pills and dug in for the short haul. Late in the afternoon he ran a temperature of 102 degrees, but he'd suffered through so many fevers in the past few years, this discomfort barely made an impression on him.

He searched impatiently for each new change, each new sign of success, but it was like waiting for a pot of water to boil. The signposts of change were in constant motion within him, but too tender yet to be recognized whenever he gazed at his reflection in the mirror.

He managed a bit of soup for dinner, and fell asleep on the couch while watching sitcoms. After the rough night, his body craved the sleep it had been denied.

A happy surprise awaited Brent when he swiveled off the couch early the next morning. He stumbled into the bathroom to take a leak, and while hovering over the toilet his gaze drifted lazily to the mirrors.

His whoop of joy caught him in midspurt. He rushed up close to the mirror, ignoring his dribbles onto the bathroom floor.

"Yes," he whispered, his green M&M eyes flashing their approval. "Yes!"

2

Captain Kirk pulled Brent aside. "My god, man, what have you been taking!"

Brent managed a smile that was not too smug. "Vitamins."

"Like hell. Come on, give. You look fantastic!"

Which he did. Brent basked in the attention of his boss, the first person to pay homage to what had happened to him. His co-workers had said their hellos but then kept an awed distance, their faces screwed with confusion.

"Thank you," was all Brent would say, choosing modesty as his escape.

But Captain Kirk would have none of it. "I've never seen anything like it. Two days, and you look like a million bucks. Not that you looked awful the last time you were here, but ... oh, hell, you know what I mean!"

Yes, Brent knew. And what fun it was to watch his boss squirm. He pulled over his own face a carefully neutral mask.

"What'd you do?"

He opted for the truth, lightly veiled. "I tried something new. It seems to be working."

"I should say so! Is this going to last, or..."

Brent shrugged.

"So what are you going to do?"

He indicated his desk. "I'm here to clean out my things. I know I was supposed to drop by yesterday and take care of it—"

"Oh, relax. Relax. Don't be so hasty."

"You're the one who fired me," Brent said, hoping the truth stung.

The heavy man lowered his head with that hound dog expression and nodded his shame. Suddenly he glanced up, eyes flashing with an idea. "Why don't you come into my office?"

Fifteen minutes later Brent was out on Market Street, whistling. His unguarded laughter bubbled out of him. It had been hard to hide behind a poker face as Captain Kirk stumbled all over himself to offer him his old job back. Part-time hours, but that suited Brent just fine. His initial impulse had been to say, "Fuck you," and just leave. Common sense held his tongue: after all, he still needed money, right? He couldn't just sit around drinking the cocktail, could he?

So he'd accepted his boss's offer and played the role of grateful employee. Something better was bound to come down the pike, but until such time he'd keep his mouth shut. Maybe he could take a vacation soon using some of those vouchers he'd racked up. (He'd given up on trips last August, after he'd spent his whole Puerto Vallarta vacation not on the beach, but in bed, sleeping with misery.)

It was cold outside as he walked, with rays of winter sunshine struggling to poke through sluggish clouds. The ocean-scented breeze filled Brent with vigor, the weak sunshine a pleasure upon his ruddy, handsome face.

His body was a source of a thousand pleasures, now. Little things. He did not walk like someone out of tilt with the world, like someone balancing on a high wire between life and death. The stiffness in his joints, especially in his hands, was gone. Good-bye, arthritis. Good-bye, too, the hammer-dull aches in his calves and thigh muscles, a common ailment from years of taking AZT. He marveled at the spring in his step, at his confident walk. Shoot, maybe he should go dancing tonight! When was the last time he'd put on his cha-cha shoes and torn up the dance floor? Oh, what endless, endless possibilities was this gift of health!

The third dose of the cocktail all but restored him. His complexion lost the last of that dirty, mottled look, free of eczema and scaly white patches. His blond hair regained luster and body, no longer a thatch of dry straw sitting atop his head. His shoulders continued to round out, as though he were a slowly expanding balloon. His cheeks gave up that sucking-on-a-lemon look. His green eyes were vital, alive. His droopy rear end had firmed back into a bubble butt. No one could accuse *him* of not knowing how to pack a pair of Levi's.

He had been thirty-six going on a hundred and two, but now his appearance belonged to a 25-year-old. The glow of good health surrounded him, a palpable thing.

With much ceremony and fanfare he cleaned out his medicine cabinet. What a trembling joy coursed through him to pick up his white container of AZT — oh, the fantasies of performing this very act — and throwing it into the trash. The acyclovir followed right behind it, and half a dozen other medications that had kept him in a twilight world of marginal good health. It crossed his mind that perhaps he should give these away to some AIDS groups, but the deliciously flagrant act of simply tossing the bottles into the trash was too intoxicating. Time enough to work good deeds. Right now, he had the right to celebrate his good fortune any way he chose.

Still, his hand hesitated when he reached up to the top of the medicine cabinet and grabbed hold of his special aspirin jar. His last resort, his final option of barbiturates. Did he want to throw them away? Surely he would never need them. And because of that very reason he put the bottle back onto the shelf. He would keep it as a reminder of where he had been, of his desperation — and as a promise to himself not to squander this second chance.

3

"Why not?"

"We've already been through this, Brent. Don't make me say it again."

"I'm much better now. Really. It's amazing, the changes in how I look."

"I'm glad to hear that. Steve and I, we've been so worried. And Clayton, he asks about you all the time. Talks about some kind of big wish he makes every day. Wondering when his uncle is going to come see him."

"Then *let* me come."

"The last time — you remember what happened—"

Brent shut his eyes. Yes. He remembered. Words like butcher knives, thrown with careless abandon. She'd had no right, no right at all, to treat him that way. He'd stormed out with his dignity barely intact, and hadn't really spoken to his sister until now, nearly five months later, when a sudden impulse drove him to pick up the phone.

"I'm sorry about that, okay? Mary Ann? You hurt me. We hurt each other. It's what families do to each other when they aren't paying attention." He thought she'd laugh at that, breaking some of the tension. She didn't. "I want to see Clay. I won't scare him this time. Honest. I'm on a new medication. It's worked wonders.

I'm at least twenty pounds heavier, and my complexion is great."

"What about your lesions?"

For a moment, he stumbled. He couldn't remember if he still had them, that small purple cluster around his left ankle and pad of his foot. Very quickly he lifted up his pant leg and pushed down the white athletic sock. A faint smudge, like a bruise on the mend, was the only tattletale sign where KS lesions had once found a home. This discovery fired Brent's enthusiasm.

"They're *gone*, Mary Ann. Honest to god gone."

Skepticism. He'd heard it in her voice — in her silence — all their years together, growing up in Southern California. "How can that be?"

"I'm telling you, this new medicine is fantastic."

"What's it called?"

"Doesn't matter. The important thing is that I'm better. I feel great. I look good. I want to see my nephew. There's no reason now to keep us apart."

Silence.

"Mary Ann?"

He imagined her mind working. Imagined excuses, large and small. Anything but the zinging truth:

"I'm happy for you, that you're feeling better and all. But don't you see, in the long run, it doesn't change anything. You're still sick."

"Maybe I'm *not* sick anymore. Maybe I've been cured. Who knows?"

"Oh, Brent. I have to endure enough fairy tales reading to Clayton; don't you start, too. I don't know a lot about this illness. There's still too many unanswered questions. The only surefire thing I do know is this: when you have it, you die."

"Thank you, Dr. Mary Ann." His tongue felt sour with acid. Here it was, one more time: that wall she threw up, preventing him from entering, his wallflower younger sister who had always resented the attention his exceptional looks had brought. She who now secretly gloated over the success of her marriage to a pudgy accountant named Steve, and the union that had brought them, quite by accident, the most adorable boy in the world: Clayton Baker, age four and a half and turning five this summer, as he would tell anyone within earshot. At thirty-two, Mary Ann hid behind her normal existence of husband, house in Daly City, and child. No one — least of all her older brother — was going to challenge that existence.

Their silence spun out, neither one daring to speak. It was too full of old hurts.

Then Brent heard it: a commotion of running feet on his sister's end, and a barked-out command: "Mommy? I'm thirsty!" Brent took his chance. "Let me talk to him."

"I don't think that's a good idea."

"You can't catch anything over the phone! Come on, now. Have a heart."

"Who are you talking to, Mommy?"

"Never mind, honey. Go watch TV and I'll bring you some Kool-Aid."

"Clayton! It's Uncle Brent! Tell him his wishes worked!"

"Stop shouting or I'm hanging up right now," his sister hissed.

Brent held his tongue. Here was that same superior tone she'd used on him the last time, Halloween night. Something inside himself broke a little against her hard edge. He felt weary against it. "Please. Sis. Just let me say hi."

"You don't understand," she said, her voice surprisingly full. "It won't stop with a hello. I know it won't. He'll be talking about you for weeks, wondering when you'll come visit. Pestering me the way he does. And ... there's something you should know."

"What?"

"I'm pregnant. I just found out."

"That's ... that's wonderful, Mary Ann." But his thoughts were spinning, trying to see how this all fit together.

Sudden tears. "Don't you see. I can't have you at the house. My doctor said to be careful about who I'm around ... Oh, Brent, there's still so much to learn about your disease! And you scared Clay at Halloween, don't deny you didn't! I won't have that again!"

"Mary Ann—"

"I have to go. I'm sorry. Let me ... let me think on it. Okay? Good-bye."

Brent stood in his den, a dial tone ringing his ear. The buzzing was like a time line, drawing him back. Halloween. Yes.

He'd ridden BART out to their house in Daly City, offered to walk Clay around the neighborhood for trick or treats, a fun evening between uncle and nephew. They hadn't seen each other since the first of summer. Mary Ann had opened the front door with a smile that had quickly frozen onto her face, like shaved ice. Steve lumbered up beside her and his mouth pursed in that funny way too. They gawked at him, at the ten pounds he'd sweated off since his last visit, at the circles below his green eyes, and the mottled tone of his skin. He'd been blind, too deep within his own denial to recognize what was so blatantly apparent: Uncle Brent had the Look.

But then Clay had appeared, slipping through and demanding a hug, his excitement a contagious thing that glued them all together. During dinner, Clay dominated their conversation. He was trying to figure out how this magical thing worked, this going up to a door, shouting, "Trick or treat!" and then having gobs of free candy tossed into his plastic jack-o'-lantern. Mary Ann laughed about the year Brent had gone as a Chinaman and lost the ponytail wig Mom had lent him because it got hooked on a mailbox. And how it was returned the following day, and now everyone knew she wore a wig, how could she face her neighbors? And Brent spun a story of his little sister in her southern belle outfit, the queen of graciousness, until the sudden thunderstorm doused them all and ruined most of their candy. Brent had looked at his sister and her family, everyone laughing, anxieties momentarily forgotten, and thought, *We may not be a close family, but we have our moments. Can't ask for any more than that.*

Clay was anxious to show off his pirate costume to Uncle Brent, so the two of them excused themselves from the kitchen table and went to Clay's room. Brent was going to be a pirate too, since it was a costume he easily scrounged together from old jeans, outdated vests, and colored handkerchiefs that would have made his sister furious if she'd known what their original purpose signified.

With lots of giggles and squeals Brent helped his nephew out of his clothes. He noted with approval the muscle that replaced baby fat, marveling at this captured moment where his nephew straddled toddler and young boy. Emotions rose in him, blooming in his chest. It gladdened him to be a part of this, to see it. The love he felt for Clay was unconditional, a first for him. And the fact that it was reciprocated, that Clay asked for nothing in return except hugs and his presence, made him dizzy with a happiness he had never known. Oh, it was all too corny — and wonderful — for words.

Clayton slipped into a pair of ripped blue jeans. The cuffs were cut-out triangles, the teeth of a Halloween pumpkin. Boots would have been perfect, but his nephew explained very seriously how Mom had thought tennis shoes best, since they'd be doing so much walking. His shirt was blousy and gaily colored, and with much pride he applied a fierce, black eye patch. The final touch was a plastic dagger bought at Walgreen's. "Now you!" Clay encouraged.

Brent had lugged his costume in a big Macy's sack. He handed out the colored handkerchiefs which would go around their necks and removed his shirt while Clayton played with them. His costume shirt was also blousy, an old polyester thing with puffed sleeves and nonsensical designs. It was ripped in strategic places. He joined Clay on the floor and proceeded to kick off his shoes and socks. Brent had his old cowboy boots to put on over cotton socks. He adroitly shimmied out of his regular jeans while on the floor and yanked on an old pair of black 501s with patched knees and slitted cuts. Clay looked up from his red and blue handkerchiefs and pointed. "What's that?"

Brent followed his gaze. His cheeks flushed. He hadn't paid much attention to his KS lesions, there on his left ankle. It was so easy to ignore them, especially when his heart wished them to go away. But there they were, lumps of swollen purple.

Clay scooted closer. "They look like blue moons," he said, and Brent nodded at the kid's observations.

"They're bumps," Brent explained. "Sort of like bruises."

"Do they hurt?"

"No. Luckily, no."

"Will they go away?"

"I don't think so. Maybe if we wish hard enough, they'll go away."

Clay obediently shut his eyes, taking his cue. He mouthed words, then reopened his eyes. "Can I touch them?"

He shook his head, nose wrinkling. "You don't want to do that."

"Uh-huh. Blue moons." He scooted ever closer, and stuck out a chubby hand. His tiny fingers pressed against the bumps.

"They feel like soft rocks. Where'd you get them?"

His chest tightened. "I don't know, Clay. I've ... been sick, and they're a part of it."

"Are you better now?"

There seemed a light shining upon his nephew's face, the boy bathed in that glow of pure innocence. Again, that clutch in Brent's chest, the war between truth and half-truths. "No," he admitted, shaky and dizzy that he had said it, aloud. "But I feel good tonight, so don't you worry. We're going to have a lot of fun trick-or-treating. Right?"

"Right!" Another light bulb went off. "Uncle Brent, what if I wished real hard for you to be well? What if I promised to wish every day — would that help?"

Oh, it was dangerous, this. The rush of unguarded emotions, spilling one atop the other. The urge to hug, to cry, to hold this moment forever. Maybe if *he* made a big tall wish, they'd freeze into a snapshot, permanently together, uncle and nephew with a Norman Rockwell logo underneath: Sharing a Halloween Moment.

"Would it help, Uncle Brent? Huh? Would it?"

"It wouldn't hurt," he replied, and cleared his throat.

"Then I'll do it!" Clayton patted his uncle's misshapen ankle in an oddly paternal gesture. "I'll make giant wishes every—"

The scream sliced through the bedroom. Brent and Clayton flinched under its sudden assault. Brent looked to the doorway and saw his sister, a frenzied apparition of howling teeth, scarlet cheeks, and murderous eyes. Her hair was an electrified halo swimming about her face.

"What in hell do you think you're doing!" Mary Ann shrieked. She rushed into the bedroom, hands clawing the air out of her way. "Get away from him! Get away!"

Clayton's hand snapped to his chest and cradled there like a scorched limb. Brent yanked his leg away, instinct jerking him: he thought his sister was screaming at *him,* not Clay. Into their guilty circle she swooped, reaching for her son right as he burst into frightened tears. With Clay in her arms she lashed out with a mother's protective fury.

"What were you thinking!" she shouted. "You let him *touch* you? Why?"

"He wanted to feel them, Mary Ann. There's no harm—"

"No harm? *No harm?* For god's sake, you have cancerous bumps popping out on your skin, and you say there's *no harm?* How dare you make that kind of decision without consulting me! You have no right to put my son in jeopardy."

Brent held out a hand. "He was curious about them, that's all. Now calm down a minute and reason this out. The lesions look scary, I admit, but they aren't contagious."

"No one knows that for sure," she said archly.

"Of course they do, Mary Ann!"

A shadow in the doorway. Steven. "What's going on here?"

"Brent's frightened Clay."

"Now, Sis, you know that isn't right."

"He showed Clayton those ... things ... on his foot and it made him cry." She turned on him again. "How could you? How could you callously expose him to disease without once thinking of the consequences? Oh, I'll never forgive you, never!" Mary Ann jerked like a trapped animal under a headlight's glare, pacing. Clayton was a bag of laundry in her arms, an object of weight, nothing more.

Steve lumbered into the room. He stared pointedly at Brent, who sat in his silly pirate outfit on the floor, one hand camouflaging his accursed ankle. "Look here. If we can't trust you with Clay, what's the point? Right? You put us into a very delicate situation where no one can win."

Brent shook his head in disbelief, and stifled a chuckle at the snowball that was rolling and rolling, getting bigger every second.

Steve puffed up. "You think this is funny?"

"I think it's hilarious. Hilariously *stupid.* Why don't you guys take Clay out, let me finish putting on my costume, and we'll talk about this in a few minutes, when we've all had a chance to calm down. And I did *not* frighten Clay; *you* did with that banshee entrance of yours. Isn't that right, Clay?"

The boy started to nod his head but then stopped in confusion, trying to figure out why his father was so angry. He squirmed in his mother's arms, demanding to be put down.

Mary Ann glared at her husband. Steven coughed into one hand. "I don't think so," he said.

Now it was Brent's turn to look confused. "What are you talking about?"

"I don't think this is a good idea anymore."

"What? Trick-or-treating? Oh, it'll be fine. We've looked forward to it all—"

"I'm not talking about trick-or-treating." Steven cleared his throat. "I'm talking about coming here to see us, when you're sick."

Mary Ann lowered Clay to his feet. She pushed a stray lock of dishwater hair out of her eyes. "I know we can't get it through the air, but letting Clay touch you like that was really irresponsible."

Brent sighed. "I didn't molest him or anything."

"I know that."

"Then why does it sound like I did? Why am I suddenly the heavy?"

He looked into their faces. *Diseased. You are diseased.* There it was, unspoken, but ringing in his ears with the force of a shout. Underneath this veneer of a family portrait was this fear, waiting like a piranha in still and deep waters. Waiting for some prey to slip into its murky waters. And oh boy, had he slipped.

"Come on, Clay, let's go wash our hands," Mary Ann said, and began to lead her son out of the room.

"Is Uncle Brent leaving?"

"No," Brent said, but he was drowned out by the simultaneous "Yes" from mother and father.

"I'll take you trick-or-treating," Steven piped up to Clay's inquisitive backward glance.

"You don't have a costume." It was the worst offense the boy could conjure. "I want Uncle Brent to take me."

"Uncle Brent has to go home early," Mary Ann explained. "He isn't feeling well."

"Don't lie to him," Brent snapped. "I'm not sick."

But'cha are, Blanche. But'cha are. It was indisputable, hanging in the air between them like a foul smell. He could never explain this to them as long as he didn't *feel* sick. All they saw was what Brent tried desperately to ignore: the Look. The rising face of his own skeleton pushing up against his skin. And the fear that this skeleton was going to contaminate their family by its clattering presence among them.

An ache in his arm pulled Brent back into the present: the phone, still clutched between fingers that had gone bone white. In that shorthand known to the mind he saw himself changing out of his pirate costume and leaving his sister's house in a huff. Words no longer mattered; he had been aware only of his hurt, and his fury.

But never, ever, had he assumed it would be the last time he saw Clayton. Like any good storm, the blowout should have passed, clearing the air. Only it didn't. His repeated phone calls had been met with cloudy indifference. So he had retracted, waiting for her to call, to apologize. Nada. Zip. A terse thank-you for Clay's Christmas presents.

Nothing, until he had broken the silence once again with this phone call.

"I'm not sick anymore," he whispered into the still air of his home. And his thoughts finished: *I'll never be able to convince you of that, will I? Because the truth is more fantastic than the lie. And the truth can never be spoken aloud.*

He hung up the phone, and felt the first pieces chipping away at his honeymoon happiness. While new doors had opened to him with this second chance, he had to remember that other doors were locked, no matter how hard he raised his fist against them.

4

He rented dozens of porno movies, three and four at a time, and jacked off with the abandon of a twelve-year-old. His body, which for so long had joined sides with the enemy, had become a playground filled with endless erotic opportunities. Brent felt he had to embrace it again, become friends with himself. And oh, what astonishing delights his body gave to him! His sex drive, which had withered away to rare dribbles now and then, rebounded with a vengeance. Three, four, five times a day his body came alive to his touch.

He started going to bars again, a single man out on the prowl. Not that he was ready to deal with having sex with another man. No, he was content to feel eyes follow his progress as he wound through a crowded bar. To be admired, adored, and somehow untouchable: it was a heady mixture for his bruised ego. Strange men bought him drinks, and asked for nothing more than a smile in return.

Everywhere Brent went, he raised eyebrows. Members of the Scarecrow Club watched him with a sullen envy — or outright astonishment, if they had known how he'd looked less than a week earlier. Their frosty glances demanded answers from him that he was unwilling to give. But to Brent, their resentment was only one more indication that he had permanently slipped their ranks. He understood their resentment completely — but secretly gloated how their suffering no longer touched his heart. If they wanted his secret, they would have to travel their own paths to get it, just as he had done. No one had handed it to him: he'd had to take it.

On the street one night, the strangest thing. A man walked toward him, browsing the shops in the Castro. He was tall and robust, the perfect picture of health. Suddenly around his head and shoulders pulsed a faint light that rippled off of him like heat waves rising from hot asphalt. Their eyes met. The man nodded at him, and smiled with one corner of his mouth, as though he'd seen something amusing. They passed each other without a word.

But now Brent knew. He chastised his own stupidity. He had kicked himself out of the Scarecrow Club and been inducted into the ranks of a *truly* secret club: those with the Look. Only now, the Look was this cocktail-induced glow of exceptional health. Somehow, they could spot each other, just as most gay men could use some hidden radar to recognize others of their tribe.

Oh, it was wonderful, all of it. Even drinking the cocktail didn't seem so bad anymore. In fact, despite its unappetizing smell and gritty texture, he reluctantly admitted that it didn't taste half-bad.

5

"But why won't you come see me again?" whined his psychologist Dr. Anthony Able, who seemed genuinely alarmed at Brent's absence.

"Because I did as you suggested," Brent answered. "I've made friends with my illness. And my illness says, 'Fuck you.' *Ciao.*"

6

The Castro Street bar was crowded. Back in the sunshine days of his past, he remembered, Wednesday nights had roosted just beneath Friday and Saturday in terms of cruising popularity. Tonight's crowd seemed to share his restless spirit. The day had been surprisingly mild, the first to hint at spring, and had pulled in a sizable group.

Brent meandered through the pools of light and dark. Men in leather and t-shirts eyed him as they clutched highballs and beer bottles between antsy fingers. He glided through their numbers, a golden god, and settled onto a ledge where others could easily approach him, if they dared. He would not make it too easy, tonight, despite his anticipation.

Soon enough, a few screwed up their courage. The first was a mousy man, tall and beanpole thin, who spun a constantly lit cigarette in Brent's face like a frustrated baton twirler. Brent ignored him, and felt the crowd's approval as the man finally fluttered off to nurse his wounds.

A second man immediately swept into the void vacated by the butterfly man. This one was attractive in a bulky way, solid and compact. A black crew cut sharpened the corners of his head. He reminded Brent of an aging drill sergeant. All was fine until the man opened his mouth, and the gaps of his numerous missing teeth grinned a weird jack-o'-lantern hello. Uh-uh. Sorry. Brent wanted perfection tonight, or as close to it as he could get.

The third time was the charm. A quiet but intense type settled next to him, and pretended exaggerated interest in the pool game going on in front of them. He had wavy black hair, which was receding into angel wings. A proud face, with dark European features and neatly trimmed mustache. Handsome, Brent had to admit, but not necessarily someone who would stand out in a crowd. Like a fine wine, he improved with each glance, each tiny sip of conversation. His name was Fritz, and no, he had no plans tonight. In fact, he pointedly admitted, he did not have to be at work until noon the following day.

He offered to drive them to Brent's place. Fritz owned the current popular rage of mini jeep, which seemed in perfect sync with his somewhat manicured but butch, masculine image. Their hands roamed each other's thighs, and their smiles were lusty with anticipation. But as they drove to Brent's house Fritz began to crinkle his nose. He sniffed the interior of the jeep. "Do you smell something funny?"

"No."

"Do you mind?" He rolled down the driver's side window. The snap of cold air that blew in was invigorating.

It was all going so well. Fritz even managed that wonder of wonders in San Francisco, a parking space in front of Brent's house. Everything moved along like well-oiled machinery, as though following some rehearsed script. Brent gave a cursory tour of his house, which conveniently ended with the two of them standing in the bedroom. Fritz began to nonchalantly unbutton his host's shirt. His fingers suddenly froze, buttons in hands. He sniffed the air, puzzled.

"What's wrong?"

"Do you smell that?"

"Smell what?" Brent was too preoccupied with his own excitement to desire a real answer. The candles in the corner, the soft music on the stereo: the mood had been set, and the hell with funny smells.

Fritz made a face. "Something — bad. Rotten."

"Thanks a lot."

"Hey, I'm sorry. I know how it sounds. Maybe a cat crawled underneath the house. Got stuck. You should have it checked out."

"Yeah. Sure." All this talk was not exactly setting Brent's libido on fire. Fritz had a very agreeable line of hair bisecting his chest, and he was curious to see how and where it finished. He stepped closer to run his fingers through the curly dark hair.

Fritz flinched. A hand reached up and captured Brent's roaming fingers. He pulled them away.

"What's wrong?" A thread of irritation now ribboned Brent's voice.

The older man swallowed hard. His eyes were big in the flickering candlelight, full of what his throat did not want to announce. He took a breath. "It's you."

"What?" He tried on a lopsided grin and chuckled with sarcasm, determined in some shadowy way to keep this arrangement between them light and frivolous. After all, he didn't smell anything unpleasant. "Too much smoke and alcohol from the bar?"

Fritz nodded.

"How about a shower, then?"

"What a good idea," Fritz beamed, jumping upon the solution. "Why don't you get it started, and I'll join you. How does that sound?"

Brent undressed. Fritz wore a pained expression, like he was suffering with gas but trying to hold it in. Even so, he whistled with obvious admiration at Brent's golden body in the candlelight.

"You like?"

"Very much."

"Now it's my turn. I want to see *you* out of your clothes."

"Go start the shower. I'm right behind you." Fritz finished unbuttoning his shirt.

Brent padded naked to the bathroom and flipped on the water. He was already sticking out at an angle, his excitement barely contained.

He was in the shower only a few minutes when he heard the front door open and close, like a jail cell slammed shut for the night.

7

The next day at the travel agency, a note was discreetly dropped onto Brent's desk when he went to refill his coffee cup.

Why don't you do your co-workers a favor, it read. *Take a bath, like a normal human being. P-U!!!*

8

A little smell indeed. What was the point of looking your best if you couldn't get close to anyone?

The next time Brent saw Skettle, he decided, he would have a talk, man to man. There must be something he could do about it. He himself noticed nothing out of the ordinary, but every day in the shower he scrubbed his body judiciously. Applied talcum powder between his legs, the crack of his ass, and under his arms. Deodorant. Splash of cologne — and he hated queens who doused themselves with phony scent, who announced their arrival into a room by this potpourri wave of flowers and musk.

His co-workers were fastidiously discreet about avoiding him, except for the tacky bitch who had left him the note in the first place, may he rot in hell. No time to lunch with you today; errands to run. Maybe next week. Workers would drop something off at his desk and retreat with a rabbit nose, as though trying to hold in a sneeze.

With yet another hound dog expression Captain Kirk reassigned Brent's duties. He no longer dealt with the gay couples coming in to talk about cruises. Now he was stuck behind the computer, punching in dates and times, printing out tickets. The shit detail, with none of the benefits of at least attempting to flirt with the customers.

At first he stewed. Then he thought, What the hell. He'd be out of there soon enough. With his renewed health and vigor, there was no telling what he couldn't accomplish once he set his mind to the task.

That afternoon he found the envelope waiting for him at home, his name a thin web of scrawled ink. The sight brought an unexpected film of sweat popping out across his forehead. With a jolt he realized this was his seventh day. Tonight's dose of the cocktail was his last.

With fingers slightly atremble, he broke the wax seal and tore into the envelope.

Ten p.m. Be ready.

9

At a quarter to ten, Brent was pacing. He'd changed clothes twice, unable to decide what would be appropriate for this outing. He settled on a pair of stone-washed blue jeans and a red plaid flannel shirt over a t-shirt. Very Brawny-paper-towel man. He passed on tennis shoes and slipped into the pair of cowboy boots he'd worn twice during his western phase. If he was going to be stuck out under a moonlit field at midnight scrounging for mushrooms or some such, he was at the very least going to look butch.

With something embarrassingly like cold panic, he'd boiled up his final packet of the cocktail. He felt like a coke addict discovering this was his last fix. What would happen to him, if he didn't get his fresh supply for the next week? His mind sketched in all the horrible possibilities. What if he wasn't cut out for the kind of job they had lined up for him? What if Skettle said, Sorry, big mistake, no more cocktail for you...

So Brent paced, and fretted, and watched the hands of his clock in the living room crawl toward ten o'clock. Ten. Only one week ago he would have been sound asleep by this time of night, having dozed off watching TV shows. He could not — *would* not — go back to that living death. This decision curbed his nervousness a little as he waited, a mantra he held before him. There was no going back.

At ten after ten Brent heard the swing of the front gate, and a quick rap on the front door. Ludicrously, it reminded him of a secret coded knock for entering a clubhouse. He was off the couch in a flash. He arranged his face into an expression he hoped simulated a pleasant greeting, and opened the door.

John stood on the other side. Behind him, on the street, was a Honda Accord with blinking hazard lights.

"Oh," exclaimed Brent. "It's you! That's a relief. You want to come in for a minute?"

John shook his head. He hooked a thumb toward the double-parked car. "We're already late."

"Okay. Let me get my coat." Brent's pleasure at being paired with this old dating buddy dimmed slightly. Did he have to be all business? Especially after their last meeting, when he had been so desperate to learn John's health secrets. They were on the same side of the fence now, for goodness sake. Brent went to the closet and pulled out his good leather jacket. He thought better of it and switched to an older, more durable letter jacket.

John was waiting in the darkness beyond the front door. As Brent joined him, he saw the double negative surge that was the glow spark up around John and steam off into the dark air. John watched him looking, and nodded with understanding. "It catches you off guard the first couple of times. You'll get used to it."

They climbed into the Honda.

"How come I don't see it on me?" Brent asked. The car shot forward into the night.

John shrugged. "It's a good thing you don't. Otherwise it'd drive you crazy."

"Kind of like this smell thing?"

His companion snorted. "You've noticed that, huh?"

"Yeah. I can't get close to anybody. No one will let me near them."

There was a silence as John maneuvered the car through the narrow dark streets on the outskirts of the Mission. He waited, suddenly cautious about saying anything more, and wondered if his friend had forgotten — or had simply chosen to ignore — his question. John cleared his throat after a minute, his words so quiet they may have been only for his ears. "You're alive, aren't you? Isn't that what you wanted?"

"I guess so."

"A little too late for guess-sos." John hung a sharp left and aimed toward Folsom Street. "That day on Market Street, when you stopped me: I knew Skettle had been in contact with you. You had a bit of the glow, just enough for me to notice as I stood talking with you. I thought perhaps I could turn you away—"

Brent cut him short. "Hey. I don't regret what's happened. Not one bit. I was a walking dead man."

"And now you're not?" A smirk played on John's full lips.

Brent cupped his hands in a gesture that seemed to say, *C'est la vie.* "I feel better, stronger, than I ever have in my whole life. I'll gladly deal with the side effects of the cocktail if it means keeping my health."

"Goody for you."

Brent frowned. This sullen nature to his friend was beginning to be a real drag. Back when they had briefly dated, John had been all smiles and jokes, eager and sexual and fun.

John waved a hand. "Aww, don't mind me. I'm just not in the mood, tonight. Don't forget, I've been at this longer than you. Sometimes ... I do what I have to do and take my supply of the cocktail. And if you're smart, you'll do the same."

Brent shook his head. "What's with all this secrecy? What is Skettle worried about?"

"First of all, we'd better stop saying his name so much. He doesn't like it."

"So? This car's not bugged, is it?"

His partner's face rippled with alarm, as though this was a possibility he had somehow overlooked, or forgotten to consider. "We're not supposed to talk too much. We do our jobs, and we keep silent."

"Sounds dull and boring."

John bit his lower lip.

"So where are we going?"

"*We* aren't going anywhere. I'm just your chauffeur. We'll split up once we arrive at the warehouse. Far as I know, you've got a cush job tonight. He always starts you off slow, your first time."

Brent shifted in his seat, pins and needles tingling his arms and legs. "So: don't keep me in suspense. Tell me. What's my job?"

"Transport."

"Transport?" He wrinkled his nose. "It sounds so ... army official."

John shrugged.

"Not to mention illegal."

"That is the *least* of your worries," John said. They had driven through the Mission and were now South of Market, a neighborhood of mostly narrow back-alley streets, faded Victorians, and box-shaped warehouses, with a few specialty restaurants and leather bars clinging like jewels on a strand of dirty pearls. Despite the quiet streets at this hour of the night, John preferred to stay away from Folsom and the more trafficked streets. He took them down alleys with no names, past buildings with shuttered windows that probably never opened to daylight. Brent gave up trying to orient himself. Someday soon, perhaps, he would be able to navigate these mazes of streets, but not tonight. Tonight, he was content to be an observer.

John hooked a right down another alley with no name. Industrial buildings loomed past in the dark. All at once he whipped into a gravel parking lot wedged between two brick buildings and parked beside a van and a Country Squire station wagon.

"This is it?" Brent asked.

"This be the place." John killed the engine and stepped into the night. "It's showtime, folks."

Brent followed. He wasn't quite sure what he expected, but somehow, not this: all was dark and apparently deserted. But as he circled around the Honda and the other parked cars he suddenly heard the whisper crunch of feet upon gravel. A shadow disengaged itself from the blood red brick wall. A man. The glow bloomed around a face steely and square-jawed. He may have been a man in his fifties, but he had the Look from the cocktail, trimming his appearance by a good fifteen years. With a shock Brent realized the man had been to his house. He'd helped Skettle out of his chair, and he'd handed Brent his first week's batch of the cocktail.

"You're late," the man snapped.

John nodded. "It won't happen again."

"You better get with the program. The boss man isn't in a good mood. So is this our driver?"

Brent stuck out a hand. "Hi. I'm Brent—"

The man slapped his hand away. He turned on John. "No names! For Christ's sake! Didn't you teach him anything? Huh?"

"Lay off. It's his first time."

"If he keeps this up, it'll be his last." The stranger shook his head with derision and then briefly massaged his eyes. "Okay. Do you know where the boardwalk is in Santa Cruz?"

Brent nodded. Santa Cruz, over two hours away, south. "Yeah. Is that where I'm going?"

The older man reached into an inside coat pocket and produced a map that was wrapped with white paper. "There's a man waiting down by the boardwalk. He'll be standing near the roller coaster. Load up the cargo and bring it back here. We'll take care of it from there."

"I need my drink," Brent suddenly blurted out.

"He's a brazen one, isn't he?" The man shoved the maps into Brent's hands. "Have no fear, hotshot. Bring back the goods like a smart little boy and you'll have your supply. Fuck up, and — well — believe me, you're better off not knowing. Understand?"

Oh, how he wanted to knock loose a few teeth from that smug, square-jawed face. Brent's free hand jiggled at his side. Beautiful men should not have to take this kind of crap.

"How will I know this guy?" asked Brent. "The boardwalk is a pretty big place."

The man turned to John once again. "He really *is* wet behind the ears. Don't worry, pup; you'll know."

"He'll have the Look," John explained. "So what about me? What have you got lined up?"

"The usual."

Brent saw his friend struggle against a frown. He wondered what could possibly be "usual" in this situation, which was rapidly becoming more and more bizarre. Here they were, three men whisked from their deathbeds by the miracle of the drug, doling out mysterious errands in some parking lot South of Market. Huddled against the dark. No: perhaps huddled *with* the dark, embraced by deeds that could not stand the scrutiny of daylight. Despite his jacket, Brent shivered with nervous anticipation.

"Take the station wagon," this pseudo-sergeant said. He dug keys out of his pants pocket and slapped them into Brent's palm. "Don't let the box slide around too much when you put it in the back. Wouldn't want to damage the merchandise. Any problems, call the number on the map. But take a hint: no problems."

Brent nodded.

"So what are you waiting for, Christmas? You've got over five hours' worth of driving ahead of you. Out with the lead, huh?"

Brent stifled another urge to rearrange this creep's face. He grasped John on the shoulder. "Thanks for the orientation lesson, John."

"No problem."

"Again with the names!" hissed Squarejaw.

10

It was well past three a.m. before Brent hooked back onto Highway 101 for his return trip to San Francisco. The wagon only picked up AM on the radio, but he'd managed to find a late-night jazz station that played decent music without putting him to sleep. Sleep. He had to smile to himself at the irony. This was one of the few times in literally several years that he'd stayed awake past the dawn side of midnight. Three in the morning is what he used to see when he'd startle awake in pools of his own sweat, his bladder aching like an old man's. Now here he was, putt-putting along in a custard-colored Country Squire with chipped wood paneling (did people still *drive* these things in the nineties?) on Highway 101, with god knew what kind of cargo spirited within the huge box in the back.

He realized with a sort of dull shock that he was craving the cocktail again. He hadn't meant to blurt it out, when he'd talked with Squarejaw — in retrospect it seemed a weakness of character. But the ache was there, deep in his gut, a craving that could only be satisfied with the drink. Again he had to laugh at himself as he remembered the effort required to down the first few doses. Right now he felt as if he could chew the stuff down raw and unboiled. Slap the ingredients onto a slice of bread and butter and munch himself into a healthy glow...

Something thumped from the backseat.

Brent glanced into the rearview mirror. The wooden crate sat where he and Joe had pushed and shouldered the heavy son of a bitch onto the flipped-down backseat. Its sides were draped with blankets. Perhaps one end of the blanket had slid off, coaxed by the steady vibration of the car.

He turned down an Anita Baker song on the radio and listened to the silence of the car. After a few minutes he chuckled at his nervousness and cranked the radio back up. Nothing. Of course, nothing. Whitney Houston filled the car with her voice.

It had been a pleasant enough drive down to Santa Cruz. The highway free of rush-hour clogging. Full tank of gas. He'd rolled down the windows and reveled in the sting of cold air whistling past. Alive, and full of purpose. He stuck his head out the window and grinned at the white-pepper spray of winter stars. He felt like a teenager.

Years had passed since his last trip to Santa Cruz. A date named Mark had accused him of being a stuck-up snob, and they'd ridden home in stony silence, each one scooted as far from each other as possible in the front seat. Mark had been too taken with himself, unable to appreciate Brent's unique charms and beauty. A doomed affair from the very beginning. He was probably dead, now. The thought — for just the tiniest moment — made Brent unaccountably sad.

He'd wound up and over the Santa Cruz mountains on 17, one of the most treacherous stretches of California highway, and then straight-shooted through town to the amusement park on the boardwalk. A few high school kids milled around by parked cars, drinking beer in the requisite arrogant stance of teenagers and catcalling to each other. There seemed a million different places where his contact could be waiting, and Brent was very aware of the ticking clock. He'd smacked the steering wheel a few times in his frustration.

On his second ride through, trawling the streets like a cabbie in search of customers, he caught a glimpse of a thickset man off by himself in a parking lot. He stood next to a beige van, a cigarette dangling from his mouth. He made a little wave to Brent. Quite unexpectedly the glow surged up around him, an eclipse of light steaming off flesh. Brent swung right and entered the parking lot. He pulled up alongside the van. His heart was beating very fast.

"You're late," the man said. He sized up Brent with a calculated once-over as Brent slid out of the car. There was none of the mean-spirited tone to this announcement as from Brent's earlier encounter with the man he now dubbed Squarejaw. "Any trouble getting here?"

He shook his head.

"I'm Joe," the man said. He tossed aside his cigarette and stuck out a beefy hand.

"I thought we weren't supposed to use names," Brent said as they shook hands.

The man shrugged. "I'm Joe. You're Joe. We're all Joes, in my book. We have to call each other *some*thing, don't we?"

Brent nodded, and felt himself relaxing just a little. He liked this man. There was something of the ox about him, brutish and pleasantly dull. He sported a hefty solid build, oak-thick and strong, but the build was softened by a bit of a paunch hanging over a belt. Brent had a sudden suspicion that Joe had been fat before his illness, and before the cocktail. Late thirties, though he could be much older.

Joe went to the van and slid open the side door. Out of its gloomy interior Brent caught sight of a wooden crate. It stood about three feet high, wide as a door. He could not estimate its length in the dark.

Curiosity tugged at him. "What's in it?" Brent whispered.

Joe looked at him with a cockeyed, you-must-be-crazy expression.

"I'm new at this. Tonight's my first night. No one has told me anything."

"That's 'cause they're smart." He crooked a finger, and Brent leaned in. "All you need to know is that whatever's in there is keeping us going. Ingredients for the cocktail. You just be content to take this back to the factory and let 'em grind it up into next week's supply. Now give me a hand — it feels like someone stuffed a couple of dead cows in here."

He was right, too. The box was appallingly heavy, as though stuffed with wet sand. They opened the tailgate on the station wagon and lowered the backseat to make room. Brent still didn't trust his new strength. More to the point, he feared he would be too weak, his muscles counterfeit.

Joe must have sensed this about him, this reluctance at war with his desire to perform well on his first job. So he coaxed Brent along, guiding his hands on the box, offering encouragement. There was a frightening moment as they wobbled between the vehicles when Brent was convinced he'd drop his end. He felt the deadweight sliding through his fingers, tugged by gravity, the ground eager to crack open the crate. But Joe reached the tailgate with his end, the pressure eased, and together they grunted and pushed the five-foot-long box into the back. Mission accomplished.

They grinned at each other, breath sharp in raw throats.

"Thanks," Brent gasped, and clapped a hand upon Joe's thick shoulder. "I wasn't sure I could pull that off—"

Joe lurched clumsily forward and kissed Brent. His lips tasted of whiskey and cigarettes. He stepped back, his eyes flashing. "You're a real looker," he huskily whispered.

Brent said nothing. Dumbfounded. In an earlier time he would have socked this guy's lights out. But something held him back.

"You done it with anyone yet? Since the change?"

"No."

"Of course not. No one can stand getting close to us, 'cause of the smell." Joe leaned in. "But we can do it with each other..."

"Joe..."

"How about it, huh? Right here in the van."

"It's really getting late."

"No harm in a quickie," Joe countered. He stared at Brent, his longing a naked thing between them.

Brent stared back, at this big ox of a man, and felt raw emotions tug at his heart. The depth of Joe's obvious loneliness scared him a little. It reminded him of his own hunger for contact which, like his craving for the cocktail, had settled into a dull unfulfilled ache in his belly. Being rejected by Fritz had hurt more than he'd wanted to admit. And that whole lonely stretch of last year's battling his illness: the only hands that had touched him were those of his doctor, as he checked for swollen lymph nodes.

"Okay," he said. "What the hell."

Thinking back on it now, as Brent drove toward San Francisco, the quick encounter seemed unreal. It had been dark and furtive and sweetly sad. "Thank you," Joe kept gushing as they prepared to leave. "Oh, thank you." It was touching and embarrassing, all rolled into one. Ten minutes of groping inside a dark van should hardly engender such an outpouring of emotion. He had been relieved to get away, to start back.

Now, with the brisk wind riffling his hair, jazz on the radio, the whole night since John's picking him up at the house seemed bathed in dreamlike hues. He was sure to wake up tomorrow morning convinced it had never happened. He grinned at his own private joke, and relished the idea of having this entire night behind him. Ahh, to sleep until noon...

Something thumped from the backseat.

Actually, "thump" wasn't right. Thump was the sound he'd heard the last time. This noise was more like—

No. The thought was an ice pick, jabbing into his brain in all its horribleness. He tried to push it aside and couldn't. With a trembling hand he reached for the rearview mirror. A wave of déjà vu flooded over him, water-cold and mysterious as though drawn from a hidden well. Even in the shadows he could see the top of the crate as it peeked out from beneath its draped blanket. Undisturbed. Or was it?

It would certainly take more than a pothole or two to cause that stone-heavy crate to scoot all the way across the back. And so far, except for the windy descent of Highway 17 down through the mountains, his trip had been smooth sailing.

Get a grip, Brent ordered himself. His hands tightened on the steering wheel in reflex. *Keep that stupid imagination in check. Do your job like a good worker bee and everything will come up roses. Promise.*

He readjusted the mirror and then fiddled with the radio; the jazz station was fading off into annoying bursts of static. He discovered an oldies station, and the bright cheerful bebop instantly cleared his head. Better. This was better. Another twenty minutes and he'd be winging his way through South of Market.

Brent was whistling along with the Beach Boys when he heard it, clear as the tune on the radio. Something like an electric shock raced up his spine, tingling nerves with spiky heat. His cheeks flushed. Should he pull over and check? What if...?

But there were too many what-ifs, the biggest one of all canceling out all the others. What if the police drove by? What if they asked him about the contents of the crate? He had no idea what was inside, but already he felt guilty and somehow sullied, in reaction to everyone's secretiveness.

His flannel shirt was glued to his skin. He mopped his brow. Keep driving. It had to be his imagination. For there was no reason, no reason at all, to believe the sounds he heard were weak kicks against the sides of the crate.

And as soon as he allowed that thought to puncture his consciousness, in a bit of karmic synchroneity, the moans started. It was a low, foghorn sound, dark and wet and animal. Ghastly. It came in short bursts, a Morse code based in the language of pain. Brent went lightheaded with disbelief. He snapped off the radio and listened, but his heart was banging against his chest, blotting out sight and sound. He felt as though someone had jabbed a pitchfork through his back. He sat ramrod stiff with fright.

Suddenly the moans — if the mournful cries had actually been moans, and not simply the whistle of wind through his cracked windows — ceased with the same abruptness as their arrival. In its place, so faint Brent unconsciously tilted his head to hear, came soft scritch-scratch noises. Claws — or fingernails — pawing from the interior of the crate.

Traffic thickened a bit as Brent zoomed past Candlestick Park and shot toward San Francisco. His mind was gray fog, nothing clear or distinct. Anytime something clear wanted to loom out of the mist he detoured down different corridors. Getting back to that alley, back to the gravel parking lot and warehouse: these were his only guideposts in the fog swirling through his brain.

He took the Seventh Street exit and unfolded the map Squarejaw had given him. Finding the Santa Cruz boardwalk had been a breeze; finding his way back to the unmarked alley was his real problem. Not to mention whatever might be clinging to life inside that crate—

The fog rolled in. He drove.

He found it, eventually. After many wrong turns. After cursing at all the one-way streets that forced him to take the opposite direction he wanted. In all its blandness the neighborhood had suddenly revealed landmarks he could follow. A coffee shop here, that he remembered passing as John drove; a futon factory outlet on the corner. He dipped and turned and suddenly, bingo, here it was. He crawled to a stop, then pulled into the gravel parking lot. There was a van parked off to the side — the same van he had seen upon his arrival with John. Brent dared himself to wonder about its own nocturnal journey. What cargo had *it* brought back? As he watched, the side door to the van slid back. A young man in overalls stepped out, his clothes a spotted ruin. He held an aluminum bucket in one hand, a sponge in the other. Even though the morning sky was just beginning to lighten, a pair of dark sunglasses perched on his nose. He stiffened as Brent got out of the wagon, his feet spread in case he needed to break into a run. But Brent's glow must have reassured him he was safe. He beckoned him over.

"Are you Santa Cruz?"

Brent nodded. This was no man, but a teenager stuck with some sort of cleanup detail. Despite the bloom of health and his perfect though wiry physique, the boy looked drawn. Tired. His face was pitted with old acne scars.

"What took you so long? You were expected back over an hour ago."

Brent had a sudden image flare before his eyes, Joe zippering himself back up, with a self-satisfied grin. "What can I say? I was detained."

"Makes no difference to me," the boy said. Then he whispered, "But they don't like it. They want everything shipshape, if you know what I mean. They don't want anybody to be able to point any fingers. I swear, it's worse than the army." And he glanced into the interior of the van, its floor still glistening from where he had washed it down.

Brent followed the boy's gaze and felt his nostrils prickle. A slightly sour, coppery smell wafted out, despite the scrubbing. He saw the look of equal disgust on the teenager's face and took a gamble. "I think — I think something's alive in the crate I just brought back. Do you know what's inside?"

The boy's eyes went big behind the oval, owlish sunglasses. He jerked his head toward the warehouse, then looked at Brent. "Cows."

"Cows?"

"They're all cows."

Brent frowned. "Kind of like we're all named Joe?"

"Huh?"

"Never mind." It was hopeless. This kid was just one more link in the fence, content to do his part for the glory of the cocktail. Up this close Brent saw the strings of needle marks riding both arms.

The crunch of gravel. Brent swung toward the brick building, his heart leaping into his throat. Squarejaw sauntered toward them. Behind him was a black slot of a doorway, where he had materialized as though out of the brick and mortar. He made a shooing gesture at Brent. "Leave our young friend alone. He has work to finish up, don't you, son?"

"Yes, sir." He emptied the dirty water from the bucket and hurried through the door.

Brent faced Squarejaw. "So what happens now?"

Squarejaw dug into his pants and produced a twenty-dollar bill. "You go home. Take a taxi."

"Where's John? Can't he drive me back home?" As soon as the words left his lips, Brent realized the Accord was nowhere to be seen. For some reason, its absence gave him a twinge of concern.

Squarejaw glanced at the lightening sky, reached into his shirt pocket, and slipped on a pair of low, jet black sunglasses. His cruel lips imitated a smile. "John's indisposed, at the moment. We're not finished with him yet."

"I want to talk to him."

Squarejaw jabbed a finger against his chest. "You've done enough talking for one night. If I were you, I'd learn to keep my big mouth shut, pronto. That is, if you want to last long in this operation. You're new, so it's been overlooked. This time."

Now the twinge had become a snake in his belly. Brent winced as it coiled around his intestines. His mouth wanted to explode with questions. He was afraid to even part his lips, for fear of what might come tumbling out. In that moment he knew he would say nothing about the kicking sounds against the sides of the crate. Nothing about the moans, or the whisper-thin scratch of nails. And that's what he filled his mind with: nothing.

The teenager returned with a fresh pail of sudsy water. Squarejaw snapped his fingers. "Be a good sport and go get our friend here his supply. It's on the table." The boy disappeared.

Brent indicated the wagon. "What about...?"

"We'll take care of that. Next time you can help us bring it inside."

"Next time?"

"In a few days. We've got to step up our operations. Too many of you recruits clogging up the works. Like that kid. Acne Andy, we call him. Hooker trash from Polk Street. He doesn't belong here, but nothing to be done about that now. Don't you worry. We'll ease you in, gradual. Kinda like a good fuck. It may hurt at first, but pretty soon you'll be begging for it." He snickered.

The teenager stepped out of the building. In his hands was a large Safeway sack. He cradled its bottom as he handed it to Brent. Heat seeped through the brown paper into his hands, as though what he held was something freshly baked from the oven. The craving stirred within him. He was ashamed to find his mouth watering. Feeling himself dismissed, Brent turned to leave.

"Walk up to Market," Squarejaw instructed. "You take a cab anywhere within these blocks and I keep your balls as souvenirs. Got that?"

Brent nodded. His feet began to move. He broke into a trot. Never had he wanted to get away from a place so badly. Never had he wanted to put aside a night so badly, to blank it utterly from his conscience. And with guilty panic he realized he had never craved anything as much as he craved the cocktail, right now. Its weight burned through the sack into his hands. It took all his reserve and strength to sit patiently in the back of the cab he flagged down on Market Street. Waiting until he was home.

The eastern sky was glowing orange as the cab pulled up in front of Brent's house. He paid the driver and practically jumped out in his anticipation. He squinted as a shaft of sunlight tore free of the dawn clouds, making him blink against its light. It was going to be a beautiful day. He hurried inside.

Without bothering to remove his jacket, he raced into the kitchen, rummaged for his saucepan and measuring cup, and started heating the water to a boil. Painful tremors were shooting up and down the length of his body. His legs felt as if they were about to cramp. Brent realized this was the longest he had gone between doses of the cocktail, well over twenty-four hours. What would happen, he wondered with shivery horror, if he hadn't been able to drink this dose?

He yanked off his jacket and draped it over the back of the kitchen chair. Opened the paper bag and reached in. He was expecting the wet-mud feel of a sealed baggie beneath his fingertips, but his hand encountered a rectangular box. He pulled it from the sack. It was no more than four inches long and about two and a half inches high. It looked like something you'd use to hide a necklace in, some piece of fine jewelry. Attached to the plain white box was a smaller version of the vellum envelope he had come to recognize. It was held against the box with a red ribbon.

Brent peered into the sack and saw his next week's supply, neatly packed into the bottom. Okay. Obviously, he was supposed to open this first. His fingers undid the ribbon, which he let flutter to the table. Unlike the other times, this envelope was blank across its front, his name nowhere to be found. He flipped it over. The waxy seal was warm beneath his thumb. He brought it close to his face, suddenly paying attention to an aberration he'd never noticed.

Squashed into the red were what looked like hairs. Brown hairs.

His mind ordered fog to roll back across his brain, but he remained paralyzingly alert. If a mirror had been brought to his lips, he would have given no indication of breathing. He slid his thumb beneath the seal. It didn't feel like candle wax anymore. Not that it ever had. Before going any further, he scooted out a chair and sat down.

He peeled open the paper folded inside.

Remember what our friend John had forgotten. Remember, or pay the same price.

Behind Brent, water boiled against the aluminum sides of the saucepan. It burped and splattered over the rim, making sizzling noises on the stove.

Gently, he lifted the top of the box. Inside lay folded tissue paper, pearl white. It was like a present from Tiffany's, gift-wrapped for his private pleasure. The fog decided to roll through his brain after all, descending with a cottony swirl, and that was good, the cotton stuffing his mouth: it kept him from screaming. But it did not prevent his fingers from tugging back the tissue paper, finishing their mission, and revealing the pink, hacked-off remains of a tongue.

PART THREE

A slip of the tongue

1

"**W**hy is it so dark over here?"

Brent shrugged at his boss. "The fluorescent lights are bothering my eyes."

"Come'ere a second."

Captain Kirk pulled Brent into a corner by the computer printouts. His face was glazed, as sweet-looking as a doughnut. Little beads of sweat clung to his receding hairline.

"I've got to talk to you," he whispered. He clutched Brent in his agitation, his hand like the pincers of some frantic sea creature, grasping and ungrasping at his arm.

"Let go of me," Brent said coolly. His boss obediently removed his hand from his arm, but his eyes swiveled in their sockets as though unable to focus on one thing. He had never seen him in such a lather.

"This drug you're taking," Captain Kirk said. "You've got to tell me where I can get it."

Brent relaxed a little. At least he wasn't getting fired for the second time. The lie came easily to his lips. "I don't know what you're talking about."

"Don't play games with me, man. I'm desperate. Your miracle drug."

"If there *were* a miracle drug, believe me, nobody would keep it a secret. It's what everyone is waiting for, for god's sake."

"I know you're taking something different," Captain Kirk snapped. His eyes burrowed into Brent. "I know how you were. I know how you *looked*. And, I know how it's changed you."

Brent said nothing, but a blush of heat rose up his neck and cheeks. Changed him?

"That smell. It's a side effect, isn't it?" His boss waved a hand dismissively. "I don't care about that. Look at me: it's not like I have dozens of dates lined up or anything. I can deal with a little smell. You have. And I've kept you working, given you a job even when some of the other employees wanted me to fire you. You owe me." He was breathless.

Brent shook his head. "There is no miracle drug. I'm taking AZT just like everybody else. Combining it with ddC. That's it."

"Bullshit."

Brent glanced around as if for the first time. The two of them, standing off by the computers, were the only ones left in the office. Everyone else had quietly slunk out of the office and headed for home.

"Now, Captain, why don't you calm down—"

"I'm getting sick," his boss suddenly blurted with a miserable cry.

"What?"

"I was at the doctor's two days ago. My lab work is shit. Shit. I've been HIV-positive for several years. But now it's getting serious."

"You never told anyone."

"Yeah. Well. Some things you keep private for as long as you can, know what I mean?" He backhanded the beads of sweat off his forehead. "I'm picking up speed on that long slide downhill. One lousy cold right about now would put me into the hospital. This is it, Brent. It's do or die time. Nobody ever gets better." He jabbed Brent in the chest. "Except *you.*"

"I'm just lucky—

"Luck has nothing to do with it. You're on to something. More to the point, you're *on* something, and it's turned you into a fucking god, for Christ's sake. The picture of perfect health. So I wanted to ask you, bottom line, no bullshit: what's it gonna cost me?"

Brent shrugged helplessly. Beads of his own sweat were beginning to drip down his hairline.

"I'll do anything. Pay any price. It can't cost a fortune, or you wouldn't be able to afford it. Just — tell me how I can get some for myself."

Brent shuddered at the echo of his own words from Dr. Anthony Able's office. *Be careful what you ask for, Captain. You might just get it, after all.*

"I can't help you," he said with a sigh, but his tone held a razor, sharp and final.

"Talk to your people," Captain Kirk urged. "Or your doctors. Or whoever the fuck it is giving you ... whatever it is..." He wagged his head. "I can keep secrets. I won't tell a soul. I just want to get in on it, is that so bad?"

"That's not how it works," he said, the words slipping out before he could catch them, before he realized what his words implied. He started with surprise. They stared at each other, neither one breathing. Brent flushed hot and cold, his skin pricked with icy needles.

"I knew it," gloated his boss. "I knew it."

"There is no miracle drug," Brent reiterated with as firm a voice as possible, while inside, scolding himself: *What have I done? What if they find out?*

"Then why do you smell so bad?"

"I don't know what you're talking about."

"You don't, huh. No one's bothered to tell you that you smell like an old pork chop left too long in the fridge? Is that what you're saying to me?" His hands were claws again, snipping at the flesh of Brent's arms.

Brent wrenched free. "I think I'd better go."

"You *owe* me, you little shit! It isn't fair that you should get off this merry-go-round while the rest of us have no choice but to hang on till the bitter end!"

Brent marched over to the coat stand and plucked his leather jacket from the hook. He glanced back at Captain Kirk. His boss's face was strawberry red, livid.

"I'm sorry," he said, his apology sawdust in his throat, coughed out because the truth was too buried, too complicated. All he could offer was this glibness, words with all the comforting weight of straw. He walked toward the front entrance of the agency.

"You walk out that door, you're fired."

Brent halted in his tracks, but this time did not turn around. Well. It was inevitable, this parting of the ways.

"You're condemning a man to die, you know that, don't you?"

Each step hurt a little, but he forced his legs to move toward the door. He heard words hurled at him as his hand grasped the marble knob, heard the venom and anguish and snake-pit hiss of disbelief. Just as he heard the sob gush out of his ex-boss's mouth, the moan of the damned, as he closed the door on Captain Kirk's Travels to the Beyond.

2

That's not how it works.

A slip of the tongue. No big deal. It wasn't like the office was bugged or anything. Or was it...?

It was bound to happen some of the time. Snatched from death back to life, how could suspicions not be aroused? What was he supposed to do about it? Skettle had given him no guidelines, no instructions, save one: silence.

And his hand went to the pliant flesh beneath his throat, his tongue a stick of deadwood in his mouth, as though anticipating the knife...

He'd stared at the gray stub of John's tongue for a long time that morning, now two weeks past. Stared with the grim fascination of a survivor, of an observer at a terrible accident. He'd drunk the cocktail, liquid searing his throat, too hot but he didn't care, he needed it, knew its hooks were in him but good, and he'd stared at the mushroom gray thing in its cotton-candy wrapping and swore to himself that, yes, he would take its message to heart, he would never be so stupid, never ever ever.

He put the lid back on the box and took it outside, holding it away from his body as though the tongue were alive and might somehow bite him. Took it to his garbage can in the alley next to his house and dumped it on top of Hefty's best trash bags, leaving the lid askew in his haste to get away. He retreated from the winter-spring sunshine and crawled into bed, sleep his merciful blanket. He felt himself rearranging a bit, his muscles relaxing with a quiet sigh as the elixir worked its magic.

Hours later came a bang from outside, the garbage can lid a cymbal crash against concrete. He lurched out of bed, disoriented, blurry with four hours sleep, and staggered to the front door. The sight took his breath, just snatched it away.

The tomcat stared up at him from the sidewalk. In an act of brave defiance it didn't move, just grasped the lump of tongue between its golden paws, guarding its prize from the garbage can.

"Leave that alone!" he had shrieked, the sight galling, awful, unfair. He jumped up and down like a witch doctor performing a voodoo dance. Suddenly he became aware that he was standing on his front step in his Calvin Klein's, morning traffic skimming by on the street. He retreated. The tomcat nonchalantly dipped to the lump of tongue and grasped it firmly between its jaws, then bolted suddenly in that lightning way of all cats, hopping up and over the picket fence to the sidewalk beyond.

No, Brent had decided right then and there. He would never be that stupid. Never ever.

And now...

Now, there was an envelope waiting for him when he got home from work, sealed with bow-tie strands of brown hair, greasy red wax seal that was no wax. *Tonight*.

He hoped its message only meant the usual ten p.m. pickup, Acne Andy his chauffeur the past few times, John nowhere to be seen, and he never asked, was too afraid to ask.

But that one word. *Tonight*.

Tonight, you're gonna get it.

Tonight, you learn a few lessons in silence. Permanent silence, hee hee.

Brent's fear was a black hole, insatiable. Whatever he threw into it was gobbled up with the threat of some new surprise they had yet to reveal. Maybe he would simply disappear the way John had disappeared, only there had been nothing *simple* about it, face the truth.

He could not eat. His thoughts whirled with half-formed strategies, shadowy, shapeless things that never firmed into something he could grasp. Perhaps he could approach Square-jaw tonight and say he knew someone who wanted to join their ranks. For all he knew, John may have gone to bat for him in that very way. How else did they recruit among themselves? Who decided who joined and who was kept out?

Brent fretted, and paced, and turned on the TV to fill his house with noise. If he looked nervous when they came for him, if he acted like he'd done something wrong, a guilty five-year-old...

He was sitting on the couch, TV on but unwatched, some sitcom with laugh track and jiggling breasts, when he heard the snap of twigs outside his bedroom window. The hair at the back of Brent's neck stood on end. He rose from the couch and slipped through the shadows of his hallway in stockinged feet. Approached the closed shutters of his bedroom window, and waited. He could hear the wind whispering through the cherry trees just beyond the gate. The hiss of his own blood rushing through his veins. If it was them, come for him, here he stood, defenseless...

He clicked off the lamp beside the bed and felt better wrapped in the dark. With infinite care he peeled back one of the louvres and squinted through the slats. A breath of cool air blew toward his face, the glass frosted with February cold. He held his breath, not wanting to further obscure his view.

But saw only the ordinary.

This is stupid. Scolding himself, and these jitters, he pushed away from the window and wandered through the house, unable to sit back down on the couch. Eventually he found himself in the kitchen and decided to boil up tonight's dose, yum yum. It helped these all-night affairs, he'd discovered, to drink the cocktail just before leaving the house. Kind of like downing a protein drink before a grueling workout in the gym. A booster. And of course, the high. Don't forget that. Nothing like the rush of cocaine, or feel-good marijuana. This was more like a sharpening of senses, no blurry edges, everything crisp and defined. A sensation of lightness. How he loved it.

He was about to take his first delectable sip when he heard a can skitter across his back porch. An old Coke can he'd forgotten to throw away? No crunch of dry leaves, this. Someone making a boo-boo of a noise, there on his back porch.

Not someone. Them. Come to teach a lesson.

He waffled between downing his cocktail while it was too hot or stepping outside onto his porch. He was no coward — well, maybe just a little bit of one — but he would confront them, head-on, if that's what it came to. He set the cocktail on the counter beside the stove, steam haloing its boiling contents. Next to it, the hot soup pan used to boil it all up. Brent moved briskly to his back door, unlocked it, and swung the door open into cold night. His breath puffed before him.

"Who's out there?"

Waited. Images of the neighborhood tomcat — out for a late-night snack, perhaps? Tongue sandwich on rye, hold the mayo. He took cautious steps outside. The night sky was frosted with fast-moving clouds or fog, hard to tell. The pine trees at the end of his lot moaned in the breeze, a sad and prickly sound.

He tried again. "Anyone there?"

An empty can answered him, yanked by a gust of wind. It clanged down the steps and rolled to a stop in the grass.

Brent shook his head. What a jerk. What a silly frightened jerk. Only ... where had the can come from? He never left trash out—

The shape bullied over him, black, locomotive huge, pushing him headfirst to the wooden porch. He fell with an embarrassing sprawl, too surprised to even cry out. Smacked his head and saw stars. A hand grasped the blond hair at the back of his head, roughly, and slammed his chin against the splintery wood. Amazing pain roared through his head and exploded out the back of his skull. Between clenched teeth a moan of his pain gurgled out.

Despite his surprise, some instinct told Brent to play possum. He lay still with his eyes closed, even as his assailant wedged him to the porch with a firm knee in the back. His right cheek was scratched from splinters.

Suddenly the knee lifted off his back. He heard labored breath, panic-hot. Backward steps as the figure stumbled away and slammed into the kitchen door swinging on its hinges. A little cry, despair or desire — Brent couldn't tell and didn't want to know, just so long as his assailant moved far enough away to allow him to jump up and beat the son of a bitch to a pulp.

The man dashed into the kitchen. Brent took his chance, springing up on his arms and then to his feet, dizzy, but that would pass, pass like the pain in his chin. He lurched into the doorway, spitting fire at the indignity of his home violated, his fear burned from him, how about that. And stared. He saw the glass with the cocktail first, highlighted there in the man's hand like a strip of color celluloid in a black-and-white world. Half its contents had been drunk, gritty liquid dribbling down that round chin in the haste to down it all in seconds. His assailant saw Brent and faltered, eyes ballooning with fear and just a touch of shame. He made a mewling sound from low in his throat.

"Please," Captain Kirk implored.

Brent stepped into the kitchen. Even though several feet separated them, his boss shrank with apprehension.

"Now you know," Brent said. His voice was like old soda pop, flat and resigned to what was.

Kirk nodded vigorously. "Yes. I'm sorry if I hurt you. I knew there was something special you took, and I took a chance that you'd have it, at your house..."

"Go ahead. Drink up."

"It tastes so awful. How can you stand it?"

"You'll get used to it." A smile, like a gash across his face.

Uncertainty. And then Captain Kirk grasped the glass with both hands, greedy for its benefits. Tilted back his head, and began to drink.

Brent glided toward him, smooth as unfurling silk, no thought, raw instinct. He picked up the soup pan from the stove. Its handle was still warm in his hand. Kirk was busy finishing the drink, his face a grimace. He noticed Brent standing close to him and offered a look of gratitude before he saw the pan swinging in an aluminum rainbow of movement. An amazing gout of blood spurted from Captain Kirk's temple as Brent whacked it against his skull. The empty glass slipped from Kirk's pudgy fingers and fell to the floor, shattering.

The second blow spun him into the kitchen table. Kirk sank in movietone slow motion, one knee grinding into the shards of glass scattered across the floor, a look of such dumb surprise on that doughnut face it was almost comical. Weakly he threw up an arm to protect his face, but the temple worked so nicely that Brent was content to hit that again with all his might, all his mettle thrown into it. A shocking spray of red flew out of Kirk, painting Brent's shirt and jeans. His nostrils flared with the hot copper scent of blood.

Kirk looked up at him, through him, off on his own travels to the beyond, up up and away, eyes glazed with confusion or was it the terrible truth of his mortality burning before him, so bright he had to duck his head. A word plopped out of his mouth — it sounded like "Why?" — and then fell to the floor along with the rest of him. He rolled onto his back, glass crunching underneath. His lips puckered with simulated kissing motions, like a fish out of water kissing his life good-bye. Brent didn't mean to giggle, but it was suddenly so funny-looking, you just had to be there.

And then it stopped, nothing sharp or dramatic but an ebbing away to silence, and stillness. A fog was trying to push across Brent's brain, but the foghorns heralding its approach hurt his head and kept his thoughts clear.

"I'm sorry, Captain," Brent whispered. A weird curiosity gripped him; he'd never stood so close to a dead body. Blood still bubbled out of the wound near Kirk's temple and trickled down the fat man's face. Its smell tickled his nose. His tongue tasted iron. Kirk looked asleep, there on his kitchen floor. But, of course, nobody sleeps with their eyes popped open like that, with that what-have-you-done-to-me? expression. Brent's right hand ached, and when he looked down he saw the soup pan clenched between white fingers. He placed the pan back onto the stove top and massaged feeling into his colorless hand. His legs began to wobble in the most alarming way, so he pulled out a chair and sat down.

"I had to," Brent said into the air. He couldn't look at Captain Kirk's eyes — they didn't seem so funny anymore. "I couldn't let you in on it, not without their permission—"

A knock on the front door, three quick raps. Acne Andy had come to drive him to the hidey-hole South of Market.

3

The teenager surveyed the wrecked kitchen with a long, silent stare. He didn't even bother to remove his black, coin-shaped sunglasses. Absently he scratched at his pockmarked face. "Where's your phone?"

"Andy, there was nothing I could do about it, he broke in, he drank the cocktail—"

The kid lay reassuring fingers onto Brent's shoulder. "The phone."

Brent pointed him into the den. The fog in his brain had managed to roll in a bit after all; even he couldn't stop something as implacable as that. But even through this cool haze he noticed that things were not happening the way he thought they would.

"We have an emergency," Acne Andy said into the phone. Murmured yeses and nos. Hung up.

Brent was waiting for panic, hot and metallic like the spilled blood of his boss, but there was nothing, no feeling, just this strange calmness.

"Did you have your drink yet?" Acne asked him. It took a moment to register what the hell he was talking about. Brent shook his head. "Okay. Sit tight." And casual as could be the teenager washed the soup pan ("The murder weapon," Brent heard a Perry Mason voice inside his head say) and set about boiling up another batch. He took a broom and swept up most of the glass while waiting for the water. He had to step over Captain Kirk's feet whenever he checked the pot on the stove, but Acne didn't seem to mind. He seemed more concerned with the dented soup pan. "Gonna have to find a new pan," he chirped. "This one wobbles too much."

Brent drank his medicine while Acne puttered around him, this kid with needle marks riding up both arms suddenly donning the Jewish-mother routine. *Are you comfy, drink up, I've got everything under control. We'll take care of it.*

And they did, too. Two strangers entered his house. They didn't even bother to knock. Acne led them in and pointed. The strangers wore navy jumpsuits and looked at each other with a let's-get-cracking expression. Plastic gloves were pulled from their pockets and slipped over their hands. Acne instructed Brent to go stand out on the porch and "stay out of the way." They dimmed the overhead globe lighting the kitchen to make sure no pesky neighbors from across the way could catch a glimpse of their party. One of the removal men, a black guy with powerhouse shoulders and hands the size of dinner plates, still wasn't satisfied: too much light. So they killed the overhead and clicked on the 15-watt above the stove. Brent tried his damnedest to figure out how these guys could see well enough to clean up but he had to admit the softer light was easier on the eyes, not to mention a smart idea.

They unfolded an official-looking vinyl body bag, unzipped its top, and had a hell of a time grunting and pushing Captain

Kirk inside. For somebody worried about dying, he certainly had the girth and looks of a healthy person, discounting the spilled blood and the amazing raspberry explosion above his right temple. At least he'd gotten part of his wish, tonight: cheating the rapid deterioration of his body to illness.

The rest of the house lights were killed, the front door flung wide, and like some nocturnal creature secreting away a cocooned prize, they crept out and past the gate to a waiting van. Brent glanced above the street and saw that the streetlight next to his house had been shot out. An unfamiliar darkness pooled the street where pieces of glass lay glimmering on the asphalt like fallen stars.

Then: back to the kitchen, the dry-twig whisk of a broom, whisk whisk, getting all the glass Acne Andy hadn't been able to reach. Men reaching into the blackness underneath the sink for Comet and sponges — got to clean up the blood, leave no traces.

Brent watched from his perch beside the back door. Shivered from the cold. Shivered from his fear. For he knew it could not be as simple as all this, his trespass. The cocktail pushed some of the fog out of his head, enough for him to realize that when punishment came it would be swift and absolute. Hold out your tongue for a moment, would you dear boy?

He shivered, and the cold ran like spiky needles up his spine. He realized in the same frozen moment that someone walked toward them down the hallway. Someone new added to this black absurdity. His throat clutched when he saw who it was.

Squarejaw sauntered into the kitchen. Acne Andy and the two removal men stopped what they were doing. Andy shut off the tap water at the sink, where he'd been cleaning sponges. Their silence, their deference, made Brent think of his meeting with Skettle.

"Where is it?" Squarejaw asked. He adjusted his ever-present sunglasses. They were very new wave, unusually stylish, shaped like upside-down ice cubes, black as tar.

The black man decided to take charge. "He's in the van. Ready to be removed."

"Then stop pussyfooting around. How long do you think a van in this neighborhood can be out on the street without calling attention to itself?"

"Yes, sir."

They were finished anyway, the tile floor cleaner than Brent had gotten it in months. The two men handed Comet and dirty sponges to Acne and then skedaddled, their retreat radically different from their officious entrance.

The tiny light above the stove cut harsh lines onto Squarejaw's face. He moved past Acne Andy, who pressed himself against the counter, even though there was plenty of room for the man to pass. Squarejaw shook a cigarette out of his shirt pocket, a one-handed movement as he walked. He cupped it between his fingers but did not light it — a deliberate omission Brent noted with his own mounting fear.

They stood in that semidarkness, Squarejaw less than a foot away. The breath that blew upon Brent's face was chalky, and full of old smoke.

"Well, well," the big man said.

Brent stopped breathing. Here it comes.

"Our little Goldilocks killed a man. What do you know about that."

"I had to. He ... he found out about the cocktail. He knocked me down, onto the porch, and broke into my house—"

The man held up a hand. Brent killed his babbling, his lips snapping shut so fast he almost nipped the tip of his tongue.

"Good job," Squarejaw said. And he did an amazing thing, truly amazing. He patted Brent on the shoulder and smiled at him, honestly smiled at him, with the first glimmer of newborn respect. He lit his cigarette and blew out a stream of smoke.

Brent was stunned. "You're not ... upset?"

"We can't have people poking their noses where they don't belong, right?"

"Right."

Another drag on the cigarette. "But, Goldilocks, let me give you a piece of advice."

"Okay."

Squarejaw reached out and wrapped Brent's left hand into his own, caressing it with a sudden intimacy that made him uncomfortable. He tried to read an expression in the man's eyes, but the sunglasses got in the way. "Don't let it happen again." And he nonchalantly buried the lighted end of his cigarette into the palm of Brent's hand.

PART FOUR

Little compromises

1

Little compromises. That's what his new life had come down to. Compromise. You see what you want to see. Hear what you want to hear. Everything else, the little bits and pieces that refused to fit into the equation — what had once represented life in its stubborn bland normality — somehow didn't matter anymore. Those pieces just broke off, tossed away because they no longer fit. They had been replaced by the sounds of feet kicking against wooden slats. Hands scratching themselves raw, fingernails ripped to the quick. Muffled cries. And in his dreams, right before falling off the edge into sleep, that cringing look of gratitude in Captain Kirk's eyes just before the soup pan caught him above the temple and knocked him to the floor.

Little compromises.

Do your work, get the cocktail. It was exactly the position Skettle and his gang wanted him in, he was sure.

Only ... it wasn't Skettle and *his* gang anymore, was it? As if "they" were the outsiders, and not him. No. It was *our* gang, now. He had joined up, been initiated because he had protected the cocktail's secret. And the truth, which he tried to hide from himself for as long as possible, was this: in some deep mysterious way that pleased him greatly, he was proud to belong.

He had to face it. He couldn't stay around normal people for very long. Their faces pinched as the smell hit them. They acted like rabbits, small funny rabbits with twitching noses and scared charcoal eyes. It was fun, to wield this unexpected power. He could clear out a long line in the grocery store in two minutes flat. Glide right to the front of the line at Eureka Bank as customers encouraged him to step ahead, they had to finish calculating their deposits and withdrawals, be my guest.

He enjoyed his difference, and the power the secret of the cocktail gave him. His attractiveness, before illness had chewed into him, had always set him apart. Now, he could be different *and* belong. For the first time in his life he truly belonged to something larger than himself, outside of himself. He hadn't asked to belong to the Scarecrow Club, so they didn't count. But Skettle: he had sought Brent out, heard his plea for help, and welcomed him into their ranks. Here, he served a purpose within their secret group, and yet he could remain a free agent, able to move between both worlds.

True, he was beginning to become a bit of a night person. He avoided the bright sunshine of afternoon hours; midday sun ripened his smell, he'd discovered. That was okay. No big loss. He preferred to tend to his errands in the early morning or late afternoon. There were fewer people about, which he liked. Also, midday light was really getting to bother his eyes, even after he went to Walgreen's and bought himself the blackest pair of sunshades he could find. With so many all-night trips, it was becoming not just easier but a necessity to sleep during the day and stay up all night.

Yes. Many trips now. Promoted from lowly gofer to full-fledged underling. And paid, too.

Squarejaw had had him report to work at the travel agency the next morning, business as usual. Skettle's orders. It wasn't until afternoon that the office began to buzz. Where was Captain Kirk? Did he take off on a trip, ha ha? Leave another message on his answering machine.

Two days later someone finally called the police. Everybody was worried, but privately embarrassed that they were over-reacting. Brent shrugged his shoulders along with the rest of them and offered his opinion if anyone got close enough to ask. By week's end it was apparent some real mischief had taken place. The jokes stopped, replaced by hushed speculation about whether any of them still had a job.

The gay papers and even the *San Francisco Chronicle* reported on the sudden disappearance. When rumors surfaced that Captain Kirk had been ill, there was a lot of head wagging. Ahh. Here lay the answer, like so many who had gone before. The old "taken a powder" routine. No one faulted him for it, but there it was. A brother-in-law from Georgia showed up to straighten the accounts, pay everyone their last checks, and figure out if the business would continue.

Brent accepted his check and waved good-bye with his healing hand. He had another job now. He did as he was instructed, and kept his mouth shut. For the rest of February and most of March they used him to run down to Santa Cruz. Obviously the town was a midway point for the cargo coming in from southern California, just as San Francisco was an end stop for most of northern California. The meeting place in Santa Cruz routinely changed, but always Brent was met by that big lummox of a man, Joe, who greeted him with sly winks.

They'd load up the station wagon, transferring the wooden crate with grunts and groans, huffing and puffing over the weight. Grin at each other when they were all done. Joe would lick his lips and tilt his head toward the empty interior of his van. What the hell. It was the only sex Brent could get these days. Joe's worshipful stance, his eagerness to please was a little on the pathetic side, but certainly arousing enough if Brent shut his eyes and fantasized about someone else.

And whenever he heard something struggling within the confines of the crate on his way back to San Francisco, he'd simply crank up the radio, roll down a window, and drown the sound out.

2

He called Mary Ann at odd hours in the hopes that one day Clayton would answer the phone. But it became clear his nephew was still too young to be picking up the phone without his mother.

"Hello? Who is this, please?"

Brent could hear Clay's laughter in the background. He held his breath, afraid to speak. Desperate to speak.

"This isn't funny," Mary Ann said, "and I'm calling the police if you do this again." She slammed down the phone.

Sometimes Brent drove past his sister's fog-shrouded house on his way back from Santa Cruz. Even though he would arrive at the dead hour of four a.m, he always waited for signs of movement within the house. It pleased him to imagine Clay curled in his bed, sheets and blankets in riot. Another hour and he'd be up watching cartoons, if Mary Ann let him switch on the TV.

Once, a small light came on as someone stumbled through the house. He never saw who made this predawn excursion, but he hoped it was Clay, awake and unable to go back to sleep. Perhaps one morning the boy would stick his head out the front door, checking to make sure his red wagon hadn't wandered off during the night. And Brent could surprise him, could—

Yeah. Sure. Come to smelly old Uncle Brent at five in the morning.

It stirred up old wounds, doing this, but he was lost to the compulsion. Even if the possibility of their getting together again was just a fantasy, he would try. And hope. He'd never let Skettle — or Mary Ann — steal that hope away from him. Never.

On this particular March morning he lingered longer than he usually dared. He'd been fooled by the steel wool fog scouring the aluminium sky. But an inner clock, which had grown so acute in the past weeks, able to detect the first stirrings of a coming morn, suddenly rang a warning alarm. A boy bicycled past, adroitly tossing newspapers against the front doors of the neighboring houses. His presence electrified Brent into action. He started the station wagon and sped off with all the enthusiasm he could muster from the Country Squire.

A moan of discomfort from the crate in back.

"Sorry, buddy," Brent mumbled. He called them all buddy, though as far as he was concerned it was animals inside that box, cows and goats and maybe a few stray dogs. They kicked, and scratched, and were just as capable of making humanlike groans as any Polk Street derelict that may lay inside that box.

Over by South of Market the fog was already in retreat. Wispy fingers hung in the springtime air. Brent could see the dawn lightening into morning. With his breath hot in his throat he pulled into the gravel parking lot and mentally prepared himself for a tongue-lashing because he was so late with his shipment. Or a tongue removal—

Acne Andy hopped out of one of the two vans, a bucket of sudsy water in one hand. He saw Brent getting out of the wagon and waved. That's a good sign, Brent thought. He and Acne had become comrades in arms, of a sort, ever since that unpleasantness with Captain Kirk. But he still missed John. John's absence frightened him, and made him feel just a touch of guilt. After all, what had John said to him that had warranted such a severe punishment? All his friend had done was try to show him the ropes. Acne Andy was an easy ally because he spoke only when something needed to be said. It was safer that way.

"Where you been?" the teenager asked. He hooked a thumb toward the warehouse. "They've been waiting for you."

At that moment Squarejaw came wobbling out of the building. Brent watched him approach with astonishment — and not a small dose of fear. The cigarette burn on his hand had finally healed (he'd poured small amounts of the cocktail onto it), but it still ached in the most awful way. Especially whenever he was in Squarejaw's presence. He came toward them as though balancing on a circus high wire, hands like wings at his sides. Was he drunk? Suffering some sort of withdrawal? Impossible to tell.

"Morning," the man grumbled. Brent thought he was offering a salutary hello, but then he realized Squarejaw was frowning at the orange-streaked sky with an open expression of disgust. His nose wrinkled, and he kept adjusting his punkish, black sunglasses as though a bright light were shining upon them.

"I'm sorry I'm late," Brent stammered. He retreated into the excuse he'd made up on the drive from Daly City. "The car—"

"Is it late?" He ran a hand through the sharp spikes of his steely flattop. "Yes. I suppose it is. Late for all of us, ha ha." He stared at them blankly.

Brent glanced uneasily at Acne, who shrugged imperceptibly. His glance asked, When did *this* happen?

"I've been talking to the nicest fellow," Squarejaw said in a neutral, dreamy voice. "He's just inside the door. Do you want to say hi?"

Brent shook his head. He didn't know what to do. This change in personality was too strange to ignore. Then again, how sudden was it? Squarejaw had always acted like a drill sergeant with not all of his screws tight.

They stood there in uncomfortable silence. A tall man suddenly walked through the sliding door panel of the warehouse. Brent turned to stare. He wore a full-length brown raincoat, the collar turned all the way up around his neck. A good portion of his upper face was obscured by a pair of mirrored sunglasses, which completely camouflaged his eyes. Shaggy black hair spilled out from all sides beneath a dark gray rain hat. The man reared back a little in surprise when he saw he had an audience. But just as quickly he composed himself and marched over to Squarejaw, taking his elbow.

"Tony," the stranger said. His voice was low in his throat, tough as iron. "Look at me."

"Look at you?" Another chuckle, like grinding glass between teeth. "I can't look at anything anymore, you know that." Squarejaw turned on Brent. "How are *your* eyes these days, Goldilocks? Staying out of the sun? Bought yourself a few pairs of shades? It won't help. The light still gets in, you know. It burns. Oh, how it burns—"

"Enough about that," the man snapped with irritation. He was increasingly annoyed with Squarejaw, and tugged on his arm to move him away from Brent and Andy. "Come with me. I'll drive you home."

A bit of Squarejaw's old self flickered. "We have transport to take care of..."

"Our friends here will take care of that," the man said dismissively. "You two can handle bringing that inside, can't you?"

Brent nodded, and an odd thrill rippled through him. Finally, he'd have his opportunity to see what lay inside these crates. But as he watched the two men walk across the parking lot, the rain-jacketed stranger supporting Squarejaw as though the man was drunk, he was nagged by a rush of unanswered questions. What in the world had happened, for Squarejaw to be reduced to such scrambled helplessness? And if this weirdness could happen to someone as formidable as Squarejaw, could it eventually happen to him, too?

A Mercedes was parked next to one of the transport vans. They moved toward it.

"Don't make me," they heard Squarejaw whine. "Let me stay."

"You need some rest, Tony." The man unlocked the passenger side and all but pushed his charge into the car's interior. "Really, this is for the best."

Brent watched them drive away. Questions upon questions stuffed his head. And that man, camouflaged as though a single ray of sunshine would reduce him to a pile of smouldering ash, like some modern-day vampire.

"Come on," Andy said. "Let's pull this crate inside."

"Wait a minute. What's going on with Squarejaw? And who was that guy? Have you seen him here before?"

"We can't worry about that now."

"Andy—"

The teenager leaned close. "Look," he whispered. "It happens, sometimes. Guys can't handle light anymore. Or they go off their rocker. Or a little of both. And if they hear me telling you this..." He made a motion with his tongue that was all too clear.

Brent nodded. He wanted to talk about it, wanted answers, but Acne was already at the station wagon door, opening the tailgate. The orange sky was now streaked with lemon. Any minute, full dawn. He turned to the task at hand, his enthusiasm clouded by questions that would have to wait.

"There's a dolly just inside the door," Andy said.

Brent fetched it, and snuck a peek into the warehouse. But all was dark, and he saw nothing. He rolled the dolly to the edge of the platform, then jumped down to help his friend. This particular shipment was lighter than usual, for the move onto the dolly took little effort.

They rolled the crate through the doors. Brent, tingling with anticipation, stepped inside. *Here we go...*

His first impression was that of an amusement park funhouse — which made no sense. All was dark. Windows had been painted black from the inside. There was a hum of activity, the sense of many footsteps, many hands busy with missions known only to themselves. Almost immediately his eyes adjusted to the nonlight, and he became aware of a phosphorescent, black-light glow that had no particular source. Long tables ran the length of the warehouse, each one crammed with the accoutrements of a high school chemistry lab: Bunsen burners, short and long test tubes, pans filled with bubbling mixtures that burped and simmered. There were racks filled with bottles and jars, liquids and powders, all arranged like an exotic spice rack. Almost invisible were the caretakers in dark blue smocks or white lab coats, men and one or two women who glided silently back and forth, fiddling, adjusting, fine-tuning. A huge ant farm, hidden not in earthen tunnels but man-made darkness.

His nose crinkled at a moist, earthy mushroom smell he recognized as one of the cocktail's ingredients. Along with the powders and liquids, he saw trays of herbs and squat, leafy plants. This dark harvest was in full cultivation, with workers diligently pruning only the best.

All of these observations flashed through his thoughts with just the turning of his head. In that moment he realized he was vaguely disappointed. This was like learning how your favorite special effect in a movie was accomplished, and once the truth was out, wishing for the ignorance of magic once again.

"This way," Acne Andy said, and indicated they should roll their cargo to the end of the first table.

There was excitement in the air. Some of the workers stopped what they were doing to exchange eager glances or to watch the progress of the crate. Brent felt their eyes upon him and fought against a budding unease. With a chill that whispered up his spine he noted that most of the workers, even in this darkness, wore sunshades.

They rolled the crate to the end of the first table. On its corner sat a large black cauldron at least two feet high — the kind of giant pot needed in soup kitchens to feed the hungry. The pot was half-full with a simmering liquid, its contents heated by the two hotplates beneath the kettle. Hanging on the paneled wall just a few feet away was a crowbar, a hammer, assorted butcher knives, and smaller scalpellike instruments.

"What's wrong?" It was Andy, speaking without moving his lips.

Brent answered in the same fashion. "I — I don't think I want to be a part of this."

"Just follow my lead. You've got to make a good impression."

"For who?"

Acne walked over to the wall and picked up the crowbar. In a louder voice, as if he were addressing an audience, he said, "Let's get this show on the road, shall we?" He attacked the crate's lid with a practiced precision. Nails squealed under the crowbar's assault.

Sweat trickled down the sides of Brent's face. His underarms were wet. He glanced up and was surprised to see an office built into a second-story loft. The first third of the office wall was made of wood, which gave way at about waist height to huge sheets of glass. The office door also sported a glass window. All the better to keep an eye on things, he supposed. A man stood next to a plush leather chair and surveyed his domain, the red dot of his lit cigarette like a firefly fluttering around the man's head. He noticed Brent staring and nodded a greeting. They had met only the one time, but Brent had not forgotten the imposing presence of Skettle.

Another surprise awaited him. A man was descending the staircase from the office. He wore a blue smock, its front a splattered stew of stains and discolorations. The zombie face was a mask of unexpressed emotion, flat as a becalmed lake's surface. It rendered the face waxy and almost unrecognizable. Almost.

The name whispered out between his lips. "John?" And underneath that, afraid to be spoken: *What have they done to you?*

And then the squeal of nails brought him back, and Brent's attention refocused upon the opening of the transport. Too much was happening. Too fast. Why wouldn't this slow down, like it did in the movies? Too many firsts, happening all at once: seeing the inside of the warehouse. Skettle. John. The crate. Dear god, the crate—

The lid came off.

Brent craned forward.

She looked so peaceful, there on her bed of straw and dirt. The thumb of her right hand was plugged firmly into her tiny mouth. Somehow he noticed that before seeing the wrists bound together with thin white rope, like clothesline. Her ankles were also bound, the rope like ankle bracelets over her pink cotton pajamas. Giraffes and fuzzy lions, playful chimpanzees, waltzing hippos, and frolicking pandas played together in a friendly zoo upon her pajamas. Even the padded feet of her outfit were adorned with cute animal hooves.

Her shoulder-length brown hair lay in a sweaty tangle about her head. Pieces of straw poked through like spikes. She could not have been a day over five years old.

"Damn it," Acne Andy growled. Brent startled at the sound. "There were supposed to be two of them. What happened?"

190 ✦

Brent was immobile. He willed himself into a statue. His nostrils flared but he would not open his mouth for air, even though that's what he desperately needed, fresh air. No telling what would spill out of his mouth if he opened it. Was he supposed to be *honored* by this, this fellowship of secrecy, the veil now lifted?

A low groan. The little girl began to stir as the air revived her. Her feet wiggled. She rolled her head to the side, and her thumb popped out of her mouth.

"Let's put a move on it," Andy whispered, "or we'll have to use the chloroform again." He looked at Brent. "Pick her up."

Brent shook his head. "This doesn't bother you?"

Something crossed the teenager's face, a look that said, *We're trapped, don't you know that already?* Just as quickly it was replaced by a sneering disdain, a shield held up for protection. "It keeps us *alive*. Now don't be a fool. Skettle's watching. We're helping them out of a jam. This is your chance."

My chance for what? Everyone's eyes were upon him. It made his skin crawl. He had no choice. With a father's grace he reluctantly reached inside and hoisted the limp girl into his arms. She folded into him, head resting upon his shoulder, without waking up. His lips trembled. He thought he might melt. Little Clayton had clung to him like this, once upon a time.

There was a sound behind him, steely and sharp. Brent turned around and saw John waiting patiently, a serrated knife held within his right hand. His face was scary in its nonanimation, as if real emotion had been pushed so far deep that nothing remained but this waxlike mannequin, a counterfeit. Did he even recognize Brent? He gave no indication. He motioned for Brent to step over to the cauldron. Step over, and hold the girl out.

At last, Brent's wooden tongue came alive. He looked at John, and then at Acne Andy. "You can't be serious," he sputtered.

But he saw their faces, alive with anticipation. He saw the nameless lab technicians pausing in their duties to watch. And last of all, Skettle, lording over his domain. He thought of the first communication from Skettle, the letter written in that spider-thin script:

Would you really, truly, kill to have your looks back?

"Please," Brent gasped. "Don't make me. I — I can't do this. She's a little girl, for god's sake."

"Just hold her," Acne instructed. He nodded at John. "He'll do the rest. It's his job."

Before Brent could protest, John yanked on his arm. He arranged them over the cauldron and twisted the girl off of Brent's shoulder so that she faced the simmering brew. Steam wisped her face, playing with her hair. Suddenly her head lolled. Her fingers twitched and jerked.

Brent's legs were rooted to the floor, chained by their expectations of him. *Make this go away. Make this go away.* He shut his eyes.

The girl began to struggle against her bonds. There came a mewling sound from deep in her throat. "Mommy?"

John stole up from behind, pressing himself into Brent's back. Suddenly the girl stiffened in his arms, followed by a choked, gargling sound. And then she was everywhere all at once, twisting in Brent's arms, convulsing.

Andy hissed, "Over the pot, you moron! Look at the mess you're making!"

Hot liquid splashed onto Brent's hands. He tried to step back, his revulsion a huge live thing, more alive than this squirming doll in his arms. John must have sensed this because he leaned in and pushed them all forward. With one hand he yanked back a fistful of her brown hair, widening the slashed throat into a V. Little pajamaed feet kicked against Brent's thighs. Her hair whipped into his nose. She kept making a wet, stuck-in-mud sound, her chest heaving for air. Blood continued to froth over his hands like hot shampoo.

In his grief, he shook her. *Stop fighting it! Just die, damn you! Get this over with!*

The zoo menagerie was trying to run away on her pajamas. Chimpanzees hopped onto the backs of lions, but the lions would not retreat. Perhaps they wanted to stay, as witnesses. Brent did not stay. He welcomed the wave of fog that blew across his brain. He welcomed John taking the rag doll from his arms, and allowing him to step back. He had red paint all down his front, and he smelled awful. Now how had that happened? He looked up to ask John where all the red paint had come from, forgetting that his former friend could not answer him, and instead watched as John set the doll onto the table beside an assortment of scalpels. Balloonlike dots floated in his vision. As

John picked up one of the instruments, Brent silently mouthed, *Adios,* and folded to the warehouse floor.

3

It made the six o'clock news the following night.

There were frantic, tearful interviews with the distraught parents. Has anyone seen our Angelica Marie, who disappeared from her bedroom? Volunteers were preparing to flood Fresno with printed flyers, vowing never to give up their search. This was followed by a picture of the little girl, brown hair neatly combed, a pink ribbon off to the side of her head. A proud smile with one missing front tooth.

Brent shut his eyes, thumbed his remote to a game show, and downed the last of his cocktail.

4

He thought he could never be shocked again. He'd seen it all, now. This hole he'd been digging for himself would never get any deeper.

But he was wrong.

A few days later, Skettle called him into his office and set the proposition before him.

Brent blanched at the idea. "Why me?"

"You're perfect. Good-looking. Nonthreatening. You should have no problems."

Brent shook his head. He glanced out of Skettle's office and down into the hive of activity in the warehouse. Some of the workers were watching him with envy. That was a laugh — envying his proximity to Skettle, lord of all, when all he really wanted was to get out, and get away. Did people disagree with Skettle? He wasn't sure, but he took the chance now. "Get someone else to do it."

The big man stroked his goatee through a pair of thin black gloves. His tailored suit had never looked more impressive. His shoes gleamed with polish. He drew in a breath. "Your friend John worked out for a while. He also had the right look, a friendly neighbor type. Unfortunately, he just couldn't keep his mouth shut. Asked too many questions and demanded too many answers. Now — well — he's better suited to his current job, don't you agree? I mean, he can hardly entice our transport when he has no means of speaking. And he doesn't seem to mind his new job anymore, what with the added pills we've been giving him. But you. Blond hair. Green eyes. Friendly face. I think you'll do quite nicely."

"What about asking Squarejaw?"

"Who?"

Brent snapped his fingers, trying to aid his memory. "What's his name. Tony. He seems like a big chief around here."

A patronizing smile. "Squarejaw. An amusing nickname. And very appropriate. But I'm afraid his services are no longer required with us. He seems to have suffered ... a setback," he said through a thinly veiled contempt.

That gave Brent pause. If an imposing man such as Squarejaw had been secreted away, or more to the point, done away with, then he had better make damn sure he did not offend Skettle in any way. "You have a whole warehouse full of people," he said, and gestured down at them. "Can't one of them take over the job?"

"Most of them don't go outside anymore. Certainly not during the daytime. Their eyes have become too sensitive to light. It's a problem that afflicts a minor portion of our community."

Minor portion? Whatever you want to believe, Skettle. Brent had yet to run into any of them that didn't protect their eyes with sunglasses, even in the dark.

Skettle waved a dismissive hand. "It's more an improvement of the eyes, actually, than any sort of defect from the elixir. Your eyesight improves so dramatically that light becomes almost unnecessary for you to see. It's quite remarkable, in its own way. But where were we?"

Brent decided he'd better play along, for now. "So what, exactly, would I have to do?"

"If you use your head and your wits, there's nothing to it. You'd be amazed at the number of kids left unattended. Elementary schools are a good choice, except that mothers often show up to drive or walk their kids home, so you have to be watchful. Public parks are often fruitful. And homeless shelters — they're a gold mine. The trick is to spread out the disappearances, which we do, all across the state, so as not to arouse undue suspicion. We can't have a flurry of activity just in San Francisco, now can we?" His white face cracked into a genuine smile at his own joke.

Brent leaned forward, and dared to ask the question that bothered him the most. "Tell me something. Why do they have to be so young? I'll be frank with you, I think I could handle this a lot better if I were dealing with — you know — street hustlers. Someone older, who's already been tossed out, and broken all connections with their family. Why can't we go after them?"

"Their blood is spoiled."

"Huh?"

"Don't you get it?" Skettle picked lint from the arm of his expensive suit. "It's not just that we need blood as an ingredient for the elixir. We need the blood of *innocents*. Why it makes a difference, I haven't the foggiest notion. A few times in the early attempts I tried someone older, with disastrous results. That's why the kids can't be too old. The cocktail requires their naivete, their innocence. It's a purity that, mixed with our other chemicals and herbs, keeps us healthy and strong. Street kids have been ruined. They've corrupted themselves in order to survive. It makes them worthless to us."

Brent felt the color run from his face. Skettle could have been discussing the latest detergent he saw advertised on television, that's how much he seemed to pay attention to his own words. But for him, the effect was like a noose tightening around his neck. As though his words maneuvered through a dangerous minefield, he said, "I'm not trying to be difficult here, but I really don't think I have it in me. You need someone to handle transport, I'm your man. I'll go wherever you need me. I'll even take over Squarejaw's old job, if you want. But ... enticing kids into a car? Chloroform? Tieing them up?" He hadn't expected to, but he shuddered at just the thought of it.

Skettle's powdered cheeks rippled with the first signs of irritation. "Since when have you discovered such high morals?"

"I'm not a prude. This is a matter of ... decency. If I had known—"

"What? Would you have died quietly, wasting away to a skeleton in your house? Would you have gone gently into the night? I think not."

"You don't know," Brent sulked.

"Let me refresh your memory. 'I would kill to have my looks back.' An exact quote, spoken from your own lips."

"I was desperate. Please. How can I make you understand—"

"No. How can I make *you* understand," Skettle thundered. It was the first time Brent had heard the man raise his voice, and the effect was hair-raising. "Who ever said you had a choice in the matter? If this is what I need you to do, you'll do it. Got that?"

Brent hung his head.

Skettle cleared his throat and shifted in his desk chair. "We'll talk in a day or two. Trust me, you'll be singing a different tune by then. Now go home."

Brent looked up in alarm. "Wait a minute."

"What?"

"I'm — I'm out of the cocktail."

"Are you?" A smile crept onto his face. "How unfortunate. Good-bye."

5

The pain was like a slow burn over a flame. An ache that bloomed out from his deepest core, blossoming into an agony that knew no bounds. His bones hurt. His muscles cried out. Every gesture, every turn of his head elicited knife stabs of pain. Sunlight swelled his eyelids. Even the artificial light from his lamps cut into his eyes, so he kept the house dark.

But the real agony was in his head. He'd surmised all along that he was addicted to the drug. No surprise there. What he hadn't counted on was the waves of craving that turned him into a sweating, shivering mess. Hot and cold flashes. Nausea. A pinprickly restlessness that kept him always uncomfortable, always unable to find a position he could relax in for more than a few minutes before the twitches started up.

It was now a day and a half without the cocktail. Brent grew so desperate he splashed water into the new saucepan he used for boiling up the elixir and drank it down, hoping that any residue would ease his discomfort and pain. It didn't.

And worse yet, he found himself contemplating Skettle's proposition. Okay, so he had denied the fact that people were being sacrificed for the drug. He'd known that the occasional moans or scratches he heard driving back from Santa Cruz did not belong to stray dogs stuffed into the crate. Deep down, he'd guessed there was a person inside. But kids?

Then a voice would whisper into his ear, so much like his own.

You knew what you were getting into. You accepted all terms, unconditionally. You're alive. And as long as you're alive, you can make choices, make changes. But you accepted the fact that when you stepped through that first door, other doors were closing behind you.

Afternoon melted into a fever dream twilight. Shooting pains began to cut the lengths of both arms. It came without warning, and caught him so off-guard he groaned with anger and surprise. He held his arms out to see and knew he must be having a delusion because arm muscles don't ripple and roll, undulating like William Hurt's arms in *Altered States*. He watched in shock as his skin puffed like a cooking bag of microwave popcorn. His shoulders suddenly ballooned beneath his t-shirt, straining the cotton fabric to the ripping point. Muscles tore. He shrieked in agony, then caught his breath as the muscles deflated like a fallen cake. He rubbed his hands along his arms and shuddered at the unyielding shell of his skin texture. Before his eyes, his arms were hardening into a mannequinlike artificialness that was the unappetizing color of a bruise. Even though he could bend his elbows and wiggle his fingers, he felt like he was moving a pair of dead sticks. His veins were the color of red ropes of licorice.

He rushed into the bathroom and beheld the cruel gashes and markings his withdrawal was carving upon him. His skeleton was back in his face, a ghoulie mask pushing from inside out. Chapped lips split open into sores when he opened his mouth in disbelief. His teeth were black with disease. The tendons on his neck were dark and stringy, like knotted ropes.

"I'll do it!" Brent shouted into the empty air. He slammed a fist down upon the counter and the skin cracked open on that side of his hand. Something dark and unpleasant wriggled just beneath. It made his stomach heave.

"Whatever you want me to do, Skettle," he gasped, broken. For he knew in his gut that the horror of these changes was only the beginning of his real withdrawal. Another day without the cocktail and — well, it was too ghastly to think about.

He wrapped his hurt hand with a washcloth and staggered out of the bathroom. His legs wobbled, unwilling to support his weight. He swayed into the den and jerked back in surprise at the firefly cigarette zigzagging through the dark air. The statue released a stream of white smoke and turned its head in greeting.

Brent almost fell to his knees. "Skettle. Thank god."

"And not a moment too soon," the man chuckled. "Withdrawal, so I've been told, can be quite painful. Worse, even, than the initial change."

"You bastard."

"First it's 'Thank god' — now, 'You bastard'? Which is it? For I can leave just as easily as I arrived, my friend—"

"No!" Brent sturdied himself. He could not let this man see how much he was despised. His head felt weighted by the chains of his entrapment. "Stay. Please. I'll do as you want."

Skettle cocked his head. "What was that?"

"I said, I'll do what you want."

The statue eased back into the rocking chair. "That's a wise choice, Brent. A very wise choice. You can see for yourself what happens when you forgo the benefits of the drug, and believe me, what you've experienced is, to borrow that old cliche, just the tip of the iceberg." He took another drag from his cigarette. "But you see, I still find myself in a bind."

Brent waited. Just sitting in Skettle's presence again had brought fresh waves of craving for the drug. The tidal waves rolled over him. Colored lights seemed to flash before his eyes.

"In your condition you'd say just about anything for another dose of the elixir. Promise me the moon, if that would help."

"No! Honest!" But of course it was true.

Skettle shrugged. "So I think to myself, how can I judge his loyalty? Granted, he's been an efficient worker, and is still good with dealing with the outside world. Many of my friends in the warehouse have lost that ability, you see. Only a select few, like yourself, manage to keep a hand in both worlds. Do you understand what I'm saying?"

Brent nodded. A new pain attacked his gut, doubling him over with cramps. Sweat dripped from his brow.

"So you will be willing to help supply us with that most important ingredient?"

"Yes." He hated himself at that moment almost as much as he hated Skettle.

"And if I say, we need this person or that person, you'll do it out of loyalty and appreciation, no questions asked?"

"Yes! Yes!" he exploded. "What do I have to do, sign it in blood?"

"My dear boy, we've already taken care of that little formality."

A cold hand squeezed Brent's intestines. "What are you talking about?"

"Surely you haven't forgotten the end of our first meeting?"

"What?" And then the memory was in front of him, Skettle gripping his hand, fingernails digging into the soft pad of his palm to draw blood. The expensive handkerchief, dabbing up three drops of blood before being refolded and tucked back into an inside vest pocket.

"Just — who are you, Skettle?"

The man took a final drag of his cigarette. He glanced around for an ashtray, saw none, and casually ground the cigarette out between two gloved fingers. He tossed the butt into a potted plant. Brent watched in mute surprise, and when Skettle saw him looking, he smiled and said, "I'm just a chemist who cut a few deals of my own."

There was a pause. Brent wanted time, time to access what Skettle's words truly meant. He thought of the well that had been his illness, containing him on all sides, and then he thought of this new hole he kept digging for himself, deeper, nastier, and more horrible than anything he could ever have imagined. Now he understood all too clearly John's melancholy on their first night's drive to the warehouse.

"Well," Skettle said. He steepled his fingers. "Let's get back to the subject. You say you'll be our local recruiter, and I have to decide whether to trust you or not. Oh, I don't think you'll run away, or anything so melodramatic. Even if you survived the withering up — and that's exactly what happens, without the drug — you'd be an outcast, shunned by all who come in contact with you. No; we have to devise a way that satisfies both our needs."

"I said I'd do it."

Skettle nodded. "So you did." He reached into his vest pocket and produced a photograph. "After I leave tonight, someone will bring you two days' worth of the cocktail. Two days. That's how long you have to bring the transport to the warehouse."

"Fine," Brent said, head bobbing, willing to say, to do, anything, knowing he was minutes from his next batch of the drug. He'd sort this all out later. But one question nagged at him. "Who am I looking for? And how do I find him?"

"Oh, I don't think you need worry about that." Skettle grinned a barracuda grin, all teeth. "No, I don't believe you'll have any trouble at all." He handed him the Polaroid snapshot.

Brent's vision blurred. He blinked to make it go away, but the photograph remained stubborn, unchangeable. A pain stabbed him in his chest.

His nephew Clayton had never looked more adorable, sitting proudly in his red wagon in his driveway, waving to Mary Ann.

PART FIVE

To what depths, desperation

1

The Tiny Tots Preschool playground was like an empty snapshot waiting to be filled. Riderless swings creaked in rusty anticipation. Teeter-totters stood at crazy right angles. One by one cars pulled up in front of the school, emergency flashers blinking. A virtual parade of working-class Volvos, Chevys, Hondas, all with baby seats strapped to the backseats and Bart Simpsons and Garfields stuck in silly postures to the rear windows. Several of the mothers got out of their cars and chatted with each other while they waited in the chilly noontime air.

Brent did not get out to chat. He'd been parked in this spot across from the school for over an hour, perched inside the station wagon they'd lent him when Acne Andy brought his doses of the cocktail. His eyes were shaded by the blackest pair of sunglasses he owned, and still his eyes ached. Even though the spring sky was a delicate blue laced with high clouds, the sunlight seemed harsh, glaring into his eyes like a giant cosmic lamp trained onto his face.

He felt like a pervert. He knew he certainly looked the part. He was dressed in black jeans and dark shoes with rugged soles for running. His long-sleeve black shirt was buttoned at the wrists, to better protect his arms. They were still healing, even after last night's restorative dose of the cocktail. Hopefully tomorrow's final dose would flesh out the deep ruts in his arms, neck, and sides of his face. On the seat beside him was an old maroon parka. One of its pockets contained two Snickers bars.

The other held a bottle of chloroform and a red handkerchief.

Shouldn't be long now, and that was a relief. He felt dark and suspiciously out of place with all these mothers around. The Country Squire was probably not such a great idea either. With its custard yellow paint and fake wood panels, it would be easily remembered, a target for speculation. Oh well. Perhaps he was making too much out of this. From the bits and pieces of conversation floating to him through the open window, these mothers were concerned with new hairdos, sexless husbands, and potty training. No one had turned to stare at his car. No one had singled him out. Yet.

As if on cue he glanced down the tree-lined street and saw his sister approach. Mary Ann wore a flower-print maternity dress, her middle bulging out as though she had hidden a cantaloupe beneath the dress. Another month and she would really show. Her long, mousy brown hair was tugged back from her face into a ponytail, held by a rubber band. Someone should tell her she is much too old for ponytails, he thought. But that was his sister, blind to what was obvious. Despite a certain weariness due to her walk to the preschool, her face was animated by that special glow known only to pregnant women.

Brent ground his teeth. If only she had not been so afraid of his illness. If only he had not felt so abandoned, perhaps he would not be faced with this predicament. If only, if only...

A school bell shattered the noontime stillness. Immediately mothers ground out unfinished cigarettes and faced the swinging doors that perched at the top of the main stairway. From inside the building came a rumble of spontaneous voices and activity. A matronly woman swung open and latched the doors. A spray of confetti blew out, little boys and girls in red and blue and green and yellow tumbling all over themselves in their glee to escape.

Brent sat up straight, his pulse quickening. He searched the swarm of schoolkids. Their cries were like rainbow flags thrown into the sky, joyous and wonderful to behold, an instant reminder from his own past of what it had felt like to hear that last school bell of the day.

Clayton came spilling out with the others, a Forty-Niners cap on his head. He had on a red windbreaker, blue jeans, and spanking white tennis shoes, which were obviously brand-new.

He spotted his mother and ran to her for a hug. He talked to her with animated gestures, something about pictures they had hand-painted that were now hung on the classroom's walls.

Brent watched, his delight melting into a waxy ball of bile wedged in the back of his throat. He could not step out of the car, could not throw his arms open wide and shout his nephew's name, and that inability caused him to writhe with frustration. At least he'd learned the obvious, that Mary Ann walked him home from the preschool, and just as surely walked him to the school in the mornings. Too bad. If only there was a moment when Clay was alone, when he could draw the boy close enough to the car to use the chloroform they'd lent him—

Like a steel trap his mind shut down, refusing to take the scenario any further. He was sick to his stomach with a queasiness that had not left him ever since his confrontation with Skettle last night. He had to do what he had to do. Period.

He started the engine, and as discreetly as possible trailed them back to Mary Ann's house. He had hoped that Clay was big enough to walk home alone from school. It would have made everything so much easier. Now he had to set another plan into motion, a plan that was hazy and ill-defined, and needed quite a bit of good luck to succeed. He reached into the glove compartment, took out a bottle of Advils, and dry-swallowed a couple of pills. The pain was coming back, his tortured skin trying to reassemble itself without the benefit of another dose of the elixir.

One bit of luck was with him: finding a parking space across the street from the house. After Mary Ann and Clayton went inside, he squeezed the station wagon into the space and killed the engine. He kept his thoughts trained on as little as possible.

A wind had picked up, blowing in off the Pacific. A curtain of dense fog was erasing the blue afternoon, transforming it into the cold steely hues of twilight. The front door opened, and Clay popped out. He squatted on the front steps, reached into his windbreaker, and began to play with several small rubber dinosaurs.

Now? he thought. *Should I take the chance...?*

Mary Ann came outside. She struggled into a sweater. She stood for a moment, hand absently touching the small of her throat, as she scanned the street. Brent shrank into the front seat.

He recognized that dour, disapproving set of eyes and mouth, an expression that had been aimed at him and his lifestyle many times throughout the years. She was looking for trouble, looking to reassure her motherly instinct that all was well.

Oh honey, Brent thought. *If you only knew...*

His sister's dander was certainly up. Call it instinct. Luck. Premonition. She bent low, as low as she could in her present condition, and spoke to Clay. He caught a bit of it, something about playing on the swing set out in the backyard until lunch was ready. Clay dutifully nodded and clomped into the house. Mary Ann got to her feet with a grunt. She was still scanning the street, still disturbed in such a way that knitted her eyebrows and made lines on her otherwise smooth face.

Brent wondered half-jokingly if his sister could smell him. He raised his face for another quick glance at their door and felt his silly grin swiped from his face.

She was staring at him. No: staring at the station wagon. Staring because she had never seen it before in their quiet neighborhood, could not pin it down as one of their neighbor's cars, so why was it parked across the street from her house?

Brent cursed his luck. His scheme, which he hadn't really thought all the way through, was rapidly unraveling. If he wasn't careful he'd have to do something to his sister ... He waited in his uncomfortable half crouch until Mary Ann gave up her post and went back inside. She might try to peek through the curtains in the front room, so he had to hurry. Slipping into his parka he scooted out of the car and dashed across the street. He angled for the narrow alleyway separating his sister's house from her neighbors. He could still be seen from the street, if someone walked by, and that bothered him. Then again, who walked sidewalks in this day and age of cars? Who besides his pregnant sister, that is. Still, the tight space between the two houses comforted him. The open sky had made him feel too exposed.

Clinging to the wall, Brent inched toward the backyard. He could hear the steady back-and-forth creak of a swing, and with that sound, ever so softly, Clayton singsonging a nursery rhyme. Brent pulled the plastic bottle of chloroform and the red handkerchief from his coat pocket. His plan was simple. Get Clay over to the corner of the house. Give him a big hug, as though his presence was a huge surprise that was their own little secret. And then press the chloroform-soaked hanky into the boy's face before Clay got a whiff of the new and improved Uncle Brent.

He peeked around the corner of the house. The swing squeaked energetically. Clay was aiming for the sky, feet pumping with a determined rhythm. In a toneless voice he grunted out between pumps:

"I'm a Rocket Man, off to the moon,
Catch me if you can, varoom, varoom!"

Something tugged at Brent's heart. It came from deep inside, from a place he had wrapped with heavy gauze for protection, a place he had thought under lock and key. He pushed it back down, no room for this, not when his own life counted on success. So he filled his lungs with air and in a stage whisper called out, "Clay!"

His nephew didn't hear him.

"Rocket Man," called Brent. "Come'ere."

The swing slowed. "Mom?"

Brent reached into his other pocket and took out a Snickers bar. He tossed it into the backyard without looking.

Creak, creak from the swing. Then, silence.

Come on, Clay. Doesn't that Snickers look yummy? Why don't you climb off that swing and find out where it came from. I've got another one in my pocket. You can have that one too, if you just come close enough to your old Uncle Brent...

Cautiously: "Mommy? Is that you?"

Brent sucked in a breath. The swing quieted its toneless song. Sneakers scraped against the dirt. He heard Clay slide off the swing. He was desperate to see him, to peek around the corner, but he waited. Get the boy close. Listen: here it came, the soft crinkle of waxy paper as Clayton retrieved the candy bar from the grass and held it in his hands. Brent's legs ached from his crouch, and his anticipation. He dug the other Snickers out of his pocket and tossed it a few feet away. He readied the bottle of chloroform.

There was a sharp intake of breath from his nephew. A whispery, I'm-not-afraid defiance: "I'm a Rocket Man off to the moon, varoom! Varoom!"

Come on, Clay. I know you love Snickers as much as me. Let that curiosity get the best of you...

The back door opened. "Clay? Lunchtime."

"Mommy, look! Candy bars. Just like Uncle Brent used to bring me."

"Now you know the rules, honey. No candy or dessert until after you eat. Where'd you get them, anyway?"

"I found them."

"Oh, Clay. What am I going to do with you?"

"It's true, Mommy. Look. There's another one on the ground."

An electric shock. Brent scrambled to his feet, out of his crouch. Twisted the cap back onto the bottle of chloroform. Nosy Mary Ann was going to peer around the house at any moment, and here he stood. Shit. He turned and fled, hugging the wall like a spider racing along its web. He glanced beyond the alleyway to the street—

—and blinked in disbelief at the patrol car gliding by. Brent froze to the spot, speared by panic. His head swiveled in all directions. This was his sister's doing. She'd had her suspicions aroused, damn her. And if she caught him between her house...

On impulse he pocketed the bottle and marched out of the alleyway and into the front yard. One of the policemen glanced his way, and Brent waved a casual hello. He spotted a rolled-up newspaper on Mary Ann's sidewalk — one of those annoying weekly papers that no one ever reads — and picked it up, shaking his head as if to say, Look at what litters up my beautiful home.

The policeman conferred with the driver. The patrol car slowed to a crawl.

Brent moved down the sidewalk with a brisk gait. A line of sweat was stinging one eye, but he ignored it and concentrated on making a happy face. He whistled as he walked. He strode toward the station wagon, and as he stood by the driver's side, turning the key, he gave the police a thumbs-up gesture of appreciation for their surveillance.

It worked. A crumb of good luck tossed his way, at long last. The patrol car continued down the quiet street. Brent adjusted his sunglasses and slipped into the driver's seat. As he pulled out of the space he caught movement out of the corner of his eye. His sister swept down the sidewalk, concerned and overwrought in her pink, button-down sweater. Brent slumped in his seat and fought the urge to floor the gas pedal.

Mary Ann stumbled toward the edge of her yard, watching the car disappear down the street. Brent almost expected her to wave an angry fist in his direction. But the big question would have to remain unanswered: had she recognized him?

2

Stupid. Stupid, and scared witless. He'd blown that one sky-high, hadn't he? Kidnapping was just not in his blood.

And then Brent glanced at the clock in his kitchen, at the sweep of hands across its face as minutes and hours ticked by, and he felt the rough weave of the noose settle around his neck, pulled ever tighter. What in hell was he going to do?

He threw his hands across his face, and sighed with a profound sadness. He could end this, all the agony and under-handedness, if he screwed up enough courage to do himself in. Surely it couldn't hurt any worse than the torment of his withdrawal from the cocktail.

Then he thought of Skettle's powdered face and barracuda grin, lips so red they looked blood-swollen. Skettle would never, ever, let him get away scot-free. Even if he managed to take his own life, what would stop Skettle and his gang from kidnapping Clayton in revenge? Especially if he stiffed them from their prize ingredient.

So, back to the equation and inescapable truth: either he killed himself, or he sacrificed his nephew to the greater good of the cocktail. Two deaths, or one. All exits closed. He thought he might stay like this forever, hands burying his face, unable to move.

And he might have, except for the sudden noise from beneath the kitchen floor. He yanked his hands away and listened in stunned disbelief.

Someone was underneath the kitchen, in the tiny basement he used for storing junk and firewood.

A raccoon. Maybe. It had happened before. Or another neighborhood cat. Except that this noise seemed deliberate, enticing, without fully giving itself away. Brent's hands tingled. He flushed hot. Who was it this time? Which one of Skettle's henchmen had come to settle the score? Or was it the ghost of Captain Kirk, with a skillet of his own held snugly in his fat hand?

A new sound, this one suspiciously like one of his lawn chairs being dragged across the cold cement floor. If ever he needed confirmation that what was downstairs was human, this was it.

He stood up from the table. Déjà vu washed over him. When was this ever going to end? He walked over to the silverware drawer and pulled it open. Not like the last time with Captain Kirk would he be caught defenseless. He dug around in the drawer and settled upon the seven-inch chef's knife with the sturdy wooden handle. As quietly as possible he slipped through the back door onto his deck. Twilight painted the sky in hues of eggplant. A few hardy stars winked back. He debated getting a flashlight but didn't want to go back into the house. Besides, in the dark, his eyes were as sharp as a cat's, perhaps giving him an advantage over his intruder.

The tall pine trees at the edge of his yard rustled in the evening breeze. As he crept down the steps of his deck into the yard, a funny thought struck him. He was falling right into horror movie cliche number three: stupid bimbo with knife in hand goes to check out creepy noise in basement. *Hasta la vista*, baby.

He went around the corner of his deck, and looked. One of the two doors that led to the tiny basement beneath his kitchen was cracked open. A strange calm settled his racing heart. After all, if the big bad monster in the basement gobbled him up, he would at least escape his present predicament.

He crept stealthily forward. Inched his body next to the hinged door. With a fluid motion that surprised even himself, he reached in and located the light switch on the inside wall. The explosion of white light startled him almost as much as it startled the figure sitting in the lawn chair in the center of the room.

The man rose uncertainly to his feet, his chocolate hair brushing the low, cobwebbed ceiling. He extended his hands, palms open in supplication.

Rage exploded through Brent. He raised the knife. "What the hell are *you* doing here?" he hissed.

His visitor's expression, and stance, said it all. Still, he implored Brent with his gaze, and mouthed two words: *Help me.*

"Forget it. I can't even stand the sight of you, after what you made me do."

The man reached into his shirt pocket. Brent pointed his knife, wary. Out came a small notepad and pen. He flipped open the cover and quickly scribbled a few words. Tore off the page, and stepped forward, arm extended.

Brent took the note.

I can't do it anymore. They'll kill me if I try to stop. Help me.

Brent's anger deflated. The knife lowered to his side. They were both pawns, after all.

"Yes," he said to John. "We'll help each other."

3

In the candle-lit cold of the basement, they talked. John was afraid to go upstairs, afraid of discovery.

"But why, John? As far as any of them know, we're friends, right?"

John's hand moved across the page.

Haven't you noticed? They want us separated. Untrusting. And silent.

"Is that why they ... hurt you? Because of that little information you gave me on the way to my first transport job?"

They were frightened of me. I knew too much.

"Like what?"

Right away Skettle had decided I was the perfect candidate for approaching kids. I was appalled. But by that time, hooked to the drug.

Brent took a bite of sandwich. He'd brought down cold cuts and bread for them to eat. "So what happened?"

I threatened to expose them. It's big — bigger than any of us dreamed.

"What do you mean?"

People pay top dollar for the drug. Politicians. Performers. Athletes. Anyone with big bucks who wants to keep their illness a secret. No way could we afford it. So we're their worker ants. Not to mention guinea pigs.

Brent struggled to swallow. "What are you saying?"

You saw those men — zombies — in the factory.

"Yes."

John flipped to a clean page.

They were the first. Warped up their brains something fierce. Impurities in the drug, too much, too little — who knows? It's unpredictable stuff.

Brent nodded. "Yeah. Skettle said something about that. Acted like it was a 'minor' problem, all this business about light sensitivity, or going nuts. Or the smell."

Look at Squarejaw. One day he's in charge. The next, carted off, never to be seen again. Probably ended up in the cocktail.

"Oh please! Don't say it. Don't even think it."

They have to dispose of bodies somewhere.

"Enough! I can't take this anymore, especially while we're eating."

John nodded his head in agreement. He folded some ham and cheese onto a piece of bread and wolfed down half of it in three bites. Then he set it aside and wrote into his notebook.

Let's run away. Take our chances.

Brent frowned with dismay. "John, they want my nephew. Clayton. Skettle's way of enforcing my loyalty to him. I tried to kidnap him today, but I screwed up. I guess my heart isn't really in it. But what am I going to do? I have one more day. Just one. I know they'll steal Clay, if we try to run away. And I seriously doubt I can survive without the cocktail."

Is it as painful as they say? Without it?

"Worse than the initial change. Worse than anything I've ever gone through. We'd be better off shooting ourselves in the head." John absorbed this bit of news while finishing his sandwich. Brent waved a hand. "The point is, whether we ran away or killed ourselves, Skettle would take out his revenge by kidnapping Clay and using him. It'd be too much of a slap in the face for him to ignore. I won't let him kill my nephew. I won't. Why are you looking at me like that?"

Sorry. It's just — this is the only time I've ever seen you concerned about someone other than yourself. I rather like it.

He deserved a smart-alecky reply to that one, but this truth cut too close to the bone. Instead, he found his lips mouthing words he had never expected to ask. "Why did we stop seeing each other, John?"

The pen scratched against paper.

Because we were both stuck-up pricks too interested in finding the next pretty face who'd adore us.

That brought unexpected smiles to their lips. They sat in easy silence, the candle between them. John reached up and slid off his sunglasses, blinking against the glare of candlelight. Brent removed his own glasses. His hand was shaking. It shook even more when his friend reached over and lay his palm across Brent's hand. Above them, the house creaked in the wind. John's eyes held steady on Brent's face. His palm upon Brent's skin was shockingly hot.

How had they met? Brent tried to remember. Was it at one of the big dance parties? In a bar? On the street? He could recall a few nights of lovemaking, with brunch the next morning at one of the Castro breakfast nooks so that everyone could see them together. There had been a fight, a spat, really, that served its purpose. Any excuse to stop seeing each other after three or four dates. After all, it was the norm, back then. So what was this? Just guilt and shame weaving them together, or something bigger, better? Out of their desperation to outwit their illness, they had fallen prey to the worst kind of blackmail and horror. Maybe they no longer deserved to be saved, after what they had done.

John seemed to read Brent's thoughts. He scribbled into his notebook.

We deserve a chance to make amends. There has to be a way.

Brent was about to shake his head *no, it's too late,* when the answer suddenly fell into his lap, full blown.

John tugged on his arm, inquiring.

"How brave are you?" Brent asked.

4

Mary Ann stepped out of her front door and locked it at exactly 11:45 a.m. Her pink button-down sweater was no match for the cold and drizzly fog, which made the day seem to hover below the brink of true dawn. She glanced at the sky and squirmed with indecision. A hand on the doorknob, key poised. But a look at her wristwatch said it all. She moved away from the door, arms hugging her belly, and down the sidewalk she hurried. She did not see the two of them sitting there in John's Honda.

"What did I tell you?" Brent said. "Like clockwork, my sister."

John answered with a nod. He was in the driver's seat, and would wait for his turn in this play of events.

Brent drew a deep breath to settle his nerves. "Hope I'm ready for this." He was back in his pervert's outfit again, basic burglar black. No jacket. In his back pocket, a ski mask, should he need it.

John gave him a thumbs-up and then patted his thigh.

"Thanks. Wish me luck." Brent slipped out of the front seat. He repositioned the sunglasses on his nose. The fog was like cold smoke, giving off an immediate chill. It had chased everyone indoors — everyone, except for his stubborn sister. She'd locked the front door, so that entrance was useless to him. On the off chance a neighbor might peer out a window and see him, he walked with purpose back to the side of the house where he'd stood the day before. He had about ten to fifteen minutes, tops.

The swing set twisted in the breeze. Brent hurried up three brick steps to the back door. Tried the knob. Damn: locked. His sister was no fool, and only fools accidentally left doors unlocked. He was going to have to break a window, just as he'd feared. No one said this would be easy.

He hunted for a palm-sized rock in the flower beds that extended out two feet from the house in both directions. His search took him back around the corner. Here was a good chunk of stone, heavy to the hand and pyramid-shaped with a pointed sharp end. He yanked out a handkerchief from his front left pocket and wrapped the stone with it. He turned to go back to the rear side of the house when he realized the window he was staring into was Clay's bedroom. If it were a snake, it would have bitten him.

On impulse he touched the windowsill. Only fools leave their back door unlocked, but a window was an entirely different matter. It could happen to anyone. He pushed. Nothing. He pushed again. With a juddering shriek the window rolled up six inches. He forced it all the way up, and then, feeling old and uncoordinated, heaved himself through the window, landing onto Clayton's Snoopy bedspread.

The silence in the room pressed against him. His nerves were a siren scream in his ears. Why did it feel so odd to invade another person's room when they weren't there? Like some primordial trespass signal firing off inside his brain. *Danger, Will Robinson!*

He felt even worse as he moved swiftly through the quiet gloom to the kitchen. It seemed as if eyes were everywhere, watching him. The yellow clock on the wall whirred its disapproval at his presence. The refrigerator was letting out a steady, protesting hum. Brent knocked it with his fist, he wasn't sure why, and obediently the refrigerator shut up. Rubbing his hand, he glanced at the array of magnets and pictures scattered across its surface. Here was Clayton in last Halloween's pirate's outfit, displaying his plastic pumpkin full of goodies. Ouch. Clay on the swing set, being pushed by his dad. Mary Ann stretched out in a lawn chair, trying to hide her face with a Danielle Steel paperback. She and Steven, dressed for a formal dance.

No Uncle Brent. There used to be, though. He remembered. A picture of Clay as a baby, held in his arms. He had his own copy at home. But not here. Not anymore. Mary Ann had neatly excised him out of their humble existence. Damn her.

He stoked this indignation, but not too much. He would use it, but not allow this fire to destroy his purpose through carelessness. Besides, he had to hurry.

There was a cold pot on the stove. Brent lifted its lid. Homemade chicken soup. The pot had been taken out of the refrigerator in preparation for lunch. Frugal Mary Ann: she wasted nothing, except her love for her brother. There were possibilities with the soup, but first a check inside the fridge. Aha! Here was a quart-sized container of milk. He hefted it, checking its weight. Too full. He'd have to pour some of the milk out, just to be on the safe side.

He brought the carton over to the sink. A drawing on one side caught his attention. He'd seen pictures like it before, seen so many in fact that the images seemed composites of hundreds of faces. This one was of a little boy, a black tyke about seven years old with a chipped front tooth. The caption screamed: "Have You Seen This Child?"

No, Brent thought. But I may have had a taste of him, just last night.

Shuddering from his own imagery, he popped open the spout and poured a good portion of the milk down the drain. He ran water and splashed it around the sink until all evidence of the milk was gone. Satisfied, Brent reached into his shirt pocket and removed the ziplock baggie he had stuffed there. Its contents looked like detergent, a coarsely ground white powder with flecks of yellow and blue — "cleaning crystals!" he heard a made-up announcer bellow.

He opened the baggie. He and John had spent the better part of an hour last night grinding this up with a mortar and pestle. His final escape plan from another world, his jelly bean soup of painkillers and sleeping pills. Working with extreme care, he took a spoon from a drawer and added two teaspoons of the powder into the carton of milk. Now came the moment of truth: how much was too much? What if they didn't drink the milk? He'd hate himself if he inadvertently harmed his sister's unborn baby.

He added half a teaspoon more to the milk and then gave it all a good stir. His glance fell back onto the cold chicken soup. He sprinkled some of the powder across its surface and stirred it in. Hot soup and milk for the both of them; that was his sister's style. The perfect all-American lunch.

From out front there came a quick, one-tap honk from a car. Brent froze. John's signal to him — already? What time was it? He jerked a glance to the clock. Disbelieving. What did they do, run through the foggy streets in a race?

He returned the milk to the refrigerator and closed the door with one smooth motion. Slammed the lid back onto the pot of chicken soup. Where was the spoon he'd used to stir the soup? In the sink? Did it belong there, or on the yellow happy face spoon holder next to the range? Think!

But there was no time to think. Footsteps upon the sidewalk, followed by ringing shouts and giggles. "I beat you, Mommy!" "You sure did, honey! Let's get inside and warm up."

Brent flushed, his face red-hot. Rooted by indecision, he swiveled everywhere at once. He dashed to the back door, tried the handle — which was still locked, naturally, with no key in sight — and spun around once more.

A key in the door. More giggles and shouts.

Brent dove through the kitchen and jumped across the hallway just as the front door swung open. Clayton spilled inside, followed by his mother. Brent rant into his nephew's bedroom and spied the window he'd left open. Was there enough time to slide back through undetected, should Clay pop into the room?

"Hang up your jacket, Clay," Mary Ann trilled. "I'll have lunch ready in a jiffy."

Brent climbed onto the bed. Cold air was gusting into the room. Behind him, he heard his nephew thundering toward his bedroom. No time to shimmy through that window. He forced the window shut and made a fast inventory of hiding places. No to the closet, since Clay was on a mission to hang his jacket there. It would have to be the bed, that most classic cliche of them all.

He dropped to his knees and pushed himself feetfirst underneath the bed. The space was low, ridiculously tight. The back of his shirt caught on the springs. He winnowed himself in right as the bedroom door banged open and Clay popped inside.

Little sneakered feet danced around the carpeted floor. Clay plopped down hard onto the floor and struggled to take off his tennis shoes. Brent held his breath. If his nephew glanced toward the bed, he was a dead duck. This wasn't in his plans. He was supposed to have gotten out of the house, and waited with John out in the car for the tranquilizers to knock his sister and Clayton into beddy-bye land. Then he could simply walk back through the unlocked front door and get on with his plan.

Clay stopped fiddling with his shoes. He kicked off the last sneaker. His nose crinkled with that rabbit twitch Brent had come to recognize, and he screwed up his face. "Mom!" he suddenly shouted. "My room smells bad."

"Of that I have no doubt," Mary Ann muttered as she walked down the hall and through the doorway.

Brent flattened himself into the carpet, willing himself to be invisible.

"Honey, I asked you to take off your coat, not your shoes," she admonished. "Now hup two. Lunch is almost ready."

"Don't you smell it?" Clay asked.

"Smell what?" But then her whole stance changed, a rigidity replacing her casual attitude. "Let me see the bottoms of your shoes. You must have stepped in some dog doo-doo."

Clay obediently held up his sneakers for her inspection.

"Nothing there. What's that on your bedspread? You haven't been standing on your bed in your shoes, have you?"

"No, Mommy."

Mary Ann marched toward the bed. Brent cringed. He could reach out and grasp her ankle, she was that close. "Then where did this mud come from?"

"I don't know," Clay answered in a small voice. He sounded close to tears, punished for something he couldn't understand.

A sigh. "Honestly, honey, you keep me coming and going. Now hang up your coat and come into the kitchen. I'm heating up that soup you liked."

"'Kay."

"We'll figure out that nasty old smell right after lunch."

She left the bedroom. Brent relaxed some of the tension throbbing through his shoulders. Yes, he thought. Have your lunch.

He stayed where he was even after Clay finally hung up his coat and left the room. The boy had left the door open, and to Brent's surprise he could hear the two of them talking in the kitchen.

"Want a glass of milk, honey?"

"No thanks."

"Mommy's having some. It sure will taste good with the soup. Gee, that's funny. I just bought this fresh, but there isn't much left. Maybe Daddy had an extra glass at breakfast. Here we go."

Brent listened to the scrape of plates against the tabletop. Chairs scooted into place. A quick prayer of thanks, from Mary Ann. And then a sound that was music to his ears: them digging in, mmm-umm, isn't this good.

He could leave the house now, if he was very quiet. Fill John in on how their plan was working, and wait out in the car. He started to slide out from under Clay's bed.

"Honey, let me ask you one more time. Are you sure you didn't see who tossed you those candy bars yesterday?"

"Uh-uh. Can I have one, after lunch?"

"I don't think that's a good idea. We should never eat things when we don't know where they came from."

"Uncle Brent used to bring me Snickers."

"Uncle Brent. Yes."

"Can I see him again?"

"Uncle Brent is very sick, Clay. He's been staying away because he doesn't want to accidentally give us what he's got."

In the bedroom, Brent squirmed with indignation. *Liar.*

"I've been making big tall wishes. He's going to get better, and come see me."

"That's nice, dear. Now listen to me. This is important. Have you seen anyone suspicious around your school?"

"What's that?"

"Someone who hangs around like they have something to do when there's no reason for them to be there in the first place. Have you seen anyone like that?"

"No."

"If you do, promise you'll tell me about it?"

"Uh-huh."

"My. That was a pretty big yawn. I know a boy who's ready for nap time. Come to think of it, I could use one myself."

If Brent had needed a signal, this was it. He couldn't stay underneath the bed, not when they'd be coming back. He scooted free, went to the closet, and made room for himself by pushing clothes to one side. He left the door slightly ajar.

"Mommy, I don't feel so good."

"You aren't running a fever. But actually, I feel a little dizzy too. Did the milk taste strange to you? Kind of bitter? According to the date, it's still perfectly good."

"My tummy hurts."

A scoot of chair. "Let's get some Pepto into you and off to bed for nap-nap."

While they were in the bathroom, new fears stole into Brent's heart. He'd given them too much. He was going to harm his sister's unborn baby. They were both going to toss their cookies. Mary Ann would call 911. Skettle was about to find out he'd failed. Shit.

Mother and son returned to the bedroom. Clay wanted to stay in his clothes and lay on top of his sheets and blankets.

"Wouldn't you be more comfortable underneath the blankets?" Mary Ann persisted. The boy shook his head. "Tell you what. I've got an afghan in the closet. Why don't we pull that out in case you get cold later on." She started for the closet.

Brent shrank into the shadows. He whipped on the ski mask he'd stuffed into his back pocket.

The door swung partway open. Daylight speared half the closet, falling onto shirts and pants. She was so close, his sister. He could see a film of perspiration on her forehead and upper lip. Her complexion was ashy, terrible. The tranqs were doing their dirty deeds. She stretched for the highest shelf, where a blue-and-gold afghan rested tantalizingly out of reach. Couldn't reach. She stood on tiptoes and tried again. Suddenly her jaw went slack. Her eyes seemed to roll back into her forehead, and she started to stumble.

"What's wrong, Mommy?"

She wiped her forehead with the back of a hand. "Looks like I need to lie down too. How about you just climb under the covers if you get chilly, all right?"

"'Kay."

Brent's legs were jelly doughnuts. His breath came out in ragged silent bursts. Jeez, that was close. The rack of clothes pressed against him suddenly. It was too hot, confined in this closet. And this was going to go on and on, this exquisite torture, until mother and son fell asleep.

Mary Ann kissed Clayton and walked out. Off to her bedroom, most likely. He waited. And Clay? He flopped around on his Snoopy bedspread for several minutes. Curled up on his stomach. His limbs twitched as sleep overcame him.

Brent slipped out of the closet. His face, in the ski mask, was sweating. The air outside the closet was better, cooler. He started toward the bed. He couldn't help pausing to soak up the unexpected pleasure of watching his nephew sleep. So fast he was growing. A dozen little changes, subtle new maturities in the strength of his face, the size of his hands, the disappearing baby fat. This boy who made big wishes for his Uncle Brent to get better so he'd come see him.

This boy, who may yet wind up being the main ingredient in the latest batch of cocktail, if his scheme failed.

Brent pulled out the note he and John had typed up that very morning. He placed it onto Clay's desk, and couldn't resist reading it one more time.

There are people who want him dead. If you don't call the police or the media, he'll be back, soon. He's in good hands.

It would confuse her. Hell, it was going to terrify her, no way around that. This was the real gamble, how she and Steven were going to react. It could make or break everything.

He went over to the bed, and crouched low. He hadn't held a child — shoot, he hadn't held *any*one — in a long time, except for that poor little girl with the animals on her pajamas. Clayton was heavier, longer than he'd remembered, but he scooped him into his arms with a natural grace that pleased him greatly. His nephew burrowed his head against Brent's neck and curled an arm around his shoulders. He stooped to pick up the boy's tennis shoes.

"Daddy?" He tried to stir.

"Shh," Brent whispered. "Go back to sleep." He carried him down the hall and moved swiftly toward the front door. John should be ready for them, double-parked, engine running. He'd almost made it to the front door when the gasp from the living room stopped him cold.

"What — what are you doing!"

Brent turned. His sister was clawing herself into a sitting position on the couch. Shit. She was supposed to have gone into her bedroom, not stop off at the couch. He stood still, her son in his arms. His mouth instantly dried up with fright. His face sweated inside his ski mask.

"Oh god, no!" Mary Ann shrieked. "Don't take my baby!" She tried to sit all the way up, but the tranquilizers and her bulging middle got in the way. She flopped around, arms waving, her stunned face the epitome of hysteria. Tears cascaded from her eyes. "Please! Don't!"

But they were gone before she'd even managed to rise from the couch and rush to the front door.

5

"Clay, do you remember how you used to say you'd make a big tall wish for me to get better?"

"Uh-huh."

"Well, I am. Much better."

"Why do you smell so bad?"

"Because I have to take this really yucky medicine, and it makes me smell funky."

"Where's Mommy and Daddy?"

"They aren't here right now. See, I made a wish of my own, for you to come see me. And here you are! We'll have lots of fun today, wait and see. And then tonight, you and I will make one more wish."

"For what?"

"For everybody to get exactly what they deserve."

PART SIX

The big tall wish

1

"Did you take care of everything?" asked Brent.

John shrugged and crossed his fingers in a let's-hope-so gesture.

There was a tug on Brent's arm. He glanced down. Clayton sat in the seat between them, his tennis shoes sticking out over the rim of seat. In the yellowish light of a nearby streetlight, his small face was harsh with fright. "Uncle Brent, I don't like this place," he admitted. His voice was brimming with unshed tears.

Brent pulled the boy next to him, and glanced to John for support.

"It's haunted," Clay said with deadpan earnestness. He squirmed against his uncle. "Don't make me go inside. Please, Uncle Brent. I want to go home. I want my mommy and daddy!" His terror had a ferocious appetite, each moment growing bigger and bigger. Tears sprang instantly from his eyes, and he was reduced to inarticulate moans and twitches.

Brent's eyes blurred with his own tears. He glanced out of the car and to the warehouse that sat about fifty feet away across the gravel parking lot. The kid was right. It was a forbidding structure, straight out of childhood nightmares. It was the kind of place that made him think of cobwebs and suffocating dark, of things that slither and burrow and wait for choice morsels of kid-flesh to come skipping their way. With its painted-over windows and unyielding facade, Brent suddenly realized it looked like a giant tombstone. God knew what horrors it conjured up for his nephew.

"Listen to me, Clay," he said. The boy's moans had turned into hiccups. "It *is* a haunted house. There are bad men in there who want to hurt us and maybe even hurt your mommy." Was this too much? Should he be telling him this? He grasped his nephew's chin and turned his head so that they could gaze into each other's eyes. It was so important. He had to be made to understand, even on some rudimentary level. "But if you follow my lead and do exactly as we discussed, we'll all be okay. How's your nose? Are you breathing okay?"

Clay nodded and sniffed noisily. The plugs in his nostrils were holding fast. It was the only way he could stay so close to any of them, without being overpowered by their smell.

"When we go inside, you're going to feel a little like you're underwater. And this pill may make you dizzy, but in a fun way." He held out a yellow Valium in his palm. "You know that spinning-wheel thing you can make go round and round in the playground? This will give you the same feeling, only better. Now it's going to be dark inside, so if you get confused just stay exactly where you are, and either John or I will get you. So here: take this."

"Does it taste bad?"

The boy could be dead within the next half hour, but his only concern was that he not have to put something bad-tasting into his mouth. "No," Brent said with a little smile. "Just wash it down with this Coke." Clay made a face as though he were about to stuff raw lima beans into his mouth, but he took the tranquilizer. Brent watched with apprehension. So much could backfire on them, if they weren't careful. So much depended upon Clay. He knew it was unfair and improper to burden a child with this responsibility, but there was no way around it. It was the only solution he and John had been able to devise. "What do you think: are we ready to do this?"

John held up a hand and pointed to Clay's ears.

"Oh. Right." Brent reached into the glove compartment and removed a small box. He glanced at the instructions. "Just remember," he said to Clay, "if you don't like what you can still hear, hum that Rocket Man song. Okay?"

"'Kay." But he looked so sad and small, eager to do his best for his uncle and afraid of what would happen if he failed. He was trying very hard not to start crying again.

"Tell you what," Brent said. "You made all those big tall wishes for me to get better, and I did. So let's all three of us make a pact right now, like the Three Musketeers." He stuck out a hand. John smiled and added his hand. Clay plopped his hand on top of the others, clearly enjoying this little game.

"For better or worse, let's stay out of a hearse."

Clay puckered his lips at that, obviously not understanding this thing called a hearse, but getting a kick out of their game.

Brent gently applied the wax to Clay's ears. With his nod they were out the car doors, into a spring night pungent with gravel, disinfectant, and a stale coppery smell he recognized as old spilled blood. His grip on his nephew's hand was absolute. They went inside.

2

"What's with the kid?"

Brent tried to push past the guard at the door, who was reluctant to let them enter. "What do you think?" he shot back. He leaned in close to the dull face and black sunglasses. "Dinner," he whispered.

The guard's lips pulled thin with irritation. "Why ain't he in a box?"

"Special orders from the top brass. He wants to meet this one himself." Brent waited. He could tell this one was trying to use what was left of his brain to sniff out a rat. "Come on," he prodded. "It's not like you don't know us."

After a moment the man nodded. He rolled back the heavy metal door. A bluish, black-light phosphorescence spilled onto the ground before the three of them.

Clay's fingers cut into the fleshy pad of Brent's hand. He didn't know a boy that young could have such a fierce grip. The two of them stepped into the cavernous room, John their wary guardian just a few steps behind. The familiar smell hit him, mushroomy and dank, of things that flourish in the dark. Instantly — and against his will — it stirred his craving for the cocktail. He glanced to John and saw the craving mirrored in his eyes. Would they ever be free of it?

At first glance the processing plant bustled with normal activity — if what these worker bee humans did could possibly be called normal. Liquids were poured and tested in clear glass tubes over the blue heat of Bunsen burners. Leaves were being pruned from squat dense plants and herbs. At the far end of this central, long table sat the huge pot containing the cocktail. Steam wafted from its stewlike surface. Brent stood where he was, wanting to give Clayton a chance to adjust his eyes to these bizarre surroundings that were bathed in tones of black light.

And as he stood watching, he became aware of something wholly unexpected: a permeating whiff of anxiety in the air. There were fewer workers than usual hanging about in their blue jumpsuits or white overcoats. They seemed distracted, their movements jerky and uncoordinated. A test tube slipped from a gloved hand and sprayed glass across the floor. Men and women collided with each other as they moved and walked. They looked like giant slugs feasting around potted plants, snipping off choice herbs and leaves, and grinding mixtures into bowls. Their sunglasses added to this decidedly buglike appearance, which was further enhanced by their insectile coldness. Nothing human seemed to remain except for this outer porcelain shell of what passed for man or woman. A clear but fleeting image came to Brent of a beehive under attack. He was about to turn to John and whisper his suspicions when there was a commotion on the stairs leading to Skettle's office.

"What is the meaning of this?" boomed an unmistakable voice.

Skettle stood at the top of the stairs, an imposing statue cut from the dark of his suit coat, Panama hat, and white gloves. He motioned angrily for the three of them to join him in his office, not even bothering to wait and see if they would follow his order. He did an about-face and stormed back into his office.

With Clay digging nails into his hand, Brent lead their troop past the bubbling cauldron at the end of the table and up the flight of stairs. He felt a little like a high school student about to be harangued by the principal. But when he saw Skettle sitting stiffly behind his desk, fingers steepled and clenched just below his face, he no longer found any amusement in their predicament. None at all.

"Shut that door," Skettle snapped. John reached behind and closed the door, but not before Skettle laid into Brent. "You stupid fool. The boy should have been brought in unconscious."

"You wanted my nephew. Here he is." Brent laid a hand on Clay's shoulder.

"Don't jerk my chain. You know how all this works."

"He's been given drugs," said Brent. His voice was very calm. "It's likely he'll pass out at any moment, especially if he keeps standing."

"Then put him in that chair and explain yourself."

Brent maneuvered the boy toward the plush leather chair near the desk. Clay stumbled the short distance, and sat down gratefully. He looked like a ventriloquist's dummy that had been propped up in a chair.

"Uncle Brent, I don't feel so good," Clay whispered.

"It's okay. Just lay back and close your eyes." Brent straightened. "I've come to ask you a favor, Skettle."

The man popped his knuckles, a dull firecracker sound in the gloves. "I'm the one who asks for favors, not the other way around."

"You asked for my nephew, and I've brought him. I'm loyal to the organization."

"That is still a matter of dispute—"

"Let me take him home," Brent said. "His life does not have to end here, tonight. I ask you to spare his life. Let me bring you someone else. If you grant me this wish, I swear you'll never have a more loyal compatriot. John and I — we both swear."

Skettle swiveled his seat. "John. Yes. Been making yourself scarce, haven't you? Secreting about. Crawling around in basements. And not taking your pills. Oh, don't look so surprised."

Brent glanced at John. "Don't you see? We're lonely. We ... draw comfort from each other's company. Maybe we even love each other, a little bit. Or will, given time." He chanced a step toward the desk. "We make a perfect team. It was only with John's help that I was able to snatch Clay. I couldn't do it myself. Why shouldn't we be a team?"

"Because John didn't have the stomach for it, and frankly, I'm not too sure you do either."

"What other choices have you left us?" Brent shrugged. "None, if we want to keep living on the cocktail. And those ...

those worker bees down there are useless for this kind of assignment, you said so yourself. Maybe Acne Andy might work out, but he's too young. He's bound to make a mistake."

"I can always bring in someone else."

"True. But they'll have to go through the change, won't they? Be indoctrinated into the group. Run a few transport missions. Sounds like weeks and weeks of hassle. I don't think you can afford the lost time. I think you need someone right away. John and I offer ourselves. All we ask in exchange is that my nephew's life be spared."

Skettle reached into his suit pocket and shook out a cigarette. His hand trembled as he brought it to his lips. "Can't be done. There isn't time."

"That isn't fair!"

"Oh, calm yourself. No one ever said life — or death — played a fair game. You just have to play out the cards dealt to you."

"Or deal yourself a new hand," Brent muttered.

Skettle pulled the cigarette from his mouth. Tendons in his neck stood out in relief. "Don't threaten me, boy. You haven't got the stuff."

Brent stepped forward and placed both hands on the desk. "And don't *you* forget, Skettle, that the cocktail has a nasty side effect of turning ordinary men into murderers. Who knows what I'm capable of?"

Skettle's jaw clenched. The closely cropped goatee bobbed with his agitation. Brent was sure he was getting the voodoo glare of death, hidden behind opaque sunglasses. A fine trickle of sweat sneaked out of Skettle's sideburn and inched a dark canal down the powdered cheek before disappearing under the rim of neck. In a voice like shaved ice he said, "The answer is no. And if you understand what's good for you, you'll take the boy and dispatch him right away."

Brent felt hands on his shoulders. It was John, pulling him away from the desk, shaking his head as if to say, *We tried our best. Let's get out of here.* But Brent would have none of it. He wrenched free. "Oh, what's the use, any of it."

"We need the boy's blood," Skettle said. He swept the surface of his desk for a lighter and lit his cigarette, wincing at the bright flame. *"You* need the boy's blood. Right away. Tonight."

"Oh yeah? What's the big hurry?"

Brent waited for a reply. Skettle looked suddenly thoughtful, his face more pensive than agitated. "There's been some problems with the transport," he finally admitted between puffs on his cigarette.

Brent and John exchanged a glance. "Why are you telling us this?"

A jet stream of smoke shot out between lips of candy red. "I am proposing a partnership. Me in management, and the two of you in recruitment and processing. We could run this business. I'm sure we could work something out."

"Let me take my nephew home, and it's a done deal."

Skettle's gloved fist hit the desktop. "No! We have to finish the elixir, right away. We need it!" He was shaking. More droplets of sweat sketched paths down his face.

Brent straightened in shock. "My god. You're going through withdrawal."

"That's absurd!" But a tremor seized him. His face and arms bulged with tension, as though he was fighting to contain something under enormous pressure.

Brent was unswayed. He knew all too well the progression of withdrawal from the cocktail. The shakes and sweats were just the beginning. In a shocked voice he choked out, "What the hell has happened?"

Something ugly and mean crossed Skettle's features. "Someone tampered with the previous batch. We had to throw it out yesterday and start fresh, with limited supplies. I think ... I think someone sabotaged some of the plants here. It was all we could do to scrape together a batch large enough for all of us." He ground out the cigarette, taking a vicious thrill in slamming it into the ashtray. "You're lucky I know it wasn't the two of you, or I'd have strung you up the moment you entered the building. So don't you see? My hands are tied. That's a brand-new batch of the elixir down there. The chemical balances bonding all of its ingredients is extremely fragile. The formula is very precise. There simply isn't time for you to fetch someone new." He nodded at Clayton, who had slumped in the chair, fast asleep. "We need the coagulating blood of an innocent."

Just talking about the cocktail was stirring desire. Brent felt a twinge, like the pain of an empty stomach demanding to be fed.

He looked at John. This was not going the way they had hoped. He felt tight, backed into a corner. He knew what had to be done, but that didn't make the doing any easier.

"Okay," Brent said. His voice was hoarse with emotion, barely above a whisper. "But I want my nephew's body back. After John and I finish with him. No usual disposal, not this time. My sister deserves to see the body. To have that ... closure. I'll personally make sure there won't be any way for authorities to trace it back to us. Fair enough?"

The tension gripping Skettle's features eased. "Get on with it."

But the task was easier said than done. Brent turned to John once again, helpless. His bottom lip quivered as he tried to control himself. His friend's eyes were shiny and bright, full of their predicament. Brent walked over to the leather chair and squatted beside his sleeping nephew. The Valium had certainly done the trick. Clay's head had rolled forward, his chin resting upon his chest. The tiniest line of drool had slipped from his mouth and created a damp stain on the boy's shirt. It was so perfectly ordinary that Brent found himself memorizing this moment. This had to be what it felt like, the love and satisfaction of watching your own child sleep. This was as close as he was ever going to get to being a parent.

From behind him, irritably: "I said get on with it."

"Go fuck yourself, Skettle," Brent muttered. He moved closer and reached out his hand to stroke Clay's hair. It was silky smooth, like a precious fabric. He ran the back of his fingers gently across the apple-cheeked face and realized with a sharp ache that this was one of the few times he'd ever touched Clay's face. He scooped his nephew into his arms. The boy was a sack of dead-weight in his arms. But when he pulled him as close as he dared and gave him a bone-crushing hug, Clay began to wiggle.

A tiny fist dug into one eye. "Uncle Brent, did I do good?"

"The best," Brent said. "You're the best. Now go back to sleep."

John had to practically tear Clay from his arms. He gestured for Brent to stay put, that he would take care of this inevitable duty. Skettle watched the proceedings with mounting impatience, his gloved fingers rapping against the top of the desk like muffled drumsticks.

"John?"

His friend turned as he opened the glass door to the office.

"Not a thing should he feel," Brent said. "Got that?"

He stood by the glass wall framing the office and watched John and Clay go down the stairs. Several of the men in white lab coats, whose earlier movements had been jerky and disorganized, swayed into stillness. The thought of them waiting with such obvious anticipation for the shedding of blood caused bile to rise in his throat. He began to pace.

Skettle broke the tension-filled silence. "You know it has to be done."

Brent shook his head. "I — I can't go through with this. I can't. Jesus, Skettle, can't you see this is tearing my guts out! Let me find someone else. I'll hit the homeless shelters. Check the streets. For god's sake let me bring you someone else!"

But the monster in the Panama hat only shook his head, unswayed.

Brent held up his hands. "I'm telling John to stop. This has got to stop!" In a rush he moved toward the office door.

"Take another step," Skettle said in his shaved-ice voice, "and I'll blow your foot off."

Brent looked. There was a pistol in Skettle's hand. Brent knew nothing about guns, had never wanted to learn anything about guns. TV and movies was close enough. He was totally unprepared to find himself staring down the barrel of a loaded weapon. If he thought his sickness had been a deep well with no way out, he was now staring down the granddaddy well of them all. And he hadn't seen it coming. Shit.

"Get away from the door," Skettle ordered.

Brent held his ground. "He's family," he said at last. "Don't you understand?"

"We're your family. Or don't *you* understand that yet? There's no such thing as ever turning back. We are your only solace. Your only home."

"If that's true," Brent snapped, "then you may as well shoot me and get this over with. Any way I turn, I'm still a dead man."

Something happened to Skettle's face. The tension seizing it released its grip. Cherry lips broke open like a wounded gash tearing apart. His body trembled, but not from withdrawal. He was chuckling. Actually chuckling.

"What's so funny?" Brent demanded, stung.

"How aptly you nailed it on the head." The big man's mirth spilled over, the chuckle transforming into a hearty guffaw. "For that is exactly what you are." Now he was laughing, enjoying his private joke at Brent's expense.

Something about the way he said that chilled Brent to the bone. He moved away from the door and ventured deeper into the office. What might or might not be happening down on the main floor was temporarily forgotten. The words did not even want to form in his mouth, but he forced himself to spit them out. "What exactly do you mean by that?"

"A smart boy like you, and you never figured it out?"

"What? What!"

The laughing jag came to an end. The hardness returned to the powdered white face. He gestured at himself, and then to Brent, totally oblivious to the gun still gripped in his gloved hand. "Exactly this. We are all. Dead. Men."

Brent doubled over. He sought the leather chair, and sank into it. For an eternity he was speechless. Brown spots danced before his eyes.

"Oh, relax, would you? It changes nothing."

Brent's eyes narrowed at Skettle. "I came to you for life."

Head and hat bobbed in unison. "Yes. And the cocktail gives it to us, constantly adjusting our bodies in a perpetual state of rejuvenation. However, before it can do us any good, it has a slight temporary side effect. It has to kill us first." This caused another chuckle of amusement. "Oh, don't give me that puppy dog look of surprise. What in the world did you think was happening during your initial change, if not the cocktail pushing life right out of you? We have to sweat and shit out all impurities, all the chemical imbalances imposed by our illness. By the second and third dose the elixir has mixed with our blood and tissues, permanently transforming our bodies. In a way, it acts as a kind of glorified embalming fluid."

Brent buried his face in his hands. That night of agony flashed through his thoughts, of waking up surrounded by the shredded remains of his own skin. *Dead*.

"So don't you see, Brent? We're a breed apart, now. Stronger and more powerful than ever we dared dream."

Brent withdrew his hands and glared at the man behind the desk. "Except that not everyone survives the change, is that it?"

A shrug. "It unbalances some, as I've stated before. Unhinges their minds, even though they can respond to orders and directions, like those simpletons downstairs. There is the matter of the eyes, of course. And the occasional smell of our own bodies decaying before we receive the next dose. A small price, wouldn't you agree?"

Brent stood up. His hands clenched into fists. He trembled with fury.

"I know what you're thinking," Skettle said. "And you're right. A bullet probably won't kill you, if you were given a big enough dose of the cocktail. But I can cripple you in exceedingly nasty ways. Blow off a hand." He aimed the gun. "Or a foot. Maybe even your balls." The barrel aimed squarely at Brent's crotch. "Are you sure you want to live out your days in constant pain, hideously scarred and crippled? If so, be my guest. There's the door."

"You bastard."

"Just looking out for my assets. Believe it or not, one day you'll appreciate my position — and yours."

"I doubt it."

Skettle leaned forward. Sweat dripped from his brow. For an instant the glow surged around his head. It was a sickly, yellowish color, like something bruised. "I conquered this disease," he hissed. "Achieved what no other physician in *the world* has been able to do."

"Yes," Brent smirked. "And paid the price with near blindness, lunacy, and murder. I—"

A startling cry of pain rose like a shot from the warehouse floor. It evaporated into a wet, gargling cough as though someone struggled to breathe through sludge. There was a shocked moment of silence, and then suddenly a spontaneous cheer echoed through the building. Brent rushed to the glass wall of the office and let out a cry. His anguish silenced all of them. He turned on Skettle, his face livid.

The man leaned back into his plush chair. "Now that wasn't so bad, was it? You drugged the boy, didn't you say? Trust me. He never knew what hit him."

Brent bunched his fists. He looked from Skettle down to the warehouse below, back and forth, back and forth. But the fire was leaving him, now that it was too late. His shoulders slumped in defeat. "Shut up," he said in a dead voice. "Just: shut up."

Skettle prudently did as he was told. He sponged his forehead dry with the back of his hand. The white glove came away smudged. "I want you to think about something, Brent."

"I told you to shut up."

"Think of the rush, as you drink the cocktail. It's like drinking liquid fire, isn't it? As the medicine flows through you. Like ... liquid sex. Gives me one humdinger of a boner, I'm not ashamed to tell you, and I bet you're the same. Nothing in the world compares to the flush of power and strength."

"Yeah. So?"

"Now I want you to think of what it was like to live under Death's shadow. To waste away, your good looks stolen, in constant agony from your ailments. Do you remember?"

Brent lowered his head. After a moment, he nodded.

"Good," sighed Skettle. He adjusted his sunglasses. "Hold on to that, and you'll see what a truly small sacrifice you made here tonight."

"That's what I'm afraid of, that one day it won't bother me anymore."

Skettle worked at the stained smudge on his glove. His efforts only smeared makeup onto both gloves. "A little late to discover you have a conscience."

"Yeah, well. I'm full of surprises."

"Has John finished?"

Brent shook his head that he did not know. He forced himself to return to the window, and look. His lower lip trembled at the sight. "He's wrapping the ... the ... with a blanket. It's over."

Skettle nodded. He lay the gun on his desk. "Let's go downstairs."

"Not yet. I can't."

"Oh, come on," the big man chided. "I know you're itching for it. Don't you want your share?"

"All right! Of course I want it. Need it." Brent stood at the glass wall. "But I have no intention of sampling this batch. I can't. It's too barbaric."

Skettle took out a set of keys. He placed the gun into his desk drawer and locked it. "You're in for an awfully long wait for the next one."

Brent smiled bitterly. "Well, I suppose I'll have to speed up operations, won't I?"

With effort, the big man came to his feet. He brushed the lapels of his finely tailored pin-striped suit. Adjusted the angle of his Panama hat. His face was still streaked by lines of sweat, and his gloves were dirty, but somehow he managed to manufacture a fairly convincing dapper look, thanks to his attitude. "Shall we?"

Brent hesitated. What he wanted was the gun, but that seemed to be out of the question, at least for the moment. He went to the office door and opened it. He waved majestically with a half bow, as though he were about to introduce royalty to the masses. But his mocking humor was lost on Skettle, who flicked his hands with annoyance and indicated for Brent to proceed down the stairs in front of him.

John lifted his eyes to the stairs. Brent caught him staring, but he could not meet his gaze. The front of John's apron was dappled a rusty red, glistening in its freshness. On the tabletop beside him lay a wrapped bundle in blankets. A white tennis shoe poked out of the folds of heavy material. Seeing it caused Brent to lose his breath. He had to stop for a moment and pull himself together.

But there was much activity around the cauldron. Acne Andy was ladling out portions of the cocktail into plastic cups. The workers, smelling blood, had swarmed into a steady line, eager for their share. The cups were hot to the touch, they had to be, but no one was complaining. They took their share, blowing cooling breaths across the steaming mixture, and found a place out of the way to drink it. As Brent and Skettle came down the stairs, the line parted to allow Skettle entry.

"Here you are, sir," Acne Andy said. He poured a generous portion into a cup and handed it to his boss. "Be careful: it's hot."

Skettle smiled. "Hot and slippery is just the way I like it," he said. Around him, people laughed. "Everyone have a glass? No? Hurry it along now, and we'll have a toast."

Andy did his best to pacify the anxious crowd. Brent watched him pour cup after cup. Now that he was standing so close to the others, he saw how many of them were sweating in the same manner as Skettle. Their skin color was ashen and puttylike, not at all the result of avoiding the sun. Almost everyone seemed to be in the first throes of withdrawal. He met John's eyes. His friend remained poker-faced. A glass was pushed into his hands. He hesitated, then finally accepted the steamy glass and set it on the table.

Skettle raised his glass. "Cheers, mates. And a toast to our new production staff, who will make sure we get our deliveries with a little more regularity."

There were some appreciative nods, and then a sudden hush as people gulped greedily at the cocktail. Brent and John exchanged a glance. Both brought their glasses to their lips. The craving hit Brent out of nowhere, as the steam tickling his nose awakened the urge to drink. The liquid touched his upper lip and caused a tremor of desire to roll through his empty belly. He wrenched the cup away.

Skettle was watching him, one eyebrow arched above the sunglasses. He had drunk half his glass. There was a line around his lips, stained by the cocktail in the same manner as a milk mustache. In any other circumstance it would have struck Brent funny. "What's the matter?"

Brent blew across the top of his glass. "Too hot," he murmured.

"That hasn't stopped anyone else."

Acne Andy came to the rescue without even realizing it. "It stops *me,*" he said with a laugh. "I'm into taste, not scalding my throat."

Skettle shook his head. "Spoken like the true drug addict that you are."

Acne grinned. "You got that one right." He brought the cup to his lips. Suddenly his expression of amusement changed. He glanced at John. "What'd you kick me for?"

John shrugged ignorance. But his face, which had become so expressive since the loss of his tongue, betrayed him.

Skettle turned on Brent. He pushed his half-empty cup into Brent's face. "Here. Finish this."

Brent pushed the cup away. "I haven't even drunk my own—"

"You mean you *won't* even drink your own," the man snapped. His head swiveled, and zeroed in on Andy. "You. Drink."

Poor Andy. He looked around in confusion. All eyes had turned to him. He glanced into his cup as though the gritty liquid could divine his next move.

"Go on," Skettle urged through clenched teeth.

He raised the cup and took one final look at John and then to Brent. His narrow face twitched, giving him a decidedly molelike appearance. "I don't want it," he blurted out, and practically pitched the cup onto the table.

"I said you'll drink, damn you!" Skettle's hand shot out and grabbed Andy by the bicep. The teenager pulled away in alarm.

"Will somebody tell me what the hell is going on?" he demanded.

Skettle pounced on Brent. He grabbed a fistful of shirt and held up his cup. The cocktail was splashing all over. "What'd you put in this?"

"Nothing! I swear!"

"Liar!" He threw the remains into Brent's startled face. Brownish liquid dripped from his chin. Skettle looked across the table and skewered John with his heated stare. "You did it. You added something to the elixir while Brent kept me in the office with his sobbing routine. You son of a bitch. I'll bet the boy isn't even dead!"

For a sedentary man, he moved with lightning speed. Skettle lunged across the table and grabbed at the folds of blanket. There was a cry of surprise and pain. In vicious triumph he ripped open the blanket to reveal the squirming, kicking figure of Clayton. The boy had been sweating under the hot wool, playing possum just as he had been instructed. Now, all he wanted was to be free of the blanket, and his feet kicked wildly.

Brent grabbed Skettle from behind. "Leave him alone."

"Get your hands off me!"

Out of nowhere workers rushed forward and pinned Brent's arms. Others surged around John. Acne Andy stood in a daze.

Skettle's gloved hands ripped at Clayton's chest. He reached underneath the boy's wet shirt and withdrew a dark, leaking package that at first made no sense. "Well, well. What have we here?" He held it up. It was a baggie. One end was still leaking a liquid that smelled suspiciously of tomato juice. A popsicle stick stuck from the baggie, having been used to pop the whole thing open. Skettle flung it onto the table. "Don't know anything about it, huh? Just two innocent lambs lost in the woods, is that what you're trying to tell me?"

"Skettle, let me explain—"

Again, the man moved with amazing speed. In his right hand he swooped up the dirtied knife John had supposedly used to slash Clay's throat. His other hand yanked at the hair on the back of the boy's head. Clayton let out a squeal as his neck was exposed to the knife. "Tell me what you put into the medicine," Skettle demanded, "or I'll slit the kid's throat."

"You're going to slit it no matter what I say," Brent answered.

Clay pulled his knees up. His eyes were huge, cartoonish. Faintly, he was humming a song. To Brent's dismay, he saw urine dripping from the boy's pants and forming a puddle on the tabletop. He had to put a stop to this, right away.

"Clay! Look at me!"

"Shut up," Skettle ordered.

"That man is a murderer. He kills people, like in cops and robbers, but for real. It stinks like a slaughterhouse in here because of all the spilled blood. And you're supposed to be next—"

"I said shut up!"

"There's no Santa Claus, Clay. The world is full of bad guys and the government could give a shit about taking care of you when you're sick. I'm a dead man. All of us here — we're all walking dead men. That medicine is nothing more than embalming fluid!"

"What are you doing!" shrieked Skettle. He pointed the knife at Brent. "I told you to shut up!"

For the first time since this change of events, Brent smiled. "Can't use spoiled goods in the cocktail, isn't that right? You need 'em sweet and innocent."

Anger puffed Skettle's cheeks. He snorted and huffed with indignation. Tendons bulged against his throat. He opened his mouth to speak but instead of words, a cough exploded out. Startled, he let go of Clayton's hair and brought the hand to his throat. He tried to suck air into his lungs, but he only succeeded in breaking into another coughing jag.

All around, as if some silent cue were being followed, men and women began to rasp and cough and claw at their throats. The cacophony of gagging was so startling that everyone seemed frozen in place. It was as if an invisible tear gas bomb had been thrown into the building. The workers tore at their throats, their efforts frantic even as they doubled over with pain. "It burns! It burns!" one man shrieked. He fell to the floor, writhing.

"You idiot," Skettle managed to spit out. "You've poisoned us."

Brent backed away in horror. He shook his head. "No! I mean — I couldn't have done it! It's only painkillers and sleeping pills, that's all!"

"It may as well be arsenic! I told you the chemicals were extremely fragile!"

Astonishingly, all around, men dropped to their knees. Their cries were more horrible than anything Brent could have imagined. Some were hunched over in pain, trying to retch the poison out of them. Brent was numb with confusion. The plan had been to convince Skettle to let Clay go. Barring that, they'd hoped to flood the cocktail with enough ground-up painkillers and sleeping pills to knock them all out. Then he would search for the cocktail's formula, steal it, and get the hell out. Anyone who survived withdrawal would have to fend for themselves.

Deaths might occur; Brent and John had already made their peace with that. But not this — not this wailing and gnashing from the pits of hell, as one after another were felled before their very eyes. And Clayton! Dear god, the boy was seeing all of it.

In the time it took for these thoughts to flash through his mind, Skettle was upon him. His gloved hands fastened upon Brent's neck. Each finger was like a knife digging into the pliant flesh beneath his jaw. Brent tried to suck in a breath but there was nothing there, nothing. In desperation he shoved Skettle back against the table. Bottles of chemicals and test tubes crashed to the floor. His own fingers sought out Skettle's face, burrowing into the man's fleshy cheeks. But then something strange happened. His hands sank into a greasy, puttylike surface. A thick coating of makeup curled away from the onslaught of his fingers as they tore deep canals into the face.

Skettle — and Brent — were so surprised that for a moment each loosened his grip upon the other. Brent gulped air into his lungs. He stared at the grooves in the other man's face. With the makeup peeled away, a ghastly vision poked through of glistening, fried cheekbones and tendons that seemed to have been seared to the bone. Brent yanked away Skettle's sunglasses. The eyes that met his were deep-socketed and gelatinous, wild with fury at this unmasking. It was a corpse's decayed face beneath this false layer of makeup and padding, an animated skull that had survived tremendous harm and yet somehow thrived. In another flash of understanding, Brent thought: *How dangerous it must have been, perfecting the formula for the cocktail. How many misses, before the lucky home run?*

Now everything exploded into a flurry of action. John had retreated with Clayton in his arms, keeping the boy's face buried against his shoulder. Brent struck out at Skettle, trying to pin him to the table. The Panama hat went flying, revealing a moonscape skull of gray and black craters, and a few errant hairs. Having downed half of his cocktail, he was still tremendously powerful, even as the poison seared his throat. Brent didn't know if he could overpower him.

All at once Skettle let out a blood-curdling scream.

"There!" shouted Acne Andy. "Take that!"

Brent looked, and felt his stomach do a high dive. Skettle's hand wriggled like a huge bloated spider, fingers twitching. It had been pinned to the table. The bowie knife protruded from his gloved palm like some evil, metallic flower. Andy had stepped back, his acne-scarred face flushed with revulsion and triumph.

Brent pressed his advantage. "Tell me where it is," he hissed.

Skettle bucked and twisted. "Go. To. Hell."

"The formula. Where do you keep it?"

The jelly eyes gleamed from within their sunken home. "You think I'm the only one with a copy?"

"Tell me where it is, or I'll personally pin your dick to this table!"

Blood was spurting from the wound in Skettle's hand. A deep red stain spread across the glove. The pain must have been tremendous. "Okay! Shithead! Of course it's in my office." And then Skettle's expression — if what lay hidden beneath the makeup could approximate human emotion — curled into satisfaction. "But you'll never get to it in time." The skeleton head gestured for Brent to look.

Brent raised his eyes. He smelled it before he saw it, the blue flames of a spreading chemical fire. Flammable liquid had spilled across the tables and dripped onto the warehouse floor, igniting puddles that seethed with flame. An oily, acrid smoke boiled into the air. Some of the wounded workers were dragging themselves along the floor, trying to get out. Brent turned to John. "Get Clay out of here," he ordered. "Andy, you go with them."

"What about him?" Andy asked, indicating the wheezing, bleeding figure of Skettle.

"He's not going anywhere. Now hurry. I'm right behind you."

With reluctance, they backed away. John wanted to stay, Brent could tell, but he glanced anxiously at the bundle in his arms and knew he had to get the boy out.

Andy stepped forward. "I'll watch Skettle. Go on, do what you have to do!"

There was a frozen moment. Brent pulled open Skettle's suit coat and snatched at the set of keys he'd seen him put there. Skettle had broken into a whole new round of gasps and coughs, his one free hand now grabbing at his throat in empty comfort. He sank to the floor, his other hand still pinned to the table. "You all would be dead without me," he blubbered. "I'll get—" A tremendous shudder seized him. His head snapped back. And at long last, he was silenced.

Brent and Andy stared in awe. Smoke wavered between them.

"Go!" Andy commanded.

Brent's paralysis broke. He backed away, stumbling over an unidentified body, before spinning toward the staircase. He covered his mouth with a hand and propelled himself up the stairs. The smoke was beginning to sting his eyes and the tender cavities of his nose. He would have a very short time.

He practically fell against the office door, pushing it open. Here, the smoke had not yet invaded with its noxious tendrils. It bought him a few extra minutes. But where to begin? He went to the desk drawers. They were locked, no surprise there, and with his third key from the chain he'd stolen from Skettle, the drawer opened. He pushed aside the gun and rummaged through the piles of familiar stationery and envelopes. Nothing.

Next, he tried the file cabinet. Another few minutes of fumbling with keys, and he had it open. What he saw shocked him. File after file of names, some of them familiar from TV and politics. He opened one of the manila folders. Inside was a picture of a dark-haired man, late forties, coming out of an apartment building. He was gaunt of face, obviously ill. A quick check of the records showed his name, age, where he lived, and when he had come into the fold. His job had been to harvest the rare herbs and mushrooms that grew along the California coastline.

A heat came to Brent's face. He's got everything in here, he thought. A man's whole life, reduced to paperwork. He flipped through the sheets of paper and came to the end of the folder. There, stapled against the back flap, was a swatch of handkerchief no bigger than a few inches. In its center, the unmistakable. Blood.

He shuddered, remembering his own first visit from Skettle, and the handkerchief that had been pressed against his palm. What could it mean? Some kind of pact with a devil, or a way for Skettle to feel he owned a piece of all of the men?

The pages slipped from his hand and splashed across the floor. He yanked out mounds of folders and spilled their guts into a paper pile. Burn. Let it all burn, and the hell with what it meant. If it was some kind of pact, some kind of one-sided contract, then he was declaring it all null and void. He tore through the pages. It hurt to see so many faces, to know that like him, they had all succumbed to the temptation of the cocktail. Some of the dates on the folders were several years old, with a big red "Canceled" stamped across the front. Brent thought of the early ones, back before the cocktail had been perfected, and of the zombielike workers who performed the shit detail downstairs.

He was mindful of his need to hurry, and knew that destroying these folders was not his urgent purpose here. But he stopped with a little gasp when his hands found his own folder. He flipped it open. Here was a picture of himself leaving Dr. Anthony Able's office. There was a lengthy biography, including his descent into illness. Notes in the margin read, "A good candidate. Desperate. A verbal willingness to kill to have his looks back." Brent couldn't read any more. And he was especially chilled to see his own scrap of bloodied handkerchief, stapled to the back of the folder.

From down below in the warehouse, explosions. Was that a shout? A cry of pain?

The hellish glow of the fire spurred him on. No time for browsing, now. He dumped the remaining folders into his pile on the floor. The cabinet was empty, and what he'd most wanted had evaded him. Damn it! In his frustration he yanked at the top drawer and wrenched it from its metal tracks. It clanged to the floor. What now? He knew the recipe for the elixir was somewhere in this office. He hated the idea of leaving it to chance, but then again, wasn't he counting on the fire to destroy all these folders?

He looked into the open maw of cabinet. Blinked. There, taped to the back, was a business-size envelope. Brent reached in and peeled the envelope from its hiding place. His fingers trembled as he opened it.

It was the formula, laid out in all its peculiar detail.

"Why don't you just pass that over here, hotshot."

Brent jumped. In the doorway stood Skettle. His scarred face was a Halloween monster mask of ragged skin and rubber. His fake goatee hung at an exaggerated angle on his chin. His injured hand was wrapped in cloth and useless at his side. But the good hand held the knife, its blade glistening with fresh blood.

"It's over," Brent said.

Skettle shook his head. It looked like a hole had been eaten open beneath his jaw. "On the desk," he rasped. "Now. The formula. Or you join your buddy in losing an eyeball."

Brent was alarmed at this reference to Acne Andy. He wanted to look down the stairs, and see if his young pal was okay. Instead, he held up the paper. "It's no good, Skettle. Everything's finished here."

"Everything but *you.*" The big man charged.

But before he had taken two steps a wire looped over his head, pulling taut around his neck. Skettle's eyes bugged with surprise. He dropped the knife and clawed at the wire, weaving this way and that. He elbowed the man holding him, but to no avail. Now his face really turned ghastly, purple and bruised. His tongue popped out of his mouth like an uneaten sausage. His eyes rolled to the back of his head. The sounds issuing out of that mouth were sloppy and gargled. Incredibly, the wire tightened even more, cutting deep and hard. Skettle's good hand flopped to his side. He dropped to the knees of his expensive suit. Only the garrote around his neck kept him upright. He implored Brent with one last look before slipping, finally, into his own infinite darkness. He rolled to his side and slumped forward like a big bag of garbage.

Brent's eyes trailed upward, beyond Skettle. He saw the white lab coat, the dangling hands of the killer, and higher still, the impenetrable ice cube sunglasses perched upon the strong nose and imposing jaw. The gray crew cut rose above the forehead like spiked nails.

Squarejaw kicked his way past the lump of body. He pointed to the sheet of paper in Brent's hand and then turned to stare at the figure coming up the staircase. "I believe this is what you're after, Boss?"

If a heart can truly stall in shock, Brent's did. He watched the second man appear out of the gloom and dirty smoke, rising, as it were, out of the ashes and flames.

"Hello, Brent," said Dr. Anthony Able. His smile was broad, amused.

Brent's head was spinning. His knees threatened to buckle. His old psychologist, Mr. Turtleneck himself. Only tonight he wore a dirty lab coat, like Squarejaw. Brent managed to stutter, "What are you doing here?"

Dr. Able made an expansive gesture. "Keeping tabs on my investments. Surely you didn't think Skettle handled all this on his own. You can see what a mess he's made of things."

A bright light penetrated the murky soup of Brent's confusion. "Wait a minute. It was you! *You* were the contact point. You waited for your patients to say the magic words, and then you sicked Skettle on us."

A shrug. "Didn't I warn you the walls had ears?"

Brent nodded with remembering. "But you aren't sick, are you? I mean, I never noticed you smelling up your office or anything."

Another shrug. "I escaped your predicament. I've never had to resort to the cocktail, if that's what you mean. My function is as manager. An overseer. I keep tabs on the flow of the cocktail, and I recruit when and where it is necessary."

Brent's glance fell into the open drawer of the desk. Pushed off to the side, in shadows, was Skettle's revolver. He quickly looked away, and focused on Squarejaw. "That was some charade you guys pulled out in the parking lot. Is this where you've been keeping yourself, with him?"

"You gotta take a promotion when it's handed your way," Squarejaw answered simply.

"And I suppose you're responsible for the recent string of foul-ups around here," Brent said, pointing at their lab uniforms. "Must have been easy to put the poison of your choice into the cocktail, right?"

"Skettle was weak," Squarejaw said with disdain. "He was so busy setting himself up as some kind of god, he forgot the business. Couldn't handle a simple judgment call. We just made him a little weaker."

"Shut up, Tony. You talk too much." Dr. Able stared at Brent, his eyes flashing. "I could use someone with your tenacity, Brent. If you had kept seeing me in my office, we might have talked business earlier on. As it is, we still have an opportunity to rebuild this organization from the ground floor. What do you say?"

"This," Brent said, as boldness struck him. He reached into the desk and withdrew the pistol. It felt alien in his hand, untrustworthy, as though it could just as easily be turned against him. "If you had honestly wanted to rebuild this organization, you wouldn't have killed everyone off with the cocktail."

"Don't make me laugh," Squarejaw smirked.

"No, you won't laugh with a bullet in your head."

"You know a gun can't kill us," he said. Uncertainty swept his concrete face. "I mean, as long as we have access to the cocktail..."

"Which you poisoned," Brent reminded. He shrugged. "I think it's going to be a long, long wait for the next batch. What do *you* think, Dr. Able?"

A flash of teeth. Enigmatic. And so infuriatingly familiar from his weekly doctor visits. "It doesn't really matter what I think, does it? The real question is whether you can pull that trigger."

"Don't tempt me, Doc. I'm not the same man who walked into your office months ago."

"No. But as usual, you deny the fact that you now belong to a secret community. First, you wanted to disassociate yourself from anyone else with AIDS. Then you were welcomed into this group, and now you want not only to deny it, but destroy it as well. It's always yourself, isn't it. Never a thought to the greater good, to working in unison with others."

"No. That's not true." But it stung, a little, to hear those accusations.

"You can't destroy this, Brent," Dr. Able said. His voice was hot as whiskey, a sure and fiery ribbon of heat aimed straight at Brent's heart. "It's too big. Too much has already been set into motion. Why fight? There's nowhere else for you to go. Except a grave."

The gun wobbled in Brent's hand. "I — I don't believe that."

"You'd better," Squarejaw interjected, "or you're dead meat."

Brent swung the gun. Squarejaw had inched himself closer during his exchange with Dr. Able. "Haven't you heard? We're *already* dead meat. Now come no closer. I can hurt you pretty bad."

Squarejaw ran a hand across his flattop. His grin was jaunty. "You have to shoot me first, Goldilocks," he said, and the words had scarcely left his lips before his whole body sprang forward, a leopard pouncing for the kill.

Brent thought he'd be prepared. The gun was aimed. But Squarejaw had the advantage of movement, and surprise. In that split second of reaction time he glanced at the weapon in his hand, willing it to fire without his pulling the trigger. And then like some fierce jungle animal Squarejaw was upon him with gnashing teeth and hands that clamped upon his wrists like claws. The gun seesawed in the air above them. Their feet danced upon the piles of folders and scattered papers.

"You never should have been recruited in the first place," spat Squarejaw.

"And I should cut out your tongue, like you did to John," Brent snarled. It suddenly occurred to him, in that odd, slowed-down way of dreams, that this bully of a man had left his body wide open, hands out to the side, grasping his wrists. This time the element of surprise was in his favor. He lunged into his attacker, as though for an embrace, and brought his knee up, hard. It connected with Squarejaw's privates in a most satisfying way.

The man staggered backward, his hands instantly retracting and covering his groin in a too-late motion for protection. His right foot skidded on the piles of paper, and suddenly he was falling against the file cabinet, dropping in a messy, flailing heap.

A movement caught Brent's eye. He swung. Dr. Anthony Able threw open the office door. Brent raised the gun, aiming dead-center at the lab coat. Again he hesitated, his hand frozen by the ingrained repugnance of shooting a man in the back. Smoke bloomed into the office, oily and hungry. Dr. Able disappeared into its embrace.

"Your turn, Goldilocks," a voice called out.

Brent saw only a blur thundering toward him. In reflex, he fired. The blast was startling and huge. So too the wail of pain from Squarejaw as he groped at his leg. Brent was no expert, but the bullet had done some pretty mean damage to Squarejaw's right knee.

"You bastard," seethed Squarejaw. Like a horse with a broken leg, he could not stand, and he only flailed his arms.

Brent was horrified at what he had done, but his feelings would have to be sorted through later. Dr. Able was escaping down the stairs. He had to be stopped. Quickly he moved out of Squarejaw's grasping reach, scooped up the envelope containing the cocktail's recipe, and rushed toward the office door. What he saw stopped him in his tracks. Half of the downstairs was engulfed in flames. Bodies in burning lab coats were writhing on the floor like slugs trying to burrow into the dirt. Without his sunglasses, the glare from the fire was blinding. And the smoke snatched away any chance of a clean breath. Its noxious fumes brought stinging tears. Every fiber of his being rebelled at charging down those stairs.

Just do it, he commanded himself. *It's now or never.*

Brent ripped buttons from his shirt and pulled one corner of the material over his mouth and nose. In one hand he gripped the envelope and his shirt, while the pistol was in the other. The roar of the fire was a thunderous din shaking the warehouse. He sucked in a huge breath and bolted. He flew down the staircase, his feet surprisingly sure and steady. A wave of heat hit him like a brick wall. He took a second to remember where the exit was; if he followed this wall, it would lead him to the rolling metal doors, and freedom. Perhaps Dr. Able had gone this way. Surely he'd be cooked in this inferno, if he was still inside. Brent crouched as low as he dared for balance and shot forward, using the wall on his right as his reference point. He skirted the huge table, which was entirely engulfed in flames. The cauldron containing the poisoned cocktail had fallen to the floor and lay on its side, abandoned. Another few steps—

But the shape flew at him, tackling Brent to the floor. His breath spewed out of his mouth, and when he gasped for a fresh breath, he was rewarded with a searing burn down his throat. Hands pried the gun from his fingers. Brent reflexively made a fist with his other hand, mashing the envelope tightly. He rolled to his side and stared into Dr. Anthony Able's singed face. It was mangled by the fiery light, orange and monstrous and absolutely terrifying. His eyebrows had burned off, and so had the hair on one side of his face. Blisters were rising like a witch's brew along his neck and cheek.

"The recipe," whispered Dr. Able. He pointed the revolver at Brent's face.

"Go to hell," he said, despite the pain his words caused his throat. Again the dream world blew over him, distorting time into a slowed-down fog. If it was all going to end here, he had one last card to play. He mustered his aim and threw the crumpled-up envelope into the glare of fire.

Dr. Able's face twisted with shock, then immediately darkened. He raised the gun and brought it down, hard, on Brent's forehead.

His world went white with heat. He felt himself roll onto his back. His throat was in agony. He thought he heard Dr. Able stumbling away from him, cursing. There was a loud crash of splintering wood, and sparks, and a yelp of intense pain. Something in Brent broke loose, casting him adrift. Darkness beckoned, where the world was cool and green. He swam toward it.

It *felt* like he was swimming. He was certainly moving. Hands had grabbed him under each arm, and there were sounds of screaming, and popping wood, and of his body being dragged. Suddenly the heat gave way to cool, and night air brushed against his bruised face like a wonderful kiss.

"Over here!" someone shouted. A van door rolled open with a clang. In the distance, but gaining, came the peace-splitting blare of sirens and fire trucks. Brent was raised into a standing position and half carried across the gravel. Other arms grabbed hold of him as he was hoisted and then laid out on the floor. And the floor: blessed, cool metal, cool, cool, good-bye heat, good-bye fire, good-bye consciousness.

Brent pried open an eyelid, saw John's smoke-sooted face grinning down at him, and let go into the cool cocoon of darkness.

3

"This is the place," said a voice. "Better wake him up. See if he wants to say good-bye."

Didn't I already say good-bye? thought Brent, rising from his exhausted dozing as a hand shook his shoulder. The movement of the van had been so soothing, so comforting. And lying next to him, curled and content in his blanket, was his nephew, Clayton. Brent swam up from the deep, his head stuffed with cotton. It hurt to breathe.

From the driver's seat, Acne Andy whispered, "Brent, wake up. Don't you want to say good-bye to the kid? Hurry it up, now, before someone hears us."

The van door slid open, but as quietly as was possible. John stuck his head into the interior. Brent managed to focus his eyes long enough to recognize the front of his sister's house. Of course. Clayton.

He turned to the boy. Clay was deeply asleep. Passed out from the Valium, most likely. Despite all he had gone through that night, his little face was relaxed with sweet dreams. At least that's what Brent wanted to think. Maybe the boy wouldn't remember anything at all, just a drug-induced fog that would cloud and distort.

But remember this, Brent thought. *You must remember this, somewhere, let it imprint your brain, let it be a comforting hug.* "I love you, my brave Rocket Man," he whispered to his nephew, and brought him close for a kiss on the cheek. Clay stirred, mumbled something, and was quiet.

John took the boy from his arms. Brent watched as they loped across the dark front lawn. There were no lights on in the house. It must be very late, the middle of the night. Onto the indented porch next to the door, John carefully lowered himself and arranged Clay in his blanket upon the cement. He straightened, turned, and got the go-ahead signal from Andy. John thumbed the doorbell with several quick jabs and then fled back across the lawn to jump into the van's interior next to Brent. He pulled the van door closed as Acne Andy hit the gas pedal.

What do you know, Brent marveled, already being lulled by the drone of the engine, by the knowledge that they had actually succeeded. He reached out and took John's hand into his own. There was a reciprocal squeeze. *What do you know.*

Shades among men

1

Always and forever, pain.

Pain as a living, breathing entity that enfolded, embraced, and would never leave them. Never. They could only adapt to its constant presence, to its cocoon of suffocating threads. The pills they used to control the pain — the last of Brent's stash — brought flashes of relief, nothing more. To live meant to be in pain, to endure, to accept. It was still a kind of living, after all.

But not for Acne Andy. He died on the third night in a spasm of convulsions and skyrocketing fevers. Despite their own agonies, Brent and John managed to wrap Andy's body with a sheet and bury him in the backyard. It had taken most of the night. Only the breezy, stirring air of morning and the sight of orange-topped clouds persuaded them to leave the grave. Poor Andy. In life he had showed a wiry tenacity, but his years with the needle out on the streets had betrayed him in the end. He simply was not strong enough to survive the appalling effects of withdrawal. Plus, the gash on his cheek, where Skettle had almost gouged out an eye and left Andy for dead, had never healed. It was a terrible blow.

Each night Brent cracked open his front door and snatched the evening newspaper. He would sit with John in bed while the fevers cooked him, and read aloud.

At first, the warehouse fire garnered front-page news. Investigators sifted through the rubble and asserted the headline-winning conclusion that something had gone terribly wrong in one of the largest drug-manufacturing rings ever discovered in San Francisco. The fact that no one could quite figure out what illegal drugs had been made there was quietly downplayed by the authorities. The evidence, they insisted, spoke volumes: the melted remains of scientific weights and measures, heaps of melted test tubes and blackened Bunsen burners. Most puzzling of all was the varied array of vegetation unearthed at the scene. Speculation ran high about psychedelic mushrooms and huge quantities of LSD, but what few plants scientists were able to analyze revealed vegetation common to the fog-shrouded west coast, and nothing more.

And there were the bodies, burned and blackened beyond recognition. One man was identified through dental records to be a San Franciscan thought to have committed suicide seven months earlier. His distraught parents went on TV to proclaim their son would never involve himself in such illegal activities.

By the end of the first week, the story had slipped page by page to the back section, then finallly vanished altogether.

Also during that first week were the phone calls, one upon the other, day and night. Brent turned off his answering machine, and when that didn't halt the calls, he unplugged the phone. Of course it was his sister, Mary Ann. He'd known it would be her even before listening to the very first message on his machine. Their greatest fear was that one afternoon the police would come knocking, demanding entrance, because Mary Ann had alerted them with her worry. There would be no time to hide down in the basement, no time to get away.

And then one day the doorbell *did* ring, and fists pounded against the front door, and a female voice on the other side said, "Brent? Are you there? Can I come in? It's Mary Ann. Please let me in!"

They listened through their gauzy delirium of pain, huddled two to the bed, waiting for her to go. It no longer mattered, that she wanted to talk. She belonged to the larger world, while they had slipped through the cracks into the shadows. There was no going back. And certainly Mary Ann would never have gotten past the twisted shape masquerading as her brother.

A few days later, Mary Ann stood at the front gate. Her maternity dress was colorful and gay, like an extension of the spring flowers that bloomed in the front yard and all over San

Francisco in a joyous riot of color. Her brown hair hung in loose, soft curls about her face. From his hidden perch by the window, peeking through slats, Brent noted with approval these warmer, softer attributes that made his sister shine with an inner light. What could it mean?

She knocked on the door, and rang the doorbell half a dozen times (while John buried his head between two pillows). She even knelt and stuck her hand into the mail slot, peering into the dimmed interior. "Brent? Don't be afraid. If you're in there, let me help you. I think ... I think the police may try to talk with you soon. Steven let something slip the other night..."

She couldn't go on. She pulled herself to her feet and massaged the muscles in the back of her neck, turning her head this way and that. Measuring the silence, she now reached into her red pocketbook and withdrew an envelope. She pushed it through the mail slot. "Good-bye, Brent," she whispered, and hurried away, her heels clicking against the sidewalk as she walked to her car.

Brent sat beside John in the bed and peeled open the envelope. Inside was a short note, and five crisp hundred-dollar bills.

"Clayton has told us many unbelievable things about that night, most of it gibberish. But on one point he is adamant: you saved his life from what he calls the 'bad guys.' I know you're in some kind of trouble because of this, or you would have come forward by now. Perhaps this small token of thanks might help you. You should know I've been doing a lot of soul-searching, and am ashamed at much of what I find. While I haven't changed overnight, you should know your sister's eyes have been opened. But am I, now, too late?"

John hefted his notepad to his knees. His stiff and uncooperative fingers spelled out his concerns.

How much time do you think we have?

"Not much," Brent answered, and his sigh filled the room. He gently removed the pen from John's crippled hand. "Whether we hear anything or not, we'll have to strike out."

2

Their luck turned the very next night. Brent retrieved the afternoon paper, and as usual he and John scanned its headlines, page by page.

Brent found it under the national news, a two-paragraph article that was nothing more than filler for the more important stories boxing it in. Seeing it gave him an unpleasant electrical charge. All the questions, the doubts, the worries that clung to him with the pain came back into sharp focus. Somehow, deep, he'd known it wasn't over.

"Damn it," he whispered to John. His voice was thin with anger. "It's what we were afraid of."

"Search Continues for Seattle Twins," screamed the headline. "Fraternal twins David and Michelle Lawton, four years old, vanished from their parents' backyard in the early evening hours of May 21st. Despite an extensive search of the immediate neighborhood and of a creek bordering the development project, no trace of these children has been found. This marks the second such child abduction in the Seattle area just in the past week. Mr. and Mrs. Lawton have set up a $5,000 reward for the safe return of their twins, described as sweet and trusting of everyone."

Brent and John measured each other.

"Seattle," Brent said.

Seattle, mouthed John, and a sadness came into his eyes.

3

Brent packed two suitcases, one of them filled with a first-aid kit, boxes and cans of food, and various medical supplies. Buried deep under the bathroom sink he discovered an old makeup kit that an actor he had been sleeping with at the time had forgotten to pick up. (Actually, the actor had hurled a few choice words Brent's way, starting with "selfish bastard," before storming out.) It contained a treasure trove of skin tones, blush, eyeliners, powders, and one false mustache. He and John would have plenty of time to experiment.

Under a cloudy night sky they said their good-byes to Acne Andy and loaded up the van. With any luck, Skettle or one of his cronies had changed the license plates on the van. For a while, perhaps, it might be untraceable. And the van would provide them with sanctuary and a place to sleep.

They had one last farewell to take care of, so despite the long detour Brent drove the van to Daly City. He pulled in front of Mary Ann's house and killed the engine. It was almost seven o'clock. The living room lights were on, casting a golden glow against the closed curtains. It struck Brent as very Norman Rockwell, corny and humble and wonderfully comforting. It also made him sad. In life he had chosen another path. He'd had to invent other ways of nurturing his own happiness that was removed from the life he imagined behind those golden curtains. He'd bungled most of it, relying too heavily upon his charming good looks to be his ticket to happiness.

His Look. How it brought a wry smile to his lips, now.

He reached across to the passenger side and took John's left hand into his own. He thought of John — not merely the visual image in front of him, but of everything John meant to him now. John turned his head stiffly and made what could be surmised as a smile upon his ruined face. His teeth and gums peeked through the splintered remains of his chin. His lips, like Brent's own, were nothing more than a thin pink rubber band circling his mouth. The nose was sunken, still retreating slowly into the skull. John's eyes, whenever he removed his sunglasses, were like wet marbles planted into his face, milky with fluid. Brent's own eyes resembled spoonfuls of old jelly, their once-vibrant green vaguely spongy and sour. Wisps of fine hair swirled about John's head like a delicate spiderweb. Brent had only his glistening, blackened skull. In fact, he had shed just about every strand of blond hair on his body.

The withdrawal had exacted a swift and devastating punishment upon their bodies. They resembled what they were: animated corpses. High fevers had blistered off their skin in sheets and shreds, fusing it into a hardened, blackened shell like melted glass. They were bones, bones held together by the thinnest tarp of skin. Their fingers were stiff, black pencils, though every day they gained more flexibility. John was still weak on his left side; he dragged his foot when he walked. Brent had survived better than the rest of them, though he was at a total loss as to why. Perhaps his earlier encounter with withdrawal had actually strengthened him, not weakened, as Skettle had claimed. Skettle had obviously survived — and thrived — from his own bouts of withdrawal. Sure, Brent's back was stiff, and gave him problems sleeping, but his legs worked fine, and his arms were amazingly strong with ropy muscle. A few of his back teeth were loose and wobbly. He'd probably lose one or two before this was over.

And that was the great question, wasn't it? They had weathered the withdrawal, but how long did they have before their bodies craved the shadowed quiet of the grave? Would the residue from the cocktail keep them indefinitely alive?

Ahh, Brent thought. Death isn't much different from life. The questions, the wondering, were all cut from the same cloth, and came down to a simple equation: do whatever it is that gives your life purpose, and do it now. The future will take care of itself.

He patted John's hand. "I'll be just a minute," he said, and opened the door. In one hand he snatched the small paper sack he'd tucked under his seat by his feet. The open air made him feel unprotected and vulnerable. He was quite a sight, even in his dark clothes and sunshades. With the stealthiness of a cat, he slipped up the sidewalk to the front door.

Inside the sack were three Snickers bars. He put the sack into the space by the door, where it would be easily discovered the next morning. As he straightened, he was startled to hear shrieks of laughter and childish giggles. Clay was playing some kind of physical romping game with his father.

"Get off of me!" Steven bellowed in mock protest. "You're so heavy now! What a big boy you are!"

And faintly, like a tinkling bell, the delightful sound of Mary Ann joining in the laughter.

Brent lay his misshapen hand against the sturdy wood door. *Good. Let there always be laughter in this house. Always.* He scuttled back to the van and jumped into the driver's seat. John was waiting for him with a note.

Are you okay with this?

It was a simple question, but it choked him up. Loss, and letting go, and moving on, juggling for balance within him. Brent's gaze drifted to the visor above the windshield, and the picture he had paper-clipped there. It was the Polaroid Skettle had given him of Clay playing in his red wagon while Mary Ann looked on adoringly.

"Yes," he answered quietly. "Or I will be, eventually." He turned to John. "Thanks to you."

It was truly a marvel, this thing between them. Elemental. Simple. How had it eluded him, all of his life? So this is what it had all been about, the dance of courtship, of bonding with another. Much had been denied him in life, but not this. This Gift, saved for the very end.

In that moment he thought John the handsomest man in the world.

They'd drive to Seattle, and wait, and watch. All signals pointed there, a city of clouds and rain and dank hiding places from the sun. Perhaps Dr. Anthony Able had died in the warehouse fire, in his effort to retrieve the cocktail's formula. Perhaps Squarejaw had burned up on his nest of papers and folders in the smoky office. It's what they had hoped. It's what they had prayed for. Maybe this trail was false. Maybe — god forbid — this was the work of someone else, someone who belonged to the mysterious bigger picture hinted at by Skettle. But they knew Dr. Able's motives. They knew his ambitions. And if the children continued to disappear, they'd track down someone with the Look, the glow — and they would avenge. This would stop. As long as they drew breaths into their lungs, they would hunt, and search out, and destroy.

Brent flipped the visor back into its upper position. Ahead lay the road, and a trail carved through darkness. Together, they would find the right path.

"We're Rocket Men, varoom, varoom!" Brent sang, and the van moved through the deserted and glistening streets like a shadow in search of sunshine.

The Unfinished,
continued

PART THREE

Resting grounds

1

A skein of thin clouds blew a silky scarf over the moon, shadowing its light. Jiggs was glad for the darkness, not that he anticipated being spotted by any of his neighbors at four-twenty in the morning. After all, as far as he knew, he was the only one who could see his companion.

"Are you sure about this?" Jiggs asked one last time.

The corpse of Acne Andy nodded. "I'm ready."

Jiggs dug into the soft earth with the shovel he'd taken from the basement. He worked in silence, concentrating on deepening and smoothing out the grave's floor to make it as comfortable as possible. It was a kind of oxymoron, of course: to make a grave comfortable for a corpse. But it seemed the least he could do.

As he worked, the clouds raced away from the moon. Milky light filtered through the branches of the pine trees. It was time.

Andy motioned Jiggs aside. Jiggs stepped out of the hole and leaned against the shovel, resting. Andy turned his head left and right, even though the motion looked as though it caused him pain. He drew in a deep breath, which made a muddy, sucking noise. Eventually his gaze settled upon Jiggs. "It's a beautiful night, isn't it."

"Yes," Jiggs answered. "Yes, it is."

Acne crouched low and stepped into his grave. He placed a bony hand on either side of the hole and settled in, sticking his legs out straight. He glanced at Jiggs one last time. "If you ever come across John and Brent, give them a big hi for me." Andy scooted into place and lay back, eyes closed. As soon as his head touched the dirt floor, all animation went out of him. Jiggs thought it looked as though he'd been unplugged, or blown a fuse. Acne Andy's body lay in unalterable rest, unmoving as though it had never stirred in the first place.

He was not a particularly religious man, but Jiggs said a little prayer as he took the shovel and began to toss in scoopfuls of earth. He thought of Brent and John standing at this very spot, performing this very task even as their poor bodies were racked with pain from the withdrawal. He suddenly and inexplicably felt heartened. He thought of all the missing kids who disappeared each year, and whether there was truly a connection or not, he hoped that Brent and John would survive for a very long time, and be able to do some good. At least their bonds to the earth were voluntary, and did not need to be released.

Jiggs shook out of his daze and hurried to complete his task. It was hard to shovel dirt onto Andy's face, so he did not look until he knew the face was completely covered. After that worst part, the rest came easily. He used the back of the shovel to smooth out and pat the earth solid. The breeze upon his wet brow was cool as he finished. The summertime air stirred with the coming morning.

His shoulders and back ached. His hand still thudded with writer's cramp, and from the painful hooks Andy had used to take control of his hand. It made him think of Luke, and the hooklike fingers that had raised him out of that pool of darkness. He shuddered, remembering that terrible image. Jiggs put away the shovel and wearily clomped up the porch steps and into the house. He meant to take a shower and rinse off all the dirt and grit that clung to him, but midway through yanking off his clothes he fell back onto the bed and promptly sank into an exhausted sleep.

2

He went alone to the hospital, mumbling his excuses to Kate and Susie and hoping they wouldn't mind. They didn't. Even though they were concerned, they also appeared grateful to beg off on this visit. Besides, it was obvious to Jiggs that they were still badly frightened by the turn of events.

There was no change in Luke's condition. Not that Jiggs expected any, at least not until he'd had his third and final visitor that evening. The nurses had moved Luke into a new position, rolled onto his side. He could almost make believe Luke was sleeping. Almost. The cast on his leg and the webs of tubing kept getting in the way.

Jiggs settled in and took one of his friend's hands into his own. "This may take a while," he began, and Brent's story unfurled out of him, all the events of the previous night. Quite honestly he wasn't at all sure whether Luke could hear him or not, but that point was unimportant. The Unfinished were listening, and Jiggs wanted them to know that yes, he was recording their troubled stories, and was fulfilling his promise to help release them.

Just as Jiggs was finishing up, the door opened and in walked Susie and Kate.

"I hope we're not interrupting," Kate whispered. She looked at her partner. "We decided we've been acting pretty damn stupid."

"Besides," Susie grinned, "it's not butch to be afraid. I have a reputation to uphold."

Jiggs gestured to the empty chairs. "I think you're wrong. I couldn't trust anyone who wouldn't admit they were afraid. I think it shows strength. After all," he volleyed back with a wry smile, "it works for me."

3

No doubt about it: the air in his house was less disturbed, less heavy. It no longer felt so saturated with currents of unspoken emotions and unfulfilled desires. Maybe he was trying to put a label on something that never wore a label in the first place, but Jiggs was trusting this inner instinct radar that had so recently developed within him.

He napped in the afternoon, even though he'd slept the morning away and had not gotten up until just before noon. But when he awakened from his nap, expecting to feel revitalized, his body had decided to betray him. His forehead was warm with a low fever. His muscles and joints ached as though he'd napped in a twisted and uncomfortable position. Strangest of all were the wobbly, uncertain steps when he walked around the house. A trip into the kitchen and back to the living room couch left him exhausted and nearly gasping for air. He shuffled his feet as though his legs had forgotten how to take confident strides.

In such a manner Jiggs wobbled precariously into the bathroom and opened up his medicine cabinet. He reached for the bottle of Tylenol. As he found it, his gaze went to the top shelf, to the unmarked bottle of leftover pills where he'd found his glass of milk back in his first days at the house. He knew what it was, now: Brent's stash of final exit pills, which had served him in such an unanticipated and life-saving way. The Unfinished had put his glass of milk there, pointing out another subtle clue — like his old tennis shoes half buried in Acne Andy's grave.

Jiggs washed down three Tylenols and looked at himself in the mirror. His face was blotchy with fever and unusually haggard. "Great," he muttered. "Just great. My luck to come down with a cold on this last night." He shook his head and blamed that morning's foray into the backyard, and digging out the grave site. The cool air and his sweating had given him a chill.

He came out of the bathroom. All at once Jiggs stumbled as his foot somehow miscalculated the distance to the floor. It was as if ... as if he'd stepped onto a pocket of air that had cushioned his foot from the floor. What a peculiar sensation. He made his way back to the couch without any further mishap.

He had no idea when his third and final visitor would arrive. The hours dragged as he watched sitcom after sitcom on the TV, waiting. There was little nervous anticipation, which was a novelty, after last night. Instead, his thoughts were cloudy and confused. He couldn't keep track of the silly characters on the shows he was watching. His fever had broken, so that was not the culprit. He closed his eyes.

And jerked with sudden panic, his hands flying to the pillows and arm of the couch. *What in the world...?* For an instant — the tiniest instant — the couch seemed to have disappeared beneath him. He had felt as though he were (and his mind stumbled over this, still unwilling to even think it) hovering above it. Actually hovering.

That's it, Jiggs thought, and slapped his thighs with decision. *Enough of this. Time for bed. My guest will just have to wake me up.*

He moved with an invalid's slow motion, brushing his teeth and removing his clothes with effort. Once he slipped beneath his bed covers, he sank against the mattress with grateful relief. *They'll just have to understand I'm not well.*

Jiggs lay there, cozy and comfortable, his mind drifting toward sleep, when the sensation stole over him that someone else had joined him in the bed. Yes, definitely, the covers on his left side were moving.

He swam with confusion, paralyzed, but one sudden clear light shone through the fog. A voice began to speak to him inside his head. It was dignified, rather sad, and sounded like many voices rolled into one.

"I've already left a note for my friend Roy," whispered the ghost. "But it wasn't enough. I have to tell it to you, tonight. Who am I? Never mind. I am Everyman. I am Me."

And as though in a waking dream, Jiggs's final guest began to reveal his tale.

ME SPEAKS:

Gravity

1

Maybe the combination of all those drugs triggered the change. The daily doses of AZT. Acyclovir. Aerosol pentamidine once a month. Megadoses of vitamins and minerals. So much vitamin C I had to cut back because it made my palms itch. Not to mention immune stimulants, herbal teas from the acupuncture clinic that smelled up my house for days on end. My poor fatigued body: it had become an unsuspecting laboratory. The real surprise, when I think about it, is not what happened to me, but that it took as long as it did to happen.

"Your heart's too heavy," my lover Jerry said to me shortly before he died. "Lighten up."

Lighten up. That was my handsome lover, kidding me to the very end. As if I had no good reason for a heavy heart, watching him shrink away to nothing in his hospice bed. Not to mention the dozens upon dozens of friends — we'd both lost count after forty — who had already charted these unfamiliar waters. Losing friends had been bad enough, but when I lost Jerry I went crazy with grief. I come from a proper midwestern background, not given to elaborate displays of emotion. Years before the first funeral of a friend I used to sit out on moonlit nights and think, *Let me learn how to feel. Let me know deep emotion.* I thought I had to "learn" how to be moved deeply, as if Emotions 101 were a class I could take in college.

I was an artist, you see. A dabbler in watercolors and pastels. I had to suffer for my art.

"Live well," Jerry whispered to me on his deathbed. "It's the best revenge."

Jerry's family took his body back to Oklahoma City, where he was laid to rest next to his grandparents and a sister who had been killed in a car crash. They invited me to the funeral, but I shook my head. Jerry and I had already said our good-byes.

It's been over nine months now. Nine months, and tonight is the night when I leave for good. I've strapped myself into the chair in the kitchen, and if it holds me long enough I'll have just enough time to put all this onto paper. Not that I expect anyone to believe me — except for you, Roy. But leaving this note suits the artist in me who craves roundness and completion.

2

Lighten up. What I needed to do was *fatten* up — that, according to my doctor at Kaiser Hospital. Being Jerry's primary caregiver those last months had taken their toll. The pounds had slid off of me almost as readily as they fell off of Jerry. I was down to one hundred and forty pounds, from one sixty-three. My T-cell count was so low I'm surprised someone sneezing on me wouldn't kill me.

I'm a tough cookie. I really am. When Jerry's passing no longer felt like shards of glass sticking into my heart, I renewed my health regimen with gusto.

Live well, Jerry had said. I was trying. I no longer had to work my job at the hotel, thanks to Jerry's generosity. He'd made explicit instructions in his will, and provided for me through a variety of insurance policies. It was the silver lining out of all this mess. I was one of the lucky ones. My friends at the hotel threw me a going-away party as though I were off on a world cruise and not just headed back to the house. With an exchange of hugs and kisses they promised to call and come visit. Most of them did, to their credit — for a while.

I think I sensed even then that my life had to be whittled down, less reliant on the whirl of outside distractions, in order to prepare for the change. Not that I held any notions, concrete or otherwise, concerning what was about to happen to me. I knew my life had to be different, and was different, without Jerry.

I did a lot of painting — small, brooding pictures of overcast landscapes and foggy San Francisco nights. Sometimes I drew figures in the mist, silhouettes of men and women who stood and stared, as though waiting.

My pals were aghast. One by one they pulled me aside. "Lighten up!" they chorused. "Jerry wouldn't want you to be so depressed."

Depressed? Who said I was depressed?

I dutifully took my vitamin supplements and minerals. I boiled up the foul-smelling herbal teas that tasted of sludge, held my nose, and drank as many cups a day as I could stand. I gulped my three AZT capsules daily, plus a few antibiotics to control any thrush in my mouth or fungal infections. I took comfort from this routine that Jerry and I had followed — but for Jerry, none of it had been enough, ultimately. Whether it would be enough to save me, or simply buy me time, I wasn't sure. I did not mope and I was not depressed — it's important to know that — but at times I did shiver in the cool shadows of the specter that haunted various corners of the house.

I thought I was beating the odds. Then I stepped onto the bathroom scale and saw that despite all my best efforts, another ten pounds had escaped me. Curiously, I looked the same, unchanged: except I now weighed one hundred and thirty pounds.

I added protein shakes to my daily regimen.

In the night I awoke to phantom aches and pains eddying through me. My arms and legs tingled as though my circulation was blocked. Perhaps it was the change working silently within me. I'm sure it was, now that I glance back on it. Preparing me while I was unprepared.

One week after adding the protein shakes to my diet, I stepped onto the scale. One hundred and twenty-two pounds. I stared at the man in the mirror, at the man I was becoming. My hair had thinned and lost its body, a casualty from months of taking AZT. It was now a brown lackluster straw that stuck out over the top of my head. My face was slim, but not drawn with that sallow, telltale look. A little double chin rounded out the bottom of my face, saving it from being too narrow or pinched. I'd lost some of the padding, the muscle and bulk through my shoulders, but still retained a pleasant definition of features. I stepped back from the mirror for a better all-over view. Laughed — for what else could I do? — at the "droopy butt" syndrome, another consequence of taking AZT.

Otherwise I looked pretty good. Nothing spectacular, nothing to tack up on the walls and drool over, but handsome in a pleasing, average sort of way.

A hundred and twenty-two pounds, indeed. At that weight I'd already be in a hospital, hooked up to intravenous tubes. The scales had to be wrong.

When it eventually dawned on me what was going on — when I could no longer deny its intrusion into my life — I think the change had been living inside me for quite some time. It was revealing itself by degrees, starting with the puzzling drop in my weight. Hadn't Jerry's ending begun with a tickle in his throat that wouldn't go away? Most changes in people's lives don't follow the Hollywood school of dramatic revelations. Like death, it comes in inches, day by day.

So: there I was, watching Phil Donahue. Killing that stretch of boring afternoon before the local news at five. Phil was interviewing a current crop of stand-up comedians, allowing each their five minutes of national exposure. I sat on the couch, cross-legged, with a thin blanket wrapped loosely around me.

They had me in stitches, these men and women. Giggling and laughing at their jokes. There hadn't been enough laughter in the house, it occurred to me as I watched. Not when I'm the only one laughing.

So: I'm watching. I'm laughing. My laugh turned into a cough, exploding out of me.

And suddenly the couch is gone from beneath me. That's the sensation: that I'm sitting cross-legged in midair, like a guru snake charmer.

I snatched onto the armrest of the couch. My eyes were wide, my breath shallow to match my wild heartbeat. The reassurance of pillow and fabric was beneath me once again.

Chuckling over my own distress, I stood up to fetch a glass of water from the kitchen — and promptly fell. I pitched forward, my hands splayed before me. The hardwood floor zoomed up to smack me. But I landed as though on a pile of cotton, belying the velocity of my fall. I lay on the floor shaken, dazed. I wasn't laughing anymore.

After that, I began to fall with alarming frequency. One minute I'd be walking down the hallway. And the next, my foot would seemingly step off into thin air, as though I perched at a cliff's edge. Over I'd fall, spilling forward with a startled squawk, arms thrust before me to break my descent. Right when it'd flash though my head that I was about to break an arm or bruise a rib, a cushion of air would somehow catch me at the last moment.

A feeling began to grow in me, a conviction with no name. For the next two weeks I stayed away from the scale in the bathroom.

I painted the scenes outside my back windows: treetops and fog and rolling clouds. My friends were pleased.

"It's good that you're active," my buddy Roy told me when he came over to pick up a few of the better paintings for an AIDS charity auction. "Most people would envy your position."

"What position is that?" I asked him.

Roy wrinkled his brow. He was still tanned from a recent trip to the Caribbean. Tanned and in impossibly good health. "Well," he stuttered, "thanks to Jerry, you don't have to work if you don't want. You can stay around the house, and paint, run your errands. Your time is your own."

"What time I have *left,*" I muttered.

"Oh, stop. You look great."

"Do I? Roy, how much do you think I weigh?"

He looked at me oddly. "I don't know. A hundred and fifty?"

I got an idea. I indicated for him to follow me into the bathroom. I pulled out the scale. "It's been weighing me funny," I told him. "Do you know how much you weigh?"

He nodded. "About one sixty-five."

Roy stepped onto the scale. "It should have me about five pounds heavy, on account of all my clothes." The numbers blurred, then stopped at one hundred seventy-one. "Yep. That's close enough."

My face stung as though I'd been slapped.

"What does it show you?" Roy asked me.

"Light," I said — a truth and a lie, rolled into one.

After Roy left I paced for a few minutes, working up my courage. I wore hiking boots with thick cotton socks, blue jeans, t-shirt, sweater. A wallet in my pocket, along with keys and change. I stepped onto the scale.

Ninety-seven pounds.

3

The change began to accelerate quickly after that — as though dipping below one hundred pounds had broken a barrier of no return. Each day I weighed myself out of morbid curiosity, and each day I watched another five to ten pounds slip away from me. And yet, when I studied myself in the mirror, I looked the same. Unchanged. Hadn't Roy thought I weighed one hundred and fifty pounds?

But my life was steadily changing, whether I wanted to believe what was happening or not. Just walking to the corner to mail a few bills became a chore. The weather that month was particularly blustery for San Francisco. I was a toy in the wind, tossed and knocked to the ground with embarrassing frequency.

Ironically, my doctor thought I looked great. "You have a glow about you," he said with admiration. "It sets you apart. I don't know what you're doing, but keep up your regimen. It agrees with you."

That was the last time I went to Kaiser. I figured I couldn't avoid the scale the next time — I'd deliberately sidestepped the nurses while they were busy. I could just imagine them scratching their heads over my current fifty-four pounds. Or worse: keeping me in the hospital while they ran dozens of tests. I didn't need tests and I didn't need hospitals.

I had to stop driving; I could no longer exert enough pressure on the pedals. Besides, I had to wait until there was a break in the wind before trying to dash from the curb into my house.

A cough could send me careening across the room, smacking me against the far wall.

I stuffed myself with food and drink, vitamins and all my medicines, but it was as though all those calories fueled another purpose. Whatever was happening to me involved more than losing weight.

One morning I slowly came awake with the feel of sheets and blankets pressed against me. I opened my eyes to the predawn light and was confused. The room rocked and swayed, as though the house had been transformed into a boat. I rolled over onto my stomach — and stared at the bed two feet below me.

A scream stuffed my throat.

I reached out like a diver scouring coral for pearls. My fingertips just managed to brush against the mattress. The floating was quite pleasant, actually, except for rubbing against the confinement of sheets and blanket.

Down, I thought. *I want to get down—*

And like an autumn leaf twirling to its final resting place, I slowly descended to the mattress. I daresay I trembled like a leaf, too — to steal that old cliche — exhilarated and no longer frightened. That sensation of lightness, of having sloughed off all the world's weight: too late, I realized I missed it as soon as it was gone.

In the days that followed I began to practice going light. I'd fold myself into a chair, relaxed and loose and comfortable, and the mantra I held next to my heart said, go light.

Practice and perseverance won out. By the seventh day I was hovering above the chair, floating on three inches of air. To will myself to go light seemed an entirely different process than having it happen spontaneously. But even that kept occurring, like when I tripped. It finally dawned on me: I was stumbling on air. I pitched forward because I was stepping onto the air above the floor when I expected hardwood floor. Now, whenever I fell, I floated gently downward.

Soon enough, I could go light at will. Floating in the air was much more comfortable than sitting on the couch. I could hover in one place or kick my feet like a diver maneuvering through water, and swim into other rooms. I knocked over a few lamps in the process, and accidentally kicked an ivy off a tabletop. Floating in the currents of the house required a bit of concentration.

I found the nerve to weigh myself one last time. Thirty seven pounds. Impossible, but true.

I kept all my shades drawn and curtains closed. No need to startle the neighbors.

I can't begin to describe what it was like, this period. Going light touched something deeply buried, like rediscovering an old boyhood fantasy that has miraculously come true. So many things had been denied me: Jerry, good health, a hope for a future. So many people I knew were weighed down by the sheer gravity of making it through each day. So: *serious.* And here I was, floating on air. Granted, I had to keep the shades drawn over the windows. And sure, there were some mornings when I woke up shivering as I bounced against the ceiling, having pulled free of my blankets and sheets. I no longer ventured outside — the last time I'd taken the garbage out I'd ended up tangled in the branches of a tree. But the freedom was exhilarating, even if I had to contain it within my house.

Roy brought me groceries once a week.

"You look good," he told me as he set the groceries onto the kitchen table. "Why are you so ... happy?"

I responded with my best enigmatic shrug. I wondered what would happen if I went light in front of him.

And just like that I felt my feet leave the floor. I grabbed onto the edge of the kitchen table and pulled myself down. If I wasn't careful my feet would go out from under me and I'd float sideways into the air.

Roy was at my side in a flash. "You okay? What's wrong?"

I stammered out that I was having a dizzy spell.

"Sit down then," he said, and helped me to a chair. He stepped away from me with a confused expression. "My god! You're light as a feather!"

I hooked my feet around the front chair legs and gripped the armrests. "I weigh the same," I shot back — knowing I still looked as if I weighed a respectable one hundred and fifty pounds.

It required all my strength and determination to hold myself down in the chair while Roy put away the groceries. He stared at me out of the corner of his eye, his expression curious while he filled the kitchen with his prattle.

Finally there was nothing left for him to do but go. I motioned with one hand for him to bow close, and we hugged. My other hand gripped the armrest, my feet secured me to the chair. Not for much longer could I keep this up.

"Good-bye," Roy said.

"Good-bye."

"You're so ... tense. Do you want to lie down?"

"No. I'll just sit here for a while."

Roy shook his head. "You're one funny guy. Just like Jerry. Do you mind me saying that?"

"No. I'm flattered."

"You'd let me know if anything was wrong, wouldn't you?"

"Yes." And I'll keep my promise: I dedicate these pages to you, Roy. You're probably the only person who might believe what's happened.

As soon as the front door closed I released my death grip on the chair. Immediately I slipped into the air, my knees banging against the kitchen table as I floated free. My head rapped against the ceiling fan. I was so exhausted I allowed myself to just float in the currents.

I tried not to think about the obvious: that I could no longer weigh myself down.

4

Staying light was a whole lot more complicated than going light. I dug old belts out of the closet and tied them to different chairs. Have you ever tried to float and eat dinner at the same time? At bedtime I tucked in the sheets so tightly I scooted in and out as though into a body bag. I couldn't paint anymore, and somehow that was the worst wound, to lose my art. I could not hold myself steady in front of the easel.

The days slipped into autumn, presenting new problems. Whenever I turned on the central heat, the blast of warm air could spin me from one corner of the house to the other unless I was strapped in.

But hey; we're adaptable people, we humans. I was perfectly content to keep going, despite the occasional discomforts my condition presented and the cabin fever settling in — until the voices. Once that started, I knew I could no longer cling to the life I had carved out for myself.

5

One night I startled awake in my pitch black bedroom to voices under the wind. I glanced at my alarm clock. Three a.m.

I heard it clearly:

"Come..."

"We wait for you..."

"Join us..."

I slipped out from under the tight sheets and swam over to the window. My bedroom window is ten feet from the street, and oftentimes anyone strolling by or walking a dog will wake me up. But the yellow glow of streetlight pooled onto deserted sidewalk. A low fog prowled the street and made visibility a murky soup. No one was out there.

Yet I heard the whispers, like someone blowing smoke into my ears. I kicked away from the window and paddled down the hallway to the rear of the house. There, I floated by the back door which gave onto the patio deck.

"Come — be with us..."

"Who's out there?" I shouted — or rather, squawked; my voice was swallowed up by nerves. I was shivering. I had a sudden image of who very well might be out there: too many of my former companions come to take me away. Too many ghosts more than willing to lead me to the promised land. I ached for Jerry, suddenly. I half expected to see him materialize out of the fog, one hand extended.

But my dead lover did not venture out to say hello, and the fog offered up no explanations to the voices under the wind. Eventually I gave up and swam back to bed.

The next night low moans, like the urgent warning of a foghorn off the bay, woke me up. I felt a strange tugging deep in my heart, my emotions stirred.

"Don't be afraid," whispered a voice outside the window.

"There are many of us," whispered another.

"Go away!" I shouted at them. "Go away!"

I looked across the bedroom at a recent painting of mine I'd hung on the wall. The room was impossibly dark — and yet I saw them, the figures I'd drawn in the mist, beckoning me with their hands.

I buried my head beneath the sheets and clapped hands over my ears.

The next night they scraped fingernails against the glass to wake me up.

"Are you dead?" I blurted out. Again, I felt a sadness surround my heart. As though I had to say good-bye before I could say hello.

They chuckled at my distress, though there was no maliciousness in their laughter.

"No," they chorused on the other side of my window.

"Am *I* dead?" For it had occurred to me: how else to explain my weightlessness and the bizarre circumstances of my present condition? Perhaps my body lay somewhere in the house, but like something out of a bad "Twilight Zone" episode I could not see it — and was in fact doomed to this strange purgatory until some outside force discovered my body.

Again, the patient laugh.

"You're very much alive," one of them said.

"So are we..."

"Come..."

"You belong with us."

Something wet stung my cheeks. Crying. I was crying. After my isolation, to be so wanted, and to discover I was in fact among friends...

I opened the shutters to my window and beheld my guests.

6

That was last night. I almost went with them, Roy, but I couldn't, just yet. I wasn't ready. I had to put this down onto paper — for you, or for anyone else who finds this notebook. I know how it's going to look: the house empty, my things undisturbed. Lots of people are going to have questions — I just don't think anyone's going to be ready for the answer.

Anyway, I'm almost finished. Physically, I'm done in. The straps on this chair have dug creases across my thighs. I can only sit strapped in for so long before my weightless body rebels against confinement. I've already gone through the house one last time. The only items you'll find missing are a jacket to keep me warm and a favorite picture of Jerry that I had taken when we met seven years ago. Somehow I'm confident that anything else I'll need will be provided.

It was only after I truly realized they were alive, as I was alive, and full of purpose, that I knew I had to go with them. They must have learned how to maneuver in ways I can only guess at, skillfully adapting to their change. I'm afraid of being buffeted by the wind, afraid that once I fly above the houses I'll be a pawn of nature, unable to control my altitude or actions. Perhaps that is the whole point: that only through surrender will I find true direction, and true companionship with my new friends.

They're tapping at the back door now. A dense fog is laced with the silver of moonlight; we should have no problems slipping away undetected. They are eager for me, and I, them. When I open my back door it will feel more like a reunion than a first meeting. After all, I have been painting them for months now.

Live well, Jerry said. It's the best revenge.

But who has time for revenge? And as for living, I'll take whatever is offered, in whatever form. I'll

7

Roy puts down the notebook. It gets to him, every time: that dangling last word, the sentence unspoken. The scratch of ink across the page, so like someone rising up, up, unable to keep pen to page.

He wants to believe. His refusal sits like a knot in his stomach demanding to be untied. But to believe would invite his undoing, somehow. His lover, Winston, scoffed it away the first time he saw the notebook. "He went crazy," Winston said. "Dementia. What else?"

What else indeed.

Except for the facts. Two months, and the house still stands empty. His friend, vanished. No phone calls, no body, nothing.

Nothing, except for that occasional odd dream, the tap tap tapping at his bedroom window, and a whisper that had to be the wind.

Roy stands up from the table. Winston is in the bedroom watching the news on the portable TV. He walks down the hallway of their flat to join him, the need to feel the comfort of arms around his shoulders strong in him.

And he utters not a sound when his feet go out from under him and he falls, featherlike, to the hardwood floor.

The Unfinished,
continued

PART FOUR

Finished

1

"So I'm not really sure where he went," Jiggs admitted. "He kept insisting he was alive, and that these people were alive, and that's why he went off with them."

Luke scooted into a more comfortable position on his hospital bed. He'd been taken out of the intensive care unit and brought to a regular hospital room on the sixth floor. "Damn mattress," he muttered with a smile. "My tailbone is sore from all this having to lie flat. Anyway, maybe he *did* die in the house. He just couldn't understand what had happened to him. He got ... confused, and that confusion carried over into death."

Jiggs digested that, then added: "I checked with the police early this morning, and sure enough, they have no official record of a death. They never found a body."

Luke scrunched his forehead. "Then why did he come to you, if he wasn't dead like the others?"

Jiggs had wondered about that too. He'd awakened that morning feeling terrific, as though an enormous weight had finally been lifted from his shoulders. As he thought about his last visitor, he realized that the aches and pains of last night, and the brief episode of feeling weightless, were all indicators of how this man had felt from his illness. It had been his way of establishing communication with him.

"Well," Jiggs said at last. "I guess I'll never know the real answer. All I know is he never frightened me. He was ... happy, Luke, really happy. Maybe some of that happiness was still

+ 279

somehow imprinted into the house. Maybe he wanted to prove that not all interrupted lives were full of pain and discomfort. That it was possible to be filled with ... joy."

"It's a nice thought," Luke answered. His face grew suddenly grim. "But I certainly never felt any of that where *I* was."

Jiggs leaned in closer. What a miracle, the phone call from the hospital telling him that Luke had awakened from his coma, and was anxious to see him. He'd taken a taxi straightaway, hoping his prayers had been answered, that the Unfinished had kept their side of the bargain. And when he saw Luke, awake, his tired but battered self acting perfectly normal, his heart just overflowed.

Now came the tricky part, the darker side of the past few days. Jiggs lay a hand upon his friend. "What do you remember, Luke?"

He was still grim about the mouth. "Everything. I remember everything."

"What was it like? Were you in pain?"

Luke swished his mouth around. "I couldn't move. I just ... floated, like I was on the surface of a dark lake. Sometimes I heard voices. I know I heard *your* voice, and the stories you were relaying to me. They seemed to like that. They approved. And so even though it was painful in the beginning, by the end it was peaceful in a weird sort of way."

They sat in companionable silence, each thinking their own thoughts. This experience would never leave them. It was going to color their lives, be an influence upon any future decisions. That was fine with Jiggs. He'd already made his decision.

As if reading his mind, Luke stared at Jiggs with panicky alarm. "You're going to leave, aren't you." He said it as a statement of fact.

Jiggs felt his cheeks burn. "Yes."

"Where to?"

"Texas, at first. Then ... I don't know yet."

Luke nodded, disappointed but trying not to show it. He surprised Jiggs by reaching out and clasping his hand. "Will you stick around long enough for me to get out of this dump?"

Jiggs smiled, sad and happy at the same time. "You betcha. And you know I keep my promises."

2

"I suppose I knew this might happen," Kate sighed two weeks later. She turned to Susie for support. "Looks like we'll never find a tenant who'll stick around."

Jiggs shook his head. "No. We're breaking the lease at Luke's old apartment. He only had a month to go on his lease, and the landlord, with a few extra bucks, was amazingly understanding."

"Where's he going to live?" Susie asked. "He's going to need a lot of help, hobbling around with that cast on his leg."

"Exactly. That's why I'm moving him in here. The house is clear, now. There's nothing to be afraid of. I was hoping the two of you would keep an eye on Luke, make sure he stays out of trouble. I'm going to leave him some money to help with the rent. Besides, I may be back, one day. I've grown rather fond of this place."

"I think that's terrific," beamed Kate.

"She's always wanted to play mommy," Susie kidded. "Now she'll smother him with kindness. By the way, when *is* Luke getting out?"

"A few more days. You should see him, hobbling around with that cane of his, walking the hallways for exercise. He's one determined guy."

"Before you go, is there anything we can do for you?" Kate asked.

Jiggs could tell she was still rather embarrassed by some of her behavior over the past weeks, even though he'd made it clear there were no hard feelings. "There is one thing you could do for me."

"Shoot."

"Get some packages of flower seeds and sprinkle them in that patch of dirt underneath the pine trees."

"Why? It's always been rather barren there. What's so special about it?"

"Believe me," Jiggs said with an enigmatic smile, "you wouldn't want to know."

3

The heat of this late July morning was already turning brutal as Jiggs climbed the gentle slope through the cemetery. Austin,

Texas in the summertime was not very kind to visitors used to a more moderate climate. He had certainly sweated through many a blazing summer here, while attending the School for the Deaf. The temperature was already in the high eighties, and yet it was not even ten o'clock.

Now Jiggs could admit to a case of nerves, as he drew close to his parents' gravestones. He'd been fine in San Francisco, Luke and Kate and Susie hugging him farewell as he boarded Southwest's airplane. And his resolve had tightened even further when he watched the late news in his hotel room last night.

But this was going to be tough, if his worst fears were realized. Strangers were one thing. His parents were something else.

He saw their markers just up ahead. A medium-sized oak tree was nearby, casting a shadow upon the carved stones. He liked that. It seemed appropriate, something alive and growing, next to this resting place.

If they were resting. It was his purpose here, to end his wondering, to end his nightmares.

Here he was. The markers before him, simple and dignified, their names and dates etched in stylish printing. He drew a deep breath. He was sweating a little from his walk. Ever so cautiously he inched up between the stones.

"Hi, Mom and Dad." He wasn't even aware he was speaking aloud. Tremulously, he gently lay a hand upon each stone. Waited. Listened.

All was quiet. No whispers spoke into his ears, no frightening rush of terrible images. For the first time in a long time, he felt a deeply buried coil of tension begin to unwind. His shoulders slumped.

"Thank god," he whispered. "Thank you."

He patted the gravestones as if they were live things and walked a short distance away, sitting down cross-legged facing their names. For several minutes he just sat and stared, reading their names over and over, as though this mantra might bring them back.

Of course, they would never come back. He knew that now, relaxed in the knowledge. They had paid a terrible price in the fiery accident, his parents, but they were at peace. They had gone where they were supposed to go. It's what he had yearned to know.

"I'm going to leave now," Jiggs said. "Last night, watching the news, I saw a videotape of a plane crash just outside of Pittsburgh. For just a second I heard some of the Unfinished. I think a few people are confused, and angry. They don't understand they've died. So tomorrow I'm going to fly up and see if I can help them."

He stood up, stretching in the sunshine. Half a mile away he watched a steady stream of cars zipping along Highway 35. So many people, leading their lives. And Jiggs thought, *We are all of us, unfinished. Some of us have our lives interrupted, and some of us live on to a ripe old age, but our time is always incomplete. All we can do is be our best. And if completion is denied us, at the very least there is the telling.*

Jiggs blew his parents a kiss. "Good-bye," he whispered, knowing their gift to him was who he was, and his gift to them was the man he had become. He trudged down the slope of manicured lawn under the bright glare of sunshine, his heart full, as he walked toward his rental car at the bottom of the road.

Other books of interest from
ALYSON PUBLICATIONS

STEAM, by Jay B. Laws, $10.00. A vaporous presence is slowly invading San Francisco. One by one, selected gay men are seduced by it — then they disappear, leaving only a ghoulish reminder of their existence. Can anyone stop this shapeless terror?

VAMPIRES ANONYMOUS, by Jeffrey McMahan, $9.00. Andrew, the wry vampire, was introduced in *Somewhere in the Night*, which won the author a Lambda Literary Award. Now Andrew is back, as he confronts an organization that has already lured many of his kin from their favorite recreation, and that is determined to deprive him of the nourishment he needs for survival.

SOMEWHERE IN THE NIGHT, by Jeffrey N. McMahan, $8.00. The realms of nightmare and reality converge in eight tales of suspense and the supernatural. Jeffrey N. McMahan weaves eerie stories with just the right amount of horror, humor, and eroticism.

EMBRACING THE DARK, edited by Eric Garber, $9.00. Eleven chilling horror stories depict worlds of gay werewolves and lesbian vampires, and sexual fantasies that take on lives of their own. Contributors include Jeffrey N. McMahan, Jewelle Gomez, Jay B. Laws, Jess Wells ... and nineteenth-century gay rights pioneer Karl Heinrich Ulrichs.

THE GAY BOOK OF LISTS, by Leigh Rutledge, $9.00. A fascinating and informative collection of lists, ranging from history (6 gay popes) to politics (9 perfectly disgusting reactions to AIDS) to useless (9 Victorian "cures" for masturbation).

UNNATURAL QUOTATIONS, by Leigh W. Rutledge, $9.00. Do you wonder what Frank Zappa thinks of lesbians and gay men? How about Anne Rice? This collection of quotations by or about gay men and lesbians reveals the positive and negative thoughts of hundreds of celebrities and historical personalities.

THE FIRST GAY POPE, by Lynne Yamaguchi Fletcher, $8.00. The first gay pope, the earliest lesbian novel, the biggest gay bookstore, and the worst anti-gay laws are all recorded in this entertaining new reference book.

HIV-POSITIVE: WORKING THE SYSTEM, by Robert A. Rimer and Michael A. Connolly, $13.00. Your life is too important to be left in the hands of your doctor. In this lively handbook, two AIDS activists — one of whom was diagnosed with AIDS in 1986 — tell how to make the system work for you.

THE COLOR OF TREES, by Canaan Parker, $9.00. What is it like to be gay in a boys' boarding school? What's it like to be black, and from Harlem, when you're surrounded by privileged white boys? A story of young love that crosses racial and class boundaries, this hauntingly erotic first novel explores the limits of freedom and loyalty.

DAUGHTERS OF THE GREAT STAR, by Diana Rivers, $10.00. The daughters of the Great Star, all born in the same year, soon found themselves estranged from their villages and even from their families. But they found one another, and created their own world of strong and sensual women.

BI ANY OTHER NAME, edited by Loraine Hutchins and Lani Kaahumanu, $12.00. In this ground-breaking anthology, over seventy women and men from all walks of life describe their lives as bisexuals in prose, poetry, art, and essays.

A LOTUS OF ANOTHER COLOR, edited by Rakesh Ratti, $10.00. For the first time, lesbians and gay men from India, Pakistan, and other South Asian countries tell their stories of coming out and of challenging prejudice. Together, they capture the exhilaration of finally finding a sense of community.

BROTHER TO BROTHER, edited by Essex Hemphill, $9.00. Black activist and poet Essex Hemphill has carried on in the footsteps of the late Joseph Beam (editor of *In the Life*) with this new anthology of fiction, essays, and poetry by black gay men.

GAY MEN AND WOMEN WHO ENRICHED THE WORLD, by Thomas Cowan, $9.00. Gay history springs to life in these forty brief biographies, illustrated with the lively caricatures of Michael Willhoite. Cowan's subjects offered outstanding contributions in fields ranging from mathematics and military strategy to art, philosophy, and economics.

GOLDENBOY, by Michael Nava, $9.00. When a young man is accused of committing murder to keep his gayness a secret, Henry Rios agrees to defend him. Will new murders, suicide, and a love affair keep Rios from proving his client's innocence?

THE LITTLE DEATH, by Michael Nava, $8.00. When a friend dies under suspicious circumstances, gay lawyer Henry Rios is determined to find out why, in this novel by award-winning writer Michael Nava.

FINALE, edited by Michael Nava, $9.00. Murder and the macabre are explored in these carefully crafted stories by some of today's most gifted mystery and suspense writers. Michael Nava, author of the Henry Rios mysteries, has selected well-known authors like Samuel M. Steward and Katherine Forrest as well as new-found talent.

REFLECTIONS OF A ROCK LOBSTER, by Aaron Fricke, $7.00. Aaron Fricke made national news when he sued his school for the right to take a male date to the prom. Here is his story of growing up gay in America.

ONE TEENAGER IN TEN, edited by Ann Heron, $5.00. One teenager in ten is gay. Here, twenty-six young people from around the country discuss their coming-out experiences. Their words will provide encouragement for other teenagers facing similar experiences.

THE MEN WITH THE PINK TRIANGLE, by Heinz Heger, $8.00. Thousands of gay people suffered persecution at the hands of the Nazi regime. Of the few who survived the concentration camps, only one ever came forward to tell his story. This is his riveting account of those nightmarish years.

GAY SEX, by Jack Hart, $15.00. This lively, illustrated guide covers everything from the basics (Lubricants) to the lifesaving (Condom care) to the unexpected (Exhibitionism).

SOCIETY AND THE HEALTHY HOMOSEXUAL, by George Weinberg, $8.00. The man who popularized the term *homophobia* examines its causes, and its disastrous but often subtle effect on gay people. He cautions lesbians and gay men against assuming that universal problems such as loneliness stem from their sexual orientation.

THE ADVOCATE ADVISER, by Pat Califia, $9.00. Whether she's discussing the etiquette of a holy union ceremony or the ethics of zoophilia, Califia's advice is always useful, often unorthodox, and sometimes quite funny.

SUPPORT YOUR LOCAL BOOKSTORE

Most of the books described above are available at your nearest gay or feminist bookstore, and many of them will be available at other bookstores. If you can't get these books locally, order by mail using the form on the following page.

Enclosed is $_____ for the following books. (Add $1.00 postage when ordering just one book. If you order two or more, we'll pay the postage.)

1. _____

2. _____

3. _____

4. _____

name: _____

address: _____

city: _____ state: _____ zip: _____

ALYSON PUBLICATIONS
Dept. J-51, 40 Plympton St., Boston, MA 02118

After December 31, 1994, please write for current catalog.